DULY NOTED

by H.M. Shander

Duly Noted
Published by H.M. Shander at CreateSpace
Copyright ©2016 H.M. Shander

Cover Design: ZH Designs
Editing by: PWA

Shander, H.M., 1975 – Duly Noted
ISBN: 978-0-9938834-4-6
First Edition
Printed by CreateSpace

You took a chance on me with Cat & Drew, and
I hope your time spent with Aurora and Nate
is just as magical and wonderful.
Thank you for reading.
This novel is dedicated to you,
the readers, who believe in happy
ever afters and the magic of falling in love.

HMS

Table of Contents

❤ Chapter One ❤

The laughter died in a split-second. No one saw it coming. Metal snapped, scrapped and twisted. The air reeked of something salty and mercurial.

Life changed forever. May 24. 10:17 p.m.

The rain poured down, blanketing everything in its path with a cold wetness that chilled to the bone. The dark sky blew up with arcs of forked lightning, lighting up the area for miles. In the distance, sirens wailed, getting louder on approach. Gasps and inaudible sounds came from the onlookers who stood around drenched yet watching. Unable to help. Unsure of where to start.

Aurora drove through the pounding rain, with her momma in the passenger seat, and Carmen behind her. Normally Carmen would drive, as she attended the University there, but tonight she let Aurora take the wheel. They enjoyed a perfect girl's weekend– eating more than normal, staying out late and shopping.

Laughing, and singing off key to an old country song on the radio, they headed back to their hotel after an exhaustive but successful search for the perfect dress. Aurora's high school graduation was less than two weeks away. Carmen, her older sister, said the ball gown made the blue in her eyes dance, and Derek would think she was the most beautiful girl at the ceremony. But Aurora knew he'd think that anyways. He always told her that.

Still blocks from the hotel, Aurora drove down the scenic one-way street and thought nothing of checking for traffic approaching the stop signs. A set of white lights, bright enough to blind her peripheral vision, appeared out of nowhere. No time to react and slam on the brakes.

"Momma!" she screamed, as her head cracked against her mom's shoulder, which was now closer than it should have been. When the vehicle stopped moving, Aurora's head smashed into the driver's side window, shattering it into millions of pieces before her world turned dark.

Coming back from the dark, she slowly pieced together what she saw. A dark grey dashboard, the cream colour of the airbag puddled on her lap, and several red blinking lights in the distance. Not a fender-bender, but a major accident. She was involved in a car crash. The kind she'd watched on her favourite medical dramas. One day she hoped to be on the other side as the ER doctor. But today, she'd be the patient.

Her jeans, cold and wet against her skin, made her shiver, bringing her back to the present. Were her ears deceiving her? All around her, an eerie silence stretched out– like the kind you get when you wake in the middle of the night from a nightmare. Yet as she strained her ear, murmurs could be heard. A gasp here and there. And some gargled breathing. And *that* sound chilled her even more than the cold. Because it was close. Too close. It didn't help her stay calm when the smells surrounding her were as frightening– strong and overpowering, but also unfamiliar as there was no textbook or literature on *that*. And without a moment's hesitation, she never wanted to smell them again. They reeked of fear and death.

"Momma," she said in a painful, whispered breath.

Her head leaned on the edge of the window, the rain mixing with her tears. She tried to lift her head, but it weighed at least fifty pounds. And it ached. Like every other part of her body. A quick roving body search confirmed that she was alive– the indescribable pain told her as much. Pushing against the door to right herself, she screamed in agony, blacking out again.

Awaking later as warm fingertips palpitated her face. A soft male voice said, "My name's Jordan and I'm here to help you."

A clap of thunder overhead startled Aurora more than the hands that slipped something solid and plastic around her neck. "Momma? Carmen?" she called out in a hoarse whisper. Forcing her eyes open, she tried to twist her restrained head to search for her mother and sister. Even straining from the corner of her eyes, they weren't there.

"Don't move." Jordan's voice spoke with such calmness that for a moment she thought the situation wasn't as bad as it was. Momma wasn't there, no sound from Carmen, and yet Jordan spoke as if he were simply removing a splinter from her finger. *Maybe I'm dreaming.*

Lightning split the sky into two distinct pieces and ground-rattling thunder immediately followed. It lit up the empty passenger seat with a missing door. "Momma?"

"She's been removed from the car already," Jordan said. His warm fingers caused an involuntary shudder to course through her body. The shaking hurt her in more ways than she could count, or wanted to count. It made her nauseous. It made her nervous. *Carmen?* Surely she could hear her?

Aurora returned her focus to the person talking to her. What was his name? Joe? Jordan? What in hell was he doing on the hood of her car? Where was her windshield?

She focused on his face. "You've been in a bad accident, and your mom's already en route to the hospital. We're trying to get you out. You're pinned against a railing, so once we have you properly protected, they'll pull your car away, so we can get better access to you. Shouldn't be much longer."

She performed some version of a nod, but it was hard to gauge with her immobile head.

I remember seeing the headlights. Bright and almost on top of us. I don't remember hearing the squealing brakes from that vehicle. The sliding lasted forever, but I think it was only three or four lanes. I don't remember seeing a brick wall, but I do remember suddenly stopping. Straining her eyes to the edges, she tried to take in her surroundings. Like something on the news, blue and red lights flashed around, belonging to a firetruck and an ambulance or two? It was hard to tell. The area was lit up with beams of light and there were voices everywhere.

"She's secure," Jordan called out as he turned his head. To her he said, "They're going to pull the vehicle back so you'll feel a deep shaking."

Oh fuck. She understood what that meant. More pain. Because it wasn't enough to hurt from head to toe already. Unlike the crash, she knew what was coming. Preparing for it was another matter. *I need to focus or I'm going to black out. Think, Aurora, think. Look at the man. Jordan, was it? Don't think about the pain that's coming. I'm in good hands.* She focused on the paramedic as he slid off the hood and stepped back, nodding to someone.

The vehicle vibrated as it skidded and scraped against the ground, the noise deafening. Unable to cover her ears, it invaded her soul. But the worst was the horrible metallic sound of a saw blade cutting into metal surrounding her. This time she figured she'd go deaf as the noise pierced her ears. Reactively, she jerked and blinding pain radiated through her before she blacked out again.

♥ Chapter Two ♥

Two Years Later

Sure, make the new girl do the dirty work. With a long list in her hands, Aurora limped to the elevator and mentally prepared herself for the task; searching through dozens of sealed up boxes for specific titles to go back on the library's shelves. *They said it would be easy. Two hours at most.* But they laughed when they said it, so she wasn't expecting a picnic.

The teen and middle grade novels had been boxed and moved to the basement while that section was under reconstruction. They were expanding the area to make it bigger and cosier, and more inviting for the teens. Adding a soundproof room with a big screen TV and the latest video game consoles would be a huge draw. Aurora thought it sounded awesome, and hoped when it was finished, she'd be able to hang out along with the teenagers. She could take them all on, especially in any combat games. She rocked those.

Shuffling into the elevator, she thumbed the down button and waited as the age-old doors closed. She sighed and leaned against the back wall, waiting for her arrival into the dungeons.

She'd heard the whispering from the other staff members about the importance of locating all the titles, but couldn't figure out why someone else wasn't searching. Yes, she was new, and yes, it was grunt work, but still. She'd been hired to shelve books and keep the library neat and tidy, so why was she selected to sort through the boxes? As much as she wanted to complain about it, she bit her tongue. If she was going to keep her job through the summer, she'd better suck it up and make the best of it.

The elevator chimed, and she stumbled out into the noisy foyer, making a quick right turn. A peek to her left told her the construction crew was down here, strengthening the joists or whatever it was they needed to do before the expansion could begin. Plugging her earphones into her phone, she fired up the latest podcast on organic chemistry, putting the volume up to a level she wouldn't ordinarily have it at. Some would find her choice in podcasts dry and boring, but to Aurora, chemistry was soothing and interesting. She spent as much time as she could learning, because she wanted to, not because she was forced to like her dorm-mate Kaitlyn would say.

Aurora made it to the stack of boxes, and stared, wondering how long this search would truly take. *A couple of hours? Really? There's like a hundred boxes here.* Spotting a cart, she pushed it over to the boxes and ripped open the first box.

Sometime later, she was head deep searching in one of the final boxes, when a finger tapped on her shoulder. Ripping her earbuds away and standing taller than the towers of boxes, she stared breathlessly at the man who stepped away from her, his hands raised up. "What the hell?" she snapped.

"Hey, it's okay," the construction worker said, inching away. He was younger than the old gruffs she'd seen earlier. This one appeared around twenty, close to her age maybe. If he didn't seem so alarmed, she might have thought him cute. "See that door there?" She turned in the direction his stubby finger pointed. "Your boxes are blocking it. That's the stairwell and our fire escape."

"Is there a fire?" Sarcasm rolled off her tongue, and she folded her arms across her chest after taking a quick whiff of air.

He frowned as he looked around. "No. Not that I saw."

"So what exactly is the problem?"

"It's a violation of fire code." He stared at her as if daring her to challenge him. "So you should probably move them out of the way."

"What are you? A fire marshal or something?" He'd have to have a badge or something, right?

"No. I'm just letting you know."

Cute or not, she didn't need that tone from him. "Well, if it's so important to do it right this minute, then move them. Otherwise I'll do it when I'm done here. I'll only be a couple more minutes. I think." She sat on one of the boxes she'd been using as a makeshift chair and rifled through the box at her feet, trying to ignore the glare he fired in her direction. "There's only two boxes left and I promise I'll move everything back." An insincere smile crossed her face. Pulling out a title, she tossed it onto the cart, missing it completely. "Dammit."

He bent down and picked it up, placing it on the trolley.

"You're seriously going to stand there and make sure I keep my promise?" She studied him. He was tall. Mind you, everyone seemed tall. She was all of five-foot-four, so she supposed he could be average. No, he was taller than average. Maybe it was the boots he wore. Regardless, he was easy on the eyes for sure, with his light brown hair fanning the edges of his eyebrows, and deep brown eyes staring at her, with what? What was that look on his face? Disgust? Hostility? No. Amusement. Because a small smirk teased the edges of his lips.

He huffed and narrowed his eyes and gave them a thorough rub. "I can help you move the boxes back. I'm finished for the day, and since you only have two more to go through–"

"Thank you, but I don't need your help."

"I can see you've done a thorough job." He leaned on a stack of boxes and crossed his arms. "However, the library closes in an hour, so I–"

Ignoring him, she glanced at her phone, and checked the time. *Dammit. I still need one more title.* She flipped faster through the open box, and finding nothing she needed, heaved it and added it to the pile.

"What are you looking for?"

"Books, obviously." She rolled her eyes and smirked. This construction worker couldn't be that obtuse, could he?

"Specifically?" He leaned over and peered into the box on the floor.

"Books by Matthew James. Yesterday he announced he's coming here on Friday for a presentation, and they want all his titles prominently displayed. It's my job to retrieve these books," she said, waving the list, "from the boxed up ones so you and your crew can renovate the teen section."

"And why's it so important that *all* his books are back upstairs?"

She massaged her temples, not having time nor the desire to explain this. Sighing, she said, "Because Matthew James does a lot for libraries and he's very encouraging at getting the kids in the door. You know for reading and such."

"Doesn't answer *why* all his books need to be displayed. Go with what you have here." He pointed to the full cart. There were dozens upon dozens of his titles piled up.

"As easy as that would be, it's not how I roll. I was given a job to do, and I'm going to finish it." She rooted through the box again, tossing out another title. "Because the branch manager *wanted* every single title up there. Then after the presentation, those who can't afford to buy his brand new books, can borrow them from us."

"So why isn't he at a big chain bookstore selling his books and making oodles of money?"

"Do you even know who Matthew James is?" Disgusted she even had to ask. Everyone knew who Matthew James was. For crying out loud, he was a rock star in the literary world.

"No. But he's already sounding somewhat pretentious."

"Matthew James is single-handedly responsible for getting teenage boys to read."

The man before her whistled. "Wow, single-handedly? Does he wear a cape when he arrives?"

She slumped over the box at her feet, hiding her oncoming smile. "Shut up. You're so out of touch." Finding another title, she waved it around. "Haven't you ever read, *Mocking Me?*"

Staring at her like she was some kind of psycho, he said, "Umm, nope. Can't say I have."

"It's fabulous, and should be required reading for pre-teen boys–"

"Well, I'm hardly a pre-teen boy." He produced a close-lipped smile as he raised his eyebrows.

Her eyes roved up and down his body. "Obviously." Displaying the book, she carried on. "It's educational, full of fantasy and fun without being preachy. It rocks." She added it to the growing mountain of books. "Plus, his organization–*The MJ Association*–donates thousands of books to the inner-city schools and the less fortunate."

Sighing at the unconcerned look on his face, she added, "He's like Tony Hawk to skateboarders, or Jeff Gordon to NASCAR."

With that his head snapped up, and he leaned on a box. "Really? So odd you would choose Jeff Gordon to NASCAR." He laughed. A sweet laugh really although she knew he was mocking her. Bastard. "So which two boxes are left? I can go through one."

Pointing to the two nearest her, he reached over and effortlessly pulled the box onto the pile before him. "Matthew James, the Rock Star God of Teenage Boy Books." He ripped open the box and rifled through, pulling out a couple. "Any particular titles? Or everything and anything that bears his name?"

"Everything." Her checklist had thirty titles on it, with at least ten copies of each, but she hadn't crossed off how many of each she'd located.

He added his finds to the huge pile on the cart. "Who the hell packed this? A kindergartener? What a mess. No wonder it's taking so long to find anything."

In spite of herself, Aurora found herself smiling. "I know, right?" She turned her attention back to the box, searching and moving books around but came up empty.

After the last box, Aurora straightened herself up, and rubbed her back. The dull ache that started a podcast ago grew in fury. She needed her pills, and fast, or she'd have some real explaining to do when she could no longer move because of the pain. The sweat headed along her temples, and she wiped it quickly away.

"You okay?"

"Yeah, why?" She pulled down the sleeves of her shirt when she saw him staring at her arms. It made her self-conscious to have her scars visible, as it always lead to prying questions, most of which were no one's business.

He turned his reddened head. "No reason." He moved a box against the back wall, and added another on top of it. "Let's start replacing these, and get you out of here before they lock us in."

"Would they do that?" she asked in a panic, her voice suddenly shaky. *I mean, they'd check first to make sure everyone had clocked out, right?*

"No." He laughed, checking his watch. "But I wouldn't want to find out I'm wrong."

With that, Aurora moved the boxes as fast as she could. Pain crept into the depths of her bones, and her back ached more than she'd ever vocalise, especially to a stranger, no matter how cute he was. Without some medication, she'd seize up tight enough to require more help than her muscle relaxers could provide.

"Done," he said, lifting the last box onto the top of the pile.

With the precious stairwell door he'd blasted her about visible again, she sighed with relief. But she was only relieved that the boxes were moved. She still needed to get upstairs and grab a muscle relaxer, and likely a pain reliever too, as the pain stabbed her repeatedly. "Thanks for your help."

"My pleasure. I'm sure Mr. Rock Star God of Teenage Boy Books appreciates you digging through this disaster of a filing system." His gaze travelled over her body, and rested where her hands firmly massaged her back. "You sure you're okay?"

Dropping her hands, she forced a smile through her grimace, hoping it appeared sincere. "Absolutely, why wouldn't I be?" She stepped around him and grabbed the cart with enough force to turn her knuckles white. *Oh please, let me make it upstairs before I scream out in pain.* She pushed it towards the elevator, biting the inside of her cheek until the metallic taste danced on her taste buds.

The doors opened to the elevator and limping as little as she could, she entered. The man who'd been helping her also stepped on.

"Thanks again for your help–" She trailed off, waving a hand around in hopes he'd fill in the gap.

"Nate."

"Yes, Nate."

"And you are?" He turned to her, his long lashes blinking up and down.

"Aurora."

Something akin to a smirk settled over his face. "Like the northern lights?"

She groaned. "No, like the fairy tale." She refused to make eye contact. After all, she had no choice in her name. It was decided before she had any input. Her mother had been a true believer in happy-ever-afters.

"Well, it's very pretty, like you."

The elevator doors slid open. "Oh, puh-leeze. Spare me the pickup line." Grunting with the effort to push a full cart of books with a pained back and a bad limp, Aurora stumbled out.

"What? It wasn't a line." His heavy boots thumped behind her.

"Good night, Nate." She rolled the cart away from him and into the back room. Sighing, she signed out and bid her co-worker adieu.

❤ Chapter Three ❤

Putting her coat on, she blinked back tears and stepped outside into the cool of evening. The sun had set and the heat of the day present five hours ago, seemed long gone. Thankful for the crisp, fresh air, she breathed it in, expelling the library basement's stagnant mustiness.

She sat on the bench outside the library and rooted through her purse, desperately searching for the much needed pills. The intense pain, stabbing and pricking her throughout her back, no longer confined to the small area above her hips. It wrapped around her mid-section as its tentacles reached up her spine, and spread like ivy down her leg. Although she lived less than half a kilometre from the library, the walk would seem endless in this much pain. Popping a couple and swallowing them dry, she grabbed her phone and dialled, needing a mental distraction.

"Hey, Daddy."

"How's my Princess?"

She rolled her eyes. Always the same start to every conversation. "Tired and sore." Instinctively, with her free hand, she gave her throbbing lower back a rub as she crossed the parking lot and headed for home.

"How come?"

"I moved a bunch of heavy boxes at work."

"Aurora," he said, his tone sad and pained. "You know better. Your body can't handle that. Tell your boss."

"Thanks for the reminder. I wasn't aware." Her tone filled with sarcasm. "Like I'd tell them that. It's a miracle to have found something so close to home. I'll make it work, and I promise I'll try to go easy tomorrow." *You never let me forget my limitations, even though* I'm *not allowed to dwell on them. Push past and move on.* "When I get home, I'll have a hot bath and relax."

"That's my Princess." There was a long pause on the line. "I'm not able to make it there this weekend."

She picked up her pace and bit through the pain, hoping to make the light at the end of the street. It was a decent neighbourhood, but with her back aching as much as it did, she didn't want to be an easy target. She wanted to get home. "That's okay, Daddy. I don't expect you to be here all the time. You helped me move two weekends ago into the apartment."

"I know, but I need to keep checking in on you. As your only parent, it's my duty."

Sadness descended on her like a wave. There was no answer, no response to make either of them feel better. So she simply said, "I love you, Daddy."

"You too, Princess."

Stashing her phone into her pocket, she hurried to the main doors of the apartment tower, everything aching more from the rush.

Blinking rapidly, Aurora awoke to a sharp, piercing of needles being shoved in the base of her back and hips. It wasn't a haunting memory, nor a bad dream, but real life.

"Fuck," she cried. Slowly and gently, she pushed herself into a sitting position and glanced at her nightstand. The clock flashed 3:24. It had been six hours since her last pill, so she hobbled into the bathroom, and blinded herself as she flicked on the light switch. "Dammit." Shielding her face for a moment until she focused her tired eyes on the pills stacked in her medicine cabinet, she read the labels. Xanax. Flexeril. Tylenol-3s. Ah–the good stuff–Percocet. *Oh thank God.* In haste, she twisted the cap off and poured two into her hands, and then changing her mind, put one back. "Fuck it," she said and dug out another, swallowing them both.

Making her way back to the bed, she pulled open her diary and grabbed the nearby pen.

April 30 – 3:28am – 2 percs. Awoke to nasty back pain from overdoing it at work. Hot shower and heating pad seemed to have only lessened the pain. Will try harder tomorrow to not aggravate things. Might be hard if Mr. Over Helpful Nate is there again. Don't want to be a weak girl. Don't want to be seen as a weak girl. Even if it kills me.

She closed her book and lay down, trying desperately to find a position that didn't hurt, or ache. Finding none, she screamed "Fuck" into her pillow waiting for the Percocets to pull her under.

❤ Chapter Four ❤

The next morning, after a comatose sleep, Aurora woke still sore but manageable and readied for work. She stumbled the half-kilometre to the library, hoping today would be a better day.

Hanging up her coat in a locker, she met with the senior library assistant, and found out today she'd be shelving books. Excellent. Much easier and cleaner than going through dusty boxes in the basement. The archaic dust and musty scent followed her into the shower last night, and she was hopeful to not deal with it again tonight.

As she placed a group of graphic novels onto the shelf in the temporary teen section, a voice whispered behind her. "Good morning."

She turned in place, slowly, so as not to make the Flexeril she took earlier work harder than it needed to as her back still throbbed. Before her stood the handsome Nate. The daylight worked in his favour, making his dark hair a touch lighter, as if it had been kissed by the sun. His eyes were an interesting shade of brown– like melted chocolate with flecks of crushed up peanuts. "Hey," she said, as she removed her gaze from his face and focused on his attire. The beige coveralls and a white t-shirt showed off sun-kissed skin.

"So, I've been pulled from the renos in the basement to work on an elaborate set up for your Mr. Rock Star God of the Teenage Boys." His placed his hands on his hips like a child does before a temper tantrum, and a hint of a pout played on his full lips. It was amusing to her, but she bit back a giggle.

"Well, I've seen the way you can stack boxes against the wall."
She leaned back and rested her elbows on the shelf.

"Have you seen your rock star's list of demands? He may do a
lot of good for libraries and the love of reading as you claim, but he
really is a bit pretentious. Actually, he's a lot pretentious. And I have
two days to build something wonderful, and submit it to his agent for
approval." A silver ball that could only be part of a pierced tongue
announced itself as his lips parted and his teeth held it in place.

Momentarily rocked by the sight, she travelled up to his eyes,
and raised her own as she spoke. "So what are you doing here standing
and talking to me then?"

He inched back, dragging his boots across the carpet. "Just
thought I'd let you know that Mr. Pretentious is a pompous ass."

"Duly noted." Nate continued to stand there, scrutinizing her,
and it heated her up, turning her insides into jelly. "Anything else?"

He put one foot in front of the other, but hesitated with his
words. "Yeah. Oh never mind."

With a smirk on her face, she said, "Okay. I won't." Quickly,
she gave a side-eyed glance in his direction. After a few books left the
cart, she heard the scuffling from his boots recede. She sighed and
rubbed her lower back. *I'm not worth it, Nate. Trust me on this. My
problems are more than skin-deep.*

Her noon break rolled around and she grabbed her bagged
lunch, sitting outside in the garden area. The day was heating perfectly,
and she turned her face up to the sun, hoping the natural light created a
few freckles on her face and give her a colour other than ghost white.

"May I join you?"

She sighed without opening her eyes, she recognized the voice.
"I don't own the space."

"Great." Ripped away from her inner thoughts by the sound of
his boots and the crinkling of a paper lunch bag, he sat beside her.

Aurora opened her eyes, and turned towards the noise. "Nate."

"Expecting Prince Charming?"

"Every. Single. Day." Closing her eyes again, she pointed her
nose towards the sun.

"Not eating your lunch?"

A glance to her lunch bag still sealed up beside her. "Not hungry for what I packed. It's grocery day." Before she could stop him, he grabbed and opened it.

"Let's see. You have a bagel and an orange. Nothing wrong with that. What's this?" He held up a container and read the label.

She snatched it from his hand. "If you wanted to know my last name, all you had to do was ask." The sarcasm rolled with ease.

"I didn't need to. It's written all over your lunch bag."

Concerned that maybe it was written on her bag, she checked. It wasn't. *Jerk.*

"Gotcha," he said and turned serious. "You take Percocet? That's some serious shit."

"Just never mind."

"Are you sure you're okay? Last night you were rubbing your back. Today you're…" His eyes held worry.

"Yeah, I'm just hunky-dory." She softened her tone. "Look, I don't mean to be a bitch about it, okay? I have a bad back and… We'll leave it there. Last night was too much and I'm paying for it today." Shoving the pill container into the depths of her lunch bag, she glared at him. "Happy now?"

Nate moved away silently, and unwrapped his sandwich. "So, about that Rock Star God to the Teenage Boys."

"His name is Matthew James."

"Well, it seems like he needs quite the display. His requirements are incredible."

"So what?" She stretched out her legs, crossing them at the ankle. It hurt her hips to cross them more lady-like at the knee.

"Hmm, I sense a defensive tone." He chewed a piece of sandwich loud enough to make her cringe. What was in it? Metal? "Do you know this guy personally?"

As she turned to face him, she opened her mouth. "Not personally, no. But as I've told you before, he's done incredible work."

"Yeah, he donates his books to underprivileged children, who probably can't read anyways, but it still makes him look good. Have you ever looked into where his donations actually go?" He raised his eyebrow at her.

She'd never checked, but always needed to defend whoever was being attacked. But Matthew James didn't know her from Adam, so why was she hell bent on protecting his image? She felt dumb. Shaking her head, she said, "No."

"You should. You'd find it highly interesting."

Tugging her sleeves down until they covered half her palm, she defended his actions. "Perhaps he sends out tutors and such to help those kids read?"

"Not that I've read."

"Well, what do you know?"

"More than you think I do."

Avoiding his eyes, she admired the nearby flowers. Crocuses and daisies. "Did you come out here just to rag on Matthew James, or was there another reason you came out here?"

"You looked lonely. Thought you might like the company."

"Well, I don't. I don't need anyone." She closed her eyes and faced the sun again.

His lunch bag crinkled, and his boots scuffed against the ground.

Sighing, she turned slowly in the direction he walked. "Nate?"

"Yeah?" He paused and faced her, his hand on the door.

"I'm sorry. That was uncalled for."

"No, I'm the one who's sorry." He opened the nearby door and disappeared inside.

"Fuck me," she growled, grabbing her un-eaten lunch. "Why do guys have to be like that?"

She hobbled back into the library and returned her lunch to her locker, glancing at multitude of hanging posters. All highlighting Matthew James' upcoming visit– one he sprang on the library two days ago. Perhaps non-profit organizations were willing to bend over backwards for funding or something, so the lack of notice from him wasn't a big deal. For her, it was. She wasn't big on last-minute changes.

Back on the floor, she sought out Nate in the construction area, confused as to why she needed to search for him. It was better to burn the bridges before he had a chance to even cross them. There'd be no future with her, she was too damaged everywhere to be acceptable girlfriend material.

That's why Derek left her. Once her knight in shining armour, and always by her side, he missed their high school graduation party to be with her in the hospital while she resembled a pin cushion, tethered to the bed and unable to move. But Derek couldn't handle it, not really. Couldn't handle the change in the relationship, in the way she looked, more Frankenstein than Mary Shelley. She'd told herself it was his loss, but those were her Daddy's words. She didn't honestly believe it was Derek's loss at all. If anything it was for the best he'd left. All her dreams were snuffed out in an instant, and her life changed forever. There was no point bringing anyone into purgatory with her.

❤ Chapter Five ❤

The remainder of the week flew by without a word from Nate. He worked nearby, usually within view. Pretending not to care while stocking the shelves, she'd kept her ears open wide enough to hear his workmates comment on Nate's craftsmanship. He got along well with everyone, and had the most heart-warming laugh. The moment the hearty sound hit her ears, she'd snap up and look in his direction.

Busy decorating the tables in Matthew James' strict colour scheme of gold and purple, she'd paid no attention to the weather. However, a crack of thunder shook the building, and terrified, Aurora dropped to the ground, covering her head. Shaking in her spot, a warm hand on her shoulder caused her to scream.

"Hey, it's okay. It's just thunder." His face a mixture of curiosity and amusement.

Hunched on her heels, her hands slowly moved off her head, and she stared at the ceiling. "Yes, I know." Another crash sounded overhead, and once again she cowered.

"It's right overhead too." A broad grin settled on his face as he asked, "Not a fan of a little storm?"

Shaking her head, she whispered, "Not in the remotest sense."

He crouched down beside her, his hand rested on her shoulder, and sincerity on his face. "Okay. Duly noted." He stood and extended his hand. "What would help?"

"Xanax."

He laughed, stopping only when she didn't return his grin. "Oh, you're serious?"

"Like a heart attack. Which I may have soon if I don't get some relief." With her eyes fixated on the ceiling as though a lightning bolt would strike her down, she quickly limped her way into the back room where her locker was. Breathing heavy as her heart pounded in fear, she poured two pills out, catching them in the nick of time as they bounced out of her shaking hand. She let them melt under her tongue.

Another loud boom rattled the building, and cowering she found herself wrapped in Nate's strong arms. "Easy there," he smirked, which irritated Aurora, although he did not lessen his hold on her.

She pushed out of his embrace. "I'll be okay now, thank you," she said as she stumbled backwards and fell with a thud onto the nearby bench.

"Sure you will." Relaxing on the seat beside her, he said, "I've never known anyone as terrified of a thunderstorm as you are."

"There's lots you don't know about me, Nate." She bit her lip and kicked the door of her locker shut.

"I'm sure there is." His smile widened, showcasing a dimple on his left cheek. His chocolate brown eyes twinkled under the florescent lights of the staff room. "However, I kind of like that the storm bothers you."

"You're a very strange man." She pushed herself up and staggered for the door, pausing as the door creaked open. Curiosity overcoming her, she turned and asked, "Why?"

"Why what?"

"Why do you like the fact that it bothers me?" She hoped he couldn't see her veins pulsing beneath her skin in such close proximity to him as he closed the distance between them.

"Because, it's neat that I can... umm..." He shrugged a shoulder. "Never mind."

"You *are* a strange man."

"Duly noted." He held the door for her. "Ready to head back out?"

She nodded, and as another clap of thunder boomed overhead, Aurora only flinched moderately.

Nate whistled. "Wow, that stuff works well."

"It would fail cataclysmically if it couldn't do its job, and therefore wouldn't be an effective means of reducing my anxiety," she said as she exited the room.

As he walked beside her to the special Matthew James area, he never said a word. Another bang, and instinctively, she cowered a touch. Nate stepped a little closer to her, but he never touched her. Almost as if he understood her. But he couldn't because he'd only met her a week ago.

Aurora, Nate and a few staff members were almost finished decorating when the branch manager came rushing over. "No, no, no," he bellowed as he waddled his girth over to the stage and removed some of the potted plants from it. "No. Didn't anyone read this?" He waved around a thick booklet of stapled pages bound in purple with gold writing across the cover. "This is his rider. If we don't have everything set up exactly as dictated, he'll cancel on us."

Aurora stole a glance at Nate who was trying to hide a laugh under his hand. He caught her eye and raised an eyebrow.

"There can only be two planters on the left, not three." The manager balanced on the edge of freaking out and maintaining control as he speed-wobbled across the small stage, flicking his gaze between the rider and what the crew had done. In haste he threw the papers on the table nearest Aurora which she immediately peeked at.

The requests made her eyes jump out of their sockets.

Pursuant to section 15.1, the following agreements shall be in place before Mr. James is to take the stage. These will be expertly combed through by his assistants, and baring no 'mistakes' Mr. James will follow through with the meet and greet after the show. Failure to provide the details, and the event will be cancelled without further notice. Everything must be in place no less than five hours preceding said event.

    All plants on the stage must be real, and only two can be on the left-hand side.

    A purple, coil bound notebook of 80 pages must be on the table with the names (last, first) of the winners of the prize draw(s).

    A gold bowl full of purple M&Ms must be available for Mr. James to munch on prior to taking the stage.

She wanted to continue reading, but the manager snatched it from her hands. "You're free to go, Aurora, and re-stock books or something."

"But I–"

"Thank you," he said curtly.

She wanted to give him the one-finger salute but thought the better of it. After all, no matter how much she wasn't enjoying her job, at least she had one. Forcing herself to behave, she bit her tongue to put up with a little attitude.

She laughed though as he also dismissed the rest of the staff, and muttered something about "Doing it all himself."

"Good luck," Aurora said as she hobbled away. At least the problem was out of her hands and nothing could be blamed on her.

Moments later, Nate leaned on the cart she'd propped against a shelf of romance titles. "So, did I call it?"

"What's that?" Pretending to be absorbed in reading the back of a novel, she avoided eye contact. She knew he saw her read the rider.

"Mr. Rock Star God of Teenage Boys, is he overly pretentious or what?" He flipped through a book on her cart. "I mean really. Only two plants on the left side? Who does that?"

Aurora placed a few books on the shelf. "He really does a lot of work. You're just seeing what you want to see. You think he's an ass, so you'll see every little thing that makes him one. However, if you saw the good in him, and the wonderful work he does, perhaps you'd change your mind."

"And perhaps you should really listen to the words that escape your mouth." He arched an eyebrow and tipped his head back.

She gasped and slammed a book harder than she wanted onto the shelf, admitting to herself that he could be right, as she never had done any deep-seated research on him. However, she'd never give him the verbal satisfaction of saying it aloud, so she continued to re-shelve books with covers of half-naked people and ignored his smirk. That smug little smirk she wanted to kiss off his face.

"What? No smart-ass comeback?"

She shook her head. "Must be the Xanax."

"Ah yes, perhaps." He stood close. Too close. Close enough to breathe in a heady mixture of cologne and sweat. Nate nudged her arm, and broke the spell.

She stepped to the side when a group of giggling girls walked by holding a pair of books with half-naked men on the covers. "Girls," she said, as they covered their mouths and tried to act casual in flipping the pages, probably trying to get to the good stuff. A fit of giggles erupted from the young girls.

"What they want to find out about love, they'll never find in a book. They need to experience it in the real world."

"And why not? Some of these books help young girls figure out what they want in a man. Whether he be dashing and daring, or strong and domineering–" She trailed off in a dreamlike state.

"Is that what you look for in a man? Strong and domineering? Or do you prefer dashing and exceedingly handsome?" He swished his hair off his face and leaned on the shelf, striking a pose like one of the models on the nearest book cover.

"Not funny," she said, although it was. Endearing almost, and most definitely charming. "What I look for in a man, I'll never find. So there's no point in even trying," she added without filtering, and she said it in a way that caused the corners of Nate's mouth to turn down.

"Ouch."

"Well, it's the truth," she said matter-of-factly.

"Guess I'll have to prove myself to you." His fingers steepled together in thought.

"You'll need to do more than that, because I'm not interested." She turned around and walked away, hoping her wobbles appeared sexier than they felt.

Later, after Aurora finished her shift up, she sat outside under the overhang of the building, waiting and willing the rain to pass. The thunder and lightning had thankfully finished their dance, but with the absence of an umbrella, she preferred to wait until the rain stopped. Otherwise, she'd be a drowned rat of a mess when she finally made it home.

Tucked under the canopy, the cool concrete snuck through her thin pants, chilling her to the bone. Nate emerged from the building, laughing with a small group of guys while she continued to shake. He seemed relaxed and clapped another on the back before rushing out to his car– an older red one that seemed well cared for. About to open his door, he glanced in her direction and jogged over.

"I thought you left hours ago." His fingers slipped through his rain-slicked hair.

"Hah, not quite. More like half-an-hour ago. I just finished up the Matthew James exhibition area."

"They let you back in? Lucky you." An arched eyebrow created her as he stepped under the canopy. "What are you still doing here? Waiting for a ride?"

"Nope. Just waiting for the rain to let up a little before I walk home."

He cocked his head towards his car. "Don't be silly, I'll drive you. C'mon."

"No thanks. I'm good." She gazed out beyond the overhang. The rain wasn't falling in sheets, but it hadn't let up either.

"I promise, I don't bite."

"Whew, that's a relief." She mockingly wiped her brow. "See, it's letting up." Scratching her nose, she rose, gathered her purse and tucked it under her jacket.

Nate shook his head. "I don't think so. C'mon, I'll give you a ride. You can't live far if you're walking."

"No, you're right. I don't live far, but I'm not getting into a car with you." *I don't have the right medication and there's not enough Xanax in the world to make a ride home bearable.*

"Okay." Pouting, he thrust his tongue stud against his teeth. "You sure are a strange duck."

"Duly noted." She winked, tucking her hands into the pockets of her coat.

He studied her, and opened his mouth. Instead of speaking, he sighed as he held back whatever it was he wanted to let roll off his tongue.

"It's okay," she said earnestly. "There's nothing you can say that I haven't heard before."

He tipped his head to the right, and studied at her. "Well, that does raise some concerns about what you may have heard. But what I was going to say had nothing to do with your comment."

"Okay, so spit it out."

"Wow. You *are* direct, aren't you?" A slight flush crawled up his neck and covered his face.

"Always."

He stared at his hands and kicked at the ground. "I was going to ask if you wanted to go out tonight. With me." His chocolate brown eyes latched onto hers.

Her eyes widened. "I can't." Rejection fell across his face, and she raced to explain, "I'm meeting my bestie at Urban DC, you know that new dance club that opened?" Smiling, she added, "You're more than welcome to meet me there."

His face lit up as his dimple deepened. "Okay, where do I meet you once I'm there?"

With a wink she said, "You'll find me." Aurora stood with a smile on her face and pointed it towards the sky. "See? The rain's letting up. Time for me to go." Hobbling away, she hummed.

"What time?" he called out from behind her.

She turned and shrugged. "After nine?" Raindrops cooled her hand as she waved and walked away.

❤ Chapter Six ❤

Aurora snuggled onto her worn-out brown sofa, and held her phone in her hand. Time for another check-in. Dialling, she waited for a man's voice.

"Hello, Princess."

"Hey, Daddy."

"How's my little girl doing? No more back problems?"

The pill bottles on the coffee table stared at her. "No, it's all fine. Had a bit of anxiety at work today over the stupid storm." Lifting a container, she counted the pills inside.

"Well, Dr. Roberts said that would take time to get over."

"I know, I just wish—"

"I know you do. I do too." Cole MacIntyre lost his wife and a daughter that night, and nearly lost Aurora too. "I'm coming to town on Monday."

"Great. I'll get the place cleaned up for you." She glanced around the tiny apartment, eyeballing the space. Everything needed a shine and polish to help it look less... unwelcome. A stack of unread mail sat near the door, and a basket of freshly washed laundry begged to be put away. "And I'll make dinner too." She made a mental list of groceries to pick up on her way home from work tomorrow.

"How's work going?"

She huffed, not completely hating her job. "Great. Been putting together an event for a huge, well-known author, so that's been a lot of fun. I've made a new friend there, but since he works in construction and is part of the renovations, he'll likely only be there for a little bit."

"A guy? Who?"

It's what fathers were supposed to do, right? Check in on their daughters. "Nate." Unwillingly, her face lit up at the mention of his name. She liked the way it naturally rolled off her tongue. Her tongue. His tongue. That barbell stud in his tongue. Mmm.

"Nate who?" He sounded agitated. Had he already asked?

"Nate Somebody, Daddy." She heard him growl in his paternal way. "But he seems nice, and he's a hard worker too. He's going to meet Kaitlyn and me at the new dance club."

"Have you had any pain pills today? You know what happens if you mix them and alcohol."

"Yeah, because I'm a heavy drinker." She'd never had a drop of alcohol. It was the drink that poisoned the mind of the asshole who ran the stop sign and killed her family. And she had enough problems within her own life without adding alcohol to the mix.

"Princess, you remember what the doctor said, right?"

"And you should know, Daddy, that's not who I am. That shit can mess you up." *Or kill innocent people.* "I'm many things, but I'm not stupid."

"Never said you were. I just want you to be safe."

"I know," she sighed. There was a long pause, common when they chatted on the phone as they both wanted to say more, but knew it would be difficult. Both had a bad habit of holding back.

"See you Monday." Cole hung up.

Aurora put her dance club outfit together, and threw that and her shoes into a backpack. Makeup on and hair styled, she hobbled out the door in runners and jeans.

It didn't take her too long–about thirty minutes–to walk from her apartment to the mall where the new dance club was located. The walk would be hard on her body, so she took a Percocet. The pain receding, she popped into the nearest bathroom on arrival and removed her runners and jeans, opting instead for the silver high-lo dress and matching heels, and took another perc to keep the pain away. Heels were always painful, and as sexy as she felt in them, they made her hips ache in new ways. But dance night was a night to escape who she was. A night to be free, thanks to the drugs, and unhindered.

Tonight, she resembled her mother; her long, brown hair piled up on her head, with a wispy hint of bangs. Her eyelashes long enough to touch glasses, if she wore them, paired with eyeliner made her blue irises dance. A touch of gloss was enough to cover the pale pink pout of her lips.

"You rock it, girl," a voice echoed throughout the bathroom, and Aurora stared at the reflection in the mirror.

"Kaitlyn," she said, surprise in her voice as her girlfriend strolled into the bathroom, always as fresh as a model off the cover of a magazine. "Thought we were meeting at the club?"

"Pee break, couldn't wait," the gorgeous blond said as she squeezed her way into a cubicle and locked the door. "I'm so glad you decided to stay this summer. It'll be a lot of fun, us going clubbing like this."

"I'm glad I stayed too." *Being home means seeing reminders, and not being able to discuss it because that'll never happen.*

"When's your dad coming to visit?" Her voice echoed throughout the tiled bathroom.

"Monday."

"That'll be nice, no?" A loud, pleasant sigh escaped the stall before the toilet flushed.

"I suppose. It's been a couple of weeks." She leaned against the counter, waiting for her best friend. Kaitlyn understood. She knew all about the accident and her subsequent fears.

One night in a drunken stupor, Kaitlyn confessed she harboured a huge crush on Aurora's father, blaming the whole widow thing he had going for him. That thought gave Aurora the heebie-jeebies. Cole was approaching his fifties, and Kaitlyn was in her twenties. Too much of an age gap in Aurora's mind. Plus, it was creepy as fuck.

Kaitlyn emerged from the stall with relief on her face. "That's better. I swear that cabbie hit every red light."

Aurora laughed. "That's why I walk." She dabbed a little more gloss on her lips. "Shall we?" They linked arms together and sauntered over to the dance club.

After dropping her backpack at coat check, Aurora surveyed the floor. Lights twinkled in a rainbow of colours as the music boomed beneath her feet. Crowds of people mashed together on the tiny dance floor, grinding and moving in time to the beat. A cluster of men and women lined the edges, drinks of stupidity held in their greedy little hands.

"Let's dance," Kaitlyn screamed into her ear, her blond head cocked towards the floor.

The ladies strutted their bodies, slinking through the crowd to a less compacted area on the dance floor, where there was a little more than a knife's edge to dance in.

Kaitlyn turned towards Aurora, and whispered, "Let's pretend and make heads turn." This was a fun game for Kaitlyn when they went out– playing pretend. Kaitlyn always wanted people to think she was gay, and maybe she was. Aurora had often wondered if she wasn't a bit bisexual. After all, she harboured a crush on her father and often flirted with him, but she loved women too. Aurora was completely confused by the whole thing and wondered if Kaitlyn was too.

Aurora, never one to judge, always agreed to play along. Besides it was fun, and it made her feel good. She missed the connection dancing close to another person brought; feeling her heat, smelling the sweet intoxication of her perfume, hands of another wavering up and down her body. The notion of getting lost, and not having a care in the world.

Kaitlyn shimmed up behind and her spindly arms embraced her. Kaitlyn's fingers danced upon her bare arms, and it electrified Aurora, freeing her from her hang-ups. Tonight she was *the* Dancing Queen. The sensations of touch beat through her like the bass of the music, rhythmic and slow, inviting and begging for more. She threw her head back against Kaitlyn's shoulder, and closed her eyes to the stares of the strangers. She didn't care. She wasn't the girl from the accident, she was free. Nothing to do but absorb the music into her soul, letting it run in her veins, making her come alive. In this moment, she was in tune with the music, becoming one with it.

Enjoying herself more than she anticipated, she turned around placing her hands on Kaitlyn's shoulders, and threw her head back so far she thought she was floating. Her body swayed in time to the music.

Lost in the vibrations, she slowly opened her eyes to the upside down view of people walking on the ceiling as she rubbed against her friend. Then she saw him and righted herself. Even upside down she recognised him. *Nate.*

Across the floor, he leaned against the bar scanning the crowd while talking with a light-haired male. Thankfully, she appeared different than her normal, mousy way, and wouldn't be so easy to spot. Her hands held firmly onto Kaitlyn's shoulders and she tried to get back into her rhythm, pressing harder into Kaitlyn and lowering her hands down to her waist. Another quick glance towards him, only this time their eyes connected.

She peeled herself out of Kaitlyn's embrace. "I'm getting hot," she yelled towards her friend. "I'll be back." Ducking out of the way, Aurora shimmied and slinked herself off the dance floor, to the opposite side of where Nate stood watching her. He nudged his friend and cocked his head in her direction.

Stealing a quick peek back, he tried to follow her, but a young girl pushed herself into Nate's arms and distracted him. It was all she needed–those few precious seconds–to help her fade into the background. After taking a moment to calm her racing heart, she peered around the column to look for him.

He'd advanced enough towards her that she could read his lips as he mouthed, "No, thanks," and he pushed the young girl away. Like a fox on the prowl, he hunted through the throngs of people, but she wasn't about to be found. In fact, she was more than a little surprised he actually showed up. She scurried to the back of the club and up a flight of stairs, enjoying the hunt. But tonight she wasn't about to be the prey. She merely wanted to watch.

On the second level, she managed to push herself to the balcony, and surveyed the dance floor. Lights of blue, green and purple danced in time to heavy beats of the thumping dance music. Now *she* was the hunter, and she searched through the people, trying to find his brown-haired head, only with the mystical lights and bad angle, it seemed an impossible task.

Finally, only at the end of a song did she spot him. A woman with short blond hair, in a skirt short enough to barely cover her ass crack, pressed into Nate, grinding against his leg. His hands hung awkwardly in the air as his eyes darted along the edges of the balcony, connecting once again with hers. A sly smile played on his lips as he spotted her.

Flushing from the smirk, she backed away and made her way through the crowd of beer swilling, and mostly drunk, college-aged people. Glancing around, she hightailed it down another set of stairs. Her foot slipped on the step, and trying to correct herself before falling down the last two steps, she threw her back out.

"Fuck!" she yelled to no one and cursed some more as she righted herself. People stopped and starred, but no one approached. Her back contracted in the worst spasms while her hands pushed deep into the tissue, hoping to alleviate some of the pain, but it was futile. The night was shot, and fighting against the people to leave pissed her off more. Her hand slammed against the counter, she redrew her ticket from her bra, thrusting it at the old lady manning the coat check. She dug her nails into her palms, and bit her lip to try to fight the urge to scream out some more.

When her backpack arrived, she rummaged until she found the little bottle and popped two pills into her mouth. She fired off a text to Kaitlyn telling her she needed to go home ASAP although she knew she'd get it later. There was no place for Kaitlyn to store her cell phone in her tiny dress. Kicking out of her heels, she exited the club barefoot and slowly, painfully, made her way to the bathroom where she cried and waited until relief settled in.

❤ Chapter Seven ❤

A desperate call from her boss rattled her out of bed. One of the staff was ill, and they needed her to fill in. Nothing hard, nothing complicated. Line control. Watch the people in line and make sure everyone waits their turn to see Matthew James. Easy, right? The extra cash sounded appealing, so she agreed.

Aurora arrived at work in her usual wear– jeans and a simple white long-sleeve t-shirt, with her most comfortable runners. She'd flung her heels into her closet somewhere after she managed to make it back home. Her back still ached today.

Preparing to wear the standard-issue library vest, she was a little put off to find out she had a uniform to wear. "For real?" she asked.

A manager passed her the purple velvet attire. "You slip it on over your clothes. It's not so bad." She turned and left Aurora alone in the locker room.

"Not so bad?" She pulled out one of two pieces. A long *and heavy* purple cape with gold trim. Did Matthew James not realise it was supposed to hit 25C today? She was going to be hot enough as it was in her long-sleeved shirt. Another groan rumbled from her as she pulled out the last piece. "Fucking awesome," she growled, unfolding the purple velvet hat. "I'm going to look like a fucking weirdo wizard."

She popped another perc and locked her locker. Slamming the ridiculous garb onto her head, she stormed out of the locker room, preparing herself for Nate's taunts. No doubt, he'd give her a hard time. With a heavy sigh, she plastered on a fake smile and headed out into the main part of the library where hundreds of eager guests– mostly pre-teen children, awaited the arrival of the guest of honour.

Aurora searched for Nate, wondering if he was somewhere in the corner, laughing at the whole event. He seemed to have no respect for the one he nicknamed "Rock Star God of Teenage Boys" and even asked if he wore a cape, and here she was dressed in a cape and sporting his colours. She could imagine the words he'd say, and the digs he'd get in. But to be honest, right now, she felt and looked foolish, and didn't care about all the wonderful goodness Matthew James did, she was on Nate's side. This was fucking ridiculous.

Aurora's portly manager waddled himself onto the stage, raising his hands in the air. "Boys and girls," he said. "Matthew James will be taking the stage in a moment. Who's excited?"

The sizeable crowd of people screamed and hollered. Wanting to cover her ears, but knowing she shouldn't, she instead pulled the wizard hat down lower, tucking her ears into it, and moved further back from the stage. Her sole purpose today was line management, and she could do that job without being close to the front where the crowd was tightest. Plus, the cape and hat get-up sucked out the positive feelings she had for Matthew James, and she wondered how long she'd have to wear it. If it was an all-day thing, she figured she'd hate his guts by the end of her shift.

"Boys and girls," the manager said a few minutes later. "May I present... Matthew James!"

The crowd applauded wildly when Matthew's name was called, and Aurora found herself momentarily caught up in the excitement as well. Turning in his direction, she saw him. Clearly comfortable in his own skin and exuding the confidence of a dozen men, he sauntered onto the stage, waving to his fans below. With a crisp white dress shirt and black jeans, he looked, well, like a rock star. Exceedingly handsome, with his long wavy hair blown off his tan and sculpted face. A hint of stubble gave him an older, sexy refined appeal.

She clapped and cheered with the fans. Her attention on him as he walked across the stage and shook hands with the manager, his megawatt smile unavoidable. She forgot about her job, and her reason for working. People were getting pushy and trying to see, and a violent shove against her aching back, made her stumble and lose her footing. Tumbling to the ground, she closed her eyes as pain blanketed her.

A loud voice boomed over the PA system. "Hey," the voice said, "is that how we treat people? Pushing others out of the way?" Although the volume on the PA remained the same, the voice who held it became louder. "Are you okay?"

She opened her eyes and there he stood. Right in front of her. His gorgeous hand outstretched. Following the line of his arm, upwards until she focused on his green eyes edged with the longest lashes she'd ever seen. He was even more gorgeous up-close, breathtaking really. Being so close to a real celebrity, she trembled as she accepted his hand. His perfectly soft and manicured hand. "Yes, I'm okay." With his help, she stood back on her feet.

He turned to the crowd while holding her hand. "This," he pointed to her, "is not how I want you treating your fellow brothers and sisters. We are all on this Earth together, and need to watch out and protect each other. Help, not hurt." He scanned the crowds. "Is everyone else okay?"

The crowd cheered, and Aurora wanted to join in, forgetting for a moment *she* was part of the reason the people applauded. She went to clap and stopped– he still held her hand. A stab of pain, and she pulled free of his hand. She rubbed her back, which had long sailed past aching. It throbbed.

"Now, my lovely lady," he bowed to her, "please come with me on stage."

"I can't," she whispered, heat flooding her cheeks. "I'm working." She bent down to retrieve her fallen hat.

"She's working," he announced into his headset with a laugh that sung through the walls. "Well, my lady, that is correct. Today you will be helping me directly. I insist." When he smiled at her, his teeth actually seemed to reflect the overhead lights. "I'm sure your bosses won't mind either." He flashed her a knee-buckling wink.

"Sure, Mr. James. What would you like me to do?"

He turned off his mic, and lowered his voice. "You're going to get me books from the boxes, and open them to page three, not page five. Not the first page but page three, and have them ready for me to sign when these sweet boys and girls come up. Understand?"

She nodded and studied the table where the boxes were stacked. Sighing internally that they were accessible, she smiled back.

"Good." He switched the mic back on and released her hand. "Ladies and gentlemen, now that that issue is resolved, who wants to have some fun?"

The crowd clapped wildly behind her as Aurora stepped up to the table and pulled out a few books. Under his orders, she opened them to the correct page, and placed them face down. Lost in the moment as Matthew James worked the crowd, bringing the group to their feet. She mouthed along as he recited moments of total brilliance from his books. Every bit the rock star, she became enchanted and searched for Nate, wondering if he was a witness to it all. He wasn't.

Aurora spent the remaining time passing the books to Matthew as guests and customers lined up to get an autographed copy. She noted that all the books were brand new, and not the ones she had been tasked with finding in the basement. Where were all those books? The distraction slowed her down, much to Matthew's chagrin.

"Where are my books, beautiful lady?" He said it in such a way that Aurora didn't take it as a compliment, and heard the underlining hiss in his tone.

"Sorry." She grabbed another stack, giving her aching back a quick rub. She hoped her back pain wouldn't reduce her to tears in front of a celebrity.

"Quicker please! These adorable children shouldn't have to wait."

She glanced from the lineup to Matthew and back again, passing another book as she did so. The longer she stood by him, the clearer she saw him. The shine of his star faded drastically with each little backhanded compliment.

Eventually, and thankfully, it ended, and she was forever grateful. She couldn't wait to toss the cape and hat getup into the nearest trash receptacle. As she was about to step off the stage, he called out to her. "Oh, my lady." He reached for her hand. "Thank you for your assistance. You are truly remarkable."

For what? Opening a book to the right page? Yeah, that would classify me as fucking remarkable, wouldn't it? Wanting to leave as fast as she could, she curtsied in return, plastering on an insincere smile, and said, "My pleasure." Even though it wasn't. Far from it. She wanted her pills. She *needed* her pills.

"May I have the honour of knowing your name, my lady?" Holding her hand high, he kissed it delicately on the top, his soft lips like a feather.

For a moment, her tongue ran away with her brain. "Aurora," she finally said recovering.

"Ah, like the princess in Sleeping Beauty." He escorted her off the stage, and continued to hold her hand while they walked to the back room, avoiding the lingering fans.

Completely spellbound, she followed the enchanting older man. Matthew James was well established in his thirties, maybe even older. At any rate, he was certainly older than her nineteen years.

He wrapped his fingers through hers, and although it wasn't uncomfortable, it wasn't altogether pleasant either. "My lady, I'd like to take you out for dinner tonight, to celebrate today's success."

Flabbergasted she mumbled, "Why?"

"Why? Because today you were my staff, and I reward my hard-working staff with dinner and drinks."

Rolling over his answer, she thought about it. Nothing special, just a dinner with Matthew James. Probably everyone would be there. "Okay, as long as it's close enough for me to walk."

"Oh, silly girl. All your transportation needs will be taken care of, trust me." His green eyes held hers.

She shrugged. "Yeah, but I don't get into vehicles with strangers."

"Infantile that thought is. Regardless, I am hardly a stranger. You know my name." His dazzling smile lit up his face.

"But that alone does not make us known to each other." What the hell? Why was she talking like him?

He sighed. "My lady, you probably know more about me than I do of you, so in this case, it is you who are the stranger to me, and yet, I've extended a dinner invitation to you."

Touché! She rolled over that statement in her head. As attractive and charming as Matthew James was, something was setting off bells in her head. Large ringing bells with flashing neon signs. But he was a celebrity, and she'd be foolish to say no. She debated. Yes or no. "Fine,

I'll accept your invitation, but I insist on it being nearby. There's a Brewster's a couple of blocks away."

He stared at her, his eyes lighting up and he waved his hand about. "Interesting," he declared to the surrounding people. "This girl, this woman–" he corrected after giving her a once over.

She shuddered violently under the cloak of purple, hoping he didn't notice. It was unlikely given he was talking to the select few privileged enough to be nearby.

They all turned in his direction as Matthew James carried on. "Is making the rules. Interesting indeed." He stared at her further, his roving gaze moving up and down her body as if determining whether she was worth it. "Fine, I, we will go with you to this Brewster's. I need time to freshen up though, so I'll meet you at the front of the library in thirty minutes."

"Actually, I'll be walking, so I'll meet you there in thirty minutes." *Take that!*

"Hmmm," he said, as he rubbed his whisker-laden jawline with his free hand. "Okay. I like this feistiness." He let go of her hand after giving it another kiss. "Thirty minutes."

Aurora turned and walked away, unsure of her feelings. Confusion mostly. Ten minutes ago she was ready to leave him in the dirt, but now? Now she was going to have a dinner date with Matthew James for crying out loud! How in hell did that happen? She'd rack this up to an unusual day for sure. She grabbed her purse, and choked down a couple of muscle relaxers. *Shit.* She forgot to give him directions to where the restaurant was, and spun back towards the special visitors room they'd set up for him.

Hand up, poised to knock on the slightly ajar door, she heard laughter and the soft, expressive voice of Matthew James. "You saw that, eh? Such a princess." He laughed a deep throaty laugh. "These young girls are so easy to charm. Give them some attention, puff them up a little and they eat out of my hand."

"Or further south," said another voice, which burst into a laugh. "Just make sure this one is legal. She looks young."

"I will, don't need that following me around again," Matthew said.

Shocked, Aurora stood there. She couldn't believe her ears. Clearly he was talking about her. He was using her, and she was no more special than anyone else. God, she felt so dumb having fallen for his charm. *I wonder if he's ever been stood up before.* She turned and marched herself home, hating herself, and hating Nate because he was right– Matthew James was pretentious.

❤ Chapter Eight ❤

"Asshole," she repeated over and over on the way home. She hated what he'd done, made her feel special when it was all an act. All lies. He was so fucking cocky and so self-assured. He'd been manipulating her with his charm and despite the back-handed compliments, like an idiot, she'd fallen for it. She knew better than that. And she certainly wouldn't be going 'further south' on a stranger.

She threw her purse across the kitchen when she entered her apartment, angry with herself. "Bastard," she yelled and grabbed her laptop. Google would provide more information about this jerk. As she started typing, her cell rang.

"Aurora!" The female voice yelled after she said hello. "What the hell? You just leave without saying goodbye?"

"Kaitlyn, I'm–" *What? Sorry, because I'm not. Well?* "I'm sorry for leaving without saying goodbye. I hurt my lower back and needed to hightail it out of there."

"I looked all over for you."

She buried her face into her hands, cradling the phone against her ear. "I'm sorry for that, but I hurt so bad, I couldn't look for you. I knew eventually you'd get your phone."

"Are you okay now?"

"Better, yes. But not a hundred percent."

Kaitlyn huffed. "Good. I'm sorry you got hurt. I was having a really good time with you."

Aurora smiled, recalling the closeness. "I was too. It was almost–" *Erotic? Is it weird to think that?*

"Yeah?"

"Yeah." Sometimes your bestie understood what you wanted to say, even if you never said it.

"Cool. So you want to hang tonight?"

Slumping against the back of the kitchen chair, she said, "Yeah, it beats researching a major jerk." She launched into discussion about her day with Matthew James.

"I should swing by and see if he's there waiting."

Aurora glanced at the clock above her TV. "You wouldn't make it in time to check."

"Actually, I'm not far away. I should. Text me a pic of the rat-faced bastard."

Aurora laughed and fund a quick pic. "There you go."

"Great, thanks. Oh, here it is. Wow, he's handsome," Kaitlyn said. "A jerk still, but a handsome one."

"Yes, he is."

"Okay, I'm going to have some fun. I'll come over when I'm done."

Kaitlyn hung up and Aurora pondered the possibilities of what her friend would do. She almost wanted to be a fly on the wall, but she'd never make it in time. Instead, passing time, she tidied up. The scattered clothes were picked off the floor and she kicked the rest down the hall into the bottom of her closet, before she loaded the dishwasher and ran a cloth over the counter, and stacked up a pile of textbooks in the corner of the living room. It wasn't Kaitlyn clean, but it was an improvement.

She'd finished when Kaitlyn buzzed and came up holding her belly.

"What?" Aurora asked.

"That–" she said between quick breaths, "was a lot of fun."

"What did you do?" Aurora narrowed her eyes as Kaitlyn fell into the living room.

"Oh I met him, walked right up to his booth and told him to Fuck Off and Die."

"What? You didn't."

"Told him, and I used the words you told me, 'That's not how we treat our fellow brothers and sisters' and then I told him if he ever touched you again, I'd break his neck."

Aurora's eyes bugged out. "Kaitlyn!" She shook her head. "Well, thankfully he's not coming back to the library, it was just today."

"Meh, whatever, it was still fun. You should've seen the look on his face."

"I wish." Aurora sat on the couch, pulling a leg underneath her. Her bestie flopped down beside her, her hand falling on Aurora's leg.

"It was awesome." Kaitlyn threw her head back on the couch, deep in thought.

Aurora relaxed. "Want to watch a movie then?"

"Sure, something scary." Kaitlyn laughed when Aurora gasped. "Kidding. I know you hate anything with gore. What would you prefer?"

"Something that will make me cry."

Kaitlyn cocked her head as she flipped through the expansive collection of DVDs. "Seriously, what's up with that? You always want a tear-jerker."

"Sometimes, a girl just needs to cry to feel better." And to let her emotions run freely without being judged. It hurt the way Matthew treated her. As much as she wanted to cry, she couldn't. But a good tear-jerker would be a great excuse.

"Fine. I'll put in that Hazel and Augustus movie you love so much."

"I'll make popcorn."

❤ Chapter Nine ❤

M onday rolled around as Mondays always do. Way too early, and full of piss and vinegar. She hated Mondays, and today she'd hate it even more. Fucking Matthew James.

As she staggered down the hall, she was rather proud of her efforts the previous day. Her home, for the first time since she'd moved into it a few weeks ago, sparkled. Clothes were washed and put away, dishes sat neatly stacked in their cabinets, as opposed to piled beside the sink. She even managed to hang up a few personal pictures but passed on displaying a family portrait. It'd be too hard to see daily, especially with her Daddy coming for a visit, so she hung up one of Carmen's canvas prints. From the room that still housed her belongings. The room she wasn't supposed to enter, and yet, wasn't allowed to empty. Carmen's storage closet. *I wonder if Daddy has a whole floor he doesn't touch at home filled with Momma's stuff.*

With a huff, she sighed and made herself a cup of coffee. Nope, she wasn't looking forward to seeing anything related to what she thought was a Matthew James sized fiasco. Maybe, hopefully, Kaitlyn's sudden appearance was hushed up. She really hoped no one heard the jerk ask her out. Cause that's what he was. A class-A jerk. A quick Google search revealed only his age– thirty-seven, nearly twice hers. It grossed her out knowing his age, and it made her shudder. Constantly.

Finishing her coffee, and taking a couple more pills, she left for work with a grocery list in her purse. She wanted to make her Daddy a special dinner, his favourite– homemade mac and cheese.

Aurora couldn't get over how different the air was here in the big city versus Fort Mac. She expected it to be smoggy and smoky, but instead it was clear, tainted with the hint of blossoming flowers and leaves. Summer was slowly approaching, and she couldn't wait to spend her summer months here.

The stage dismantled, she was beyond pleased to see the area back to a regular section of the library. Gone were the plants, the chairs, the tables, anything purple and gold, and the boxes of pretentiousness. Relief washed over her.

Steps away from where the display had been, she glanced through the poly film blocking off the newest addition, hoping to steal a peek at Nate. However, the opaque plastic wall made him as easy to find as sharks in a river. Growling, she marched away.

"There you are," a voice called out behind her. Spinning around, she expected to see someone else, and instead came face to face with her boss. "I've been looking all over for you."

"What's up, Sarah?" She didn't like the overly excited expression on her face. Something was up.

"We wanted to thank you for your help on Saturday with Matthew. You helped us out in a pinch."

"Really?" Aurora raised an eyebrow. "I didn't do anything more than pass him books." *And wear that ridiculous cape and hat.*

"Regardless, you were there to help. The lines ended up being more than we expected and we sold out the books we had here, and the others have all been checked out."

"Great?" She wondered where this was going.

"He was rather fond of you, and told us how much he appreciated you."

I'm sure he did. She rolled her eyes.

"He's coming back. At the end of summer for a huge two-day event. And he's personally requested you to assist him. Isn't this wonderful?" She clapped her hands in excitement. "We're going to push hard to get the new addition open by then. We're calling it the *Matthew James Wing*. Isn't it great?"

She surely didn't think so, but nodded an affirmative.

"Oh, he left this for you on Saturday. He took off quickly, and returned before we closed for the night to share with us the good news about a return visit. Here." Sara thrust a beige envelope towards her.

"Thanks," she smiled weakly as she flipped the envelope over and over. "He's really coming back, eh?"

"Yes. And with more time to plan, we can make this visit HUGE. The board's meeting all this week to think up wonderful ideas. You should join us since you've been requested and all."

"Nah, I'm good, but thanks."

Sarah turned on her heels, dancing her way to the back office.

"Well, at least someone's happy."

Even with her back to him, she heard his smirk in his voice. "Nate."

"Aurora." A twinkle formed in his eyes before he thumbed in Sarah's direction. "Is she always like that?"

"As long as I've known her." *Which really isn't very long since I've only been here a couple of weeks.* "Crazy, isn't she?"

"Better than a bitchy boss, I suppose." Nate stared at her hands, at the envelope. "What's that?"

"Have no idea, but I'm not interested in it either."

"So let me have it." Having grabbed it, he ran his finger across her beautifully handwritten name. He waved it in front of her. "Who's it from?"

Aurora cringed. "Matthew James."

"Ah." He lowered his hand a bit and leaned against the wall. "And? How was the show?"

Heat flooded her face in a fraction of a second, and a ribbon of disgust ran through her. "It was… unpredictable." She searched his face for a sign of emotion, any emotion. "It went so well that he's coming back at the end of summer for a two-day celebration."

"Whoopee doo," Nate said. "Glad I'll be done here by then."

"Wish I could say the same." She kicked the cart with her foot. "Dammit. I hate that you were right."

"About?"

Those brown eyes of his danced as she spoke. "Oh, shut up. You know. Mr. Pretentious. He really is a class-A certifiable prick."

"Such language, and from one of his biggest fans too. What happened? Mr. Pretentious forget to sign your book?"

He laughed, but she didn't return the feeling. Instead she ripped the envelope from his hand and stormed away.

Soft footprints approached from behind. "Hey, I was kidding. Geez, lady, take a joke."

"I'd rather not, thank you very much."

"What did he do to make you turn on him?"

She wanted to tell him it was none of his business and yet, she also wanted to tell him everything. As if keeping this a secret from him would be a terrible thing. Her face flushed, and she fanned herself with the envelope while she debated telling him.

Again, he stole it from her, but this time opened it. His face screwed up and tightened. "You had a date with him?" She avoided his eyes. "Really?"

She hung her head in shame as the ripped envelope and card fluttered to her feet. "It wasn't a date, really."

"So you'll go on a date with Mr. Pretentious, but when I show up at the club that *you* invited me to, you take off. Guess I know what you go for in guys."

A sharp inhale before meeting his gaze. The moment she did, she wished she hadn't. Betrayal hung over him, washing clean his normal chipper expression and replacing it with disgust. The silver ball of his tongue piercing perched between his teeth and made him sexy, but it was overshadowed by the air of sadness.

"And I thought you were different."

Although he marched to the construction area, she hoped he'd turn around. He didn't. She fetched the mess at her feet, and opened up the card.

Dearest Aurora,

Sorry about the way our dinner turned out.

I'm not sure where things went wrong, but I'd like to make it up to you.

Please call me. My personal number's below.

Yours, Matthew

"Ugh," Aurora grunted and walked over to the nearest recycling container, tossing in the envelope and card. "Fucking jerk," she added as she shoved it to the bottom of the bin.

Overextended emotionally, she backtracked to the staff room and rooted through her purse. *I need a quick fix.* The container where relief should be was empty. No matter how many times she shook the container, nothing spilled out. "Dammit," she cursed and slammed a palm into the door of her locker. A quick glance to the clock. Still two hours away from a lunch break when she could run home and get more. Double checking in case one pill hid in the depths of her purse, she dumped the contents across the bench.

Wallet. Phone. Notebook. Emergency tampon. A pill bottle with a dozen Percocet. A few coins. Lipstick tube. Another pill container with five Flexeril. A set of keys. An empty Xanax container. No little blue pill. *Fuck.* She stared at the two pills she did have. Combined, they would work and take the edge off. A little annoying voice in the back of her head, likely the pre-med voice she once listened to, told her to never mix them. However, at this moment, she wanted to escape her emotions. To feel blah. To not care. She stared long and hard, debating.

"Fuck me," she growled and cleaned up her personal mess. It wasn't going to happen today.

After restocking her travelling containers with more pills at lunch, she returned a little lighter in her steps. Keeping an eye roving about for Nate, she did her work at a distractingly slower pace than normal. *Where was he hiding?* She didn't see him. Anywhere. And she desperately wanted to talk to him. Explain things better. She hated that Matthew James had interfered in something between them. But what was between them?

Nothing, really. A bud of friendship, maybe something romantic. It had only been a week or so but she was intrigued by him. Yes, intrigued was a good word. He had no love for the rock star that was for sure, and he let those feelings show. He comforted her during that wicked storm and didn't think she was acting childish. Derek never understood her fear of storms, and always laughed at her cowardliness.

Plus, Nate was cute too, in a handsome way. That dark hair, those brown eyes. She shook her head.

Although he'd already asked her out, it would never happen. She was too damaged to ever make a relationship work. She never needed the reminders, but Derek proved it. She'd been with him for two years, her high school sweetheart. Then after the accident, he couldn't handle the way she'd changed; physically and emotionally. Everything changed after that day. Everything.

"Hey, Aurora, phone call for you. Long distance," Sarah called out to her.

For a heartbeat, she worried it was about her father, because otherwise he'd call her cell. Plus, he was due to visit tonight. Panicked that something bad had happened, she raced to the phone and pressed the blinking button. "Hello?"

"Aurora?"

"Yes, this is she."

"Ah, great." The voice on the other end paused a moment. "It's Matthew."

Her heart sank. *For real?*

"Matthew James."

"What do you want?" Her voice changed from panicked to irritated in a microsecond.

"I wanted to talk to you. Find out why you stood me up and sent your demonic friend in your place."

She tapped her foot, and glanced around. No one was around. Two staff members out of earshot were the closest people. "I heard what you said about me. How easy I was to manipulate and how you'd have me eating out of the palm of your hand." Anger built in her core and she turned her back to the open door. "I'm not that type of girl, so go fuck yourself."

The receiver was away from her ear, but she heard him call out, "Wait, Aurora, please." She put the phone back against her ear. "Geez, you are feisty."

"What do you want?"

"Please, my lady, understand that I meant no harm. I was talking to my manager, and that's how things are with him. It was all in fun."

"Whatever."

48

"No really, I wouldn't have asked you out if I didn't mean it."

"You're just a typical jerk-faced toad. You like an easy score at every place you visit." She stood tall, as she cradled the phone against her shoulder, stealing glances towards the door. Which was now closed. Great. Someone had overheard her conversation.

"I'm not. I swear."

"How am I supposed to believe that?"

"Well, for starters, I'm across the country calling you."

"So what? That proves nothing."

He sighed. "Fine, do you have a pen handy?"

"Sure–" She grabbed the one nearest the phone and ripped a receipt off the till.

"When you go home, Google 'Rebecca Gordon' and then call me."

"Why would I do that?"

"Well, my feisty one, when you do, perhaps you'll understand."

"Humph."

She said goodbye, more politely this time, and hung up. Thinking hard, she remembered she'd thrown away his card. She raced to the recycling bin and dug through it, searching through the mounds of paper. Finally, she found her prize and pulled it out, flipping it over and staring at the back of the card. The number was within her local area code, and although that could put him anywhere within northern Alberta, it meant he lived closer than she expected. She folded up the card and tucked it into the depths of her pocket.

"Daddy," she exclaimed, dropping her belongings by the door. "What are you doing here?"

He rolled the newspaper he was reading down and looked her squarely in the eyes. "Princess, I told you I was coming."

"I mean, what are you doing in the apartment?"

"Since I'm the one that pays rent on this place, don't you think I'd have a key?" He folded the newspaper perfectly and set it on the table. His demeanour changed from amusement to chagrin.

Shaking her head, she walked into the kitchen, needing a glass of water for her dry throat.

"How was work?"

Conversations were always so limited to such trivial topics. Work. School. The weather. That was about it. Never anything personal. They avoided those discussions as the couple of times they tried, it was awkward and weird. Daddies weren't for sharing private thoughts. Mommas and sisters were. "It was good. Not overly exciting."

"Well, that's life. Sometimes it's good when it's not exciting."

Walking back in to the dining area after downing a full glass, she worried about her father. He looked terrible. His eyes were bloodshot and red-rimmed, and his skin more sallow than normal. "I suppose." Aurora's eyes bugged, and she slapped herself in the forehead. "Oh shit, I forgot to pick up some groceries on the way home, and I totally meant too."

He stood and headed for the spare room, a sparsely decorated room since its abandonment a few weeks ago when its former tenants, Carmen's friends, moved out. "Let's go out for dinner, then. You can show me what's good around here."

"Well, there's not much in terms of sit down places, but there's the standard fast food."

"Ugg, no thanks."

She placed her hand on her hip, and the other on her back, giving it a quick rub. "Well, how about?" *Brewster's? Ha, no.* "Let's go to Donny's."

"What's that?"

"Pizza and burgers, at least according to the flyers. I've never been there, but it's close by."

"Great, let's go." Her daddy grabbed his keys off the table.

"We can walk."

"Aurora, this is unhealthy."

"What do you mean? Walking is great exercise." She rolled her eyes, knowing exactly where this conversation was going. Again.

"You need to get over this irrational fear for cars."

She clenched her fists and narrowed her eyes. "Irrational? I don't think it's irrational to be afraid of what killed people I loved. They are death mobiles, and I'll have no part of that." Her father's face paled.

"Aurora–"

"Have you seen motor vehicle accident statistics? They're outrageous, Daddy. And we're part of that stat." She stomped her foot and crossed her arms over her chest.

He sighed and ran his fingers through his thinning salt and pepper hair. "You need to get over this."

"I won't, and it'll never happen."

"This place you mentioned has to be less than a five minute drive. Try."

She pressed her lips together into a tight line. "It'll never happen. Besides, you didn't bring any special pills with you, did you?" The only way she'd been able to get into a vehicle since the accident was to be so drugged she didn't remember. Her daddy had a special pill that caused her to block the trip out of her mind, like selective amnesia.

"You can't keep taking those pills to hide from it."

"Yeah, and I wouldn't have survived the trip from the dorm to here without them." The magic pills had come in handy for that trip.

"Speaking of pills, how's your supply doing?"

How was she supposed to answer that? She used them, but *only* when she needed them. "I guess it's good?"

"Do you take them every day?"

"Not *every* day." It wasn't a lie, really, it's only been lately that something has necessitated their use. "I've only taken them when my back or hips ache, or something causes me massive anxiety."

"How often is that?"

"Not as often as I think you're trying to lead me to admit." She picked at her cuticles, and tore off a strip of hangnail.

He shook his head and placed a firm, yet fatherly hand on her shoulder. "Watch it, okay? So you don't become addicted to them."

Frozen in her spot, her mouth hung open. "I'm not–" Her hands covered her mouth. She couldn't even say the word, mostly because it wasn't true. "I write down each time I use them, and why." She paused and thought a moment. *Except I haven't, really. The last few days I've not recorded. I need to do that, account for each pill used, otherwise it looks bad. Like I'm addicted or something.*

As if he could read her mind, he asked, "When's your next appointment?"

"End of the month." Aurora had regular visits to an orthopedic doctor on campus, to check that her pelvis, her left hip joint and both legs functioned to the best of their ability. She still limped but there wasn't much they could do about that anymore. Her hips had healed slightly out of alignment, but with intense physical therapy, he told her, there could be hope. If she went. Which she didn't.

In the new apartment, there wasn't a physical therapist nearby, and no hope of getting back to campus. And without regular visits to a PT, her doctor was a hard man to convince that she needed more pain pills, because that was the whole point of the physical therapy visits– reducing her pain. It was a vicious cycle.

Frustrated with her doctor's lack of house calls, she'd found a new doctor nearby. This one had no issues treating her chronic pain with pills, and good ones too. Without any pressure to see a physical therapist or even discuss pain strategies. She liked him. An easy fix. Five minutes in and she'd get a couple months' supply of happy little pills. So appeasing him, and to prove to herself she wasn't an addict, she kept the diary and tried to remember to keep it updated.

Her daddy wrapped his arms around her. "That's my princess. Now, let's go eat. I'm hungry."

❤ Chapter Ten ❤

Aurora left a note with her work schedule taped to the spare bedroom door the next morning, not daring to wake her father. Slipping out the door, she walked to work, enjoying the fresh air.

Despite the weather and all-around good morning, she woke to a misery the sunshine couldn't melt away. Her father always had that effect on her. She missed the pleasantness of her momma and Carmen. It had almost been two years since the accident. Two years without feeling a part of something.

She pushed back the impending tears. *Not today.* As she approached the library, she remembered she forgot to Google the name she'd written. Oh well, she'd do it after work. Her daddy was meeting an old friend for supper, so she'd have time without pretending to be interesting. Resting on the nearby bench to catch her breath, a van of construction guys jumped out and headed around the back of the library. A red car pulled up beside, and caught her attention.

One man in specific stopped, and nodded at her as he approached.

"Hi, Nate."

"Good morning."

Her skin tingled as it warmed, and her breath quickened in response. "Well, good to know you're still talking to me."

"Yeah, we never said we were exclusive." He stepped closer.

"What? We're not even–"

His fingers made a gun, and he clicked it at her. "Gotcha."

A smile broke across her face. "Oh, ha-ha."

He approached her and sat beside her on the bench. "What are you up to after work?"

She cocked her head. "You are a persistent one, aren't you?"

"Duly noted." He smiled. "So?"

"Well, not much I guess."

"Not much you guess? There's enthusiasm for you." He rubbed his legs. "Want to grab a coffee? There's a GrabbaJoes over there." He pointed towards her apartment.

She was familiar with it as she passed by it to and from work. "Sure," she said, seeing the way his smile crinkled a little, and his brown eyes sparkled with joy. "It's a date."

"A bona fide date?"

"Yes, and I'll even stay this time." Aurora laughed.

He raised an eyebrow. "Perhaps I should escort you so you don't bolt."

Heat flooded her cheeks, and she whispered, "Perhaps."

"Great. I'll meet you here. Right here."

As he walked away, she took in his fine form, even in the overalls. None of the other guys suited those, but Nate... wow. They showcased a slim silhouette. For the briefest moment, she wondered what he wore under them. Underwear? Or a pair of pants? With a shy smile, she rose and headed in through the main doors.

As promised, she met the waiting Nate at the bench. "Shall we?" he said as he waved his hand and pointed towards the coffee shop.

"We shall," she replied.

When she wasn't as fast as he was, he slowed. "So, tell me, what's your aversion to cars?"

She stopped walking and faced him, arms crossed. "I have no aversion."

"Oh yes you do, but I'm truly curious as to why?"

"Why? What does it matter?"

"It matters because if I want to take you out somewhere, I'd like to pick you up and drive you, the way a proper man should. None of this meet you there, BS."

She resumed walking, and a funny impish smile tugged at her face. "'Fraid I'll take off?"

"Well, you didn't this time, so I'll say that there's only a fifty percent chance of being ditched."

"What can I say? I'm unpredictable like that." She shrugged and tugged at her sleeves, pulling them over her palms.

"Indeed. Playing hard to get too."

"I do no such thing. I'm an open book, with nothing to hide." Smugness crossed her face.

He folded his arms across his chest. "Really? So then, why are you afraid of cars?"

She squinted her eyes at him in mocking disapproval.

"See," he pointed, "right there. You're a closed book."

They reached the open door of GrabbaJoes and entered. "What do you want?" she asked after giving her order to the barista– a maple macchiato.

"Nothing pretentious," he joked as he scanned the boards and ordered a flat white.

"Outside?" Aurora tipped her head with her warm coffee in her hands. "The patio's open."

"Sure, why not?" After they located a free table, he stepped behind her, and pulled out her chair.

Aurora laughed. "Seriously?" When he didn't laugh, she bit the inside of her cheek. "Sorry, I'm not used to that."

"Apparently. You never dated a guy who did that for you?" She didn't answer. "My dad always did that for my mom. Lead by example, he'd say, show the lady she's worth it."

"Oh? What happened to him?"

Nate twiddled his thumbs, and when he responded, he avoided her. "Dad died a few years back. Cancer."

"Oh, I'm sorry. I truly am." She reached for his hand, and gave it a squeeze. It was an honest thing to do, but it felt good. And judging from the way he glanced from their hands to her eyes, it must've felt good to Nate too.

"Thanks."

"I know how tough it can be to lose a parent. I lost my mom and sister almost two years ago." She welcomed the voice she gave her own loss, but took little comfort knowing someone else had survived that.

People held their fancy coffees as they walked by, laughing loudly. It annoyed her. They were sharing a personal moment, and she would've preferred privacy. Her metal chair scraped against the concrete as she scooted closer to him.

"Yeah, it's tough. The first year was the worse, but after a couple of years… Well, you develop new routines, different ones and you make the best of it. Mom's doing well though. She's tougher than I give her credit for. She's always talking about him, even something little. The other night, while making cream of chicken soup, she added a sprig of parsley to the top. Just like he did." Nate glanced around and squirmed in his chair. She wondered if it was hard for him to talk about his father.

"Wish Daddy would."

"Daddy? Really?" He smirked, and his smile was the most beautiful thing to lay her eyes upon.

Embarrassed, she pulled her hand away and picked at the raw cuticle on her finger. "Anyways, my father," she said as he leaned closer to her. "He never talks about it. Dismisses it as if it never happened."

He reached for her hand, stroking the finger she'd tormented. The warmth coming from his hands soothed her although his skin was quite rough and callousy. It shouldn't have surprised her holding the job he did.

"We should get our parents together, Mom never shuts up about it and she can make anyone talk about anything."

She recoiled. "That would be… weird. Our parents getting together."

"Only weird if something were to happen between us."

"Because us happening would be weird?"

"Are you always like this?" He cocked his head, a smile breaking out across his face.

"Like what?"

"Twisting everything anyone says?"

"Perhaps." She nodded and pulled her hands back, to take a long sip of her drink. A hint of a smile leaked out of her lips. A matching one played at the corners of his, pulling the left side up enough that his smile was lopsided.

"You're funny."

"Oh yeah," she rolled her eyes, "A real riot act."

His eyes grazed over her, down to fingertips, and up her arms, landing on her blue eyes. "You're very pretty, in an understated kind of way."

"Wow, you really are the master of cheesy pickup lines." She took another long drink of her coffee.

"Not really. I just tell it like it is."

"Well, understated is a good word."

He leaned back against his wrought-iron chair. "You're incredibly difficult to read, you know."

"I prefer it that way. Lends itself to a little mystery."

"Yes, it does." He took a drink, the foam sticking to his pale pink lips. "I like mystery. Means there's more to you than meets the eye."

"And there you go again, Mr. Cheesy Pickup Lines." She laughed, a good throaty laugh, tipping her head back in the process.

He licked his lips, and matched her smile. "Hmm."

"Hmm what?"

"Trying to think of what to say that won't necessarily bring on a quick little comeback." His voice full of curiosity.

The weight of his stare was like a hundred pounds, so she gave her coffee a swirl.

"You claim you're an open book, which you're not because you managed to completely avoid my questions. You have a witty sense of humour, which I'm rather fond of. You have a genuine fear of cars, which I'd like to get down to the bottom of, and you have an interesting fear of thunderstorms. And you have a mouth like a sailor."

"What? I do not."

"Yeah, you do. I heard you on the phone. Shame, shame." He waggled a finger at her in jest.

Laughing, she shrugged. "Well, we can't all be perfect."

"I agree, perfection is boring."

He stretched out his long legs, and rested them beside her chair. "So tell me, Miss Aurora, what is it you like in a man?" He paused and leaned forward, and arched a sly brow. "It is men you're interested in, correct?"

With that, her cheeks flooded with a stinging shame. She could only imagine the way it had appeared to him. Her tongue failed to move and her brain could only say, "Shit" over and over.

"I only ask, because I saw how you danced with that other girl at the club. That's not how someone dances with just a friend. I'd never dance that way with my buddies."

No witty comeback available, she went with the truth. "Kaitlyn's my best friend, and was my roommate in the university dorms. We're close."

"*That* I saw." His face displayed raw interest as he stroked his stubble covered chin.

"Well, if you must know, no I'm not into girls, not that way." She flashed back to Friday night, and heat coursed through her core as she remembered their dancing. "We're just friends."

"Hey, it's cool."

"Sure it is. Because it's every guy's dream, right? Two girls getting it on, fighting over a man." She rolled her eyes.

"Maybe for some, but I'm not particularly fond of sharing. A bad habit I developed as a child. Ask my mother."

Aurora laughed as she imagined him as a child. How cute would he be?

"So," Nate said, "back to my question, Miss Avoidance. What do you find appealing about men? Shall I continue to chase or not?"

"You really are direct."

"Well no point in beating around the bush." Aurora raised her eyebrows suggestively, to which Nate laughed. "Touché." He took a drink. "So?"

"I'm not going to be able to avoid this, am I?"

"Nope. I'm very curious."

Aurora leaned back on her chair, and crossed her legs. After a half second of stabbing hip pain, she uncrossed them, cursing in her head and instead, crossed her legs at the ankle. "Well, I like a man who respects women." He nodded. "Someone who knows how to treat a lady and yet doesn't pamper her like a princess."

"Okay."

She watched his face as she spoke, observing the way his tongue stud danced over his teeth when he contemplated her words. "I like him to be strong, and yet gentle spirited. Someone who knows his way around the female body, and knows what makes her tick." She winked, and he edged his chair closer. "A man needs to be loving and compassionate, honest and trustworthy. He shouldn't give up when the going gets tough, either." *Like Derek did.*

"I'm so close on this one." He smirked.

"Oh yeah, which part are you faulting on?" She licked her lips as she leaned towards him.

"Wouldn't you like to know?"

She cocked her eyebrow. "Yes, I would. Very much indeed." Her eyes searched his face, waiting for an answer that didn't come. Pouting internally, she said, "Oh, yeah, one other thing. He can't have a tattoo."

"Well, there goes that. I'm out." He leaned back and pulled up the sleeve of his black shirt, revealing a gorgeous colour tat. It extended over his shoulder and onto his back.

"Are those feathers?" She ached to run her fingers over it.

"It's an angel, fighting the devil. My dad's the angel, cancer's the devil." After she admired the complexity of what she saw, he recovered his arm. "Guess we can only be friends."

"Guess so." She stared at him through the fringe of her lashes, and wondered if the playfulness was still there or if it had packed up ship and left harbour. Another long gulp as she waited.

"Well, is there anything else?"

"Huh?"

"Anything else you desire in a man? Anything else, physical?"

She smiled. Game on. "Of course. He has to be hot, real fucking hot." She fanned herself. "So hot that I can barely keep my pants on and the anticipation nearly kills me." Seeing him wiggle in the seat spurred her to keep talking. "Dark hair and eyes are a must, and a killer smile. One of those panty wrecking smiles."

"Like this?" His dimple appeared with his lopsided sexy grin, and she wanted to scale the table.

Body and soul on fire, she whispered, "Want to come back to my place?"

He leaned even closer, and his breath tickled her ears. "Nope." Falling back against his chair, sultriness written all over his face. "Keep your pants on and allow the anticipation to nearly kill you."

Pouting, she leaned back and crossed her heaving chest with her arms.

"Ah, two can play this game." He winked.

❤ Chapter Eleven ❤

The next day, Aurora left work and found herself staring at Nate. He sat on the hood of his car, the sunshine lighting him up as if he were a gift from heaven. An intoxicating smile and radiated charm called her over when they made eye contact.

"I didn't think you were working today. I didn't see you," she said on the approach.

"They have us working on the exterior for now. You know, make hay while the sun shines and all that."

She nodded. "Gotcha."

"So I was thinking," he breathed out, "about yesterday and this car fear you have, but won't talk about."

Taking a step back, she glared at him.

"And I think I figured out what's going on, although I'm no rocket scientist." He slipped off the hood and walked closer to her. "Correct me if I'm wrong, and feel free to tell me to shove it."

"Oh, I will." There was a lot of seriousness behind those brown eyes, yet apathy too. Words failed to escape her mouth, for once.

"So based on the bit of info you've blessed me with, I highly suspect you were in a wicked automobile crash, which killed your mother and sister. Am I close?" He searched her eyes, holding them and she couldn't look away.

Shocked beyond comprehension, she stared at him, unable to blink. Or breathe.

"Okay, I figured I was on the right track." He reached for her hand. "And I want to help you get over this fear."

"It will never happen," she said, her voice falling.

"I'll still try. Because if something becomes of us, I'd like to eventually take you places, and show you more of this wonderful city." He waved his arm about.

"If something becomes of us?" She licked her lips while smiling.

"Yes, if something does, I'd like to show you off."

"There's nothing you can do. My therapist told me I may never get over it."

As he stepped closer, he said, "And I get that I'm no therapist, but I have ideas. If you're willing to try."

Her hands shook and her voice trembled as she whispered, "How?" Horrible visions of him strapping her into a car and taking her for a spin filled the forefront of her brain.

He reached for her hand and held it. "Simple. Baby steps."

Blinking slowly, she tried to comprehend. "Baby steps?"

"Yep. I have a plan. Today we'll try something and we'll see how it goes."

She backed up, quivering with each step.

"Today, what I want you to do is simple." He guided her towards the side of his car, but she put the brakes on, pulling hard against him. "Easy. Today, we touch the car. That's it."

Her eyes darted from him to the car and back again. "That's it?"

"Honest to God truth." He crossed his heart with his fingers.

She swallowed and stared at the car. It sounded so simple, so easy. With trepidation, she slowly extended her shaking hand. She glanced at him. No hint of impatience on his face, he locked eyes with her, letting her make the move.

A cold sweat built up along the base of her neck, and her legs turned to mush. "I can't." Her hand raced back to her body, shaking violently. Instinctively, she covered her eyes. "I can't."

"Sure you can. I'll help you."

Her eyes flashed open as his rough hand touched the top of hers, no doubt feeling the tremors, but he laced his fingers through regardless. Slowly, he guided her hand until they touched his car first with the edge of her palm. The metal was cool to the touch, but didn't aid in slowing down the shakes. However, she was touching it. She closed her eyes, trying to block out the smell of blood, the sound of grinding metal, the popping of glass. The screaming that came from her mouth only. Breathing hard and sweating profusely, Aurora kept her hand on it, speed counting in her head. When she hit fifteen, she yanked back.

"Wow. That was great."

After opening her eyes, she focused on him. Pride radiated from his eyes and a genuine smile lit up his face. Free of his hand, she thrust it into her pocket. "Yeah, I did it." Not believing it, she stared at the spot where her hand was moments ago, unable to blink. *Holy shit! I fucking touched the car. I can't believe I actually did it.*

"How was it?"

She inhaled a huge gulp of air. "Scary as hell." Against her better control, her hands shook in her pocket.

"Baby steps. That's all we'll do." The handsome devil leaned back against his car with his crossed arms over his chest. "Your therapist, did he or she ever discuss PTSD with you?"

"Duh, of course."

"Good."

She shrugged and tilted her head, gazing into his eyes, his cheerful-looking eyes. "Yeah, I'm aware of what I have. However, she said some never get over it, and others do with time."

"I think with time you will."

"You don't know me."

"You're right. If you weren't willing to try, you would've told me to fuck off or something."

Eyes narrowed, and with a heart still beating out of control, she said. "There's still time for that." Her arms crossed over her chest, but she smiled when she said it. "So now what?"

"Well, we can go out for dinner, or you can go about whatever else you had planned."

"Umm, let me check." She grabbed her phone.

"Do you have a busy social calendar?"

"Why yes I do." She laughed. "No, my daddy... dad..." She expected a hint of a grin from him after correcting herself, but there was none. "He's in town." Thumbing through her text messages, she sighed.

"Everything okay?"

"Yeah. He's left already. Typical." Beneath her breath she said, "Without even saying goodbye. Thanks a lot." Readjusting her backpack, she speculated on the new choices she had. "I think I'd like to go out for dinner. You know, baby steps." She winked. "And I know just the place."

They walked the short distance to the Brewster's; the place where she was supposed to meet the Rock Star God of Teenage Boys. It was one of two decent sit-down restaurants in the neighbourhood, and she figured fast food wasn't an appropriate last minute date venue.

After ordering drinks, she asked, "So, tell me about your previous girlfriends."

He nearly choked on his own spit. "Well, there haven't been many." He wiped his mouth. "Why do you want to know?"

"Well, you know what I'm looking for in a man, and I'm curious, *real* curious, about the women you've been with. I need to know if I'll measure up or not." She tucked a stray strand of hair behind her ears and tried hiding a smile.

He raised an eyebrow. "Don't you think I should be the judge of whether or not you'll measure up?"

"I like to know my odds."

"They're good."

"So you're not going to tell me?"

"Not really." He shrugged. "It's not like they're beating down my door or anything."

She whispered as she leaned in closer, "I highly doubt that." In a louder voice, she asked, "So, ballpark, more than ten?"

"I'm not saying anything. Obviously, they weren't important, or they'd still be around."

One point to Nate. "Fine. No past info on the girlfriend situation." She stared at him, thoughts swirling in her head. "School? Can I ask you about that?"

"Sure."

She waited for a few heartbeats. "So?"

"I'm waiting for you to ask." He grinned a sexy, toothy, grin popping that damned stud between his teeth again.

Although she wanted to launch herself across the table, she restrained herself and took a more formal approach to their conversation. "So, are you in university?"

"Yes," he said and took a long drink from his pop. "Civil engineering. Just finished third year."

So, you're about twenty-two. Good. Was hoping you weren't that *much older than me.* "Cool. So what, you design bridges or something?"

"Something like that, or will when I graduate."

"Right on."

"And you?"

"Me? I'm quite behind. Thanks to the accident and recovery, I just finished my first year. In science."

"Hmm," he said, rubbing his chin. "Science chick, eh?"

She slyly arched her eyebrow. "Totally. I love all sciences."

"What field are you studying?"

"Pharmaceutical Sciences."

Nate chuckled. "How ironic."

"How so?"

"You take some pretty hard-core drugs."

She pressed her lips together into a fine line, letters unable to form proper words in her brain. Slamming the menu shut, she placed on the edge of the table.

"Does it pose some challenges for you?"

"I'm not sure what you're getting at?" Blood pumped through her veins.

"How do you get there each day?"

"Oh." Her shoulders slumped. "Well, I was living in the dorms on campus, so everything was within walking distance."

"But you're not now." She shook her head. "So, how will you get to campus?"

"I won't."

"You're giving up?"

"No!" She leaned forward towards him, squinting her eyes. "I'm doing most of it online, and when I have to attend in person, I'll cross that bridge when I get to it." The tension in her neck gave her the start of a headache.

"Hmm."

"What?" she said, slamming her palm against the table. A table of two turned in her direction.

"You're cute when you're angry." He laughed and rested against the back of the booth, a devilish grin teased her.

It softened her, but she needed to turn away. "You haven't seen me angry yet."

"I'm sure someday I will, and it'll still be cute."

"You're a jerk."

"I know." He winked at her. "My brother tells me all the time. You should meet him."

"Why? Is he a jerk too?"

"Actually no. He's the total opposite of me." He twiddled his thumbs. "Reddish hair, blue eyes. Total babe magnet. Super smart, can do anything he wants. He'll graduate this year, top of his class with tens of thousands of dollars in scholarships."

"Doesn't sound like my type at all." She huffed.

In a low and husky voice, he said, "And once again, we're back to what it is you look for in a man."

"Ha-ha." She played with the straw in her drink their waiter had dropped off. "As long as he doesn't give up on me, then it's all good."

"Is that what happened with your last boyfriend?" He leaned closer, appearing ready to take in every detail she wasn't going to share with him. Not today.

She glared at him and then softened. "Yeah, something like that. He couldn't handle the changes."

"What, do you turn into a werewolf or something?"

"I wish. No. After the accident, I was immobile for weeks and then had to wear a pelvic external fixator while my smashed pelvis healed."

"What's that? The pelvic thing."

"A fucking nasty device. It had pins extending out of my skin, attached to rods across my pelvis. Very attractive. I took first place in the Miss Pin Cushion Competition. Mind you I was the only competitor around."

He scrunched up his face. "That... thing... sounds terrible."

"It was, I won't lie." She paused when the waiter appeared, resuming after they'd given their orders. "I didn't want to go out with this ginormous device sticking out. I looked like fucking Frankenstein. And then I realised I *couldn't* go out. I was terrified of ever leaving. He couldn't handle any part of that, so he ended it."

"Wow. He sounds like a jerk."

"Not really. Just immature. I mean, I was seventeen, he was a year older. I figured it wasn't going to last anyway as he wasn't the one. May as well kick me when I was down."

"I'm so sorry." The atmosphere changed between them. Now a dark grey cloud hung over them.

"Whatever, fuck him. I didn't need him anyways. He was simply a toy."

Nate gasped. "What?"

"Oh come on. You heard me. He was a plaything, and damn good at it." Those brown eyes of his bored into her, many questions behind the stare, including curiosity. The truth of the matter was it hurt when Derek left, it made her feel worthless and unattractive. Who leaves someone twenty-three days after losing half her family? Even though she knew he wasn't her forever, she'd still loved him, and wanted him to stay. A small sigh of heartache as she remembered. "It was like I knew something major was coming and I'd need to get in all the hot sex beforehand. Because it sure as hell wasn't happening afterwards." *Not for a long while, anyways.*

His cheeks flushed, and he fiddled with the napkin.

"It's not like I'm a slut or anything."

"I never said that."

"You have that look. There have only been two, no three, that I've been with."

"That's not obscene."

"Clearly, it must be if you use that phrase. So you must be less than that."

"And what makes you think that? Maybe I've been with dozens of ladies."

"Perhaps, but your expression spoke volumes. And that's okay, I like a man that's selective." She reached out to touch his hand.

The chill from his hands shocked her although she wasn't sure why. And she liked the rough texture, and imagined what those strong hands would feel like touched against the softest parts of her. Her desire for this man flared up from deep within her core, spreading like wildfire to the tips of her extremities and then pooling in her pelvis. The way he stared at her, like he was doing right now, fanned the flames, keeping her hot. And wet. Oh so wet. She was afraid to move for fear it would be noticeable on her seat. Grabbing a napkin, she tried to cool herself down.

"You okay?"

"Yeah, it suddenly got real hot in here."

"I noticed that you flushed." He smiled a knowing smile.

She closed her eyes briefly, trying to imagine his cool hands caressing her flaming cheeks, his fingertips sliding down, drawing across her collarbone. *Take me* a sultry voice said. "What?" she asked.

"I didn't say anything."

She narrowed her eyes. "For real?"

"Yeah."

"Hmm." Aurora gazed at him, attraction pushing her to him. But was it only carnal desire, or was it more? She'd certainly have no issues whatsoever jumping into the sack with him to see how he worked. She imagined it would be a helluva ride.

♥ Chapter Twelve ♥

Friday rolled around, and Aurora skipped with excitement at seeing Nate after work. As he had for the past couple of days, he perched on the hood of his car waiting for her, wearing a pair of beige overalls, and a skin-tight black tee underneath. Fuck if he wasn't sex on a stick.

Smiling impishly, she sauntered over to him as he slipped off the hood. "So, what's the game plan for me today?"

Yesterday, she touched the outside of the car for sixty seconds before a wave of panic hit her from the insides, beating out the destruction her mind threw at her. The smells, the sounds, the fear– they were ready to close in on her when Nate pulled her back.

"Something a little different."

With each step back, her smile fell. "How so?"

"I want you to sit on the car."

"I can't sit in it." Repulsed by the mere thought of sitting in the car, enclosed by the metal and plastic that killed her momma, she sneered in the car's direction.

"You're right, that's why I said sit ON it. I'll lift you up, hold you close." His eyes twinkled.

She shook her head. "Not going to happen."

"Which part?" He smiled. "Although I do love a good challenge," he said, whispering under his breath.

It made her heart flutter. "Come again?"

"Do you trust me?"

"It's not you I have the problem with, Nate, it's me and my mind."

"Yes, I get that. Still, do you trust me?"

Body trembling, she attempted a weak nod and dropped her purse to the ground.

Nate walked over, closing the distance between them in a heartbeat and slipped his hands around her waist. "Ready?"

"Not in a lifetime," she breathed out. She clutched onto his strong, well-defined arms, holding on for dear life. He didn't make a move to lift her, so she leaned her cheek against his chest. She could swear his heart raced as much as hers. "Was this just a ruse so you could touch me?" She tried laughing, hoping it would push her swelling fear away, but it failed. Miserably.

"No, but I'll admit it feels good holding you this close." His chest rattled as he spoke.

Suddenly weightless, she instinctively wrapped her legs around his waist. Like a cat about to be dunked in water, she clawed at him and tried climbing over his shoulder.

"Easy there. We're not even near the car." He cocked his head and following his gaze, he was correct. They were still a good few feet away. Relaxing the tiniest bit, she pressed into him, and his hands readjusted, moving to under her bottom.

"Excuse me?" She arched her eyebrow.

"You'll slip out of my hands otherwise."

With his face so close, she saw a glimpse of fear reflected in his eyes. Was he afraid he'd drop her or was there more to it than that? She stared at his full lips, seeing the faded hint of a scar above the right side. Her eyes washed over his face, taking in every detail from the unfair length of his lashes to the way his eyebrows would be almost one if it weren't for the lightest hairs between. His cheeks devoid of facial hair as if he'd shaved before leaving work. She threaded her fingers together behind his neck, and pulled herself tighter into him, her breasts flattening against him.

His head leaned closer and the sweet lips she'd just studied, brushed across hers. Hungry for him, she brushed back, parting them, daring him to seek her out. Unclasping her hands, she ran one through his short hair, the bristly ends tickling her palm. She pushed into the kiss, unaware he had moved, until the cool metal touched the back of her thighs, and the sensation of his hands moved up along the small of her back.

"Oh my god," she said barely breathing when she realised what had happened and what she now sat on. "Oh my god." She clenched onto his arms again, trying to pull herself up and off. Her eyes widened, and her breathing hitched as she held her breath.

"Breathe, Aurora. It's not going to bite you."

"Yes it will." Her voice pitched higher. His arms wrapped tighter around her, not in an attempt to keep her there, but in a way that made her feel safe.

"The car's not alive, I promise."

"Please," she begged, tears threatening to erupt. "Get me off." Air swept underneath her as she lifted towards the sky. Like a delicate piece of china, he set her on the ground. Taking a step away, she folded right back into his arms.

He pulled her close, and together huddled on the curb, her back towards the red car.

"I want to be mad at you for that." She beat lightly against his chest with her fists. "But I don't have the energy." The worn soft cotton of his t-shirt nuzzled against her cheek as she breathed rapidly.

A firm hand wrapped around her waist, landing on her thigh. "Don't be mad, I'm trying to help."

"I know you are." She closed her eyes. "But I can't be helped. It's so obvious."

"Tell me something, when you moved from the dorm to your apartment, how'd you do it?"

"Drugs. Great drugs."

"What kind?"

The buckle on his coveralls became a play toy for her fingers as she tried expelling the nervous energy. "They're special, and I only get them for the immediate trip. Since it's usually my dad that I travel with, he keeps them."

"And what do they do?" His hand stroked her back. Could he feel the dampness of her shirt? She certainly thought it was wet as she'd become a little sweat-making factory during his little experiment.

"Block it out, basically." Returning her gaze up to him, he took in every word she said. "Essentially, the doctor says it's like the date-rape drug. I don't remember anything that happens. Before I moved, I took one, while he loaded up his truck. By time he was done, I was ready to go– or so he says. I don't remember. Then we unloaded here, and it started wearing off. I think I get a couple of hours of darkness in that tiny little pill."

"Wow."

"Tell me, why is it so important to you that I can get into a car? And I don't want to hear the answer you've previously given."

He tightened up to her questioning. "It's important because it's my livelihood. I work on cars, I get them running and I drive them hard. I don't want the girl I'm dating to be terrified of them."

"The girl you're dating?"

"I did kiss you."

"Presumptuously."

"Oh yeah, because you didn't beg me to come back to your apartment earlier?"

"Duly noted." She stood, pushing up from his shoulder. "So we're officially dating now?"

He stood beside her and smiled. "Sure, if you're okay with it."

"Yeah, I think that's fine." She brushed off her pants. "So, a date tomorrow night? I can't tonight."

"Tomorrow night I'm busy at the–" He stopped himself. "I'm not going to be in town."

She shot him a quizzical look. "Okay then. Sunday?"

"Sure. I'll meet you where?"

"There's a park to the south of those towers over there. I'll meet you at one, and I'll bring a picnic lunch for us."

"Deal." He leaned closer to her. "May I kiss you again?"

"No need to ask, we're dating now," she said with a playful tone in her voice.

A big bowl of popcorn sat in Aurora's lap later that night, as Kaitlyn and her new friend, Jessica, were over. It was girls' night, and they watched a chick flick, one of Aurora's personal favourites– *The Notebook*.

Passing around a box of Kleenex, Kaitlyn grabbed one and dabbed her eyes. "Noah is so dreamy. The perfect guy. Everyone needs to find someone like him."

Aurora raised her eyebrow. "Really?"

"You know what I mean." Kaitlyn glanced quickly at Jessica who seemed oblivious to the comment. She was too busy sobbing into her tissue. "What about you, Aurora? We need to find you a man."

She laughed. "Too late."

"What?" Kaitlyn turned in full and sat facing her. "When? And with who?"

Jessica sidled up closer. "What? Aurora has a man?" Her blond ringlets hung in her face.

Pulling the blanket up over her legs, Aurora whispered, "We met at work."

"Ooh, another librarian? Your kids will be so smart." Jessica smiled.

"It better not be that asshole I met at the restaurant."

Aurora shook her head. "No, not him. But I do need to do some research on him. He gave me a name to search."

"What. Ever. For?" Kaitlyn clenched up her fists.

"Just because. He said it would all make sense." She shrugged off the two pair of eyes staring at her.

"What would?" Kaitlyn asked. "I'm so confused, Aurora. You're not making any sense."

She filled in her friends about the phone call she'd had with Matthew James. By the end of it, she was more than a little curious. "Let me grab my laptop." The computer on her lap, she Googled his name, but nothing juicy came up. Only the bits about his *MJ Association* and reading awards. Boring.

"Type in his name, the plus sign, and her name, and see what you get," Jessica said, sliding closer to Kaitlyn to see the screen. Kaitlyn put her arm around her friend's waist and pulled her tight.

So Aurora did what Jessica suggested. "Oh my god," she said as she scrolled through the link that listed both Rebecca Gordon's name and Matthew James.

"What? Is that an obit?" Jessica asked.

"Shh," Kaitlyn whispered.

Rebecca Meredith Gordon, of Edmonton AB, left the bounds of earth when she died unexpectedly on May 25, 2014. She leaves behind her devoted husband of 14 years, Matthew James.

"What? That's it?" Kaitlyn asked. "That's like the shittiest obit."

Aurora typed frantically, Googling the date and names. Her eyes scoured the links, stopping on one. She clicked on it. First she saw the pictures of the crumpled cars, before the headline: CAR CRASH KILLS THREE, INJURES TWO

"No, no, no," she whispered, but couldn't remove her eyes from the screen.

The Police Service Collision Unit is investigating a collision that occurred over the weekend which resulted in multiple fatalities.
On Saturday, May 24, 2014 at approximately 10:30 p.m. police responded to a report of a two car collision on 100 Ave and 117 St. It was reported that the car travelling southbound failed to stop at a stop sign before proceeding through the intersection and collided with the westbound car. Firetrucks and ambulances attended the scene to assist.
The 29-year-old male driver of the southbound car, Mr. Thomas Anderson of Edmonton, sustained serious, non-life-threatening injuries and remains in hospital. His passenger, a 35-year-old woman, Mrs. Rebecca Gordon of Calgary, succumbed to her injuries that night in hospital.
The 17-year-old driver of the westbound car, Miss Aurora MacIntyre of Fort MacMurray, sustained serious, life-threatening injuries and remains in hospital in critical condition. Her passengers, both from Fort MacMurray, 47-year-old Mrs. Angelica MacIntyre, and 20-year-old Miss Carmen MacIntyre, both died on scene.
Speed and alcohol are believed to have been factors in this collision. The investigation continues.

A gasp came beside her as Aurora slammed the lid of her laptop shut and threw it on the floor. "Oh my god," she repeated over and over, as she paced around the living room. "No, it can't be."

"Are you telling me that his wife was involved in your accident?" Kaitlyn asked after picking up the laptop and reading the screen again.

Aurora shook, rubbing her arms to generate heat. She grabbed the blanket from the couch to wrap around her body and slipped into the nearby chair. "I never knew the names of the people who ran into us. Never knew. Didn't want to know the name of the murderer, the one who took my mother and sister. How could there be this link between Matthew James and me? And why this connection? Does he know it's me? Or did he want me to know that he was married? Not that it means anything if he was married because people cheat all the time."

"Ah, might not necessarily be him that did the cheating. His wife was in a vehicle with another man," Kaitlyn pointed out.

"Are you sure it's his wife? I mean there could be another Rebecca Gordon?"

"I'm pretty sure, Jessica, that that's his Rebecca." A violent shiver racked her body, and she pulled the blanket tighter.

Jessica turned to Kaitlyn. "But the dates are off by a day."

"No, silly," Kaitlyn said, "it stated she died later that night. So technically she died on the twenty-fifth, but the accident was a few hours earlier on the twenty-fourth."

Jessica said nothing further and slumped deeper into the couch.

Aurora rocked from side to side in her seat, whispering, "I can't believe I'm connected to him. What does it mean?"

Kaitlyn walked over and put her arm around her. "It means nothing aside from the fact that he's found a way to weasel into your head. Don't worry too much about it. In fact, stop thinking about him and tell us about this new man in your life."

Nate. What am I going to tell him? Or should I tell him? Does he have a right to know that the guy he hates is connected to my past? "Auugg. I don't know what to think anymore." She stood, but her legs were weak and unsteady, so she fell onto the couch. "Fuck me," she screamed into the pillow and pounded her fists into the seat. Another scream wailed from her, and she sat up. Kaitlyn wore sympathy, Jessica seemed afraid. "Sorry, girls, but you're going to have to go home. I need time alone."

Kaitlyn shook her head. "Actually, I think you being alone isn't a good idea."

"Yeah it is. I'm going to my room, so if you want to stay, stay. But I need–"

She walked down the hall to her room and slammed the door. She didn't want to think about it, but she couldn't help herself. Visions of the accident rolled in her head as if an old film projector was on repeat. She didn't remember much about the car that hit them, just the blinding of the headlights. Her days after the accident were hazy at best, and she didn't attend the funerals. Pinned to the bed and trying to hold on as the frailty of her life threatened to have her join her mother and sister.

Life wasn't fucking fair. She'd heard whisperings that someone in the other car had died, but never heard anything further. Never looked into it. Never cared. All she'd learned was that the driver was beyond intoxicated and speeding excessively down the road.

Staring at her medicine cabinet, she debated taking something. Just wasn't sure what something to take. *What to take?* The Xanax seemed the best option and after popping a couple, she curled into her bed.

A soft knock on her door, roused her from her sleep. *Kaitlyn.* Her clock indicated it was morning.

"Aurora, I'm coming in. You'd better be decent."

She rolled over and pulled the blankets up. Not that it mattered, she was still in the clothes she wore last night. "Come in," she said, clearing her throat.

"Hey, brought you a cup of coffee." She sat on the bed and put the mug on the bedside table. "How are you doing?"

Aurora brushed the hair off her eyes. "I'm okay, I guess."

"Sorry that the night didn't end well for you."

"Yeah." She reached for the mug and took a quick sip. A little strong, but drinkable. "Thanks."

"Come on. We're going to get up and face the day. You've had your night of sorrow or grief or anger or whatever you want to call it. Time to get up and live your life."

"And it's quite the life, isn't it?" Aurora rolled her eyes.

Kaitlyn jumped off the bed. "Stop it! Right now!" She stormed over to the window and threw open the curtains, blinding her with the bright light. Turning, Kaitlyn placed her hands on her hips and stood over her. "Don't make me drag you out of bed. You'll lose."

She nodded, knowing she would lose. Not only mentally, but physically as well. "Fine, I'll get up. But you better have breakfast cooking." The blanket hit the floor.

"Already in the oven," she said, smiling before she left the room.

Splashing cold water on her face and changing into fresher clothes, she limped down the hall. The kitchen beckoned her. The aroma of bacon assaulted her nose, along with the smell of fresh baking bread. "What did you create?"

"Nothing much. Bread's nearly done. Might not be too good, though, as I'm not familiar with the bread maker."

"I have a break maker?"

"Yeah, tucked into the corner of your cupboard."

"Who knew?" The apartment came fully furnished as it had been Carmen's and a couple of roommates. However, she never really searched through the cupboards as a pot and frying pan were pretty much all she needed. "When did I get bacon?"

"You didn't. I ran and picked up a few groceries this morning while you were snoring. The bill's on the fridge."

The table was set for two in the dining room. "Thanks," she waved around, "for all this. And I don't snore."

"Like hell you don't. What did you take last night?" Aurora stared blankly at her friend. "Oh come on, I know you took something." Kaitlyn's hand was firmly on her hip again, disbelief on her face. Someday, she'll terrify her children with that look.

"Fine, a couple of Xanax. That's all."

"That's all?"

"Geezus, what are you my father?"

"Ha-ha, you wish."

"No, not really. But maybe you do?"

"He could be the man to turn me straight, but I guess we'll never know."

The thought made her want to toss her cookies, but instead she grabbed the plate of food Kaitlyn pushed at her. "So what's the scoop with Jessica, anyway?"

"I'm working on it." She sat and placed a few slices of fresh bread between them. "She's totally into girls, but I think she's never been with a girl. Still a virgin and still waiting to come out of the closet I think."

She giggled. "And you'll help her either announce it or never come out from it?"

"Something like that." Kaitlyn shrugged and nudged the butter in her direction.

"She's pretty sweet," Aurora said, taking a bite of bread and letting it melt against her tongue. "This is damn good, Kait."

After a few minutes of silence, Kaitlyn suggested, "Let's go to the mall today and do some shopping."

"For what?"

"For what? For anything. For candles. For sexy lingerie. You do have a new man now, which by the way, you haven't told me about it."

"Well, his name is Nate, and he's pretty cool." She smiled as she pictured him in his overalls and t-shirt, his dark eyes staring into her. The mental image made her damp.

"Pretty cool, my ass. He's warming you up just talking about him."

Indeed he was. She was more than a little warm. "He's very nice in a gentlemanly way. Holds the door open for me, pulls my chair out, you know, old school charm."

"You mentioned you worked with him? How does that work?"

"Well, he works at the library, but as one of the construction team. Not as part of the library."

Kaitlyn smiled a smug little smile. "Construction worker eh? That's hot."

"Do you think about sex all the time?"

"Just when I'm horny."

"So all the time then?" Both girls laughed. "Seriously though, there's something about him. He's big into cars and we've been taking baby steps with the PTSD and all." She swallowed a drink of coffee as her throat suddenly dried out thinking about what they've done.

"How's that?"

"Well, first, he had me touch the car. That's it."

"That's kind of weird."

Aurora leaned back in her chair and thought for a moment. "Not really, no. He doesn't want me to be afraid of them."

"Because?"

"It's his hobby, cars. And he wants to be able to drive me places without me freaking out."

"So he has you touch his car?"

"Yeah," she said, looking over at her best friend. "I even sat on it yesterday. When he kissed me."

"No shit! You've kissed him?" Kaitlyn playfully pushed into her arm. "You move fast." She winked.

"Kait, you're missing the big picture here. I SAT on his car."

Kaitlyn fiddled with her fork, moving it around her plate. "And?"

"And what? I survived." She shrugged and pinched her nose. "It was scary as hell, but I did it."

Her friend tapped her fingers. "Was he kissing you before or after you sat on it?"

"Before and during."

Kaitlyn smirked and then reached for her hand. "I like him."

"But you don't know him."

"No, but I see what he's doing."

Aurora cocked her head. "What's he doing?"

"Something that shitty therapist of yours should've tried." She took a long drink from her coffee. "Don't you see? He's trying to make the car less scary by putting positive images into your head about it. Kissing you on the hood of the car is fucking brilliant."

"What? It is not."

"Yeah, keep denying it." Kaitlyn snatched another piece of bread. With her mouth full, she said, "We so need to get you some lingerie, honey."

"I'm not having sex in his car."

"Perhaps not, but, well, you certainly can't sleep with him in that?"

"Kait, I changed into this." Leggings and a worn out shirt did not constitute pajamas.

"We're going shopping. Can I borrow some clothes and makeup?"

"Have at 'er. I'll clean up, you can shower first."

She watched her best friend saunter down the hall. After cleaning up, she retrieved her laptop, but only stared at it. The name like a beacon on top. Hoping Kaitlyn was still in the bedroom, Aurora lifted up the tray of cutlery and pulled out the card that Matthew had written his number on. She desperately wanted to talk to him as she had so many questions. A loud bang as the closet door rolled shut, and she quickly tossed the card back under. It'd be better later, when Kaitlyn wasn't around. She made a mental note to call him tonight.

❤ Chapter Thirteen ❤

The girls stood in visitor parking beside Kaitlyn's car after some time spent shopping at the mall. "That's a longer walk back than I expected." Kaitlyn opened her car door.

"That's why I don't do it every day." She shifted her weight between her feet. Her back and hips started to throb, and the Percocets called her name. She could hear them from the parking lot below her suite.

"No kidding. Well, you got some nice things for Nate. I'm sure he'll love seeing you in them."

"Well he won't for quite some time. I don't shack up that quickly." She hugged her friend goodbye.

"If you change your mind about tonight, join Jessica and me. We'll be at the club."

Aurora balanced her bags between her two hands. "I'm good. Going to phone my dad, and get some studying done, otherwise I'll never catch up before the fall session."

"Bor-ing," Kaitlyn said, getting into her car. "Ciao."

Her friend drove away, and she hauled her few bags up to the apartment. After setting them on her bed, she grabbed her pills and headed to the kitchen to chase them down with a cool drink of water. The laptop remained on the table, where she'd left it last. Sighing, she once again retrieved the number hidden beneath the cutlery tray.

With trembling fingers, she dialled the first five digits. Her heart raced until she hung up. Taking a deep breath, she redialed, hanging up once more. She shook out her hands and paced nervously around the living room. Finally, feeling a wave of courage, she dialled all the numbers and waited, holding her breath. She hoped he wouldn't answer but if he did, what would she say? Be all casual? Like, 'Hey, it's Aurora?' Maybe voicemail would answer. Yeah, that'd be better. Easier.

Her breathing nearly stopped when he said, "Hello?"

Jump right in. "It's Aurora."

The line was silent for a moment, and then she heard him breathe. "Just a sec." She curled up on her couch, looking guiltily around her apartment as if she had her hand in the cookie jar. His mumbling in the background was indiscernible to her. He spoke after a moment. "My lady. You finally called."

"Yeah, I did."

"I figured I'd never hear from you again."

"Yeah, well, that was sort of my plan, but curiosity took over and I Googled. So, well, here I am." Grabbing a nearby pad of paper and a pen, she started doodling.

"And that's why you're calling?"

A heart scrawled out from the tip of her pen. "Do you know who I am?"

"Excuse me?"

"I mean, you know my name. But why did you tell me to look up your wife's name?"

"So you will understand I'm married. That joking behaviour, like I said, it's all an act. I've always remained true to my wife."

The pen continued to draw of its own accord, distracting her momentarily. "But she's been gone for almost two years."

"Doesn't mean I've stopped being faithful to her."

"Her accident. Who was that with her?" She cringed asking. It wasn't really any of her business, but her inquiring mind wanted answers.

"That was her… lover." Matthew's voice fell.

Sadness overwhelmed Aurora. "Oh geez, I'm really sorry."

"I've gotten over it. I think. I have no use for cheaters, but she was still my wife."

The air hung stagnant between them. "So, even though she did that to you, you? You?" Where was she going with this? "You, act like a jerk? But you're not really?"

"Well, I am, but not in the way you think."

"Huh? I've seen your needs for the stage setup. The number of plants and all that."

He laughed, and it relaxed her a bit. "Yeah, again at the request of my manager. He's huge into Feng Shui and everything needs to be a certain way. I personally, couldn't care less. Just let me hang out with my fans. Let me get them hooked on reading and expanding their minds, that's all I care about now. Well, except–"

"What?"

"You. Something about you, calls out to me. A familiarity almost. I can't put my finger on it though, but it's like I've met you before."

She snorted. "You're fucking joking right?" Her cheeks burned all the way over to her ears.

"I'm sorry?"

"Listen, Matthew," she stopped herself from saying something vulgar in place of his name. "Do you know who I am?" Her hands shook, and she kicked the edge of the couch.

"Yes," he sighed again, "the girl from the library."

"Glad you think of me as a girl. That's reassuring." She switched the phone to her other ear, her right hand clenched tight in a fist. "Do you know I'm connected to your wife?"

"You knew her?" He sounded uptight and tense.

"No, not at all. She was killed alongside my mother and sister," she cried into the phone, "I was fucking there that night. I was driving the car he smashed into." Red hot tears streaked down her face.

"What?? No–" The line was quiet. Too quiet. No one spoke as the air crackled between them.

Aurora couldn't move as she quivered in place and made no attempt to wipe the wet trail careening down her cheeks, soaking her shirt.

"I never put it together," he finally said after a few minutes. "Never. Although I remember now where I've seen you."

"Oh yeah? Where?"

A loud sigh. "That night, I flew to the hospital. The nurse said Rebecca had come out of surgery and sent me over to the recovery area. I pulled back the curtain and saw the person on the bed. But it wasn't her. It must've been you. You looked like you were in a lot of pain, even though you were sleeping."

"My fucking pelvis was shattered. That's not a pain you can escape from, even in sleep."

"I'm familiar with pain, Aurora." Pretentiousness aside, the anger rang clear in his voice.

She settled down and answered, "Yeah, because emotional pain is the same as physical pain. Your heart may have broken in the figurative sense, but my body broke in the literal sense." A quick peek at her doodling showed her she'd drawn Matthew's name. In anger, she scribbled it out. The air cracked between them as the silence grew. "So what now?"

"That's what I'm wondering too." He took an audible breath. "I'd really like to see you again. I think we should meet, in person, and discuss this. I didn't realise that there was *that* connection between us."

"I don't know, Matthew, that's a big deal."

"That's why I think we should talk. I want to know more about you, my lady. There must be a reason I am drawn to you."

"Because you feel sorry for me?"

"Why would I feel sorry for you?"

"Because I was involved in the crash? And you want more details."

"I do want more details, if you'll share them with me. But there was something before knowing that. I need to know you more."

Forcing herself to think of something else, she drew hearts on the paper, writing Nate's name in the middle. "You're what? Thirty-seven? I'm nineteen. That's too big an age gap for me."

"All I'm asking for is dinner, to talk. Nothing more."

Why in hell was she thinking of agreeing to this? She wanted nothing further from him. "Matthew, I can't. I have a boyfriend." Which was mostly true. They were dating although she didn't know if they'd achieved couple status or not.

"So what? I'm not asking for your hand in marriage. Just dinner."

She sighed. "Fine." *It can't hurt, right?* "When? Your schedule's busier than mine."

"Okay, give me a sec." She heard him flip through some papers, and imagined he was checking his hectic calendar. "I have an appointment I can reschedule if you want to meet tomorrow?"

Tomorrow? She had a date with Nate. At one. Would they be finished their date in time for her to have dinner with someone else that night? No, it wouldn't be right. "I can't."

"Fine, figured you'd say no to the first suggestion anyway. How about next Saturday night?"

Don't couples usually go out on Saturdays? She didn't know. She and Derek went out all the time. And she didn't know Nate well enough yet to know if he was particular about a certain day of the week being an official date night. She could always tell him that she had these plans booked for a while now. *What to do, what to say?* With a loud sigh she agreed.

A sound of relief came from the other end of the line. "Great. Thank you. I'll pick you up where?"

"I'll meet you. Brewster's. Seven o'clock."

"Okay. I will meet you there. You won't stand me up?"

"If I do, you have permission to track me down."

A small laugh. "Well that's interesting."

"Saturday, seven, Brewster's."

"Perfect."

She hung up the phone and asked herself, "What in hell am I doing?"

❤ Chapter Fourteen ❤

Aurora stomach tightened and flipped after hanging up the phone. She'd accepted a dinner date with Matthew James. Matthew James, for crying out loud. Needing to clear him and their conversation from her mind, she grabbed her purse and headed out for the grocery store. She needed to pick up the picnic supplies for her real date. Tomorrow. With Nate. The one who made her smile and not scowl in anger. *Fucking Matthew James.*

She had no idea what to purchase because she didn't know much about his likes and dislikes. It's not like he presented her with a rider or anything. She chuckled at the thought. No, Nate wasn't like that. He wasn't a 'somebody' and any Google search on him would likely be less than what she'd find on herself. She made a mental note to check later, for the hell of it. Playing it safe, she grabbed a few buns, fresh veggies and cold cuts, some snack foods and a couple bottles of iced tea.

After returning home, she attempted to study chemistry. But it wasn't working. Her thoughts drifted between Nate and his sexy smile to Matthew and the way he pulled at her, almost as if by magic. At least she was honest with Matthew about having a boyfriend. She really needed to open up to Nate although he did say he liked a girl with a little mystery to her. Well, hiding a supper date was mysterious, wasn't it? And it's not like she's hooking up with Matthew James. He's way too old for her anyways. It's an innocent dinner date. To connect over his dead wife who was there when her family was killed.

She shook her head, and stepped out onto the balcony for some much needed fresh air. The air was warm, and soothing and she inhaled, debated her choice of returning to her schoolwork or heading out to the mall. The dull throb in her back reminded her she needed another pill. She'd done too much walking today, and she agreed.

The pill-popping diary open, she sat with it in hand, and tried to remember what pills she had taken and when and for what reason. She'd been horrible with the upkeep lately, and there were several of each pill unaccounted for. Not good. Not good at all. She scribbled down the two she took after her trek from the mall and one for tonight that she was about to take for the hip pain. It still left fifteen Percocets, four Flexeril and thirteen Xanax unaccounted for. *Shit.* She vowed to be better.

The next morning she rose excited for her picnic. She showered and shaved her legs although she would never wear a skirt or capris or shorts. There were way too many scars on her legs, and it was easier, no better, to hide them all away beneath leggings or jeans or whatever clean pants she had. She only wore a dress when she heading out to the bar, and that was a fancy dress that fell to the floor with pantyhose or something similar covering her legs.

It had been so long since she'd been on an official date, she debated what to wear. After calling and waking Kaitlyn from a drunken sleep, she concluded that jeans and a nice top would be fine for a picnic.

With everything packed up into a cooler bag, she headed downstairs and across the street to the park. The blanket spread out over a nice grassy spot, and she placed the bag on the corner. Plopping down, she stretched herself out, and enjoyed the rays of sunshine warming her face.

"Cute," a voice said as Aurora opened her eyes in the shadow of a gorgeous man who, with the sun outlining him, looked like an angel.

"Nate," she said, gesturing to the blanket as she curled herself up into a sitting position. "Glad you made it."

"Of course." Dressed in jeans and a plain white tee, he was hotter than usual. The white highlighted the bronze of his sun-kissed skin. He sat on the edge of the checkered blanket. "How was your weekend?"

"Good. Girls' night on Friday, shopping all-day yesterday. Studying last night. Yours?"

"Good. Busy. Hung out with family and friends. Typical weekend."

"Oh yeah, what do you typically do?" She leaned on her knees.

His eyes trailed over her while he paused. "Just things. Talk cars and such."

"With your family?"

"Why not? We're all big NASCAR fans."

"Isn't everybody?" she said sarcastically.

"Well, not everyone clearly."

"Yeah, no. Not a fan of death-mobiles racing around in circles at stupid high speeds, waiting to plow into each other."

He laughed. "That's not the goal. It's being first across the finish line."

"I know that. It's just... crazy and stupid."

He lost his smile. "I don't think so. Not at all. In fact, quite the opposite."

She stared at him, bewildered. She knew he liked cars, but NASCAR? Really? It defied her logic that someone could enjoy watching cars race at such high speeds. When they crashed, people died.

"What are you thinking?" His forehead crinkled with the question.

"Everyone who crashes at that speed, dies."

"Not true. In fact, race cars are designed to protect the drivers. For example, a few months ago, Austin Dillon got into a high-speed spin, and flipped his car over and then was run into. He walked away from the crash without a scratch. There's so much protection put into those cars. You're safer in them than you are in a street car. Even those that come with the highest safety ratings." He nodded. "It's true. Look it up."

"Not interested. I still think all vehicles are unsafe."

"And that's where I enter. To help you with that. To teach you that they're not."

"But you just alluded that street cars are unsafe."

He sighed. "Not what I meant. I simply meant with a race car, you are strapped in; harnessed in really. You wear a HANS– a head and neck support system, so that in the event you do crash, your head doesn't snap forward and cause brain damage. There are roll bars all around you, and safety systems put in place so that you can escape a vehicle with ease. You're quite protected, trust me."

"And yet, you want me to eventually get into a car?"

"Eventually, yes. But you won't be travelling at two-hundred miles per hour like Jeff Gordon does. More like sixty miles an hour, and that's only if you're on the highways."

She studied him, admiring his stupid determination to break her of her fear. But it couldn't be broke.

"So," he said, breaking the silence, "what's lunch? I'm starving."

She pulled out the sandwiches, and passed him a bottle of iced tea. "Fancy, I know." Chuckling as she set everything out. "I'm a much better cook than this. Someday I'll have you over."

"Someday soon, I hope."

Her eyebrow raised, and a smile stretched across her face. "So eager to see my place, are you? I did invite you over once, but you shot me down."

"Not a mistake I'll make again." He beamed his crooked little smile and moved closer to her.

Dampness settled into the seat of her pants. He needed to stop looking at her like that, or she won't be able to finish her lunch. She'd lunge at him and take him right there in the park. Clearing her throat, she wiped her sweaty hands on her jeans.

"Well, my apartment's right across the road. I even did a little shopping for something special yesterday." She caught his eye as she flipped her hair off her shoulder.

"Now I'm intrigued. What did you get?" He shuffled closer, the heat from the sun warmed up his skin and in doing so, released the aroma of a nice cologne.

Aurora scooted closer as well. "Wouldn't you like to know?"

"Oh, I would." His face moved closer to hers.

"It's green and slippery."

"Mmm," he whispered into her ear. "Tell me more."

"You've already seen it." She giggled and pulled back.

"What?"

"The pickle, silly."

He quickly leaned forward and planted a kiss on her lips. "A pickle? Really?" He kissed her lips, more softly this time. "I thought it would be a little more romantic than that."

She enjoyed the taste of his kiss, flavoured with lunch and a minty aftertaste. "Oh, I'll show you romantic." She threaded her fingers through his sun-heated hair and pulled him beside her, kissing his lips the whole way down.

His hand wrapped gently around her back, the other braced himself up as he blocked out the sunlight, eclipsing her face. "You're so beautiful."

"Enough with the cheesy pickup lines. Kiss me some more." She brought his face to hover over hers, and she stretched up, eager to meet him. His rough, chapped lips claimed her as they trailed over hers, down her neck and across her collarbone. Her hands rubbed along his strong, muscular back. The taunt outline of his muscles beneath the soft cotton shirt intoxicating. She pulled at the shirt, trying to free it from the holds of his jeans.

He broke the kiss. "Hey, lady. Slow down. Let's enjoy this. There'll be plenty of time for more. I promise." He resumed his kisses along the base of her neck.

Warmed by so much more than the intense sun, he drove her wild and stirred up all sorts of naughty ideas in her head. And in her core. It heated to the sensation of his parted lips pressing into her. Breathlessly, he kissed up to her ear, and gently took her lobe into the heat of his mouth, and a new wave of desire puddled around her. "Oh God," she whispered, trembling slightly from the tingling racing through her veins.

"You called," he said, gazing down at her face.

She smiled, although slightly agitated he'd stopped kissing her. She stretched out to try to connect with him again.

"I think we should finish lunch first, don't you? Don't want it to spoil after all the effort you put into it." He sat up, and straightened out his long legs.

"Fuck it, I don't care if it spoils." She rose into a sitting position, readjusted her shirt, and then gave her hair a quick fluff.

"But there are others in the park, and this isn't the place for more." He jerked his head towards the playground a couple hundred feet away from them.

She glanced in the direction of the kids, and then back at him. "So let's go to my place then. It's cooler there." She raised an eyebrow seductively.

"So eager to get into my pants, aren't you?"

"As you are into mine."

"That may be true, but I can wait. I'm not going to let it happen for a while."

"What?" Her mouth dropped open.

"I'm a gentleman. I believe in courting you first."

"Fuck the courting, just take me already."

"My, my. Such a mouth on you. I'll have to fix that." He pulled her close, and she kissed him with unabashed drive and passion.

"I'm going to swear like a trucker from now on, if that's how you plan on punishing me." She laughed and pressed her breasts against his hard chest as her lips parted. Straddling him, he kissed her hard on the lips. As he moved his lips down the base of her throat, she tipped her head back, eyes closed tight against the sun. "Oh, fuck, that feels good," she whispered and as she pulled herself closer to him, a tight bulge strained against his jeans. "And you're enjoying it too, it seems."

His pushed her back slightly. "Yes, I am."

"So, let's go up to my place." She pleaded and kissed his cheek, leaving little kisses all the way up to his ear.

"No. Not today."

Resigned that it wasn't going to happen without serious effort and dedication, she licked his earlobe, and gently sucked on it, pulling it gingerly with her teeth.

"Woman, you are driving me insane."

"That's the plan."

Taking a deep breath, he grabbed her arms and held them firmly with his hands. "But not today, okay? Let's take this slow. I don't want to be somebody you bed and leave the next day."

She was taken aback. "But I wouldn't do that."

"Maybe not, but I don't want to find out okay?" He tipped up her lowered chin. "I'm enjoying this. Each little step with you I want to be memorable. I'm not racing to the finish line."

"Okay. I think I understand." *I think. At least I'll pretend I understand. Everyone I've been with, it's happened relatively quick. Derek and I did it on the first date. Then there was that other guy after a night of dancing. What the hell was his name again? Oh well, and then there was other guy. Geezus, what was his name? Something about an airplane comes to mind. Jet? Yeah, that was it. Whew. I'm not a complete slut.* She climbed off his lap, rooted through the cooler bag, and tossed him an ice pack.

"Oh, very funny," he said as he caught it, and then threw it back at her.

She placed it on her chest, the cool soaking into her sizzling skin. She wanted to put it between her legs to cool the intense heat there, but thought he might find that strange.

After eating a little more, Nate stood and pulled Aurora to a stand beside him. "Let's go to the car."

"Wow, you sure know how to kill a mood." But her feet didn't move. They were firmly cemented into the ground.

With one hand in his, he rubbed the top with his other hand. "It'll be okay, I promise."

The car sat beyond them in the distance. "I... I... can't. I don't have my meds. What if something happens? What if I panic?"

"Then we'll go get them." His voice calm and reassuring.

Calculating the time it would take to make it up to her apartment, she grabbed her keys from the bag and pocketed them. No point needing to double back to the blanket for them, should she need them.

She slowly took the first step towards his car, parked on the edge of the parking lot nearest them. Hand in hand, she followed him over, the distance between them minimal. "Here we are. What's today's lesson?" She looked up expectantly into his face, happy to see the joy behind his eyes. It was clear he was happy she was going to try, and somewhere, deep down, she was willing to try. Maybe he *was* the key to getting over this. The power of positive memories erasing the bad ones.

"You tell me?"

"What, seriously?" She darted between him and the car, hoping an answer would appear in thin air.

"Yes. What do you want to do?"

"Umm." Avoiding his dark brown eyes, she shrugged. "Touch it?"

He smirked and raised an eyebrow. "Always about the sex."

Relief washed over her as she smiled. "That's not what I meant." Before she could stop herself she found her hands, as if by their own guidance, landing on the hood of the car.

"Tell me what you're feeling?" he whispered, standing behind her.

Her eyes slammed shut. "Heat. The metal's hot. Burning hot."

"What else?"

She lowered her head between her arms and breathed deeply. "Fear. Lots of fear." *Momma's head on my body, and my head hanging out in the pouring rain. I'm confused and scared.* First one hand, and then another caressed her shoulders. Each hand made its way down her arms, slowly, tenderly, stopping only when his hands covered her shaking ones.

"What do you feel now?" His soothing voice warmed her ear.

"Heat, lots of heat." A small unguarded smile bubbled its way to her lips, popping away her momma's image.

He kissed her ear. "What else?"

She bucked slightly, and one of his hands wrapped firmly around her waist, holding her up. "Intense heat. Lots of fear. And something else."

"Your strength. I can feel it, surely you must?" He kissed the side of her neck, causing her knees to fold completely beneath her. He caught her, and spun her around, wrapping both his arms around her. "You okay? You're shaking like a leaf?"

Her breathing came in spurts. "Yeah. Let's carry on." She glanced between the hood, and his face. Heart racing, she said, "Put me on the hood."

"You sure?"

Another quick glance back and one to the ground. If she needed to, she could puke right there. "Yes." She inhaled deeply and wrapped her arms around his neck as he lifted her. Trembling, she kissed his neck, hoping her quivered kisses were firmer than she felt.

Hands cupping her bottom, he stepped closer to the car.

"Oh God," she whispered into his ear, and gripped him until she worried her fingernails would break skin. Fear gave her unparalleled strength.

"What are you feeling?"

She shook her head against him as he lowered her onto the hood. "That I can't do this." She tried to pull herself off. The shaking built from deep inside her and radiated to the tips of her extremities. For a moment she was glad to be sitting, for she knew she'd be unable to stand. Wave after wave of fear washed over her as she remembered what it was she sat upon. Her stomach tightened and another fear, one of puking all over him, surfaced.

"Aurora? Talk to me."

"I can't. Please. I can't. Not ready." Her breathing came in gasps. A face in front of her, holding her face. His voice telling her that her mother's been taken to the hospital. But where was Carmen? Her heart pounded so hard she wondered if it would break her ribs. Her grip never lost its strength though as she continued to claw at him.

"But you are." His whisper was like an arrow shot right through her heart. "And you're doing great."

The pouring rain pounded down in her memory. She blinked rapidly as she stared at the EMT who spoke to her through the windshield as he touched her while trying to keep her calm. She blinked harder and tried to focus on him. He looked like Nate. But–

Involuntary shaking overcame her. Sweat filled her pores. Her heart threatened to explode. She struggled for air. "Nate."

"Right here."

"Please," she pleaded, and just like that, was lifted into the air. She buried her face into his chest, tears wanting to erupt. She didn't let go, and let out of small gasp when something hard pressed against her ass.

"It's a picnic table," he said reassuringly, as his hands brushed down her back. "You're okay. I promise." He pushed back on her shoulders. "Look at me. Aurora, open your eyes and look at me."

Taking a deep breath, she opened her eyes and searched his.

"I thought you were crying, you were shaking so hard."

"I wanted to, trust me. But I won't."

"Won't?"

"I refuse. Crying's for weaklings."

"I don't believe that." He caressed her cheeks with his finger for a hundred heartbeats. "I'm proud of you. Takes some guts to climb back on the horse. And you did it."

She blinked in the direction of the car. It had felt like her world had flipped upside down and yet, the world hadn't changed at all. Everything was still the same as it was before she sat on the hood. Nodding to him, she said, "Yeah, I did it. Barely."

He kissed her. "You totally did. Was it easier than last time?"

The courage was there before she hopped on and she thought she'd lasted longer than she had before, but was it easier? "No, not really."

"Baby steps."

She leaned into him, calming herself down, one breath at a time. "Baby steps."

♥ Chapter Fifteen ♥

Safe and secure in Nate's strong arms, Aurora leaned against Nate's chest, finally catching her breath.

He gently rubbed her back. "All better?" he asked after a few minutes of silence.

"Yes, much. Thank you."

His shoulders sagged, and he said, "C'mon. I'll walk you home."

Aurora sat up straighter. "No." She looked up into his patient eyes as anxiety swirled around her. "No, Nate. The date isn't over. I refuse." She jumped off the picnic table. "Let's go finish our lunch, okay?"

"Really?"

"Damn right." She tugged on his hand and pulled him over to the blanketed area. "Now sit." She pushed him playfully onto the blanket.

"Ooh, I like a girl with dominance," he said and a feisty grin replaced the concerned look he held moments ago.

She leaned over top of him. "I'll show you dominance." And she dropped her lips onto his, pushing, parting, panting.

"Whoa, slow down," he said, coming up for air and curled himself into a sitting position. "C'mon, baby steps."

Aurora groaned. "Fine, baby steps. It's our thing, isn't it?"

"Seems to be."

"So what's next?" she asked, cocking her head towards the car.

"I don't know. I think we'll continue with this for a while. Daily, perhaps." He shrugged. "And maybe next weekend, we'll try something else."

Aurora bit her lip. "Speaking of next weekend–"

"Yeah?"

Do I tell him? Or not. She sighed. *I'll probe.* "What are your plans?"

A hesitation. "Family things."

"On Saturday?"

"Yeah, always. Why?" His voice full of defensiveness.

She played with the edge of the blanket. "Just curious."

"Someday, when I think it's time, I'll show you what it is I do every weekend."

"Why not tell me?"

He reached for her head, his fingers tangling in her hair. "Because I'd like it to be a surprise which I'm sure when I show you, it'll blow your mind," he said. The pitch in his voice betrayed the smile on his face, and for a brief heartbeat, Aurora figured it was bad– whatever it was he did.

"So I'll be surprised?" Her blue eyes narrowed at him.

"Totally."

"No hints?" Her cheeks puffed.

"Not a one."

Pulling her knees to her chest, she said, "Hmph."

"Why were you asking me about my weekend plans, are you making some of your own?" He trailed a finger down her arm, and over her knuckles before holding her hand.

"Yeah. Going to go out for dinner, hang out. Try to get some studying done." She smiled.

"Sounds… fun?"

Aurora laughed. "No, it sounds boring as hell. But I like things that way." Nate lay back on the blanket, and she curled up into him, resting her head on his shoulder. Her hand stroked his chest.

"You're not giving yourself enough credit." He squeezed her hand.

"Sure I do." Her eyes shut as the sun peeked out from behind a cloud, temporarily blinding her.

"No, you don't." His fingers ran up and down her arm. "But I think you're doing great. And we're going to keep at this. You'll get through it, somehow, someway."

"I'm so glad you believe in me." She scoffed.

"I do. We'll see how the week goes, and then we'll try something new. I have an idea. For Friday, I mean."

Friday rolled around. Although they'd agreed on doing something new with the car phobia, Aurora had no idea. But in preparation, she made sure her purse was full of Xanax, Ativan, and anything else she thought to grab.

As had become usual over the week, Nate waited for her on his car. Today was a hot one, muggy too, and he was sweating a lot as his t-shirt was stained with wetness.

"Happy to see me?" she questioned as she walked over to the grinning Nate, fanning herself.

Slipping off the car, he wrapped his arms around her, and kissed her firmly. Lovingly. Tenderly. "Always."

"Good, me too." She stared at the dark grey skies. "I hope it pours. This mugginess is unreal."

"And yet, here you are in a long-sleeve shirt and pants. Why don't you wear something more appropriate?" He tugged up on her sleeves.

"Because, my body is riddled with scars, and I'd rather not be a walking freak show."

"Oh come on, they can't be that bad."

She pulled up the sleeve on her right arm, which he took in his hands. With a tenderness she didn't know he possessed, he ran his thumb across the three-inch long scar that ran parallel to her brachial artery– the main artery in her arm. Had the piece of vehicular hardware punctured a half-inch closer to that artery, she could've bled to death.

With a tenderness she'd never experienced, he pushed the fabric up a little further and revealed another faded white mark– this one two inches long and ending at her elbow's crease. Searching his face for disgust which she didn't see, she tugged the sleeve back down.

"It's not so bad. You're bound to have scars. Everyone does. Yours are barely visible but it doesn't change who you are." She narrowed her eyes, disbelieving. "See this scar above my lip?" She nodded. "Bike accident when I was ten." He pulled his shirt sleeve over his shoulder. "Underneath this tat, there's another scar. A big one."

"What from?"

"A dirt bike accident." He shook his head. "It's a long and complicated story, but it ends up with me getting about forty stitches."

"Wow, must've hurt."

"Probably did. I don't remember. Good drugs." He winked at her.

"And speaking of, since I have no idea what you have in store for me today–" She rooted through her purse, produced a slim pill container and popped it into his hands. "Part of my collection." She shrugged at the concern on his face. "You know, in case I lose my marbles or something."

"You haven't so far."

"There's a first time for everything, right?"

He stared at the container and placed it on the roof of his car. "Okay, shall we begin?"

"Aye-aye, Captain Nate." Trying to keep the mood light, she saluted him with a half-hearted smile, her hand trembling as she lowered it.

"Don't be so nervous. I'll be right here."

Her lungs filled with air, and she grabbed his hand, pushing it against her chest. "Do you feel that? That's where I need you. Here, inside me."

"I'm already there."

"Oh, Mr. Cheesy Pickup Lines."

"Says the one who actually started the whole cheesy pickup line."

She stood on her tiptoes and reached up to give him a kiss. The best part of her day was kissing him. As often as possible. She loved it when he held her close and her breasts squished against his firm chest. But try as she might, he hadn't advanced to anything further than first base, remaining steadfast in his damn baby steps theory of their relationship. She hoped deep down he wanted her as much as she wanted him.

After a few minutes of heart-racing action, he pulled away and tugged at his shirt collar. Aurora fanned herself as well. The mugginess in the air pushed on them both. "Let's get this over with. Before we get dumped on." She searched the sky as if it had somehow warned her of the approaching storm.

Nate cocked his head towards the car. "So, step one."

Taking a deep breath, she stepped closer to the red car and hesitantly placed her quivering hand upon it. "I'm doing it," she said through gritted teeth. Her eyes slammed shut, and she held her breath as she waited for him. Waited for his touch.

Nate didn't disappoint her, and once again ran his hands down the length of her arms and ended on top of her hands. She shuddered when his tantalising breath blew across the nape of her neck where a fresh wave of sweat built up. "That's my girl," he whispered.

After counting to sixty, she turned and leaned her backside against the car. With great care, he lifted her like a feather and rested her on the hood. She wrapped her legs around his waist, more in fear than sexiness. Breathing hard and hands folded into her chest, Nate hugged her tight. She was sure there would be some dampness beneath his arms where they rested against her shirt. And it wouldn't be caused because she was hot. Fear had a funny way of showing itself.

"You're doing so well," the voice said in her ear. "Keep it up, Aurora."

She held onto his voice, rather than claw at him. Listening to the rhythm of his words, she focused every ounce of her being on the little inflections, the soothing way he whispered her name, the way his breath sounded against her ears. The trembling started low, but built to a crescendo rapidly. Her heart raced, and her breath came in quick spurts, but she handled it. As long as she concentrated on him, the edges of her living nightmare stayed away, or at least remained somewhat hidden in the fringes of her mind.

A voice beyond them broke her concentration. "Get a room, Johnson," it said.

"Shut up, Josh," Nate yelled over his shoulder, as he lifted Aurora up and off the hood.

Unable to stand, she leaned against him, surrendering herself to him. "Who was that?"

"One of the crew." His arms drew tighter around her. "Sorry."

She shook her head in his arms. "It's okay. I wanted off anyways."

"How're you doing? You okay?" His eyes laced with concern.

"As good as I'll ever be, given the circumstances." A huge release of air escaped her lungs.

"Ready for step three?"

"Is it painful?"

His laughter melted the edges of her frosted fear. "I truly hope not."

She glanced over to the pill container still sitting atop the car. "I want one now. It takes a couple of minutes to kick in anyways. It'll make whatever you're wanting me to do a little easier. I think," she said, drifting off.

He twisted it open, and hesitantly poured one onto the lid. "For sure?"

Without another word, she popped it into her mouth. "Okay, what now?"

He opened the passenger side door, and waved her in.

"You've got to be fucking kidding me, right?" Her gaze flickered between him and the passenger seat. Nausea built lightning quick, and she wiped the sweat off her brow with the back of her hand. "You expect me to get into this?"

"We can try." He held out his hand.

Like a leaf in a strong breeze, she gripped it tightly and shook her head. "No. Fucking. Way."

"Just try."

She wanted to please him, she really did. But this? This was asking a lot. Her stomach did a double flip, and her mouth became dry as cotton. Tripping over her feet, she stepped to the open door and looked inside. It was clean, and well taken care of. Not what she expected. Her eyes flew between Nate and the cloth-covered seat. It didn't look at all comfortable, it looked like death. And she didn't know if she could face death today.

She squeezed his hand even tighter, and gingerly took another step closer. "This is–" she breathed out in two breaths, "insane." Nate's face was expectant, and she grimaced, biting her tongue in the process.

"Baby steps."

A wave of anger washed over and out of her, faster than her racing heart. "Baby steps, my ass. This is a fucking ginormous step." She backed in slowly, lowering herself until her legs gave out and she fell into the seat.

Suddenly, lights were everywhere, blinding her view. But her ears never stopped working. The high-pitched sounds of twisting metal rang loudly through her head. Plastic interiors snapped and ripped. Glass crunched and crumbled like dry leaves. The smell of fear was overpowering, and ripe with blood. Lots of it although she didn't know where it came from. The occasional brilliant flash of lightning highlighted the darkened area around her. But worse was the pain. Everywhere. It hurt to breathe. It hurt to move. "No!" she screamed before she passed out.

A warm arm pressed against her back, wrapping around and holding her waist. A gentle hand caressed her cheek, its trailing fingers lingering along her jawline. She blinked, and when she opened her eyes, she stared into the dark concerned eyes of Nate.

"Hey," she breathed out, noting her calm and even breathing. How? When? She turned her head, relieved that she was outside the car, on the sidewalk, five feet from the open car door. "What happened?"

He shook his head, fear registering in his eyes. "I don't know. You screamed and passed out. You'd barely even sat down."

"I'm sorry."

"No, I'm sorry. I pushed you too hard." He brushed his hand down her cheek again. "I gave you another pill from that container, so you should feel more relaxed."

Her arms were loose, and she tried wiggling her fuzzy toes, which felt miles away. "Thank you," she said, sitting up, although she would've liked to enjoy hanging out in Nate's arm under better circumstances. She shuddered and cowered under the safety of his arms when a low, distant rumble of thunder rolled across the skies.

"Time to get you home." He assisted her in standing. "I'll walk with you, since driving will be an epic mistake."

She nodded and attempted a weak smile as he linked his hands through hers. "No, I'll be okay. It's less than five minutes."

"Sure, any other time you're practically begging me to come to your place, and here I'm offering, and you're flatly refusing my offer." A feeble attempt to make her smile, but it worked.

She turned to him, and wobbled in her steps. "Fine. Maybe you'd better walk me home. I'm feeling woozy."

"Woozy? Is that your technical term?"

"Fine. I feel like hammered shit. Better?" She gathered up her belongings as Nate closed up the failed attempt to get her into the car.

After securing the car, he pocketed the keys, replacing them with her hand.

"My place is a mess, so don't hold it against me."

"How bad can it be?"

She tried to think about the general lack of order she'd left it that morning. Her alarm failed to wake her, so she slept in. She was sure her breakfast dishes still sat on the counter.

However, before she knew it, she unlocked her apartment door, and cool air hit her in the face, meaning the air-conditioner worked. "Tada," she said, stepping inside and kicking her shoes off to the side. "Make yourself at home, and please forgive my mess." Her purse thumped to the floor.

He walked into the living room, and admired the paintings hanging on the wall. "Wow, you really like this one artist. There are," he counted, "seven paintings."

"Yeah. They're my sister Carmen's, all of them. She was an art major, specialising in Monet. She was beyond talented."

He ran his hands through his hair. "Indeed. I'm sorry."

"You've nothing to be sorry for."

"Her work's amazing."

"It truly is." Aurora strolled into the galley kitchen. "Can I get you something?"

He spun around and walked closer to her. "Nah, I'm good." Glancing around again, he said, "This is a big apartment. Just you?"

"It was Carmen's and her two roommates. After she died, my... dad," she caught herself, "said they could continue to stay until they graduated, as long as they continued to pay their portion of the rent. They left in April after graduating and I moved in. All Carmen's personal items remain locked up in the third bedroom. I have the master bedroom, and when Dad stays, he uses the guest room."

"Good to know." Nate looped his index finger into the belt straps of Aurora's pants. "How are you feeling?"

"A little lightheaded, but that's to be expected." She stepped backwards towards the couch, pulling him along. "So, what now? You seemed a little rattled after phase three. Was it scary for you?"

Nate shivered, and she'd bet her right arm it wasn't from the air-conditioner blasting at full. "Since I couldn't see what was going on in your brain, yeah, it was a little scary. Watching you pass out isn't on my list of things to see again." Before she could open her mouth, he silenced it with the touch of his finger. "But we'll figure something out. I promise."

"We won't and I know it." She tapped the side of her head. "The doctor said PTSD is a powerful thing and I may never get over it. I need to learn to live with it."

"But it's so limiting. It has to be for you. There isn't much to do around here."

"I can walk to the mall in about thirty minutes, and there's lots to do." She crossed her arms over her chest. "Plus there are lots of things around here to keep me entertained. I don't need to go out to have fun. I have a stack of movies, lots of video games and piles of books. And I can get more anytime I want."

Nate sighed. "Don't you want to explore? Go beyond the boundaries of your neighbourhood?"

"No, I'm quite content here."

"Really?" he asked, and slowly turned around whispering, "It's like you don't even want to try."

"Excuse me? I don't want to try?" Her arms flailed into the air. "What the fuck do you think I've been doing every day for the past two weeks? I'm trying, Nate. God-dammit, it's hard."

"I know." His hands landed on her shoulder.

She flung them off. "You don't know and that's the thing. You think you can waltz into my life and make everything better. Fix my fears. Well this won't change. I'm afraid of cars and I have every right to be."

"Aurora," he said and lowered his gaze. His voice a low whisper. "I just want to help."

"Yeah, and I don't understand that. You don't know me. Not really. So what's in it for you? What do you get out of fixing me?"

"Nothing, I just want to have you a part of the real world." She wasn't sure, but she thought he said under his breath, "Part of my world."

She stormed over to the door, yanking it open. "Good night, Nate."

"Aurora," he said, his mouth frozen in place.

She slammed the door, and crying, dialled. "Hey, we're still on for tomorrow?"

❤ Chapter Sixteen ❤

Flipping through her closet, Aurora tried to find something nice to wear for her dinner with Matthew James. Something nice, not too sexy, not too prudish either. She sorted through her clothes at least a dozen times before finally deciding on a pair of black skinny jeans and a long, flowing royal-blue top. The top was a little lower cut, so she pulled out a push-up bra to wear beneath, although she hoped that the top colour would bring out the blue in her eyes. Then he could talk to her, not her breasts. In order to appear flawless, she dabbed on some makeup, even though the scars on her arms would contradict that. With her feet in a pair of flats, she headed out.

Her dinner with Matthew James was only a chance to get together and talk. Harmless, right? Yet riddled with anxiety. What if the filter between her brain and mouth malfunctioned? It was hard to believe a celebrity was into her, even if she wasn't entirely reciprocating the interest back.

She arrived a few minutes early, and waited. Why was she nervous? So she'd always harboured a little fan-girl crush on him, which lessened considerably after hearing him talk to his manager. But it didn't hurt that he was off the charts handsome either. She was immoral enough that his looks could exceed his less than desirable personality, and the age difference. But he was still Matthew James, and she was just Aurora.

She paced in spot another minute further until she saw him. Exiting his black sports car, well-dressed in tight black jeans, suit jacket and light blue shirt unbuttoned at the top. From a distance, he almost looked like Bradley Cooper. He didn't walk either; he strutted with swagger and purpose, like he owned the place. He radiated confidence and, although she hated to admit it, he fucking oozed sex appeal.

His face broke into the broadest of smiles when he pulled open the door. "Well, My Lady of the Library. You made it this time." He reached for her hand, and placed a kiss upon her knuckles. His lips warm and soft. "How are you this fine evening?"

"I'm good," she said, her knees buckled briefly. *Focus on the reason for being here. You're not on a date, you're only discussing the accident and the connection.*

He strutted up to the hostess. "Table for two. Someplace quiet."

The waitress appeared to stumble as she grabbed the menus and stuttered, "Yes, sir. Right this way." She led them to a table, near the back, with a view of the patio.

"After you, my lady," Matthew said, waiting as she slid into the booth. He hung his suit jacket on the hook, and sat across from her. "I sat at this exact table when your monstrous friend came over and verbally assaulted me."

She huffed, and crossed her feet at the ankles. *What a way to start the conversation.* "She was sticking up for me. You were a bit of a jerk."

His brilliant green eyes lined with lashes almost as dark as his hair, stared at her. "I wish it had been you that had come. To at least speak your mind if nothing else. Have the courage to stand up for yourself instead of having others do it for you." He nodded at her, sincerity on his face, and a flash of fire in his eyes.

She snapped herself out of staring when she followed his gaze to her breasts, which until she checked hadn't realised they were heaving. He was checking her out, and she liked it. Made her feel feminine and attractive. But she needed to focus on the menu. On something else anyways.

A waiter appeared, and asked what they'd like to drink.

"My lady?" Matthew asked.

"A coke is fine."

"A coke? Surely the lady would like something stronger. Something adult?" He cocked an eyebrow.

Aurora glanced up to the waiter. "A coke is fine, with a wedge of lime, please."

Matthew looked amused, and smiled. "I'll have," he winked. "I'll have what she's having. It's different than my usual."

The waiter disappeared and Aurora said, "What do you normally have?"

"Something laced with alcohol. It takes the edge off."

Before she spoke, she twisted in her seat. "Do I make you nervous?" She laughed at the absurdity of it.

"Yes." Adjusting the collar of his shirt, he said, "Yes, you do."

"Get out." She smirked and blinked a few times. "I make you nervous? That's funny."

"I don't understand."

"You're a celebrity, a world-famous author. People have heard of you. I've been nervous all afternoon preparing to meet you. And to sit here across from you. Well, it's inducing high levels of anxiety in me right now." She tapped her purse as if confirming to herself her Xanax was nearby should she need it.

His smile was a white, dazzling one, thanks to the companies willing to throw products at him for a couple of endorsements. No one's teeth were that white and sparkly naturally. "Hard to believe that celebrities are people too?"

"What?" Her eyes widened, and she glanced around. Surely, others had to have noticed who he was and yet no one paid any attention to them.

"I'm just as much a human as you. And meeting with such beauty and feistiness makes *me* very nervous." He peered at her over the top of his menu.

She closed her mouth, fearing whatever she wanted to say would be misconstrued and taken the wrong way. Unsure if he would get her sarcastic tongue. He didn't seem the type to have a witty banter with, like Nate. Matthew seemed light years out of her league.

"Cat got your tongue?" he asked, and placed the menu along the edge of the table.

Mirroring his actions, she did the same. "No. I'm in awe."

"Of me?" Clapping his hands, he threw his head back. "Really?"

"Yeah. You're Matthew James. And yet, you're sitting here with me. I'm perplexed by it all."

"Should I not be charmed by your grace?"

"I have no grace."

"Ah, but you do. I watched you that day. You have a way with people, but yet you don't *know* that you have that way. It's interesting to me."

"Because?"

"My team, they're as arrogant as they come. That being said, they know what they want, they know how to get it and they know how to get others to assist them. But you, you command an audience without knowing it. Your beauty is astonishing, and from what I've seen about you– your quick tongue can give me a run for my money." He winked. "I like that you won't take shit from me. And you've already told me off a couple of times. No one stands up to me like that." Matthew leaned in. "I like it."

Speechless, she barely rattled off her order when the waiter appeared with their drinks. She took a long drink, the coolness slipped down her dry throat. "So, our reason for meeting tonight wasn't about you talking about me, but rather this connection. Between us."

"Ah, yes. This connection." He tapped the side of the drink with his finger. "My wife, as I found out, had been having an affair with Mr. Anderson for some time. Nearly a year. I was in Calgary, that's where I live, and she was up here allegedly having a meeting with our banker to discuss our investments. Rebecca was my financial manager, it was how we met. Mr. Anderson was our investment broker. So, imagine my surprise to find out they'd been together." Sadness and surprise crept behind his eyes. "Then that night, two years ago Monday, my world collapsed. My wife, whom I loved more than anything else in the world was in an accident. I flew here and a waiting driver raced me to the hospital. The nurse said she'd come out of surgery and sent me over to the curtained area. When I pulled back the curtain, I was in shock. I know now that it was you, but for a moment I thought you were her. And you appeared like you were in so much pain."

"I was."

He stopped and raised an eyebrow. "I figured. The nurse came over and ripped the curtain from my hand, and opened the other one." A soft, heart crushing sigh. "Where Rebecca lay, wrapped and bandaged. I sat there until she died, about an hour after I arrived. It was only later that I discovered her affair."

"I'm so sorry. It must've been awful to find out like that."

"It was no picnic, that's for sure." His slim fingers rubbed his temples as he closed his eyes for a moment.

Breathe, Aurora. Yes, he suffered that night, and lost. But don't fall for it. The air between them grew thick and uncomfortable as she thought about that night and watched his face. Unable to look him in the eye, she noted he didn't have the same issue. The constant scrutiny made her squirm. She killed the awkwardness by flipping her attention to the hockey game playing on the big screens.

"Hockey fan?"

This she could talk about. Easily. "Oh totally. It's the playoffs now, who isn't excited?" She watched Matthew from the corner of her eyes.

He put his elbows on the table, and rested his chin in his hands. "Tell me about your mother and sister."

She snapped her head in his direction and studied him. "What do you want to know?"

"Whatever you want to share. It must be tough on you–this accident–as it removed half of your family."

What? How the hell does he know that? Her throat clenched, and she took a sip of coke, staring at the ice as it bobbed. "It was no picnic," she said, holding his gaze for a moment. "But I don't remember the first little bit. I was heavily sedated and pinned in place, so I missed their funeral."

He closed his eyes and took a deep breath, shaking his head. "I'm so sorry you never had closure."

"Life goes on," she said as she twirled her straw. "That's what my father always says. Stop glancing in the rear-view mirror, and look out the windshield. The view is bigger and better." Anger surged beneath the surface. She never forgave her father for pushing her forwards.

"And? How's that going?"

"It fucking sucks." Her hands tightened into fists. "I'm never allowed to talk about it with my dad. Ever."

"So tell me. I'm listening."

She stared at him. This is what she always wanted– to talk about it. Never in a million years would she have thought it'd be with Matthew James. "For real?" she asked, eyebrows high.

"Why not? I've read all I can get my hands on, and I talked with Mr. Anderson about it. Did you know his sentencing will happen within the next month or so?" He waved his hand about. "I can't imagine how hard it's been for you to not have any closure. It's hard to move on from something, when you've never been able to deal with it in the first place."

Unbelievable. Was she really discussing this with him of all people? Her pocket vibrated, and distracted her. Blinking, she glanced at the display. "Sorry, it's my dad."

He nodded. "Go ahead."

"Hey, Daddy, can't talk now," she whispered, hoping Matthew wouldn't hear as she covered her mouth. "I'm out for dinner."

"Okay, Princess, just wanted to let you know I'll be there on Monday. For the anniversary."

She hung her head. She wasn't stupid, she remembered what Monday was. "Yeah, I know." A quick glance to Matthew, who appeared engrossed on the hockey game. "Monday." She hit end, and pocketed the phone. "Sorry," she said.

"It's all good. I'd never come between a father and a daughter. Are you close?"

With a shrug she said, "We try. But it doesn't always work out." She bit her tongue and leaned back as the waiter dropped off their food.

Matthew cut his burger in half before taking a bite. "It must be infuriating."

"You have no idea."

They ate the rest of their meal in near silence, neither speaking much about anything more important than the current status of the hockey game, and the playoffs in general. A die hard Flames fan he bragged, which made her shudder. The Oilers would always be number one to her, even if it had been years since they'd even made the playoffs.

They finished watching the game, and Matthew picked up their tab.

"Well, thank you, my lady, for joining me tonight."

"Yeah, it turned out better than I thought." She smiled as she stood. *Awkward, but tolerable.*

He snickered. "I'm so glad." Grabbing his jacket, he pointed towards the door. "May I have the honour of driving you home?"

"No, I'm good. Can't ride in cars and all that. Besides, I only live a few blocks from here."

"May I escort you then?" They exited the restaurant as he pushed open the doors for her.

She contemplated it. As much as she wasn't as into him as he was into her, the company was nice. It was nice to chat about the accident, even briefly. At least he acknowledged it'd happened. And the relationship between her and Nate ended when she threw him out of the apartment, so she was back to the lonely part.

The apartment tower loomed in the distance and she nodded. "Sure. Why not?"

He reached down and grabbed her hand, kissing the top of it.

She wanted to pull away, but didn't, continuing to stare at the awkwardness of the whole thing. Turning towards her home, she started walking. They were footsteps from the corner of her block when she stumbled over her own feet, and the sidewalk rushed to her face. Instinctively, she shielded her face, twisting sideways as she fell. Her hip slammed onto the top of the concrete as a painful curse escaped her lips.

Pain radiated through her body as she lay on the sidewalk, blocking out his calls. Her hip screamed at her, begging her not to move. For a minute at least. She brushed away his help. "Just give me a minute please."

"People are going to think you're seriously hurt," he said as he dropped to her level.

"I am seriously fucking hurt." She winced in pain, and fought the tears battling for release.

"Should I call 911?"

After a few breaths, she pushed herself into a sitting position, her breath laboured.

"If you're that hurt–"

"It's more embarrassment than anything," she lied and took a few more breaths. *Fuck!* "Okay, let's go."

Matthew stood, and extended his hand. She pulled hard on him, favouring her right leg as she stood. She winced as she massaged the hurt, wondering how big the bruise will be.

"I can carry you."

She leered at him. "Like hell. I can walk."

He waved his hand as a sardonic expression crossed his face. "Then go ahead."

Glaring at him, she took a step with her right, and fell back into his arms.

Without a word, he scooped her up and said, "Which building?"

"The tower," she sighed as she leaned against him, her face buried into his chest from total embarrassment. "The south tower."

As if she were weightless, he carried her into the building, unlocking the door with ease, and stepped into the elevator. "Floor?"

She reached out and stabbed '17'.

They arrived in silence as she bounced along his arms down the hall. "I'm feeling better now. Can you set me down?" The screaming pain downgraded to a roaring throb.

Gently, he lowered her to the ground, and she stepped forward to unlock her apartment, putting as little weight as possible on her left leg. With a hobble more pronounced than usual, she gestured to the living room. "Make yourself at home. I need the bathroom." She excused herself and limped into her master bathroom, ripping open the medicine cabinet door. Staring hard at the choices of pain relievers, she settled on a Flexeril, a perc and a Xanax, to help her relax, before heading back fresh-faced into the living room.

"Can I get you anything?" she asked.

He had a Cheshire grin on his face. "No, thank you. Come sit."

After she got comfortable, he moved closer to her. "Feeling better?"

Breathless at being so close, she nodded. Damn he smelled good. Did he freshen up?

"Good." He dropped an X-BOX controller onto her lap. "Let's battle. I love this game."

The TV was on, and the already loaded Call of Duty awaited her player profile. "You're on," she said, grinning and wiggled herself into a more comfortable spot.

An hour later, after alternating between being so serious and laughing from Matthew's total inability to accurately hit a target, Aurora turned off the machine. It was so hard to concentrate with him sitting beside her, and she was more than happy when it was over. Feeling better, *much* better thanks to the drugs, she twisted towards him. "Thanks for the game. That was fun. My friends don't enjoy that particular game." A yawn escaped, and she covered her mouth.

He set his controller down on the coffee table, and leaned closer. "Thanks for having me over."

How did his breath manage to stay so minty smelling? She didn't recall him popping anything into his mouth. "My pleasure," she said, looking into his emerald green eyes and trailed her gaze down to his plump lips. *Stop. It.* "Maybe next time, you'll be able to hit your mark." With the pain wiped out thanks to the perc, the spasms alleviated with a nod to the flex, and all anxiety out the window because of the Xanax, she rose and stumbled for the door.

Matthew stepped behind her. "There'll be a next time?" His smile flawless.

"I said maybe." She stifled a yawn after she smiled. "Thanks for dinner. The evening turned better than I thought."

"High praise indeed." His cool hand touched her inflamed cheek, and stroked it gently. "My lady–" His voice warm and husky.

Her grip around the doorknob tightened. His touch so soft, like Nate's. She closed her eyes as Nate's fingers stroked her cheek. Without another thought, she entangled her fingers through his dark hair, the silky strands caressing her palms, and she pulled him close, wanting to taste his lips. *Oh, Nate.*

With an eagerness of a teenage boy, he bent down, his strong arms wrapping around her frail body. He pushed back into the kiss as he lifted and carried her back to the couch.

Trailing kisses down her chin, he kissed the base of her neck she exposed with her head thrown back. "You're delightful, my lady."

She moaned as she pulled her blue top off, exposing her black-lace covered breasts. She tugged his shirt out of his pants, and ran her hands along the smooth ridges of his chest.

His hands warmed and tingled her skin as they traced a pattern. A familiar one. One she had lived with for the past two years. "Ignore my scars."

"That bastard marred your perfect body."

"I'm familiar with what he did, and the marks he left." She lifted his chin, and blinked slowly, trying to see him clearly. He remained fuzzy around the edges. "For now, just take me. Fuck me hard and leave me begging for more." Her eyes draped close.

"Your wish is my command, my lady." A foil packet ripped open, and the wrapper fell to the wayside.

"Prepared, were you? Expecting something?" Opening her eyes, she raised an eyebrow. His eyes lowered as the latex rolled the length of his shaft.

"Hoping, never expecting, my lady."

As it hurt too much to focus, she blindly kissed his salty but sweet tasting lips.

"I've been fighting this all evening long." He flipped her over.

Her cheek against the couch, and her ass in the air, his hands played up and down her back. A finger slipped under the band of her bra and before she knew it, her breasts were freed. Finally. Tenderly, he pushed the straps over her shoulders and the bra fell to her hands. Her lacy panties rubbed against her skin before being pulled to the side.

"Meow," she said as the pressure of fullness filled her from behind.

A flat hand rested across her lower back, as another slipped around her waist, searching beneath her panties for the most feminine part of her. The heat burned as he found and deftly stroked a little nub. "Ooh," she moaned to his touch.

He slammed against her and she rocked on her hands to maintain balance. The harder he pushed into her, the more intense pressure he applied with his fingers as he rubbed her. Harder. Harder.

"Yes, yes," she moaned out. "Faster." She breathed so hard, she almost couldn't catch her breath. "Harder."

His finger rubbed at her apex until a moment later, he let go to grip her hips so tight she cried out in pain as he held on to the bruising part of her. He growled as he unleashed, and held her tight.

"Finish me off. I'm so close," she begged. Panting and desperately fighting to breathe, her body twisted as he flipped her onto the couch with ease. It didn't take long to return to the build-up that had been so close. It had her pleading to fall off the edge into sweet, total bliss.

His mouth ravaged her, sucking and nipping. Over and over. Warmth burned from the pit of her stomach and radiated outwards, tingling to the tips of her fingers and toes. Feeling as light as a cloud, she wondered if she could fly. She licked her lips. *Oh, Nate.* Slowly, she moved her hands over her own breasts, twisting and tugging on her nipples.

Moist heat from his mouth arrived a moment after. He flicked with his tongue. Her nipples rolled between her fingers. Seductively, her hands travelled down her body, stopping at her hips and ran her fingers through his hair. His magical tongue unleashing wave after wave of pure, unadulterated bliss. The sensations–the tingling, the build-up– made her realise it had been far too long without a man, and she wanted to, needed to explode all over him and soak him completely. And it wouldn't take much more to achieve.

Taking his hands, she pushed them down and guided him to open her further as he dove in face first. He mashed his nose into her. The motions were strong and fast and long. His tongue felt like it was as long as his– "Ahh," she whispered when he touched the spot responsible for her recent bouts of self-loving. It was fucking magical.

"Let it happen. Let me watch you come undone." He kissed and sucked and stroked. In doing so, the sensations overwhelmed her and before she could warn him, he licked her firmly and she exploded all over him. The slippery, silky fluid rushed from her and washed over his face. Like a thirsty man in the desert, he lapped it all up.

His words a whisper. "Sweet Jesus, that was heavenly." He sat on the couch, pulling her weak legs over him. His hand rested on her belly.

Too tired to move her heavy, yet satisfied body, she rested against him, chancing a quick peek. His head lopped on the back of the couch, eyes closed, and his chest rose and fell softly. Sated, she mumbled, "Good night, Nate."

♥ Chapter Seventeen ♥

H er mind woke up before her body did. She was uncomfortable. Worse than that, she was in pain. A great deal of pain. As she tried to move, the bed beneath her didn't give. The more she thought about it, the more she remembered. She hadn't fallen asleep on the bed. She was still on the couch. Naked and on the couch. And fuck, was it ever hot.

Blinking rapidly, she focused on the source of heat. Matthew James. *Matthew James? What the fuck?* Tucked in behind her on the couch, his arm draped over her. It wasn't a dream. He was in her apartment underneath a throw blanket. When the hell did that happen?

Desperate to move, and stiffer than when she'd been pinned in place in the hospital two years ago. Another move. A deep breath. Each movement sent a fresh wave of nausea-inducing pain throughout her body.

"Hey, wake up." She poked him and when he didn't respond, she poked him harder. "Get. Up." Twisting was a bad mistake as the pain sliced through her. Unable to hold it in, she screamed. And that woke up Matthew.

"What?" he asked as he jumped up with no shame in his nakedness.

"Pain," she cried and closed her eyes.

He pulled on his underwear in a hurry. "What can I get you?"

"Pills. Bathroom."

One long painful minute later, he returned baring multiple pill containers and a glass of water.

"Which one?"

Scanning them all, she pointed to the second one. "Two, please."

He popped the top, and toppled them into her outstretched hand. "Water?"

A subtle head shake. "Give me a few minutes," she whispered. *I need to figure out what the actual fuck is going on. But I can't think straight in this much pain.*

He covered her. "Do you want me to move you to your bed at least?"

Shut up. I need to think. She closed her eyes as if it would make everything better. *I remember the restaurant. Brewster's. Dinner was okay. Awkward but tolerable. We went to leave, and I was lonely, so invited him over. I fell.* Her hand instinctively went to her hip, and she palpitated, figuring the bruise was at least as big as her palm. *Oh fuck.* A quick movement and pain coursed through her. She hated this, hated feeling like this. Weak. Fragile. Fuck, sometimes she hated her body. *Pills. I had some pills. What did I have though? Definitely a perc.* Thinking hard, she tried to see in her mind what containers she moved. *Yes, a perc. Probably a Xanax. I didn't add a flex, did I? Fuck.* Her palms pressed into her eyes. *Aw, fuck.* As she opened her eyes, Matthew James' face hovered over hers. *Oh, fuck. I fucked him, didn't I?*

"Everything okay in that head of yours?"

I swear it wasn't him. All I could see was Nate. "What the hell?"

He stood before her and pulled on his jeans. A smile crossed his face. "Can I take you out for breakfast before I head home?" His shirt slipped over his head. "When you start feeling better, of course."

"I don't eat breakfast," she lied, "especially with the pills. It turns my stomach." Another lie, but she wanted him to leave. Disgusted with herself, she couldn't look at him. What was she thinking to have had sex with him? She swore it was Nate. That had to have been a fucked-up combo of pills. But they'd broke up, right? She kicked him out and was rather rude to him when he was only trying to help. And now she'd fucked someone else. If she could've felt worse, she would've. But– ah, the pain meds were starting to kick in and numb her.

He brushed the hair back from her face and placed a kiss on her lips. "Okay. I understand."

Pushing him away, she glared at him. "What do you understand?"

"I'm not stupid, my lady. And it's okay, I get it."

"What exactly do you get?"

"That you're embarrassed. I'm sure you hadn't planned on sleeping with me."

Shock registered on her face as she tightened the blanket around her. "You got that right, buddy." Grateful for working meds as the movement didn't blind her in pain.

His eyes narrowed at her terse comment. "Feel better, my lady," he said, "and call me later if you want. You know how to reach me." He sauntered over to her door, and exited her apartment.

When the door clicked, she turned her head into the couch cushions and cried. "Oh, what have I done?"

Sometime later, because she wasn't sure what time it was when he'd left, she woke up and tidied the apartment, taking care to make sure it was devoid of anything Matthew James related. She would not let on to anyone, especially her daddy, she'd had a one-night stand.

About to step out and grab a few groceries, the buzzer to her apartment sounded. "Hello?"

"Flower delivery."

Oh for fuck's sake. She pressed the button, allowing him access.

She unwrapped the huge bouquet, staring at the card. *You've stolen my heart. With you, I know it's in good hands.* The more she read it, the more it pissed her off. She stormed over to the recycling bag and after ripping the card into a million little pieces, tossed it. But the daisies and lilies filled the air with their fragrances, it'd be a shame to toss them. With the card gone, no one would be the wiser to know who they were from. So, she placed them in the centre of her kitchen table.

Wanting to talk to someone, she considered calling Kaitlyn, but slammed that idea away, figuring she'd be livid to know she'd first had dinner, and then, gag, sex with Matthew. She didn't want to share that with anyone. It was bad all over. And Nate. If they ever got back together again, Nate would be pissed, and rightfully so. It would drive them forever apart. Her daddy would think her a slut which she'd agree with at this point. And back to Kaitlyn– she'd probably march over and slap some sense into her. Yep, not going to happen.

That night, sleep gave Aurora the middle finger. The past twenty-four hours were quite the roller-coaster. She remembered the sex part, and it was great. But was it great because she thought it was Nate? As much as she fan-girled over Matthew, she wasn't into him like that. Did Matthew take advantage of her? Unlikely, since he didn't know what she'd taken, and didn't realise her altered mind. But how could he not know? She told him dinner was awkward, right? If only she'd said no to him coming over. Grrr, it was so frustrating.

Other thoughts plagued her– the anniversary of her mother and sister's death, and the visit with her daddy who would no doubt be a total zombie about the whole thing. He never talked about it and it bugged her. They both lost that night, and yet he seemed to jump right over it, as if he skipped a chapter in a book. What was wrong with him? Why couldn't he talk about it?

After tossing for hours, she retreated to the bathroom to search out something. Something chemical to help her find Mr. Sandman. Choosing the tiny pill, she swallowed it down and crawled back into bed, rolling over and over until sleep gave up fighting with her, allowing her to steal a couple of hours.

The morning greeted Aurora no better than the night had, with a nasty grin. Her clock flashed 7:00 a.m. and she smacked it off the table, growling as it bounced on the floor. Four hours of sleep wasn't enough. Even a cold shower, and a cup of coffee, didn't help her to perk up. Normally it would. Not today.

Two years ago today, she killed her mother and sister, even if documentation said she didn't. She was the driver, and ten seconds faster or slower that day could've saved their lives.

She pulled out the last family photo, taken eighteen months before the accident. All posed together in a portrait studio, trying to capture the perfect smiles for their Christmas cards. But the photographer was crafty, and made them laugh about something Aurora had long since forgotten, and snapped the picture. It turned out brilliantly, becoming Aurora's favorite. No forced smiles at the camera, instead they're all looking at each other. Perfection in a photo and Aurora begged her parents for a copy of it, displaying it with pride. Now in her apartment, it sat on her dresser. She touched her mother's head, and whispered, "I love you, Momma."

Work did nothing to ease the sadness within her soul. She'd rather have interacted with her co-workers, instead she organized and shelved the reference material at the far back of the library where no one visited much. If people needed information nowadays, there was Google. It was uncommon to see people using this section. Mostly, they pretended to read, but what they really did was remove books from the shelves and leave them on the table.

She grumbled as she reorganized the back shelves, making sure the books were in the correct order. Time alone was not good. She longed for company– someone, anyone, to distract her from thinking. Too many people swirled inside her head, and she couldn't make any headway. Thoughts about her mother would meld into thoughts about Matthew, which would then turn into Carmen and flip to Nate and start the process all over again.

On a bathroom break, she rooted through her purse needing her gold – Xanax. Disappointed in herself for not having refilled her supply, she debated what to do. Thinking all morning was not the best use of her time, but it couldn't be avoided. As she stared at the pills she had, she wondered? *Will they ease my thoughts? Settle down my mind so I can focus? I won't mix what I did Saturday, just a couple to shut my mind up. If it helps.*

After glancing around the locker area to make sure she was alone, she twisted open two containers. She hoped together, the two pills would achieve the same effect as the Xanax. *Maybe they'll even be a little stronger together and I won't have to think at all.* Nodding to no one, she swallowed the pills. *I'll be home within the hour and can get the Xanax I need.* Dumping everything back into her purse, she headed back out on the floor.

A young couple made their way to the back area where she stood. Thankful for something to listen to, she manoeuvred her cart closer to hear their conversation. They debated the merits of a recent film, discussing the direction and acting until they stopped. And stared at her. "Can I help you?" one of them asked.

She focused on the book in her hand. "Umm, no."

"Let's go. I hate eavesdroppers," the one girl said, standing abruptly.

So much for having something to listen to. Now it was back to her twisted thoughts. She held a library book, and stared at the call number. Focusing on the shelf in front of her, she couldn't figure out where it belonged. 126.758. Did it go before 126.578 or after? It was hard to tell as the numbers kept swirling. Five minutes later, she was no further ahead as she still held the book.

"Fuck it," she said, sliding it into a random spot. Her phone beeped. Lunch time. "Oh, thank god. It's time for Xanax."

Waving goodbye to a staff member who must be new as she didn't recognize him, she stumbled out the main door. Her head spun uncontrollably, and she tripped over non-existent rocks, catching her foot in the crack of a sidewalk. Her keys dropped from her hands, not once but twice. Exhausted in her efforts to walk with jello-filled legs, she leaned against the apartment tower's main door trying to unlock it. *What's wrong with me? Why do I feel so heavy? And funky?* Her. Key. Would. Not. Fit.

"Here," someone said as she left the building, and held the door for her.

"Fanks." *Fanks? This can't be good. Something's definitely wrong.* She wobbled her way to the elevator and leaned hard into the soft wall which moved against her back. *Someone ought to complain to the caretaker about this. Maybe there's mould under this wall.* The numbers on the panel blinked in slo-mo. 13... 14... 15... 16...

"Woo-hoo. Seventeen," she yelled out when her floor number flashed.

With her head rotating like a tornado and her feet moving like rubber bands, she somehow made it to her apartment door. She breathed hard and leaned against a wall as she tried to see the number on the door. Three doors later, she cheered, "Mine!" Her knuckles rapped on her door. "Hello?" she answered, her laughter echoed down the empty hall.

"I've got this," the male voice beside her chimed up, although where he came from, she wasn't sure.

"I know you, don't I?" Her speech slurred, and she attempted to focus on the vaguely familiar person before her. Definitely male. Tall. Dark hair. Ah, fuck. Who cares? She gave up trying to figure it out. It was too much work. Besides, he wasn't standing still, and moved around too much. The tug of the keys from her hand was easy. Way too easy. She sighed and closed her eyes only to throw her hands out to the sides when the unmistakable feeling of falling backwards overcame her. Until something, or someone caught her. And as her stomach flipped, she turned her head, emptying the contents outside the door.

"Yuck," the male voice said.

Her feet dragged beneath her, over to the couch. The rough fabric rubbed against her face. "My couch," she said, before her body relaxed and her mind darkened.

♥ Chapter Eighteen ♥

A loud gurgle bubbled out, as she opened her left eye, and then her right, gasping as two pairs of eyes stared down at her. One had a disapproving glare on his face, and the other wore concern.

"Hey, Princess."

"Daddy?" *Oh SHIT.* "What're you doing here?" She scrambled to get into a sitting position, tossing the blanket off. *Where had that come from?*

"It's Monday. I told you I was coming."

She rested her aching head against the palms of her hands. *Tylenol where are you? I need you. Nah, fuck the Tylenol. I need something stronger.*

"Imagine my surprise when I came into the apartment and saw him in here. With you passed out on the couch."

She removed her hands to see the other face. *Nate.*

"Anything you want to tell me?" Cole was angry, his eyes in little slits. His mouth tight and drawn.

"No." But she turned to Nate. "What are you doing here?"

He moved out of the way so she could put her legs on the floor. "I followed you home."

"Creeper."

"You're lucky he did, Princess." She hated the tone her Daddy used– the same one he used on her when she was a child. She hadn't done anything wrong, so why was he scolding her as if he'd caught her riding her bike when he told her not to.

Nate spoke. "You were walking kind of funny when you left, so yeah, I followed you. You stumbled across the road almost like you were drunk, but I think you were dizzy. You couldn't stand straight so I helped you into the elevator where you leaned on me, and I unlocked your apartment before you passed out on the couch."

She winced, but not from pain. *Oh my god, that was you?*

"Your dad shows up, which I figured out because he had a key, and you sort of look like him. Once he determined you'd be okay, he introduced himself. And then we waited. And talked." Nate stood, moving away from her over to the other chair after she shot an arrow in his direction.

"What did you take?" Cole demanded.

Aurora shook her head, not able to remember. *What did I take? I think there were two, maybe three pills?*

He grabbed two containers off the floor beside him, flashing them before her eyes. They were from her purse. "How many?"

She grabbed at the containers, and remembrance dawned on her. "A perc and some cold meds."

"Aurora!" he yelled and stood. "You're not supposed to mix them."

"I had to, Daddy," she yelled back. "The days are hard enough without being slapped with memories. And all morning long I spent walking *alone* down memory lane." Tears escaped her eyes. "Today's a really hard day, and I just needed–"

"Oh, Princess, I know."

"No, you don't." She stood to match his stance, pushing his hands away. "You weren't there. You didn't hear the crunching of the car. You don't know what it feels like being slammed into a wall and then hearing nothing. NOTHING." She sniffed and wiped her nose on her sleeve. "You don't know what it's like. Every god damn day I hear a car squeal its tires, I wonder why I never heard that sound that night. Why did he never try to slam on his brakes? Every time I see someone have a drink at the bar, I wonder if they'll drive home, and if so, how many people they'll kill on their way." Defeated, she slumped. "And it's all my fault, Daddy."

He pulled her close, wrapping his arms around her. "No, Princess, it's his. He was drunk and ran the stop sign. It wasn't your fault."

She pushed out of the fatherly embrace and stormed over to the patio door. "It was. I was driving. It was my responsibility to keep them safe, and I should've looked before entering the intersection. Maybe if I had, they'd be here today. I killed them." Her forehead slammed against the glass as her shoulders rolled inward.

"Oh, Aurora. It wasn't your fault and the witnesses agree. You did nothing wrong."

Turning to face her father she said, "I should've paid more attention, but we were laughing and having a good time. And then... and then... it was gone." She snapped her fingers. "Just like that. Not looking cost them their lives, and I have to live with that daily. So forgive me if today I didn't want to feel that pain and hurt." Huge tears fell down her cheeks.

"That's not how to deal with it." He shook his head, his hair falling into his eyes.

"How then, Daddy?"

"You talk about it. Talk through it."

She scrunched her face, staring at him. "With who? The therapist? The one who only knows me only since the accident? Why can't I talk about it with you?"

"Because, you can't. You don't understand."

"Don't I know it?" Turning back to the window, she hunched her shoulders and braced herself against the glass door. "You always shut me out. Every fucking time." She limped and paced around the room.

"Don't use that language with me."

Aurora faced him and pointed a stern finger in his direction. "Your wife and your daughter died that day." Her hands flew into the air. "How can you not talk about that? How can you pretend like it didn't happen, and they never existed? How do you make it through the day like that?" Her sleeve scratched across her nose.

Cole looked her hard in the eyes. "Work."

"Bullshit, Daddy. I work all goddamn day, and it doesn't do fuck all to help me." More tears fell. "Even weeks later, when I was studying all-day for the diploma exams, I thought about them. Then throughout the first year. How can *you* not think about them?"

"Because I CAN'T, Aurora. It's what works for me."

"Well it doesn't work for me." She poked the air in front of him, almost connecting with his chest. "I miss them so much, and I think about everything Momma will miss in my life. My university grad, my wedding, my babies. Everything. You don't think that doesn't weigh on me?" Her voice fell to a volume barely above a whisper.

"Drugs aren't the answer." Although his expression was one of concern, his tone was flat.

Falling to her knees, she said, "They're prescription drugs, they're supposed to help me." Her eyes searched his, hoping for anything else but the anger they held. Tears streamed down her cheeks realising it was hopeless. "I need them, Daddy. I need them because I need you, but you keep shutting me out. Talk to me. Please."

Her daddy pinched the bridge of his nose. "I check in with you almost daily. Trust me, I'm not shutting you out."

"Why won't you talk about her then? You act like she's at home, waiting for you."

"Aurora, there are things you don't understand."

Her voice pitched. "So enlighten me. *Please.*"

He opened his mouth, and shut it just as quick. "Never mind. You're a child and you'd never understand."

"Daddy, please."

"Call your therapist. They're trained to help you through this. Because you need to get through this, Aurora. Hanging on like this, and using drugs to diminish your pain, that's not healthy."

Angry, she stood with her hands on her hips. "You know what's not healthy? Not admitting you need help too, Daddy."

He glared at her, and stepped sideways, thrusting his hands into his pockets. "I don't. You're wrong."

"Because MacIntyre's don't dwell on things. Ever. Am I right?" Anger and heat seared into her soul as he growled.

"Make an appointment." He walked to the door.

"Hypocrite," she yelled as loud as she could before the door slammed. Grief overcame her, and she backed up to the couch, her head buried in her hands. After collapsing into the soft fabric, the couch shifted beneath her. Through tear-filled eyes, she spotted Nate. She'd forgotten about him in her rant.

Nate said nothing as she folded herself into his arms. He rocked her and held her tight, giving her back a gentle rub from time to time.

Minutes later, she pulled out of his warm embrace. The apartment remained silent, Cole MacIntyre had yet to return. She glanced towards the door.

"Do you think he'll come back?"

"Hell if I know," she said, lowering her head. Breathing deeply, she steadied herself and stole a look at the clock. It wasn't as late as she expected. It was only two. She shook her head— it had felt like hours.

Nate seemed to have read her mind. "You weren't out that long. And you were responsive."

"What?"

"Well, when you passed out, I worried. So I called the pharmacy listed on your pills and explained. They suggested I try to get a response out of you, so I shook you a little. You told me to fuck off, so they suspected you'd be okay. But if you didn't wake soon, to call 911. Then your dad showed up, and knew you'd be okay. So we waited, and talked."

As her tired fingers rubbed against her temples, her eyes closed. She exhaled. "I didn't sleep much last night, so I'm sure that had a lot to do with it." Their eyes locked together.

He raised an eyebrow. "Really? Not buying it."

She curled her lips. "No really. I had a lot on my mind." *Like Matthew, you and everyone else.* "I know what you're thinking."

"This should be interesting." He stretched out on the couch, and folded his arms over his chest. "Go ahead."

"I'm not a drug addict." Her stance defiant, her tone outraged.

"Okay."

"I'm not, because that would make me a criminal."

"How so?"

"Because it would."

He laughed. "Good thing you're not a lawyer. That defence holds no water."

"Well, I'm not a drug addict."

"If you say so. I don't believe it."

She slumped onto the couch. "I need them."

"Sometimes, yes you do." He raised an eyebrow. "So it makes moving forward tricky."

"It does." She lowered her head into her hands, breathing deeply. She wasn't an addict. The pills helped her survive the pain or anxiety. They helped her, and she only ever used them when she needed them. It's not like she took them whenever she wanted, there was always a good reason. Every single time. So, she wasn't addicted to them, right? And why should he care so much? What was it to him? She looked over to him, still dressed in his work gear. "Why are you here?"

"I've already answered that."

"No," she said, positioning herself better to see him. All of him. "I mean, why did you follow me home? We broke up." Her eyes narrowed and posture stiffened.

"Seriously?" Nate's laughter warmed her soul, until he stopped. "We didn't break up." There was truth in his eyes, and the twinkle in his eyes made him so adorably cute.

"Yes, we did. I kicked you out."

"So what? That didn't mean we broke up." His shoulders drooped as he leaned closer towards her. "Is that what you thought?"

"No," she lied. *So now that means I didn't have a one-night stand with Matthew, it means I cheated on Nate. I'm a terrible person.* Standing, she limped around the living room.

"Did you never fight with your other boyfriends?"

"Daily," she rolled her eyes as she answered.

"Aww, that's cute."

"What?"

"You thought we broke up because you closed a door in my face." A chuckle rumbled out of him. "Look, I've had more doors slammed in my face than I care to admit. It doesn't mean much, except that the person on the other side is fairly pissed off." He walked over to her and wrapped an arm around her waist. "And I get that you were upset. But really, if I thought we had broken up, would I have followed you home today?"

She shook her head. "Obviously not."

"So there you go. I care about you." He planted his lips, those perfectly soft lips, on hers. The kiss so intoxicating it caused her to forget everything. It was better than any drug she'd used. And she loved it.

❤ Chapter Nineteen ❤

They stopped kissing and came up for air.

"I want to talk to you about something." Nate held her hand and led her back to the couch. "I was chatting with your dad while you were passed out."

She shifted, suddenly uncomfortable with where the conversation was headed. Nothing good ever came out of *I was chatting with your dad.* She swallowed. "Yes."

"And I asked his opinion. I told him what I was doing with you, I mean, with the car and stuff. How we're taking it slow and I'm trying to get you comfortable with cars again." His hands twisted together.

She stared at him as anger surged within her. How dare he share that with her father? That was between them, wasn't it?

"So, I asked him about this magic pill you used when you moved." Unable to believe what she heard, she covered her ears. Warm hands pulled hers away and squeezed them. "I want you to meet my family on Saturday. And in order for that to happen, I need to drive you there. It's a forty-five minute drive away." Her mouth fell open. "So I asked if it was possible to get one of those pills."

The muscles in her face tightened, and she struggled to find her voice. "Let me get this straight. You think I have a drug problem and yet, you want me to take more drugs so I can see your family? I'm confused."

He bit his lip. "So am I. Conflicted really." His head tilted to the side as he shrugged. "I honestly think there's some kind of abuse going on." A loud gasp escaped from her open mouth. "However, and this is where it gets weird, I want you to meet my family. I know the only way right now for that to be possible is to give you this magic pill your dad mentioned. So I feel like I'm enabling you, when really I should be helping you."

"But–" She had nothing. No comeback. No thoughts. Nothing. Even her expression was blank.

"I get it. It's completely selfish on my part." A pause while he hung his head, and his thumb stroked her knuckles. "But I don't know how else to get you to meet them."

A quick check of her surroundings told her she could seat a few people in comfortably. Four at the table, a couple on the couch, one on the sofa chair. There shouldn't be any issue rounding up a few more stools from somewhere. "Have them come here. I don't mind."

"They wouldn't all fit."

She screwed up her face. "How big is your family?"

He smiled. "My immediate family is small. Just the seven of us. But my extended family is much bigger." He gave her hand a quick squeeze.

"How big?"

"Big."

Running her fingers through her hair, she gave it a tousle. "This meeting, when would it be? In a month or so?" At least with a goal, she'd work harder, although, it would be impossible for her to be riding in a car in thirty days. Maybe by Christmas? He could wait seven months right? Did she need to meet his whole family so soon?

"I was hoping this weekend." Brown eyes searched hers. "It's my birthday on Saturday."

Saturday? SATURDAY!! As in five days from now? Pill or no pill, that was asking a lot. "That's bigger than a baby step."

"I know." The gap between them swallowed up as he moved closer. "Would you think about it? For me?"

So she shut her eyes to block out the cute little grin playing on his lips. She needed to think, dammit, and that sweet dimple made it easier to give in. And she didn't want to. Shit. She needed to figure this out. This would be huge for him, more so for her. She'd be getting into a car. With him. To meet his family. And that seemed super fast, even though it was for his birthday. She was speechless.

"I can see the wheels turning in your head. Tell me what you're thinking."

"Fuck me," she whispered.

He laughed. "Always about the sex."

This time, she raised an eyebrow. "Not what I meant."

The smile fell. "I know." He lowered himself to the floor, so he kneeled before her. "It's so much to ask." Rubbing her knees, he whispered, "Let's make a deal. You do this for me, and I'll do something for you."

Hmmm, this is interesting. "It would have to be something big. Because you're asking me to take a pill that's essentially a date-rape drug, and drive me out to the middle of God knows where to meet a family of strangers. That's a lot of trust to dispense."

"You don't trust me?"

Ouch. His pained expression spoke volumes. "Obviously, especially after today," she whispered.

"So what would you like from me?"

"Anything?" She gave him a subtle wink.

"Anything."

She squeezed his hand and after kissing it, placed it over top of her breast. She hoped her racing heart beat hard against his hand. "I want–" Why was this so hard to say? She'd had no issues insinuating it before. "I want–" She breathed. "You."

His swallow was audible.

❤ Chapter Twenty ❤

"I ... umm..." He swallowed again and took a deep breath. "That *is* a big step."

She pulled his head close and kissed his lips while holding his hand to her breast. "It's what I want."

"I know. You're like a little horndog." His laughter was music to her ears.

"Fucking right." She smirked. "So, what do you say? I agree to take the fucking little pill and be surrounded by strangers in a foreign place, and you agree to make love to me."

He nodded as he tensed. "When? That night?"

"No. I want to remember it because I'm sure it'll be magical." She kissed him again. "But soon after."

He let out a breath and a moment of worry flashed in his eyes. Kisses trailed over her neck, and slowly his hand moved up along her backbone. Over her shoulder. Down her arm.

It fired up little synapses everywhere he touched her, igniting her passion in a way Matthew didn't. The sensations felt good– right, wholesome and pure through to her soul, which warmed and tingled the longer he stroked her arm. "I don't know if I can wait until after your birthday."

"You'll have to try." His voice was smoky and soothing.

"Fuck that," she said, pushing him down, so he lay on the couch. She straddled him and started to unhook his Carhardts when the unmistakable sound of a door clicked against the strike plate.

"Aurora," her daddy said, agitation strong in his voice.

"Sonofabitch," she muttered and climbed off Nate.

But Daddy wasn't looking at her, he glared in Nate's direction. Assessing him. Thoroughly. And poor Nate, his face turned the most brilliant shade of crimson.

A quick glance in his direction said it all. Daddy was still pissed, but yet his eyes wore concern, and the longer he stared at her, the softer his features became. He turned to Nate. "I thought about what you asked me and I want to show you what it does and how it works." He faced Aurora. "Has Nate discussed with you about this weekend?"

Heart beating hard wondering how this would end, she nodded. "Yes, we just finished our negotiations."

Confusion crossed his face, but he shook his head. "But before I have the final say–"

"*You* get the final say? Shouldn't I?"

"No. Because you don't know how you act while you're on it. I want Nate to understand," and his eyes narrowed in Nate's direction, "how this works." He pointed a finger at him. "And if you try any funny business while she's on it, I'll hunt you down like a dog. You have my word."

"Yes, sir." If she didn't know better, she'd swear he was shaking beside her.

Cole rubbed his chin as contemplation crossed his face while he mumbled. "A perc and pseudoephedrine five hours ago, plus the Isas…" Shaking his head, he studied her, looking her up and down. "How are you feeling, Princess?"

Confused by the out of the blue question, she stumbled. "Fine, I guess."

"Headaches? Nausea? Dizziness?" She shook her head as her eyes widened, understanding why he asked. "I think we should be okay for a demo. Are you willing to try a small dose tonight?"

A gulp. She reached for Nate's hand and searched his face. "Are you willing to see this? You're supposed to be at work still."

He turned to her, holding her hand close. "I've taken care of it. Do *you* want to do this, tonight?"

Another swallow. She'd be meeting his family. His mother. On his birthday. Putting her whole trust into him. Obviously, he proved he was trustworthy. He could've packed her in his car and sped away with her, but he didn't. Instead, he took care of her. Her head hung in shame as she realized she trusted *him* more than she trusted herself. "If it makes it so I can meet your family." She shrugged. "Wait? What will they think when I arrive and I'm loopy?"

"You don't get loopy," her daddy said. "More distant than anything else."

"What will they think?" Her eyes held Nate's face.

Nate stroked her hand. "I'll prepare them, although they already know about your fear."

What the fuck? Seriously? Does he tell everyone?

"I promise, they'll be gentle."

She sighed. "Okay. Let's do this. Let's show Nate how this works."

Her daddy pulled a small plastic bag from his pocket. "These are propranolols. We call them Isas. They're fast-acting. Each pill will give you about an hour."

"But I thought they lasted longer than that?" Aurora asked as her eyes widened.

He gave her the sideways glance. "You take more for the longer trips." He turned his full attention to Nate. "It takes about six or seven minutes to kick in. It's like flying." Her dad chuckled, and it made the hairs stand up on the back of her neck. "Its peak effectiveness is roughly forty minutes though. Six to seven minutes before you hit cruising speed, and about five minutes to landing."

"Okay." Nate's brow furrowed in deep concentration.

"So, monitor your time well, Nate. You don't want to be on the receiving end of it wearing off before arrival. Trust me on this." From the corner of his eye, she caught his look.

What? I don't remember anything like that.

"I will." Nate nodded and draped an arm over her shoulders.

"For tonight, I'll cut the pill in half. It may not be as effective, but you'll get the idea."

"May I add," Aurora spoke up, her voice dripping in sarcasm, "how much I love being a science experiment for you two?"

Her daddy walked into the kitchen and brandishing the sharpest knife he could find, expertly broke the tiny pill into two. Holding half, he passed part of it to Aurora.

"Right now?"

"Please," her daddy said.

As she had before, she placed it under her tongue and waited.

❤ Chapter Twenty-One ❤

Aurora slowly started to realise what was going on. It always took a while to exit out of the fog. Tonight was no different.

A rush of adrenaline followed as the sounds registered first. Glasses tinked, hushed voices beyond her, and speakers that played terrible music. *Focus on the voices. Who's here?* Her breathing came faster and shallower, a normal reaction to 'waking up' in a strange place. The smells hit next– nearby coffee, something spicy in the air, and fresh bread close enough to taste. A quick jump in her heart rate. Finally, the vision returned. As she blinked around, everything became clearer.

Nate sat to her left, her daddy across the booth from her. Both chatted animatedly as if she wasn't there. She was, but she really wasn't. If she had been part of the conversation, surely she'd remember. *What had we been talking about?* But that was the trick of the pill, wasn't it? No memory. And coming out of it always left her feeling like a ghost which made her insecure.

"How can you not be an Oilers fan?" her father asked Nate, who shrugged.

"Not big into hockey, really. Never had time."

Aurora stared at them both. "Hey," she whispered. They kept on chatting. Surely, she hadn't been comatose, and they hadn't grown deaf in the past few minutes. "Hey," she said.

They stopped and turned in her direction. Nate spoke first. "Hey."

"How's my Princess?"

"I'm fine, Daddy." *They were discussing hockey. YES! I remember.* "It's wearing off." A smile formed on her lips as she turned to Nate. "Not an Oilers fan, eh? Well, guess tonight's going to be our last date."

Nate laughed as Cole shrugged. "Welcome back," her daddy said.

"Did I pass the science lesson? Everything okay?" She wanted Nate to answer more than her daddy.

Dammit, her daddy spoke up first. "Yes, Nate understands." Added as an afterthought, "Clearly."

"Yeah." Nate gave her hand a little squeeze. "Considering how you reacted when you tried to sit in the car, this was a walk in the park. I think we'll be just fine on Saturday."

She squeezed his hand back. "Good. I'm glad. I hate taking that pill, but it sure does the job." Heat flashed and flamed through her cheeks. "I didn't say anything, you know, out of the ordinary?"

A scolding voice from across the table said, "It's not a truth serum, Princess. It's a beta-blocker."

Oh good. I've never had anything to hide before, and I didn't want the whole Matthew bit to come out. "Whew," she said. "So, what's everyone having?"

The restaurant they dined at was more than a thirty-minute walk back home, so once again, Aurora took the other half of the pill for the return trip. When she rolled out of another fog, she was safely home in her apartment. Nate sat at the kitchen table, with Cole holding a beer and offering one to Nate.

"I'm kind of surprised you're drinking. When did you get the beer?"

"I brought it down with me." His tone was one of finality. There'd be no further discussion.

She sighed and tugged at her shirt. "So, Daddy, how long are you here for?"

"I was going to go home tomorrow, but after your disaster today, perhaps it's better if I stay a bit longer. Keep my eye on you." He downed a swig while holding his sight on her.

Her eyes rolled. "Daddy, I'll be fine. I promise."

"We'll see. For now, I'll stay a couple of days. Then go from there." He drained the remainder of his beer before tossing it into the trash container. A pop as another beer opened. "I'm going to bed. It was nice to meet you, Nate. Goodnight, Princess."

"Goodnight, Daddy." She waited until he closed the spare bedroom door before getting up and retrieving the empty beer can. With a shudder, she tossed it into the recycling can. She leaned against the cabinets, staring out into the eating area.

Nate came and blocked her view. "You okay?"

She blinked, and searched his brown eyes. "Yeah, why wouldn't I be?"

"You got real quiet and zoned out." He wrapped his arms around her waist.

"Do you want to get out of here? I think I need to go for a walk or something." She grabbed a pen and piece of paper.

His face brightened. "Sure. Let's go." He stopped at the table. "I meant to ask earlier. Who are the flowers from?"

The pen skidded across the paper. "Kaitlyn," she said, not tearing her eyes away from the drying ink. "For the death-aversary."

"Oh," he said. "That's a nice gesture."

Breathing once more, she taped the note to the spare bedroom door, and they left the apartment hand in hand. They walked in silence across the street to the empty park. She sat in the swing and absentmindedly swung it, little by little.

Nate sat in the swing beside her. "Your dad's pretty cool."

"He's acting like a jerk right now." She drew a circle in the sand with her foot. "He knows better than to bring alcohol into the apartment." Angry at her daddy, she kicked at the circle, sending sand flying in multiple directions.

"I'm sure today is hard on him."

"Perhaps. You'd never know it though."

He pushed back and lifted his legs, swinging forward. "You scared him today. Do you think it's possible he worried that he was about to lose you too?"

"He already lost me. Two years ago. He won't talk to me, like really talk to me. It's all very generalized, like he's doing it because he has to. The check-ins are to make sure I'm not over-medicating and that my studies are going well. That's it."

"Well, he's worried."

The swing came to a halt. She pushed her hair off her face, and stared at him. "And you know this how?"

He twisted his swing and faced her. "He told me."

"Great." She jumped off her swing. "He can tell you that, but he won't talk to me?" She stormed over to the giant tree they'd had lunch at, and kicked the base of it as hard as she could.

Nate grabbed her and pulled her back as she kicked wildly. "Hey. Hey. What did that tree ever do to you?"

When her feet touched the grass, she spun around, burying her face into his chest. Her body shook with the sobs she'd held in for too long. Nate said nothing, and held her tighter to keep her from falling apart.

With her anger extinguished, she pushed out of his embrace. "I'm so sorry."

"For what? Having feelings?" A soft finger wiped away a trail of tears.

"I'm so frustrated with him."

"Yeah, I sense that." He brushed her hair off to the side. "But he loves you. Dads just have a different way of showing it." Hand in hand, he led her over to a picnic table where they sat on the tabletop. "My dad was a very strict man. But yet, I knew he loved me– even if he never said it. It's in all the little things he did for me. He was my biggest supporter although he would've been the first to tell me to try harder." Whatever memory he thought of, it brought a twinkle to his eyes. "And my mom, she's the total opposite. Wears her heart on her sleeve and everyone within a fifty-mile radius can feel her zest for life. It was so neat to see my parents interact with others. Dad rarely smiled, always so serious. But he'd also be the first man to give you the shirt off his back if you ever needed it."

"Do you miss him? Like every day?"

He huffed. "Yes, and no. The hurt I felt daily is gone. But I still miss him. There are times when I'd like to sit down with him and get his opinion, but–" he trailed off, as he looked into her eyes. "But it gets easier." He kissed the top of her hand. "And maybe that's a guy thing. We tend to handle things differently."

"Maybe." A shrug.

"What about your dad? What was he like when you were growing up?"

"When I was little, Dad would be home for one week, gone for three. It's the nature of the beast working in the oil field. So our time together was always precious, and he'd make sure to spend those evenings with us, doing fun things. Momma, Mom, was always the disciplinarian, ensuring we had our homework and chores done first. Then as we got older, the fun died down a little, because the homework demands rose.

"When Carmen moved here for university, it changed the dynamic at home. Totally. Suddenly, Mom was the fun one and Dad was the strict one, always pushing Carmen to do better, to be better. She was gone for months, and only came home at Christmas and Reading Week, but I never blamed her. It was tough being around him. Mom worked more to pay for our weekend trips down and part of her income paid for Carmen's living expenses and provided her with an allowance so she didn't need to work during the year and could focus on her studies. The same deal applies to me, but only Dad's the one footing the entire bill. It was rare, but he'd come and visit Carmen as he passed through, but never for an overnight. I used to joke he fathered her long-distance because there wasn't much said between the two of them. Mom and I came down at least once a month and it was always a girls' weekend– movies, shopping, pedicures. Female bonding stuff."

Nate's face scrunched. "Yep, sounds like a girly thing to do."

"Yeah, but, I'm not a girly girl like Carmen and Mom were. I'm the tomboy. I love video games and going to watch the Oilers. That was what Dad and I did. Now, it's more like I'm on probation and he's the warden."

His calloused hand ran over hers, soothing her. "Take him to a game."

"You really don't follow hockey at all, do you?" She laughed. "The Oilers didn't make the playoffs."

"Oh. Well–" He looked thoughtful. "You could always have a video game night with him. I've seen the stacks of games you have."

Moving closer to him, she agreed. "That'd be fun, I suppose."

He gazed at her and leaned in for a kiss. The brush of his lips fuelled her heat, burning away thoughts of her father. Everywhere he touched her–her face, her cheek, the length of her arm–the electricity snapped her cells alive and ached for more. Her body longed for him and responded well to him. It was almost hypnotic.

"Come on, I'll take you back home. We both have to work in the morning."

She slipped off the picnic table. "Yeah, I'm not looking forward to going in. They won't be happy with me."

"It'll be fine. I told them you were sick."

"You lied?"

"It wasn't a lie. Technically you were sick." He raised an eyebrow.

She rolled it over in her mind, and supposed he was right. *Technically.* They stood and walked back through the park, towards the tower.

"Where's your car?"

"Still at work. Remember? I followed you home."

Nodding, she did remember. "Well, let's walk back and get it."

"And you're going to what? Sit in it while I drive you back home?"

Snorting, she shook her head. "Yeah right. No, I'll walk back home."

"Not at night, and not when I'm right here. I'll walk you upstairs," he said, cocking his head at the tower, "and kiss you good night."

"Such a traditionalist, eh?" she asked, although secretly inside she beamed. She had to admit it felt nice to be treated that way.

They arrived at her door, and she placed her key into the lock. Before she opened it fully, he spun her around and planted a deep, lingering kiss on her lips. She pressed herself hard onto his lips and into his body, the bulge in his tight overalls pushing against her hips. Breathless herself, she bid him good night and closed the door.

Surprised to see the spare room door open, she glanced to her left and saw her father sitting in the living room.

"Hey, Daddy."

"Princess." He patted the space beside him. "Come sit."

A hesitation. "I'm surprised to see you out. I thought you were going to bed."

"No," he said, running his hands through his hair, "I wanted to give you and Nate some time alone."

"Thanks, we went for a walk though." She crossed her arms over her chest. The fight inside her roared to life in a heartbeat. "Why would you bring alcohol into my apartment?"

"Your apartment? I pay the rent on this, Princess, so watch your words."

"Watch my words? What else do I have to watch, Daddy? I have to watch so much around you, I'm afraid to do anything. I can't speak my mind, I can't talk to you. I'm a science and social experiment for you to show off to my boyfriend."

"Hey," he said, standing, "I did that FOR YOU."

"For me? Great thanks."

"I mean it. That boy, he cares about you. I want you to be with him and not be afraid. It sounds as if he's trying awfully hard to help you– the least you could do is this for him. He wants you there, and he wants you to meet his family. It'll do you a world of good to go someplace new."

"But that's the thing, I don't want to go somewhere new. I want to stay here because I like it here." Her hands retracted inside the sleeve of her shirt.

"No, you've just resigned yourself to this kind of life, and this isn't living."

"What do you mean? I'm getting a university degree. I'm working. I have a boyfriend again. I can hang out with my friends. I'm happy. I'm living." She pointed her finger towards her father. "It's YOU that's not living."

"Watch your mouth."

"Have you gone out on a date with anyone? Started seeing anyone?" He stood in front of her, anger pouring out of his beet-red ears. "Why not? You won't talk about Momma, so why don't you get out and start living?"

"It doesn't work that way for me. I'm an old man."

"Fuck that, Daddy. You're barely into your fifties." She stood level with him, not budging an inch. "When are you going to start living? Because you can't preach to me about it, holed up in your home, watching bad TV and pretending things aren't the way they are."

"Aurora, stop."

"No, you stop. I'm trying to move on. I'm trying to get into cars again, and it's terrifying. Second scariest thing I've ever done. Every time I touch his car, or sit on it, I feel like months are being shaved off my life. But I do it, even when I so desperately want nothing more than to walk away." Before he opened his mouth, she cut him off. "And it's not for him. It's for me." She slumped her shoulders when the realisation dropped on her head. "Because, maybe someday I do want to get out again and see the world." *Wow, I really do.* "And he's the person who'll help me, who *is* helping me to do that. I just didn't see it until now." She hugged her father. "Thank you."

"Although I'm not sure why you're thanking me, I appreciate the hug." He kissed the top of her head.

"I'd always thought I was happy here, in this little life I've made. But I'm not. Not really. I want to explore. So thank you for getting me out tonight, and using that nasty fucking pill to show Nate. Maybe there *is* hope for me." Tears edged her eyes. "And if there's hope for me, then there's hope for you too, Daddy."

"Well that, Princess, I'm not sure about."

"Since you won't talk to me about Momma or Carmen, will you talk to someone? A therapist, perhaps?"

"It won't help." Cole turned and slumped back on the couch.

"Because you haven't tried. Try it. You and I, we're the only bits of this family left. We need to stick together. You know that's what she'd want." A vision of her momma shaking a finger at the pair of them sprung to the front of her mind.

"I'm not making any promises."

"But you'll try? You've been pushing me, so I'm going to push back."

He sighed. "I'll think about it."

"Well, it's a start." She smiled and walked to the kitchen. "Do you want anything?"

"No, but I am interested in knowing who the flowers are from?" He tipped his head to the bouquet on the table. The ones that Matthew sent.

She waved her hand through the air. "Oh those? Those are from Kaitlyn." Lies. Lies. Lies. What possessed her to keep them? All they did was laugh and taunt her, with their smug little daisy smiles. They reminded her of her stupidity. Fucking one-night stand. She still couldn't believe she did that. Shame coursed through her mind, but not through her body which remembered Saturday night. Vividly. Opening the fridge door, she inhaled several cool gulps of air. "Why do you ask?"

"Oh, you left your phone behind, and it rang a couple of times. Some Matthew guy popped up."

She narrowly missed bonking her head on the top of the fridge. "Oh, he's just a guy I worked with." *Ha-ha, that's not a lie. A twisting of the truth, but still not a lie.*

"If you say so."

She heard him turn on the TV, so she desperately hunted for where she'd last left her phone. Lifting a few newspapers, she stole a peek underneath. Nothing. Trying to act nonchalantly, she stepped out into the living room, her eyes searching for the flipping phone.

"It's on the table," he said, amusement and smugness in both his expression and voice.

"Oh good," she said relieved. "I wanted to text Nate and say good night."

"To him or me?"

"Both, but I'll say good night to you first."

He turned his focus from the TV to her. "I'll leave tomorrow, okay?"

She felt the weight of his decision. What had changed that he didn't think it necessary to 'babysit' her? The phone flipped over in her hands.

"I think you're in good hands with Nate." For a moment their eyes locked.

Her heart fluttered hearing his name. "At least stay for dinner tomorrow night. You can leave on Wednesday."

"Only if you're sure."

"I wouldn't tell you if I wasn't." She kissed his forehead. "I'll see you in the morning." Feeling relaxed with Daddy's approval, she walked to her bedroom and took a deep breath before closing her door. She was no longer as interested in reading Matthew's texts.

8:35 Thanks for Saturday night. I had a good time.

8:37 Couldn't wait to talk to you again. I keep thinking about you.

8:40 Call me if you want.

8:45 I'll be back in town mid-June. Can I take you out again?

Oh, fuck. She was positive her father had read every single text. It was all there on her lock screen. Dammit, why didn't she think to take her phone with her? Is this why he said she was in good hands with Nate?

She hopped in the shower and washed away the yucky remnants of guilt, hoping to see it twirl its way into the sewer system. But it didn't. No matter how hard she scrubbed, the truth remained– she'd slept with Matthew and it appeared he was falling for her.

Fuck! Nate was the one she adored, even though he refused to take the next step with her. For now. She'd never been in a relationship like this. The physical always happened first, and the getting to know you came second. Confusion settled in around her, and it pissed her off. But she didn't know where to begin.

❤ Chapter Twenty-Two ❤

Before Aurora knew it, Friday arrived. The week had been a blur of activity, and she wasn't looking forward to the end of the week. The big birthday trip weighed heavy on her mind.

Cole stayed until Wednesday and the two of them had an enjoyable dinner together, and managed quality time playing video games. It was a start. Baby steps as Nate told her. When he left Wednesday morning, she was a little sad, but for the most part relieved because she could go back to living the way she liked– messy. It was hard to pretend to be a neat and tidy person when that's not who she was.

She continued to play 'touch the car' with Nate, which in a sick way she actually looked forward to. Her heart told her it was because Nate was such a fantastic kisser, but her stupid brain said it was because it wasn't as frightening to touch the car. Or, gasp, sit on the hood– as long as Nate secured her in his strong arms. She hadn't yet ventured back *into* the car.

Aurora sauntered out the front doors of the library, bee-lining straight over to Nate. A long kiss came first. The delicious taste of Nate. A fantastic way to end her work day, and she tingled all-day in heady anticipation of it. "Hey," she said, breaking off the kiss. She leaned against the car, and put her hands in the air. "Tada," she said smiling.

"I'm impressed."

"Good. Because I like impressing you." She kissed him again as he lifted her. The cool metal helped bring the hidden heat down a notch, but the way Nate kissed her back, well, it didn't stay cool for long.

Breathing fast, from both the passion and the fear, she rested her cheek against Nate's chest.

"Aurora MacIntyre," a high-pitched female voice called out behind Nate.

She launched herself off Nate's car and righting herself, stared directly into Kaitlyn's eyes. "What are you doing here?"

"I had some library books to pick up." Kaitlyn's gaze ran over the tall man.

Introductions were needed, and pronto. "Kaitlyn, this is Nate. Nate, Kaitlyn." She breathed hard as the two sized each other up.

"Kaitlyn." Nate rubbed his chin in thought as if searching a huge database of names. "Ah, yes, you're the girl from the bar, right?"

"Huh?" Kaitlyn said.

"Aurora and you were dancing that night. Although," he wrapped his arm around Aurora, "she snuck out before I got the chance to dance."

Kaitlyn looked mildly amused. "Yes, she's a great dancer." A subtle wink meant only for her. "Speaking of which, do you want to go clubbing tonight? I could meet you there?"

"Want to join us, Nate?"

"Not tonight," Nate said. "I have a busy day tomorrow. Lots to prepare for." His tight body turned its full attention to Aurora. "Pick up you at noon?"

"Noon?" she whispered, "That seems so early." Her hand trembled in his.

"It's a long drive."

"I know," she said, hanging her head.

Nate lifted her chin with his finger. "You'll be fine. I promise." He placed the world's gentlest kiss on her lips. "Noon. Have fun tonight."

"Get a room." A fit of giggles erupted from Kaitlyn. "I'll leave you lovebirds alone. Text me if you want to hang."

"Kait," she said, "come by my place in an hour, okay?"

"Sure thing. Nice to meet you, Nate." Kaitlyn blew a kiss as she walked away.

"You too," he said.

She waited until Kaitlyn hopped in her car and drove away before speaking to Nate. "Sorry."

"For what? You didn't know she would show up."

Her hands danced their way around Nate's hips to his lower back. Lacing her fingers together, she pulled him closer. "Where were we again?"

He kissed her, and once again lifted her effortlessly onto the hood of his car. "Here, I think?"

Aurora's hands moved from his lower back to around his neck, feeling moisture along the nape. She pushed her fingers through his silky hair, and her tongue into his hot, little mouth searching out that sweet stud. Moments passed as hearts pounded.

"Open your eyes," he whispered, his tantalizing mouth moving towards her ear.

Slowly, she opened her eyes. She still sat atop the car, although a moment ago, she could've sworn she was flying. With every ounce of determination in her, she remained on the hood, but pulled out of his embrace. Her hands hovered above the hood, inches high. With great trepidation, she inched them down, bit by bit until they splayed out on the hood beside her thighs. In Nate's eyes she saw pride flash behind them. She knew from his expression that she had impressed him once again.

She stared at him, focusing on him to hold her in the present and not flashback like her mind wanted. It was a battle of wills fighting inside her, and she outlasted her longest battle. With a gasp and cry she leaped off as the memories crept in, halting her progress.

"Wow," Nate said, holding her close.

Although she trembled in his warm embrace, she managed a smile. She managed to go longer than she'd ever thought possible. It had to have been at least ten minutes. "How long was I on there?"

"In total? Maybe three minutes?"

"Oh." Her face sank.

"Don't. You did so well. I'm so proud of you." He tilted her head up and placed a kiss on her lips. "That was a really long time."

"I've *kissed* longer than that." She laughed as she playfully smacked him.

"Shall I take you home? I'm sure your friend will be chomping at the bit to get you out dancing." He locked up his car and headed toward her apartment.

"Sure you won't come along?"

Her hand moulded perfectly in his. "I wish I could. But I have a lot to do in the morning before I pick you up."

"Anything I can do to help?"

He kissed her hand. "Nope. Just be ready."

"What do I wear?"

"Sunscreen, although I'm sure Mom will have some too. We'll be outside all day and the weather's supposed to be great."

"So, like, at a beach?" He laughed, but she didn't understand why. It was impossible trying to get a hint or two from him.

"Not a beach and bring a sweater as the nights can be a little cool."

"How long are we going to be out there?" Her voice ripe with concern.

"If everything goes well, I should have you home by midnight. Maybe later."

She swallowed. "So it's an all-day birthday party."

"Essentially. But it'll be fun. It gets your blood pumping." His face split with an ear to ear grin.

My blood's pumping already but I suspect for different reasons. "Hmm." She tried to read between the lines, but came up empty. She was a terrible guesser.

They arrived at her apartment. "I'll leave you here. Think you can manage the elevator ride up?"

"Most days," she said, shrugging.

After another kiss, she watched him leave, and followed him as far as her eyes could see.

Upstairs in her apartment, she was about to text Kaitlyn to see where she was, when someone pounded on her door.

"Get in here, you freak," Aurora said to her friend after a quick peek through the peep-hole.

"We've got to talk, girly. Tell me more about Nate. He's sex-on-a-stick."

She sighed. "Oh, he is."

Kaitlyn walked into the dining room, and gave the dying flowers a sniff. "Did he buy you these? They're gorgeous."

She didn't confirm nor deny who sent them, having lied enough these past few days. However, it was hard to control the flood of colour filling her cheeks as she thought of Nate– and the perfect way he made her soul soar.

"Ooh, girlfriend, you have it bbaaaaddddd."

"Fuck off, I do not." She walked to her bedroom. She still hadn't packed for clubbing.

"Look at you. You're like a Christmas tree bulb burning bright." Kaitlyn flopped on the bed. "So, is he coming tonight?"

"No. We're going out all-day tomorrow though. What should I wear to a picnic? I'm meeting his family tomorrow."

"You're meeting his family? Girl, you do have it bad."

"And it's his birthday." A blank stare into her closet. "What in hell do I wear?"

Kaitlyn pulled open her underwear drawer and flashed a corset-type piece of lingerie. "How about this?"

"No." She tore the outfit from Kaitlyn's hand and stuffed it back into the drawer. She limped back over to the closet, and rooted through it. Clothes flew out and landed on her bed.

"Where are you going?"

"I have no fucking clue."

"Typical guy. Says nothing."

She flipped through a few dresses. "All he said was wear sunscreen and bring a sweater because it gets chilly at night."

"Yeah, that's not a lot to work with."

"Would a dress be wrong? I want to impress his mom."

"Well, I'd start with your mouth then," Kaitlyn said in earnest. "Watch your language."

"Good point." *Had I ever heard him swear? Maybe once or twice.* "Ahh, what the hell do I wear?"

Kaitlyn flipped through the piled up clothes on the bed, selecting a couple. "Here. Black capris and this floral button-up. But iron it please. And you can add this," she pulled out a black sweater, "for when it's cool. It's picnic-y, but it's also not trying too hard."

She smiled at her friend and placed them on hangers. "That's great." Walking into the en-suite, she hung the hangers on the shower curtain rod.

"That won't count as ironing," Kaitlyn laughed from the other room.

"I know. But it'll help." She leaned against the doorframe as her best friend hung up her clothes. Always tidying up.

"So, how are you getting there?"

Aurora launched into details about the special pill she'd be taking, and how her daddy showed Nate what she was like while 'under'.

"Good lord, girl. This relationship had better be *the one* for you and your dad to put that much trust in Nate. He'd better not fuck this up."

"I think Dad threatened him within an inch of his life."

"Good, and then I'll finish whatever's leftover. This is some birthday present you're giving him. That's a lot of trust."

Aurora spun in the spot. "What did you say?" Her eyes grew wide.

"I said, 'That's a lot of trust?'."

"No, the other part."

"This being some birthday present?" Kaitlyn looked confused.

"Oh my god. A birthday present." She fell back onto her bed. "What do I get him?"

Kaitlyn lay beside her. "You haven't got one yet?"

"Shit, shit, shit." Aurora stood and paced around the room. "What can I get him? I have no idea."

"I'm sure he'll understand. Your relationship is new. I'm sure he doesn't expect a birthday present."

"Probably not, but he's taking me to meet his family. I need to get him something." She paced in the room. "Think, Kaitlyn."

Kaitlyn shook her head. "What did you get your last boyfriend?"

"We weren't together on his birthday."

"Have you ever dated a guy and celebrated his birthday?"

"Just Derek, but we'd known each other for months first. Not a couple of weeks."

"So get him a gift card."

Aurora tossed a throw pillow at her friend. "That's not at all romantic."

"What does he like?"

"Kisses. Cars. Construction."

"Not helpful, Aurora."

Her eyes widened. "I know." She dashed to the kitchen, and flipped through an old recipe book. "I'll make him some of the best damn truffles he's ever eaten." Ripping through the cupboards, she pulled out various ingredients. "Sorry, Kait, but I'm not going dancing tonight. I'm making these."

"Well, I'm staying to watch. And sample."

❤ Chapter Twenty-Three ❤

B y the time Aurora fell into bed, it was well into Saturday. However, the truffles turned out perfectly, at least according to Kaitlyn, and she couldn't wait to give a nice box to Nate for his birthday. She made five different varieties, and made up a smaller sample box for his mom. Aurora was more than a little nervous to meet her, and wanted to make sure she gave a good impression.

After a quick sleep, she readied herself, making sure to apply a hint of makeup to her tired eyes and take a couple more minutes to style her hair. Pinching some colour into her cheeks helped a bit too, but she still looked exhausted. Which she was.

She refilled her travelling pill containers in case she needed pain or anxiety relief. As she filled her container, she debated taking a Xanax, but worried what that might do combined with the Isas. So she held off and instead, drowned her anxiety in coffee. But not too much so she'd have to take a pee break on the road.

As she nervously paced the apartment, Nate buzzed right at noon, and she let him in.

"Wow," he said when she opened the door, "you look amazing."

"Too much?" She twirled, throwing her arms out to the side. "Figure, if they're meeting me, and know that I need a special pill to get there, they may as well get all of me– visible scars and all."

He tipped his head from side to side as if trying to figure out the best answer to that. His finger trailed down her arm, and he gave her a quick kiss. "And yet, you're still beautiful. They won't even notice your scars, they'll be too mesmerized by your beauty."

"Always with the cheesy lines." But her cheeks heated regardless.

"Are you ready?" He held up the special case Cole had given him containing two Isas– one for the trip there, and one for the trip back.

Swallowing hard, she nodded. "Yes, but first, happy birthday." She reached up and threaded her hands through his hair, giving him a kiss filled with passion and minor hesitation.

"You okay?"

"Nervous," she said, trembling.

"Don't worry. My mom will love you."

"That's only part of the worry." Her gaze fell to the container.

He sighed. "I know. It's huge. Bigger than a baby step. But I give you my promise, nothing will happen to you. I swear." He crossed his heart.

She tapped her hands against her arms, and breathed. "I know. I'm just worried."

"It'll be fine. I'm to text your dad when we leave and when we arrive. It was part of the deal."

"Okay," she said, stepping backwards into the kitchen where she grabbed a small box and pressed it into his hands.

"What's this?"

"For your birthday. I didn't know what to get you, since we've only known each other a short time, so I made you something."

With a curious look on his face, he pulled off the velvet ribbon and opened the lid. "Chocolates?"

"Truffles, actually. It's my momma's recipe."

He grabbed one and popped it into his mouth, moaning as he bit into it. "Oh my god, this is heavenly."

"Thanks." She grabbed the other box off the counter. "This is for your mom."

"She'll love it, thank you." He planted a kiss on her forehead. "We need to get going." He held up the pill container and opened it. "Ready?"

With her heart racing, no doubt due to extreme nervousness, she turned up her twitching palm.

He rolled one of the tiny purple pills into it. "I promise."

A huge sigh, and then she popped it into her mouth, allowing it to melt under her tongue. "Let's go," she said, grabbing her purse and sweater before locking her apartment.

They stood beside Nate's car, and as a test, Aurora put her hands on it. She knew there'd be a point where it wouldn't bother her, and that was Nate's cue to load her into the car. While she played tag with the vehicle, Nate put her belongings in the back seat.

A high-pitched voice screamed, while a symphony reached a crescendo. *What is that? Opera?* She stretched her ears out to listen, to find a phrase to focus on. She bounced in her seat. *Wait? I'm in a seat.* Her heart picked up speed, racing faster than normal coming out of the fog, and sweat formed in her pits and along the base of her neck. *Oh. My. God. I'm in a car.* Smell usually followed the re-introduction of sound, but she couldn't sniff much. A tiny hint of aftershave. *Who's wearing it though?*

A deep breath. A voice. "You doing okay over there?"

I recognize that voice. It's Nate. Relief flooded through her. *We must be there already, but why am I still bouncing?*

"Nate?" she asked, "Why are you listening to opera?"

"Aurora, are you coming out of it?"

"Yes." She smiled, glad the haze was dissolving. It was the worst feeling not remembering.

"No," he said, panic clearly written on his face as she focused on it. "We're not there yet."

In a smooth motion, she turned to the front and scanned her surroundings. Sure enough they were on the road still and a gravel road was responsible for the bouncing. "Fuck no, Nate. I can't be in a car!" Her voice rose an octave as she spoke. "Fuck, fuck, fuck," she screamed.

"Aurora, listen to me."

"Nate." The pull of black memories covered her. Not wanting to see the darkness come for her, she cowered into her seat. Her nails dug deep into her palms.

"Aurora," Nate said with more firmness in his voice than she'd ever heard. "Listen to me. Listen to my voice."

She shook her head and bit her lip. The darkness in her mind wavered in and out. Two steps in, one step back. It was only a matter of time before it completely consumed her.

"You can do this. We're almost there, okay?" Nate's voice jumped. "Please hang on." He paused. "Tell me about the giraffe."

What the hell? What giraffe?

"Aurora, tell me about the giraffe when you were little."

"There was no giraffe." She closed her eyes, trying to block out the sight of trees and buildings racing passed.

"Think, Aurora. Where were you the first time you saw a giraffe?"

Her mind floated back many years to when she was a little girl.

"Out loud," he pleaded.

"I was five or six," she said highly irritated, trying to see the memory clearly. Like picking through multiple file folders, she stumbled upon the correct memory. But a dark curtain hung on the edge. "It was at the Calgary Zoo."

His voice a little further away. "Good. Good. What do you remember? Describe everything."

"Well, I remember walking a long ways and my feet were sore, as I wore those cheap thongs. The day had been a long one, but Daddy insisted on seeing one more set of animals. The African area smelled terrible, but that was because it was a hot day."

His voice miles away. "Keep going."

Fighting against the black curtain of doom, she viewed the memory. All four of them were there. They looked like complete dorks in tank tops, short shorts and flip flips, but it was so hot. Everything they touched burned their skin.

"We rounded the corner," she said, "and there were three giraffes. I'd never seen one in real life before, but there they were. And they were so tall. Bigger than the buildings they stood beside. It was so neat. I wanted to reach out and touch them. Daddy lifted me on top of his shoulders as one came closer, but it never got close enough to touch. Even on Daddy's shoulders, I still wasn't as tall. They were so amazing to watch. So graceful. So calm. They never made a sound, but they did keep an eye on us. I didn't want to leave. I wanted to stay and watch them forever. I didn't care how hot it was. All I wanted to do was watch the giraffes."

"Then what?" His voice calm as it floated on the breeze.

Her eyes shut tight, she sighed. "Well, we had to go because the zoo was closing. So we stopped in the gift shop and Daddy bought me a tiny glass giraffe. It was no bigger than my hand, and I loved it. It sits on my dresser."

"That's a great story, Aurora," Nate said.

"I didn't like the lions, they were scary. And the other animals were okay. The hippos were pretty neat too, but I really liked those giraffes."

A cool breeze blanketed her, and she popped open her eyes. Nate stood with his hand outstretched and the passenger door open. Not a moment's hesitation, and Aurora pushed against her seatbelt, which Nate discovered too late, he'd forgot to unlatch.

He reached across her, unfastening it before pulling her out and into his arms. He planted a kiss on her, and she noted his lips trembled and shook. "You did it," he whispered.

She looked behind her to his car, and up into his face. His eyes were tired and worn out as if he shouldered the weight of many men. Tipping her forehead to him, she breathed out, "Thank you," and relished having his strong arms wrapped around her. "What happened? I wasn't supposed to be in the car when I came out of this."

"I don't know. We hit a bit of traffic, but it's not even one yet." Firm hands ran through his hair, and then pulled down on his face. "I was afraid you were coming out of it, so I sped up. I was more than terrified that you'd start screaming and I'd endanger more than just our lives."

"Sorry."

"It's not your fault." He rubbed her back in reassurance. "But I need to text your dad. Maybe he'll have an answer." He fired off a quick text. The phone rang back right away. "Hello, sir... We've made it, but I have a question." He explained what happened and what he did to prevent her from losing control in the vehicle.

While her boyfriend and father chatted, she took in the immediate area. They were parked beside a fifth wheel, and as she searched around, she saw another dozen more, either trailers or RVs.

And semi-trucks with trailers. And regular trucks with flat-deck trailers. *What kind of weird campground are we at?* But the noises didn't jive with a campground. A low rumble came from a distance. Engines revved, screaming at a high pitch. They reminded her of the sounds she heard late at night from her apartment when the window was open– the sound of a jerk off revving his motorcycle down the avenue, likely racing to show the world how much testosterone he had. But this sound was different, and not like a motorcycle.

Curiosity grabbed a hold of her, and she stepped out of Nate's reach, walking beyond the RVs, trucks and trailers. Billboards hung everywhere, and a giant grandstand on the opposite side of an oval shaped race track. *Oh my fucking god, he brought me to a–*

Turning on the spot, she glared as she faced him. "You brought me to a fucking race track?"

He pocketed the phone, amusement on his face. "Yes. It sounds crazy, but this–" That dimple nice and deep as he pointed to the track. "This is my home away from home." He turned her around. "That trailer, with the blue stripe, that's where my family stays every weekend."

"You live here?"

"Just Friday and Saturday nights."

"Do you watch the races?" She wasn't sure what his answer would be, but she was sure as hell unprepared for...

"Yes and no. I'm a race car driver."

"Fuck me," she said as the world darkened.

❤ Chapter Twenty-Four ❤

"Here she comes," a voice said softly as Aurora moved and sat up.

Her eyes jumped wide open as she gazed at the strange, unfamiliar people who stared at her. "What happened?" Her colour drained as she realised she sat on a gurney. *What the hell?* Beyond them were the open doors of an ambulance.

Nate chuckled. "You fainted." He rubbed her leg. "Guess I should've maybe said something beforehand?"

"About you being a race car driver? You think?"

He laughed. "Aurora, meet my family. This is my mom, Brenda."

"It's so lovely to finally meet you." Brenda enveloped Aurora in a tight hug.

Aurora dusted off her hands. "I'm sorry, I'm all dirty." She pointed to the dusty prints on Brenda's shirt.

A quick flick of her hands and the dust was gone. "Not a worry. You'll fit right in," Brenda said. "We're usually dirty in one way or another by the end of the night. Grease stains or something." One would never need to guess if Nate was her child or not, it was clear as day looking at her. They had the same brown hair with a hint of wave, and the same chocolate eyes. Her smile was nearly identical, but her lips were fuller. More ladylike than Nate's. "Are you doing okay, honey?"

Physically, she felt fine, but she was a trifle mad at Nate for not having said anything about his weekend life. *Trifle. Truffle.* "I brought truffles," she said, gesturing to Nate.

He walked to the car and brought them back their gift. "You'll love them. She made them herself."

"Oh, you shouldn't have."

Aurora said nothing and glanced around at the three other people still staring at her. Unable to meet their gazes, her own fell to the ground. There was grass, but it was in short supply. Mainly it was a dirt field. And sandals were not the appropriate footwear. Nor were the capris.

Nate spoke. "This here is my little brother, Lucas." He pointed to a thin, gawky teenager. This must be the brother he joked about her liking and he was right. With his strawberry-blond hair Lucas did not look like Nate. He must've taken after Nate's father. Nate pointed to the lady standing beside Lucas. "My sister, Chris, and her boyfriend Max. He's the on-site EMT."

"It's Christina actually," the average-height brunette said, shaking her hand. Much older than Nate, she looked more like Brenda's younger sister rather than Nate's older sister.

Aurora nodded and shook her hand back, stammering, "Pleased..." A loud sigh. "Pleased to meet you."

A beep came from behind her. Max held her arm as he started up the portable monitor. "Need to double check." He listened to her heartbeat and checked her blood pressure. "It's a little high, but nothing to worry about."

"It should be higher," she said under her breath. "I'm so embarrassed." She tucked her head down.

Max patted her arm, and whispered, "They're great people, I promise. We've been prepped by Nate to expect the unexpected with you." He unwrapped the monitor.

"Surprise," Aurora said, throwing her arms in the air, trying to lighten the mood. It worked as they laughed with her.

Nate wrapped his arms around her waist. "That's my girl." He kissed her cheek as everyone started walking away.

"Come on, we'll give you a tour," Brenda hollered out.

"Give us a minute and we'll catch up," Nate said to his mom's back. He looked at Aurora. "Feeling better?"

"A little warning would've been nice."

"I was afraid to say anything."

"So you figured the only way to get me here was to drug me and throw it at me when I came around?"

"Something like that."

She crossed her arms and pouted.

"Look, if I'd said anything, would you have even continued to see me?"

She glared at him and softened. "Probably not. Total deal breaker."

"That's my point. I didn't want you to give up on me because of this. I like you, like really like you. This–the race track–is a huge part of my life. And I want you to be a part of it."

She swallowed and took it all in. The billboards, the race cars, an entirely different side to Nate. "But... but..."

"It's not the same as driving on the street. I promise you. We're more protected in the race car than in a standard car." Her mouth fell open. "We have roll bars, and harnesses, and a head and neck system to prevent any head trauma. It's safer than jumping on a trampoline." He held her hand tightly. "No one has been seriously injured on this track and there have been a lot of accidents over the years."

"Not helping, Nate." A tremor rippled through her body.

"But no one has died or spent more than a day or two in the hospital." Leading her down the edge of the track, he pointed. "See all the cars in the pit?"

Holy shit! There had to be at least fifty, maybe more.

"Now look at the track. It's a quarter-mile track with the top speed in the ballpark of sixty miles per hour. The big races, like Daytona, they've been known to exceed two-hundred miles per hour."

"But it's racing." Her lip curled in confusion. This was so not how or where she expected to be spending her day.

"And it's fun. I'll show you."

"Nuh-uh. I'm not getting into a car." She dug her feet into the dirt.

"Of course not. I would never do that." He hopped the straight part of a wall between two rounded corners. "But I will give you a tour of the track."

"Wait!" she called out. "My pills please, just in case."

After throwing a variety of the drugs into a small pocket-sized container, she followed Nate over the wall and listened as he pointed out the complexities of the track. Where the start and finish line were–on the opposite side of where Nate parked his car–and how they were the same thing. He explained the corners and how corner one was the first turn after the start line, and two, three and four followed. They walked across the paved track, heading for the heart of the pit.

"This is Lucas's car," he said, pointing to a beat-up lime green car with the word CHASER written across the body of it and a bright orange 67 on the door. "He called it that because he's always chasing first place."

Lucas who had finished changing the tire added, "Someday I'll get first."

"Yeah, someday," Nate said, ruffling his little brother's hair. "He's in the feature stocks."

She shook her head. "I don't know what that is."

"A class of drivers. We'll leave it at that for now." He walked a little deeper into the pit. "This is what I drive," he said, proudly pointing to a white car with yellow and orange strips. A blazing 15 painted onto the door.

"You drive this?" She sounded amazed and petrified in the same breath. Her arms wrapped around her stomach. *This has to be a dream. Or a nightmare. My boyfriend's a race car driver?* The mental picture of him sitting in it made her head spin. It didn't look safe.

Focusing back on him, she missed the first part of what he said. "That's why I couldn't come any earlier this morning. I had to unload her and get her all set up before I picked you up. Then I could spend more time with you this afternoon rather than prepping the beast." He tapped the top. "She's all ready to race today."

Amazement in her voice, she looked around the pit and back to his face. "So this is what you do on the weekends, eh?"

Nate nodded, still smiling. The look on his face said this was his happy place. "The season started up a couple weeks ago, and we run until the end of September. Every weekend."

"Wow." She watched as a semi-trailer parked and a few guys ran to the back, lowering the ramp.

"Everyone here," he waved all around, "this is fun for them. Everyone loves the thrill of the race, and the social aspect of the entire family getting together."

"This is all family?" She couldn't believe it.

Nate laughed. "My surrogate family, aside from my family-family. Most of the people here are second generation racers, some third and fourth."

"Seriously?"

"Seriously." He hadn't stopped smiling. "Lucas and I are third gens."

Aurora blinked rapidly. "That's actually–" She took a deep breath. "Pretty cool."

Nate grabbed a folding camp chair from beside a rolling toolbox and gestured for her to sit. His car was close enough to touch if she wanted. Not that she did. "You may see Grams around here tonight. She said she'd drop in later."

"Your Grams races?"

"No, but she wishes. She helps out where she can. Like part of my pit crew."

"You have a pit crew?"

"Yeah. Mom, Lucas, Chris, plus the other racers if need be. We help each other out."

"The things I'm learning today," Aurora said. She was beyond thrilled to see Nate so euphoric and kept her focus on that. Otherwise, the moment she allowed her thoughts to drift, her stomach, followed closely by her racing heart, reminded her of what she needed – Xanax, with a Percocet thrown in for good measure. But the enthusiasm in his voice was almost contagious. Almost. He really did have a thing for cars. "What did Dad say, by the way, about the Isa?"

"He doesn't know." Nate pulled his folding chair closer. "He suspects that maybe your heart was beating so fast from anxiety that it burned it quicker. He's looking into it."

She slumped into her chair. "What about the drive home?"

"I don't know yet, but we'll figure it out." His hand rubbed the top of her thigh.

"We'll have to." Nervous energy swirled in her head and chest as she watched the people in the pit milling around. Turning her attention to focus back on Nate, she said, "So tell me more. You said Lucas was in, what was it, future class? What about you?"

"Feature stocks," he corrected. "I'm in the super stocks."

"And that means what exactly?"

"Each car looks a little different– like my Camaro differs from Bill's Mustang, and is different still from Caleb's Fusion–" His hand flew in different directions, not that it mattered. She didn't know what car was what as she was pretty clueless about cars in general. To her four wheels and a steering wheel made a vehicle, but it was obvious to him it was more involved than that. "But we're all the same under the hood. We all have to meet the same requirements, wheel size, engine size, etc." He held her hand. "I can see I'm boring you."

"No, no you're not. This is interesting." A true smile spread across her face.

"Really?"

"Yeah. I may change my mind after watching you race, but for now, it's interesting." Like a child in a candy factory, she was unable to focus on any one thing in particular. There were cars and car parts everywhere, men and women walking around with tools and chatting about things she'll never understand. But they all had something in common. Everyone looked happy to be there.

"May I join in?" Brenda asked, pulling up another chair. She handed Nate two colourful strips of paper and a full-sized sheet. "Today's bands and race schedule."

Nate looked it over, pointing to a few lines as he showed Aurora. "See here. I'm doing two heats, and then after the intermission, there's the feature race, where being on the podium is a big deal. It gives us points and at the end of the season determines the overall winner."

"Have you ever won?"

A shy smiled crossed his face. "Yeah, I was third overall last year and second the year before."

"Sheesh." She stretched out her legs as her hip started to ache.

"Aurora, can I grab you a drink?" Brenda asked. "It can get awfully hot in the pit so you'll want to stay hydrated."

"I'm good for now, but thank you, Mrs. Johnson."

"Oh, honey, call me Brenda. Everyone does. Not even Grams goes by Mrs. Johnson."

Aurora laughed and felt herself relaxing, which surprised her given her circumstances and surroundings. Who knew she'd ever find herself at a racetrack? She wondered if her daddy knew where they were coming.

Nate rose and placed the schedule on his chair. "Come on, I want to show you off."

"But don't the races start soon?" She hesitated as she didn't want to be shown off.

"Not until five. But we have time trials before, and those will start in about an hour." He pulled her into his arms. "But first, I want you to know where the safety area is. If–for whatever reason–you get overwhelmed, go immediately into that shack." He pointed to a small shed-looking building behind his spot. Nate grabbed a marker and wrote his name across one of the wrist bands before securing it to her. "Flash this, and someone will let you in."

"What's in there?"

"It's a small office. It's a little soundproof too." He reached for something off the top of his toolbox and showed her. "These are for you. Noise cancelling head phones." He positioned them over her ears and she was shocked by how different everything sounded. The world muffled, the background noises gone and even the rumble of a nearby engine was greatly reduced.

She pulled them off. "Wow."

"I know, right?" He placed them back. "Just in case. I want you to be comfortable here as much as I can help on my end."

"You're really too sweet, Nate."

"I know," he said smiling. "Now come on. I want you to meet the rest of the family."

She held his hand as he introduced her. There were so many people, and so many race car drivers, she knew she'd never remember any of their names. Only one she remembered, and not just because she was female as she'd met others. Marissa Montgomery was a beautiful and tall blond, who had lust in her eyes for Nate. And it wasn't hard to see. Aurora was many things, but she wasn't blind. She didn't miss the side eye Marissa gave her upon being introduced by Nate as his girlfriend.

Leaving Marissa behind, Nate crossed the north side of the track and walked up the stairs to the open gate.

He toured her around the grandstand, and bought her an ice cream from the concession before bringing her to the announcer's booth at the top. "Quite the view from up here, eh?"

She wasn't all that high up, but yet she could see the entire track with the pit tucked into the middle. "Wow." She took a bite from the ice cream bar.

"I rarely get to see it from up here. Even on my weekends off, I'm in the pit."

"Weekends off?"

"Yeah, not every class of drivers races every weekend. It's rotated and over the season, I'll have two weekends off."

"But on your race day, can you come up here to watch?" She fanned herself with her free hand. It was warm sitting in the full sun.

"It's not easy to go back and forth. They pull the stairs and guard the gate so that people don't go onto the track. It's a safety thing."

"I get that."

"I watch from the spotters' cage," he said, pointing to a raised platform in the middle of the pit. "But only when Lucas races. Otherwise, I'm tinkering on the beast."

"Where will I be?" she asked curiously.

"Where would you like to be? Mom and Chris have offered to stay with you. If you'd feel more comfortable up here, one of them will join you. If you're more comfortable in the pit, well…" Her boyfriend– the race car driver who hadn't stopped smiling since they arrived– beamed a little more. His dimple nice and deep.

"But you can only stay in the pits."

"Yes, I'll be in the pit," he correctly verified.

"Then I want to stay where you are." She linked her arm through his and rested her head on his shoulder. "You're full of surprises, Nate. I would've bet my life you'd never find me at a race track."

"You're the one who's surprising me." He twisted to turn and face her. "Who would've thought I'd actually see a smile on the girl of my dreams here of all places? I'm glad you're here."

"Did I have any other choice?" said Aurora, eyebrow arched?

"Not really."

"I haven't even needed a Xanax or anything yet." It's not that she didn't *want* one, she felt she didn't need it, yet. But patting her pocket, she made sure they were still within easy reach.

"I'm proud of you for that." He leaned forward, tipping his head.

"I'm going to enjoy the other end of this deal," she said, coming out of the kiss a little more breathless than she anticipated.

"Duly noted." Nate blushed a bright crimson colour. "But I'm looking forward to it too."

❤ Chapter Twenty-Five ❤

Her hand securely in his, they headed back into the pit.
"I have a driver's meeting now," Nate began, "so just hang here and I'll be back as soon as I can." His sister appeared. "Chris will stay with you, right?" His sister nodded.

Aurora's shoulders and neck tensed. Chris had that protective big-sister expression on her face.

"You'll be fine. She's harmless." His lips brushed against hers. "I'll be right back."

Sighing as he walked away, she folded herself into the chair and looked up at Chris.

"So," Chris started, "Nate's told us a lot about you."

She twisted in her seat with the tone in Chris' voice. "I've noticed."

Chris leaned closer. "Being part of this–" She waved all around. "Means you need to have complete trust in your team and we're part of Nate's team." Aurora nodded. "Don't worry, he doesn't tell us everything. Although," she paused, before adding, "we don't keep secrets from each other either. And Nate likes you. A lot."

"Yes, I know."

"And do you like him, a lot?"

Aurora knew the colour had drained from her face as she felt three-inches high in the chair. "Yes… very… much so," she stuttered out.

"Good. So don't do anything to break his trust. Because once it's broken, it's gone for good."

Again she nodded, not sure what else she was supposed to do. Chris disappeared into the sea of people, leaving her all alone. She tried to get comfortable in the chair but everything ached when she sat in it, her body preferred something a little softer. Standing and stretching, she walked over to Nate's car.

As far as cars went, his was gorgeous. She loved the bright colours and the way the stripes sparkled in the sunlight. It looked brand new. Hesitantly, she glanced around, confirming to herself she was all alone. She stepped as close to the car as she could, and extended her hand. Another quick glance around, and she placed her hand on the edge of the windowless door, the cool of the metal spreading across her palm. Taking her other hand, she lay it beside the first. As she closed her eyes, she imagined Nate standing beside her, and tried to feel him holding her, his hands on her hips. She counted to thirty, and in taking a deep breath, counted to thirty once more. Upon opening her eyes, she lifted her hands and broke the contact.

Proud as hell, she stepped back, smiling to herself.

"Well done." A familiar voice and a pair of hands clapped behind her.

Shit. I had an audience. A coy smile on her face, she tried acting cool as she turned and threw her hands out in the air. "Yeah, it was easy."

Nate walked up beside her, and whispered low in her ear. "Liar." But he smiled as he pulled back. "I saw you trembling. But it doesn't matter." His grin was face-splitting. "Look what you did. All on your own." He pulled her close, and finally, those arms she imagined a minute ago, wrapped around her. "I'm so proud of you."

Pride bubbled up in her. Yeah, she'd done it and done it without prodding. Perhaps there's hope for her after all.

He brushed a strand of hair off her face. "Aren't you going to say something?"

Aurora smiled as she stared at the handsome man in front of her. He now sported a black jumpsuit. "Yeah, look at you. You're not a guy who likes to wear normal clothes, do you?"

"What do you mean?" He raised his eyebrow.

"During the week, you wear overalls, and now you're in a jumpsuit."

He laughed. "It's a fire suit, actually."

"Seriously? Is that necessary?" Panic built up lightning quick since she hadn't taken anything to keep it contained. "Do you... are there... fires?"

"No." His warm touch on her arms did little to soothe her. "Another safety precaution, just in case. Safety's a big deal at the track."

"Have there ever–" Her body trembled as her mind envisioned Nate trapped behind the wheel, flames engulfing his car. A violent shudder coursed through her.

"Hey," he said, pulling her into his arms. "It's going to be okay. You have my word."

A few deep breaths after calming her heart down, she pushed out of the embrace. "Well, I wish you'd lied and said it was a jumpsuit."

"Oh yeah?" His eyebrow arched. "Why?"

"Cuz you look sexy as hell in it."

"Thank you." He blushed. "I'm one of the first racers to time trial, so I needed to suit up." He held her hand, kissing the top of it. "I'm so proud of you." He tipped his head toward the car. "Maybe you'll be my good luck charm today."

"Maybe."

"Are you going to watch my trials from the cage or stay here?"

"I think I'd like to watch it–" She wasn't sure though if she really wanted to or if she said it to appease him. "From here?" A quick look confirmed the headphones were still visible and a pat on her hip reminded her of instant relief in her pocket. She could do this.

Brenda appeared out of nowhere. "I'm going over to the cage. Come with me," she said to her.

Aurora nodded and winked. "Guess I'm going with your mom."

"It's only four laps. It's just me, and I'll be right back. Less than minute really." He blew her a kiss.

Brenda and Aurora walked over to the spotters' cage. "Up you go," Brenda motioned.

She climbed up the ladder to the top, and found herself staring out to the track. Situated six feet off the ground, an impressive 360 degree view surrounded her. "It's amazing up here."

"Yeah, it is." Brenda held onto the platform railing. "I'm glad you came."

"Well," she said, knowing full well she didn't have any say in the matter, "it's great being here. Not at all what I thought we were doing today. But it's interesting."

"Yes, it's interesting. Never a dull moment." Brenda smiled, that same put-everyone-at-ease smile as her son.

Feeling brave, she asked, "Does Nate bring his girlfriends often?"

"What girlfriends? Honey, you're the first girl he's ever brought to the track."

Brenda looked in her eyes and in that breath, Aurora understood what Chris had meant. By bringing her to the track, Nate had brought her into more than his love of racing. He'd brought her into his heart. And she knew she was in deep trouble if she ever messed with it.

An engine roared to life beneath her and ducking for cover with surprise, she crouched down low. Catching her breath, she stilled herself. Sneakily she slipped the pill container into the palm of her hands. A quick dart around, she opened it and retrieved a Xanax, slipping in under her tongue.

"You okay, honey?"

She nodded and rose, hoping Brenda didn't see her take the pill. "It scared me for a sec and I needed to catch my breath."

"We can get down if that's easier."

"I'm okay," she said, more to herself than Brenda. It shouldn't take too long for relief to settle in.

While waiting, she watched Nate slip over the door into his car. Lucas passed him his helmet and his steering wheel before stepping back as the vehicle started. Nate pulled out and waited second in line. A heart-pounding minute later, and Nate upped his car into the first spot. Aurora struggled to breathe and think at the same time, feeling this was all a dream. The roar of the white car as it thundered onto the track, gaining speed as it approached the starting line, focused her thoughts.

This is sheer lunacy.

"Each lap is monitored," Brenda explained. "Of the three laps, they'll count his fastest lap and assign him a spot in the heat."

The #15 raced around corner one. Corner two. Corner three. Corner four. Over the start line. 13.3 flashed up on the boards.

"Wow, and that's only his first lap," Brenda said.

Aurora could hear the engine roar as Nate stepped on it after each turn. She gripped tightly on to the handrail, unable to remove her eyes from his car as he zoomed over the start line again. She glanced to the flashing boards– 12.9.

His mom beamed. "Impressive, he's getting faster."

Completely in shock, she followed him around the track as concern moved between her upside-down stomach and the thoughts swirling in her head.

"He's doing well today," Brenda said beside her, giving her a playful nudge. "Trying to impress someone I think."

Aurora forced a smile, and refocused on Nate as he rocketed over the starting line for a third time. The board lit up with 12.7. Her eyes followed him as he slowed down, and pulled into the pit. Climbing down the cage, she made her way over to him. "Okay, that was pretty cool."

"You like?" his cocky voice asked as he retrieved his helmet and placed it on the roof.

"I may question my sanity a bit because, yeah, I'm surprised that I do." She reached up to tame his wild helmet-hair, and gave him a kiss.

He studied her, his chocolate-coloured eyes searching her face. With a gentle lift from his finger, he tipped her chin. "Did you take something? Your eyes are different."

Shame washed over her, but at least the anxiety over it was gone. "Yes." She closed her eyes and hung her head. "A Xanax."

Wrapping her in a hug, he kissed the top of her forehead. "Are you okay?"

"Better now," she said honestly.

"Did you want to see Max or Chris?"

"No, and I'd rather stay away from your sister," she said without filtering, and lowered her gaze to stare at the ground as the words tumbled from her mouth.

"Don't worry about her or whatever she said." Nate stroked her cheek. "She's been very helpful to me."

She crossed her arms over her chest. "How so?"

"She's working on her Master's in Behaviour Sciences. She's a—"

"Yeah, I know what that is." Aurora had had her share of psychologists over the years. She was well aware of what Chris was. A shrink.

"She's been giving me ideas on how to help you." Nate stepped back as if assessing her stance. "And it's helping. She's young, and thinks differently than the older people in her profession. She's going to change things, and not just for you."

"So she knows?" His nod spoke volumes. "Everything?"

"Don't you want to get better?"

"Yeah, I guess."

"You guess? You'd rather be afraid for the rest of your life then try?" Nate's eyes narrowed. "Really? I don't believe that, Aurora. I've seen you in action today."

"Well, I'm not big into having strangers butting into my personal history."

"What strangers? She's my sister."

"But she's a stranger to me, Nate." She huffed. This wasn't going well. It was one thing to be coddled still by her father, but now her boyfriend's sister was prying into her life and making suggestions.

"Fine," Nate said and stormed off. Ten feet away from her, his shoulders slumped and his head lowered. Turning around, he slowly came back. "Sorry, I shouldn't have walked away because it's not fair to you. You have nowhere to go to pout. At least I can take my rage out on the track. You? You're sort of stuck here."

"Yeah I am," she said, and crossed her arms over her chest. "I'm trying, Nate. You know that."

"Yes, I do."

"This is a source of contention between us."

He shrugged. "I guess that's part of being with someone, you want the best for them." She stood there, silently stewing until his arms wrapped her, and his voice whispered in her ear. "I'm sorry."

"Eww. Get a room, Johnson," Marissa Montgomery said, and they separated. Marissa flipped her hair over her shoulder and sauntered by.

"She's pleasant," Aurora said, following the beauty as she made her way to a large group of guys hanging around the barbeque.

"Oh yeah. Been ticked at me for years. Wants to expand our company relations. Thinks we'll be better teammates if we know how the other ticks, so to speak."

Aurora gave Marissa another passing glance. "So there's never been anything–"

"Not with me, at least." He leaned closer. "But she gets around." He turned her cheek back in his direction. "However, she doesn't catch my eye."

"No?" She snickered. "Who does?"

"You."

"Time for my first heat." Nate untied the arms of his fire suit from around his waist, rolling them over his shoulders. After giving her a quick kiss, he said, "I'll be right back."

She nodded as he slipped into his car and harnessed up, the belts so tight she doubted he'd move an inch. Lucas passed him the helmet and helped attach it to the harness. He gave a thumbs up to Nate, who returned the gesture after securing the steering wheel in place.

"He's good to go," Lucas said, "so time for us to go. Elsewhere." Aurora stared at Nate who refused eye contact with her. "It's part of the ritual. He needs to get into the zone."

Aurora nodded and reluctantly followed Lucas, unable to remove her gaze from Nate. *He's going out. To race. Against other cars.* Her heart started beating in her stomach. *What if?* She swallowed hard, trying not to let her brain finish that sentence.

Brenda came over and linked elbows with her. "Come with me. I could use the company."

Beyond nervous, she slipped on one of the rungs and caught herself. *Breathe.* Stabilizing her foot firmly, she finished the short climb, with her heart racing and her antiperspirant working overtime. The whites of her tightly clenched knuckles betrayed any confidence she had.

Brenda wrapped a hand over top hers. "It'll be fine, you'll see."

The super stocks roared from idle to race, and poured out onto the track.

Aurora, a bundle of nerves, debated watching the laps in rapt admiration or cowering down in the pit's office with her earphones on. If her feet weren't as heavy as cement, she likely would've bolted. This time, nine cars were on the track, not only him. And it wasn't only three laps either. It was ten. Enough to make her heart race into the stratosphere. *Be safe.*

"Nate gets pole position," Brenda explained. "He's the lead car on the inside lane. His time trial was the fastest."

She took a deep breath of air, and re-gripped the railing. She wanted more pills, but was too afraid to let go of the railing. A quick look to Brenda, she wondered if it would be weird to ask her to dig out the pills and put one in her mouth. Yeah, it would be. She shook her head.

The flag guy waved the green flag, and the stands erupted in cheers. Aurora scanned the crowd– there had to be at least two-thousand people. She had no idea racing was a popular thing to do around these parts.

Nate maintained his lead until a green car behind him gave him a tap on the driver's left side and sent him spinning.

"NO!" Aurora screamed as his car crossed onto the grassy portion of the pit. She ducked down and covered her eyes while plugging her ears.

A hand on her back rubbed it gently. After a minute of shallow breathing and battling the urge to vomit all over the place, she opened her eyes and turned to find its owner. *Lucas.*

Brenda spoke first. "It's all good, honey. It's a normal part of racing." She pointed to the track. "See, he's still in it. No permanent damage done." Brenda's voice was unexpectedly calm.

Stunned, Aurora looked from Brenda to Lucas to the track. Nate's #15 was there, moving slowly as he zigzagged back and forth. And he was in one piece.

"Caution came out. It's when they slow everyone down because of something like this. Gives everyone a chance to reset," Lucas said.

As he finished speaking, the cars roared again, and she turned to the board. Two laps remained. Thank God, because she didn't know how much longer she could watch. Hands clutching the railing for dear life, she struggled to stand with rubber bands for legs.

Lucas said, "Nate'll exact revenge on her. Maybe in the next heat, but for sure in the final."

"What?" Her eyes grew large.

Brenda laughed. "Oh, honey. Marissa's an aggressive driver, but she's got nothing on Nate. You'll see."

What if I don't want to see him get revenge? That could be... *disastrous.* With her lungs in dire need of a large gulp of air, she sighed with relief when the heat ended. The cars rolled into the pit, with Nate in seventh.

"You stay here, hon, and I'll send Nate over. He likes watching the IMCAs."

Whatever those are. "Fine." She couldn't move anyways. Her chest hurt from not breathing properly and thinking of all the what-ifs. Seriously how was she going to make it through two more races? She sat on the floor of the cage, her legs dangling over the edge, watching as Nate extracted himself from the car. He waved in her direction, but was engrossed in a conversation with his mom and sister. Aurora had the sneaking suspicion they were talking about her. She needed to get a grip on herself although it was so hard. It was damn near instinctual.

After a few minutes, Nate climbed up the ladder and joined her on the floor. "What did you think?"

"Great job," Lucas said.

She sighed and kept her eyes on Nate who, although upset with his overall placing, was definitely, thankfully, alive. However, her anger revealed itself. "I think Marissa's a bitch."

Nate chuckled. "Yeah. I figured she'd pull something like that."

"Really?" She covered her mouth in horror.

Nate's hand on her thigh did little to re-assure her. "Sure, that's her style. If she's not number one, she'll try to remove those that stand in her way. It's nothing personal." As an afterthought, he added, "Not always."

She leaned into his shoulder, the heat from the black suit warming her body but the smell of it made her pull back. It was a scary, familiar scent of gas and oil. Her stomach soured once again. "I'll be honest with you. I don't know if I can handle this. If something were to happen–"

"Nothing will happen."

"It's one thing watching you race around the track on your own, it's entirely different seeing you race against eight others. There's not enough space for that."

He sighed. "Is there anything I can say or do to prove to you that this is okay?"

The cars were a blur on the track as they ripped on by. "I don't know." Too many what-ifs played out again in her mind. The tears welled up, but she wasn't about to let him see.

His voice sounded torn apart. "Do you want me to take you home?"

Turning, she stared into his handsome face. She'd be the most selfish person in the world if she said yes. And she couldn't do that to him. Couldn't take him away from his love because of her. She shook her head. "No, I don't." She reached for his hand, running her fingers between his. "But I need another Xanax, or I'll never make it through the night." She didn't need his permission, but dammit, he had to know what this was doing to her. And he must've understood as he nodded, while she popped one into her mouth.

"Would it be easier if you sat down by the car, and not up here for the next heat? Or would you like me to see if Max has something stronger?" Although his face bore concern, he sounded upset.

And she hated herself for that. "No," she said with determination. "Please don't ask." She released a buildup of air as she turned her head and rested it against the metal railing whispering, "Fuck."

♥ Chapter Twenty-Six ♥

As relief swam in Aurora's mind, she sat in a chair beside Brenda, under Chris' watchful stance. Nate may have mentioned her pill popping as there were hushed discussions and glances thrown in her direction. At the moment though, she couldn't have cared less. Her heart rate was steady, and she could breathe again.

It didn't take long before Heat Two started, and she watched Nate's preparations, cemented in the confines of her chair.

"You'll be okay?" Nate squatted in front of her.

The Xanax had kicked in, and the headphones hung on her armrest, so she nodded. "Totally fine. Go and... have fun."

He looked at her quizzically before he bent over her, his sexy grin inches from her face. "I'll be right back."

"I'll be right here," she said before kissing him.

Once he gave the thumbs up to Lucas, she turned to look in Brenda's direction. Chris paced a few feet away but always within view. As she placed the headphones on, the sounds from the cars and crowd faded away. Now she could hear her thoughts clearly, and she wasn't sure she liked that any better. The what-ifs tickled the edge of her mind. *He said he'll be right back.* She focused on his voice as it played over and over. Her eyes shut tight, she pictured him lying on the picnic blanket, smiling up at her. *He'll be right back.*

It must've been a clean race, as the heat ended before she knew it. The setting sun reflected off Nate's glittering car as it pulled into its spot beside her. Relief washed over her as he upheld his promise. *He came back.*

Standing and placing the headphones on top the toolbox, she watched him extract himself from his car and jump to the ground, air punching the entire time. "You are my good luck charm, Aurora," he said as he grabbed her and twirled her around in a racing fuel scented embrace. "I got first."

"You won? That's awesome."

"I got first in the heat which means for the feature tonight, I'll be in second spot. That's a great spot to be in."

Nodding, because she didn't understand how that all worked, she said, "Good job?"

"Yeah, it is. I hope you'll want to watch it." His fingers intertwined in hers.

Nervous and afraid, she wasn't sure how she'd could. Part of her wanted to, but another begged her not to. Thirty laps for the feature was a hell of a lot longer than for the heats. What if Little Miss Aggressive was too aggressive, and he got hurt? She wasn't sure how she'd cope with that what-if.

They hung out in the chairs, hand in hand, neither speaking until the last of the heats ended.

Lucas parked in his spot, opposite of Nate and hopped over. "I got first!"

Pride etched itself on Nate's face. "Excellent job. That'll give you a huge advantage in features." They high-fived each other. "Don't you worry, I'll be watching." She didn't miss the quick glance in her direction. "One way or another."

"Okay, who's hungry?" Lucas said after a few breaths of tension-filled air hung around them.

"Me." She stood and stretched. "I haven't eaten since—" Morning? Really?

"So let's go." Nate opened a drawer in the toolbox and removed his wallet. "Let's eat up at the main concession. Better selection."

Lucas joined her and Nate as they crossed the track. Lucas hopped up and stood at the gate. "I'll meet you guys in a bit. There's someone I'm going to say hi to."

She waved bye and stood perplexed where the stairs should be. "You expect me to hop up?" The wall had to be at least four feet tall. Her hips ached just looking at it. "I can't do that." Unable to jump since the accident, or if she were being honest, she didn't want to jump, afraid of what the jostle would do to her hip.

"I'll help you."

"You just want to touch my ass," she said giggling.

Nate laughed. "Yeah, that too." He lifted her with ease on to the wall, and waved her to the side while he jumped. "They only put the stairs out for the racers at the beginning and at the end of the night. Anytime in between, we're on our own."

"I'll keep that in mind next time, and I'll wear my dirty clothes."

"It's probably better you do. Your nice clothes could end up wrecked."

"Well, with a little warning, I could've planned better."

"Touché." He led her past the grandstand and over to the concession. "What do you want?"

After ordering their food, Aurora spun around when a kid of eight or nine whispered, "Dad, that's the number fifteen driver. Nate Johnson."

Nate turned around, smiling. "Hey, little buddy."

"You're so awesome."

He squatted to eye level with the little man. "Thanks. You coming down into the pit afterwards?"

The little boy looked up to his father. "Oh can we, Dad? Can we?"

The dad nodded. The boy cheered.

"Great," Nate said, "I'll see you after the show." He gave him a high five.

"Good luck, Nate."

Aurora observed the conversation between the little boy and Nate, but waited until they were out of earshot from them before she said anything. "That was pretty cool."

"How's that?"

"That boy was shaking with excitement. I think you made his night just by talking to him." Aurora beamed as she spoke.

"It's no big deal, really."

"Yeah it is. You're a celebrity to him." She smiled a big, toothy grin. "And I'm dating a celebrity," she said as she playfully punched him.

"Hey, watch the food." He laughed as the guard opened the gate and let them through. He set their goodies on the wall and hopped down, extending his hands for her. Helping her to the track, they were inseparable as they ate beside his car.

Nate's race was the last of the night, but Lucas raced first. They waved goodbye and good luck as Nate escorted her back to the cage.

"Do you need any pills for his race?" There was no disgust in his voice.

She sighed and forced a smile. "I don't think so," she said, "it's just yours that gets my heart beating extra fast."

As he wrapped his arms around her, he said, "You have no idea how much I love having you here tonight."

In trying to be respectable and decent, she kissed him. Not a prolonged we're-all-alone type kiss, but a nice full kiss-on-the-lips that lasted a few seconds. When they broke apart, she saw Marissa Montgomery staring up at them, disgust smeared on her face. Feeling jovial, Aurora waved at her and grinned as she stomped away.

"Stop that," Nate said as he pushed her hands down to her sides.

"Fine. I don't want her to inflict revenge on you and hurt you in the race."

"She'll be ahead of me, so it's her back she'll need to watch." He winked.

"Oh goody." Even though she wasn't a fan of Marissa's, she didn't want to see her get hurt any more than Nate. "Just be nice. No crashing into her."

He ignored her. "Lucas is about to start." Nate pointed as the cars drove out. "Go Lucas," he yelled.

Lucas raced hard, and Nate filled her in on the lingo she was sure she'd never remember. It was impossible to not get caught up in Nate's enthusiasm and she cheered along. Lucas raced clean and placed second on the podium.

Nate jumped off the cage, helping her down as he raced to the edge of the pit to congratulate Lucas. Standing beside him, she hollered with pride as Lucas received his second place trophy from the announcer.

They coasted back to Nate's car. "Pose with me," she said. Nate's arm hung over her shoulder, and she took a selfie of the two of them in front of the orange and yellow striped car.

Aurora: *Guess what Nate does on the weekends?* She attached the picture and hit send, wishing she could see her friend's face when she read it.

Kaitlyn (A half-second later): *WTF?*

She laughed and typed. *Nate's a race driver and that's his car we're in front of.*

Kaitlyn: *STFU! Really? We're doing lunch, girl. I need the 411 on this.*

She laughed again, imagining her friend's face. Utter shock, no doubt.

Until it was time for Nate's final race of the night, they huddled together. His hand on her knee, her head rested perfectly on his shoulder. Safe and secure. For a moment, there was peace. And Chris broke it when she said, "You're up, dude."

The prospect of him out on the track had her heart rate jump again. A cool wave of sweat beaded across her neck.

"Take one," he said, and she wasted no time in popping it in her mouth.

She studied him, and saw how nervous he looked. Was he upset she needed this? Or was he nervous about going into the race in second spot, having to fight Marissa for the win? For a moment, she wanted to offer *him* a Xanax.

"You'll watch me?" Nate asked as he pulled his fire suit up and over his shoulders.

Without a lot of confidence, she nodded and glanced around wondering if anyone would join her. "Good luck." She gave him another kiss and stepped back, allowing him to finish his preparations. A huge sigh escaped her lips, and she turned with her head hung to walk to the cage.

A tap on her shoulder made her spin around. Nate stood there, holding his helmet in his hand. "I'll be right back." He leaned down and with his free hand wrapped tightly around her, pulled her in for a kiss.

His lips parted as if he wanted to say something, but held back. Something flashed behind his eyes, but she couldn't figure out what it was. Whatever it was, it was sexy as fuck.

"Good luck," she said breathless. Stumbling, she headed for the cage, pleased to see Brenda after she ascended the ladder.

"You going to be okay?" A motherly concern crossed her face.

"Already took my pill, so I should be fine." She sighed and leaned against the rail. "This will be a long race."

The super stocks roared to life once again, and the cars made several laps to get everyone in their proper spot. The longer it took, however, the more relaxed she became thanks to the Xanax.

Marissa's green car held the pole position, with Nate in second. She took a deep breath as the flag dropped. Thirty laps to go. Marissa and Nate raced side by side, going two wide in the corners, Nate on the outside as he tried to overtake her on the straightaways, gaining inches only to lose them as he slowed in the turns. Five laps completed, and no change to the race order. Marissa still out front, Nate holding tight beside her. The other cars almost seemed to hold back and fight for third, rather than take those two on. Both had a huge lead on the others.

Ten laps down. Aurora gripped the railing as a wave of nausea pitted in her stomach. A third of the way through, and the race was going okay. Nothing aggressive, so no cautions to slow everything down and delay the race from finishing. If the race stayed at this pace, she figured she'd be fine. Only twenty more laps to go. She breathed out her bad feelings as Nate and Marissa zoomed around the track.

Fifteen laps completed, then twenty.

"How you doing, honey?"

"I'm okay." And she was. For the most part. Although her heart rate climbed a little, and her breathing was shallower, she was still in control and not overwhelmed.

"This is not an exciting race," Brenda said.

Says you.

"There should be more going on between those two," Lucas said from behind her. "What the hell is he doing?"

She returned her gaze to the track, where Nate and Marissa maintained their considerable lead over the others. Twenty-five laps down, and no change. Every inch Nate gained on Marissa, he lost in the turns. If she was frustrated for him, he must be losing his mind.

"Come on, Nate," Lucas yelled, startling her.

Then it happened. Nate trailed microseconds behind Marissa until the third to last lap where he pulled a slick maneuver in corner two and managed to overtake her on the straightaway into corner three. Side by side, he was against the outside wall when she slowed. Not much, but enough that Nate floored it coming out of the turn and inched ahead of her. By corner four it looked as if Nate had the lead as he zoomed the straightaway.

"He needs to stop driving beside her and get in front of her," Lucas said. "And he may do it on the next straight."

They crossed the start line. The boards flashed and #15 was in first place, but barely. Two laps remained.

Unable to take her eyes off Nate's car, she breathed hard as Nate inched ahead in corner one, and in corner two. Again Marissa slowed enough in the corners that on the straightaway, Nate took back the lead. Coming out of corner four, his bumper just inches ahead of hers proved how close the race was, and it would be a photo finish at this rate.

Last lap. Nate sped through corner one and corner two, and on the straightaway, he pulled in front of Marissa's car, securing his lead.

"Two turns and it's his," Lucas yelled.

As Nate came out of corner four, he gassed it. When the checkered flag dropped, Nate drove over the line first. Brenda and Lucas both squealed beside her and she would've been startled, except she was screaming as well.

They waited along the infield wall on the edge of the pit as Nate parked his car on the track and exited. She waved when he turned and searched for her. His smile a mile wide as he gave her a big thumbs up. He collected his trophy from the announcer and after thanking his sponsors and family, he thanked her for being here with him tonight and for trusting him. Her cheeks burned with heat, and she inched into the shadows.

With the racing finished for the evening, she helped pack up what she could, folding chairs and tidying the immediate area. Nate tucked the headphones discreetly into an empty drawer of the toolbox. Fans from the grandstand came into the pit to greet the drivers and admire their cars. The father and son from earlier came over and the little one stared in awe up at Nate, congratulating him on his big win. Nate asked if he wanted to sit in his car and Aurora thought he'd pass out from sheer joy. The little boy smiled the entire time and couldn't squeak out a thank you, much less anything else. After a few minutes, they left.

"Okay, everything's packed up," he said to her. "I'm going to put the car on the trailer, and then I'll take you home." He kissed her. "I'll be five minutes."

Lucas rolled the toolbox out of sight.

Chris and Max stood beside her as Nate took off with his car.

"I'm glad you came out tonight," Chris said. "It was great meeting you."

"I'm glad too," she said, shuffling her feet. "It wasn't at all what I was expecting."

"Good. And you did better than I hoped." She smiled, and it wasn't a forced smile, but one of genuine warmth. "I'm sure Nate told you what I do, and I'd really love the chance to sit down and discuss everything with you. The things he's attempting with you. How you're coping with it. I'd be able to help you out, and it'd be great research for me. Think about it." She patted her arm. "Here's my card if you'll consider it."

The smooth silver card slipped into her palm. She looked at it before pocketing it. "I promise."

"That's all I can ask." They waved goodbye and strode off to say good night to everyone else.

Nate returned in normal clothes and held her hand. "Thanks for tonight. It means so much more than I can tell you. You putting that trust in me, being here, and hanging out with my family." He rested his forehead on hers. "It was such a great day." He took a deep breath. "There's been something I've been meaning to say."

She stared at him. The tone of his voice had an edge to it. "Well, spit it out already."

He rubbed the top of her hand, and then gazed into her eyes. "Today… Today was more than I could've hoped for. You put so much trust in me. I hope I haven't shaken it and jeopardized our relationship."

She shook her head, curious where he was headed with this. "You haven't, trust me."

"Good. Because–" A big sigh. "I loved, no I mean, I love having you here with me. It means," he covered his heart with her hand, "just that much more. I love you, Aurora."

Shock registered on her face as her knees weakened. "Wow. Nate–"

He brushed a strand of her hair from her cheek. "It's okay. I don't expect you to say it back. But I wanted you to know. Since you're here with me at the track, my family knows how I feel. Figured maybe I should let you know as well."

She wrapped her arms around him, inhaling a unique scent of fuel and sweat mixed with a hint of burnt rubber. Although at first, the smell turned her stomach, she remembered his motto of trying to turn a negative into something positive. He was alive, living and breathing in front of her. That was a positive enough start for her and she breathed him in again, touching him. "Thank you for exposing me to this. It's nice to see this side of you." Deep in her heart, she knew she wasn't yet ready to say those three words. They held too much feeling, and as much as she felt she *was* falling for him, she couldn't repeat them back.

"Like I said before, it's okay, you don't have to say them back."

"I… I'm just in shock."

His fingers lazily played with her hair. "No one ever said that to you before?"

"No one has said it that I actually believed."

He looked her in the eyes. "Say what?"

"I've heard it before, but I always thought they said it because they felt they needed to or because they wanted something from me. But I believe you when you say it because I know it's the truth." Her hand rested against his heart.

"I have no reason to lie to you." He leaned his forehead back against hers. "Should we get you home? It's already after eleven."

They walked to the car after saying good night to his family. Brenda gave her a big hug and whispered, "Thanks for making Nate's birthday."

In his palm, Nate held the tiny container with the Isa. "Whenever you're ready."

She swallowed. This part– she hated it. Prying open the container, she poured the only pill out and popped it in her mouth.

"Cheers to not remembering the ride home," she laughed, but her voice didn't contain an ounce of happiness.

"It'll be fine." Nate rubbed her back. "But I'm going to watch the time, so we don't get a repeat."

Nodding and breaking free from his warm embrace, she touched the car. "So far, okay."

He held her hands, linking his fingers through hers. His warm lips touched hers, and she felt an internal fire light up, taking the chill off from the crisp night air. She wanted more. More than just to be held, so she pressed herself into him, as if trying to fuse with him. A leg of hers linked around his, and she wrapped her hands around his waist.

He broke off the kiss, and gently pushed her away. "Not like this, okay?" He opened her car door. "Whenever you're ready."

❤ Chapter Twenty-Seven ❤

*I*t *smells like dirty shoes and something's chiming. I feel woozy like I'm being launched.* The elevator, she came to realise. She was in it moving higher up. Which meant she wasn't in the car anymore and she was home. Safe and sound although she had a funny feeling things could've gone south. "Nate?" she called out.

"Right here." A touch on her arm milliseconds before his voice touched her heart.

Relaxing, she melted into him, knowing he was close enough to lean on. *He really needs a shower.* He no longer smelled of body wash and crisp air. More like a mixture of sweat and something she couldn't quite put her finger on.

"Keys?" he asked.

After unlocking the door, they stepped in and full, total relief washed over her. Back on her own territory.

"You did it." Nate swelled with pride.

"Thanks to you. And we made it in the nick of time."

He checked his watch. "Under forty-five minutes. Hopefully there's no photo radar."

"Speeding were you? I thought that was reserved for the track."

"Or when I know how urgent it is to get someone home."

"Touché." She smiled. "Thank you for an interesting day." She leaned into him as the soft cotton of his t-shirt caressed her cheek.

"It was, wasn't it? Would you come again?"

She pondered for a moment. "If there was an easier way to get there."

An arm wrapped tighter around her. "What would you suggest?"

"Teleportation."

Nate laughed. "Well, since that's yet to be invented, what else?"

Smiling, she pulled out of his embrace and walked to the fridge. "I don't know."

"You wouldn't come again?"

Although there was no double meaning in his statement, she raised her eyebrow at him, regardless.

"Oh, hah-hah." He grabbed her hand, and twirled her out into the eating area. "Seriously."

"Well, that depends."

"On?" Swaying in time to music she imagined only he heard, she held on tight as he danced with her.

"On whether or not you'll want me enough to ask me."

He dipped her. "Oh. I see. Fine." He smiled. "I'll ask again."

"I'll check my calendar."

He twirled her towards the door. "I should get going. I don't want to, but I need to."

"Okay," she said sadly, knowing there would be nothing she could say that would make him stay and spend the night. Tonight was not the night, they agreed. However, that time was coming soon. She gave him a kiss. "Thanks. For today. And happy birthday. I hope it was a good one," she said between kisses.

"The best." He broke off, and waved goodbye as he exited the apartment.

She woke the next morning, stiff and achy. She'd been so worn out that she woke in the same position she fell asleep in and it wasn't the most comfortable. Arms stretched above her head, she spotted her phone, and a quick peek revealed it lit up with messages. Daddy, Kaitlyn and a couple from Matthew James.

She called her panicked father explaining that they arrived home late and forgot to call, but she was okay. Slumping on her bed, she listened to him berate her for the better part of five minutes before hanging up on him. All further calls landed in voicemail. She'd deal with him later, besides Kaitlyn had texted she was on her way over. And there was still the matter of Matthew and his texts.

The night with Matthew only a week ago, and so much had happened in that time. She debated what to do. Call him back? Ignore him? Yesterday with Nate was beyond anything she'd ever experienced and even though it was way out of her comfort zone, she survived it, and enjoyed it. Nate gave her hope. Matthew, on the other hand, had only given her sex–hot, core-bashing sex–but that was it. Matthew and Nate. They were so different. Light years apart. Nate made her feel special–alive–even without the sexual connection.

Kaitlyn marched into the apartment holding up a big bag of greasiness and a tray of coffees. "I'm not waiting until lunch, so spill it. You don't look very happy for a girl who spent the entire fucking day with her boyfriend."

"I'm just battling something."

"Whatever it is, you can tell me."

"Yeah, but not yet."

Kaitlyn looked hurt. "Oh, I get it. It's a man sex thing, like he's smaller than you expected? 'Cause I can't help you there."

She laughed with Kaitlyn. "No," she opened the bag, "nothing like that."

"So, tell me then."

"I will, just not yet. I need to figure some things out first."

"Mmm-kay," she said after taking a huge bite out of her breakfast sandwich. "Then we're cleaning up this pigsty, Aurora. This place is a mess." In their dorm room, Kaitlyn had been neat and tidy– an everything-has-a-place-so-let's-put-everything-in-it type person, so she let her. She didn't care. But now, she had to admit as she looked around, the place was kind of a disaster. She hadn't washed the dishes before Nate came over. She was rather embarrassed as she looked around.

Aurora's phone pinged and pinged, to the point where she could tell it was pissing Kaitlyn off.

"Seriously, just answer."

"Nah, it's Dad, and he's angry with me. I hung up on him this morning." She told her all about their brief yet disastrous conversation.

"I'll call him back when I've had a chance to settle down, and maybe he has too. I don't need another lecture right now."

The girls finished breakfast and Kaitlyn helped her clean up. The doorbell buzzed, and both looked at each other. Aurora was still in her jammies and put on her best 'please' look to Kaitlyn as she folded her hands together.

"You owe me." Kaitlyn buzzed back and opened the apartment door.

A minute later, a soft knock sounded. "Flower delivery."

Kaitlyn smiled. "I wonder who they're from."

She had a sneaking suspicion, but didn't want to say anything.

Kaitlyn unwrapped them, and before she could grab the card, Kaitlyn turned and read it. "My lady, I can't do without you. Call me." She fanned herself with it. "Oh la la." She stuffed the card back into the bouquet. "How romantic. Things must've gone better than you thought."

Aurora grabbed at the back of her chair. Kaitlyn was referring to Nate, but she knew better. Only Matthew would've sent the flowers.

"Aurora, are you okay? You're very pale."

"I need to sit down." She pulled out a kitchen chair. Her phone continued to ping.

Kaitlyn glanced at it. "Matthew?" Then realisation dawned on her. "Oh my god, not *that* Matthew? Not that SOB from the library– that author guy. Why is he calling, Aurora?" Her voice filled with rage.

"I honestly don't know." And she didn't because she hadn't texted him all week. You'd think the guy could take a hint.

With her phone in Kaitlyn's hand, she watched as her eyes grew bigger and bigger. Before they could explode from her head, Aurora ripped the phone away.

"Do you care to tell me what the fuck is going on between you and him?" Kaitlyn's shrill voice was pitched high enough to make dogs bark.

"There's nothing going on. Anymore. It just happened." She snapped, and it felt good to at least acknowledge something.

"You just happened to go on a date with him?" She nodded. "Aurora, please don't tell me you slept with him." Aurora kept her lips sealed. "Oh god, no." She wagged her finger at her. "Bad girl. Bad, bad girl."

"It's not what you think."

"Not what I think? You had sex with him, right?" Kaitlyn stood after she nodded. "Gross. He's like forty years old. Ewww." Her friend shook violently on the spot. "What's wrong with Nate?"

"Nothing. We're just not there in our relationship."

"So you'll sleep with that beast instead." Kaitlyn smacked the table startling her. "When?"

"Last Saturday."

"Seriously, Aurora. What the fuck is wrong with you?"

Her vision blurred as the tears built. "I was feeling guilty about Nate, and I was mad at Nate for pushing me so hard. Not that it matters, but I thought of Nate the whole time."

"You're not making any sense."

She lay her head on her arms. "The whole fucking thing doesn't make sense." Her voice was soft, the fight gone from her.

"What sort of sick appeal do you get from Matthew?" She was being sincere in her questioning.

"The opposite from the appeal I get from Nate. Matthew didn't push me and accepted the limitations I have. Whereas Nate wants more than that."

Kaitlyn flopped down beside her. "That's a problem for you, is it?" Aurora shrugged. "Let me see if I got this straight. You're confused because two men like you. One pushes you to spread your wings, and encourages you to see the world. The other is content with you living in your closed up little world, where he ultimately has control." Her friend hovered inches from her face.

"It's scary with Nate, but in a good way. But I don't know how much I can take." She sighed and lowered her head. "Or how much he can take, if I can't give anymore. If his pushing breaks me, will he still want to be around me?" The tears she held back burst free of their hold, and streamed down her cheeks. She ran her hands over her face. "Pathetic isn't it?"

Kaitlyn leaned back. "Actually, when you put it like that, not so much. I kinda understand now."

"Great." Her voiced ringed in sarcasm.

"But you need to figure out who you want. In here." Kaitlyn lightly touched her chest above her heart.

What she wanted was a big sister, and Kaitlyn was as close as she would get. And that brought a fresh wave of bitter, angry tears. "I want Nate. I'm just afraid."

"Sometimes fear is a good motivator."

"Yeah?" She wiped her nose on her sleeve. "But is it good for a relationship?"

Kaitlyn hugged her. "Only you can answer that. Only your heart knows what's worthy of it. But for the record, I think Nate's the one. You'll make cute babies."

With that, she laughed out loud, as the tears fell. "You're already talking babies? We haven't even had sex yet."

"You will."

"There'll be no babies though. The accident made sure that would never happen."

Kaitlyn rubbed her back. "I'm sorry. I didn't know."

"It's okay. It's not something I run around telling people. I'm not sure when to tell Nate that though."

"I'm sure when the time's right, you'll know."

She sat up straighter in her chair, and narrowed her eyes. "You sure like to tell me to listen to my heart. And where has it got me?"

"Where has it got you?" Kaitlyn jumped out of her chair. "Where has it got you? Oh my god, Aurora. Look at you. You have this wonderful man, who clearly adores you and pushes you to be more than *you* think you're capable of. And he doesn't do it for his own selfish reasons, he does it because he believes in you. He BELIEVES in you." Her finger came close to puncturing her heart. "He's getting you to do things, to try things that your two years of shitty therapy have failed to do. He's given you hope. If I was straight, I'd fucking scoop him up and let him take me away. I can't believe this is even a debate for you." Her best friend stormed around the living room.

"But we have a connection."

"What? You and the jerk? Because his cheating whore of a wife was in the other car? What kind of sick, fucked up connection is that?"

She had no reply. Even in her head, nothing made sense, so there would be no reason to give it a voice.

"You know what your problem is, Aurora?" Kaitlyn stood over her, glaring down. "You're afraid to let him in. Not everyone is Derek.

Not everyone will leave you when you've hit your lowest point. Those that are worthy of you, will push and fight for you. And we both know which one is doing that."

Aurora rose from the table and stormed down the hall. Her stomach in knots, her head a swirling mess of thoughts, all twisted and convoluted, and it pained her. Relief was but a pill, or two, or three away. The containers lined up in a neat little row called out to her, and she chose the one that would provide the escape she needed right now.

♥ Chapter Twenty-Eight ♥

K aitlyn sat on the edge of her bed. "Hey, feeling better?"
She rolled over and stared at her friend. "Much. Thank you."

"So what's your plan? Are you going to stay with Nate or," she shuddered, "pick up where you left off with Matthew?"

"There's nothing with Matthew. Nate's who I want." A loud sigh, and the start of a smile. "I'm falling for him but I'm really scared. What if something happens? What if during the race he's in an accident? Then what?"

"Then you deal with it, especially if you love him. Does he know about Matthew?"

"No," she hung her head. "Do you think I should tell him?"

"Yes, and no." Kaitlyn scratched her chin. "Either way, if he finds out, you risk him leaving. If you admit it was a mistake, and you thought you were broken up, maybe he'd be more forgiving."

"So either way, I'm fucked."

"In a nutshell."

"Great."

Kaitlyn passed her the phone. "You left this out in the kitchen and it's been driving me crazy." She rose. "Come out when you're feeling better."

She flipped through her messages. Most were ignorable. A couple from her daddy. A few from Matthew. A message from work with her schedule, which she didn't like. And a couple from Nate.

She texted Nate. *Hey, you.*

Nate: *I miss you.*

Aurora: *U2. Can U come over tonight?*

Nate: *No... have a meeting. 2mrw?*

Aurora: *No. I work the 2-9 shifts all week. :(*

Nate: *Bummer. When can I see U again?*

Aurora: *We can have lunch?*

Nate: *:) :) :) Perfect. How about 1, every day? A picnic behind the building.*

Aurora: *Won't you get sick of me?*

Nate: *Never.*

Feeling lighter in her mind and soul, she sent out a text to her daddy. *I'm sorry and that's the end of it. It was an oversight. End of story. You can either accept it or not but I refuse to apologise any more.*

Since nothing further came from him, she assumed he did not accept her apology. Oh well, his issue to deal with, not hers.

The next two weeks dragged. The only perk to her otherwise dole-drum day was her forty-five minute daily lunch date with Nate. The evening shifts sucked since he usually left at four-thirty and there were no after-work playtimes at his car. Granted, he spent a healthy amount of time texting her during the evenings to the point where she got in trouble once for responding.

After work, and before meeting him for lunch, she filled her free time and managed to get caught up with the summer course she'd neglected. It was boring as hell though, and didn't help pass the time as quickly as she'd hoped. Kaitlyn worked days at the department store, so she had no one to hang around. Even with the Percocet and Xanax taking the edge off, she was lonely.

Having swapped a shift, she surprised Nate by leaning against his car, waiting patiently for him to come out from behind the building. She never spoke about it at lunchtime, and his expression of sheer joy and surprise was priceless, and worth it.

He sauntered up to her. "Well, look at you."

"Yep, look at me."

He placed his hands on either side of her body, and leaned in close. "Xanax?"

She shook her head and breathed him in. "Nope. Total determination." He whistled. "And I've been practising."

"How?" He ran a hand through his hair and she saw the sweat on his forehead. Someone had been working hard. Either that or he was really hot. She'd place her money on him being hot, because he was sex on a stick.

"Random cars in the parking lot."

Nate laughed. "I can just see it too. You walking around touching different vehicles."

"Pretty much." She stepped away. "Okay, enough of that." Imaginary dust flew off her pants as she gave them a smack. Nate kept his car in unnaturally clean condition. "I've missed this."

He held her cheeks with his calloused hands, and brushed her aching lips with his. "I've missed this too."

"I'm back on days now, so we can be together all evening, every evening if we wanted too." She grabbed his damp shirt collar and pulled him closer. "Care to clear up our bargain?"

"Tonight?" He sounded surprised.

"Yeah, why not?" She'd kept her apartment clean and tidy, and this time wouldn't be embarrassed if he showed up.

"I can't. It's Friday."

Her eyes rolled. "I'm aware of what day of the week it is."

He laughed as he rubbed her arms. "I'm heading out to the track tonight."

"Oh, right," she said as she kicked at a pebble.

"I'd ask you to come, but I know you can't. You're not there yet." Tenderly he brushed away a tendril of her hair. "Not without those drugs."

"Yeah, not yet."

"Have you thought about calling my sister?"

She narrowed her eyes. "You know about that?"

"Yeah, there's no secrets, remember."

"I wish I could forget." She shook her head. "But I haven't."

"And your dad?"

"He's still pissed. So getting any magic pills from him won't happen before Christmas likely."

He pulled her close. "Racing season will be over by then."

The sarcasm rolled out. "I think that's his plan."

He kissed her, dipping her the longer their lips locked together. "As much as I love this, I need to go. Lucas is driving down with me tonight, and he'll be at my place soon."

She kissed him goodbye, and waved as he drove away

Aurora was buried nose deep in the back office on the Saturday when a strong male voice called her name. Her heart jumped a little, thinking Nate was there instead of at the track. Instead her heart skipped a beat when she saw Matthew standing there, looking adorable in tight black jeans and an emerald green top. He held a single rose in his hands.

"Matthew, what are you doing here?"

"Visiting, my lady." He stepped closer to her. "I'm checking on the building. For the big end of summer bash. I came to see how it was coming along."

A quick scan of the area before she inched closer to him, and whispered, "You can't see me."

"Yes I can, you're right in front of me, my lady."

She waved him away. "No, I mean, *YOU* can't see me." She sighed as she came around the desk. "I told you, I'm seeing someone. I'm sorry."

"I figured but hoped I was wrong and you were lying to me. This is for you anyways," he said, passing the rose. His face multiple shades of sadness. "Can you at least join me for supper tonight, and we can talk about it?"

Not wanting to be a complete bitch, she set the rose on the desk, when she really wanted to drop it in the trash. "There's nothing to talk about." Her arms crossed tightly over her chest, and she narrowed her eyes at him.

"Look, my lady, I will be here for a few days at the end of summer, and I'd rather there be no awkwardness between us."

Steadying herself against the desk, she said, "Maybe it'll only be awkward if you keep trying to make something between us. There wasn't anything there, it was just sex and there's no future for us. I'm with someone else." Her voice was low to not arouse the staff into coming into the back room. "I'm sorry. I'm not going to dinner with you."

He stepped closer. "Have you heard about Mr. Thomas Anderson?"

The name rings a bell. She shook her head, worried the direction the conversation seemed headed. "No, but I'll bet you know lots."

The tall dark-haired man stepped closer. "Do you know who that is?"

"Of course," she lied as she couldn't for the life of her figure out who he was.

"His trial starts on Monday."

"Oh, good." The lightbulb flickered. "OH. Oh," she said, unable to make eye contact. *The murderer. Momma and Carmen's murderer. And Rebecca's too, I suppose.*

Matthew stepped back when a staff member came into the room. "So I thought we could discuss what I've heard, what the lawyers are asking for. You know. That."

She sighed, and resigned herself, tugging down her sleeves as she straightened up. "Yes, I suppose I should have an idea."

"Thank you," he said, but there was no smugness in his voice. And she expected plenty. "Tonight? Same place, same time?"

She nodded, wondering what the hell she was getting into.

Why the fuck was she back here, again, with Matthew James? She was starting to think she was losing her mind. In her head only, she decided she'd get the info on the murderer and head home. Nothing more. Not looking forward to it, she popped a Xanax as she left.

She took little stock of her appearance, not wanting to give him any fuel. Her messy hair styled into a top knot, for no other reason than to keep the hair off her neck. It had been a hot day, and at the moment she was thankful for the air conditioning. Walking in the heat to the restaurant was nearly unbearable. She didn't even apply makeup for fear it would melt off by time she arrived.

As she beat him there, she sat in a corner booth, drumming her fingers in moderate frustration. Tardiness was a huge pet peeve. Just getting ready to leave, he waltzed in looking fresh and damn good. Probably part of his tactic, charm her with his dazzling good looks. Well, dammit it, it wasn't going to work. Not today. She had Nate, and he was hotter. Way hotter.

"You're late." She didn't even wait for him to have a seat.

"And my apologies for keeping you waiting, my lady." He hung up his suit jacket on the hook beside the booth. How could he wear a suit jacket? It's twenty-nine fucking degrees outside. "I had a meeting with my manager that ran longer than anticipated."

"Let me guess, you couldn't agree on the right colour of baskets for the pencils to be sorted in?"

He looked at her with confusion on his face. "No."

"Are the layout plans wrong, and everything will have to be scrapped and redone?"

"No, my lady." His brow furrowed as he studied her, a worried expression crossed his face. "I was discussing my estate. Some of the termed deposits I had set up for Rebecca matured, and we needed to decide on the appropriate management of funds." He folded his hands together. "You're upset with me."

"When we agree on a time, I expect you to show up."

"I'm five minutes late."

"Late is late."

His mouth creeped open a hair, but it shut after a moment's hesitation. Pausing, he twisted his hands while taking her in. "You look lovely tonight," he said sweetly.

"I wasn't trying very hard." Her mouth twisted into a sneer. She needed more relief than the Xanax was providing. Her core felt tense and one misstep from the man across from her, and she figured she'd throttle him.

"And you certainly don't need to," he said.

She dug through her purse and dug out two percs. "Stop, please. Just stop." The back of her hand wiped across her sweaty brow.

"What? What is it I'm doing that's irritating you so much?"

The pills slipped down her throat dry. "It's you." Sighing, she looked him deep into the eye. "You're driving me crazy." Matthew's grin meant he took her statement in a different direction than she intended. "It was only sex. One stupid night." Well, that wiped the smug smile off his face. "I'm sorry." She took a breath and carried on. "You're a great guy, but you're not the one for me. I'm seeing someone."

He dismissed her with a wave but his face spoke volumes. It was easy to see from the hurt on his face she was probably breaking his heart. "I'm sorry you saw it as a 'stupid' night."

"I was high that night. Loaded up on a combo of drugs. I honestly thought you were someone else."

"Yes," he thumbed towards her purse, "I've noticed you're a big drug user," he said with an uneasy smile while he twisted in his seat. "My lady, I've requested your assistance with my end of summer event and I don't want things awkward between us."

Her back pressed into the seat of the booth. "Did you think coming here would help?"

He nodded. "I did. I hoped."

"Then you need to stop. Stop with the weekly delivery of flowers. Stop with the texts." She wanted this over, and didn't want the possibility of this date, or the one-night stand to ever come up again. "Unless you have—"

The waiter appeared and asked for their orders.

"I'm not staying for supper."

Matthew's jaw dropped. "Oh, please. One last supper together." He smiled, but not a true smile. This was forced.

The waiter stood motionless. "Shall I return?"

"No," Matthew said, pointing to an item on the menu. "I'll have this." He closed it up and looked at Aurora. "Your turn."

"I'll be fine with a 7UP, thanks."

Matthew nodded, and the waiter took off.

"The heat kills my appetite." She glanced around the restaurant as a large group of patrons walked by. Uncomfortable in his presence, she couldn't stand it no more. "As I was saying before…" A large gulp of air filled her lungs, but in its release it left behind a breath of courage. "Unless you have news about the trial, please don't call or text me anymore."

"My lady."

"Hopefully things will be better at the end of summer when we've had some distance. But I can't stay here for supper. I'm sorry." She fished out money from her purse and dropped it on the table. "Goodbye, Matthew." Without turning back, she walked out of the restaurant. She felt bad for being such a bitch, but the man needed to get a clue.

❤ Chapter Twenty-Nine ❤

Aurora wandered around her apartment Sunday morning with a heavy heart. Holding the phone in her hand, she wondered about Nate, if he missed her as much as she missed him, although her thoughts flipped briefly back to Matthew. Should she send him an apology? She wasn't that mean was she?

Her back ached and throbbed, and she kneaded her knuckles into it. Looking up at the sky, the pain had to be caused from the darkening clouds to the west. And like her mood it grew darker.

First she needed some pain relief and later she'd swallow a Xanax for the storm. She grabbed a couple percs and settled in to her favourite chair, but after a few minutes, she didn't much care and tossed her textbook to the floor. She had a mid-term next week and was overwhelmed at the possibility of failing her test– it would be her first fail. But she couldn't concentrate with so much going on in her mind.

Between Nate and Matthew, her boring as hell job, a stack of assignments she wasn't sure how to complete and the constant throbbing of back pain, she was poised on the precipice of great peril. She hated feeling helpless. It had taken her a long while to pull out of that pit of despair and she'd be damned if it would happen again.

She texted Nate. *How'd the races go last night?*

Nate replied almost instantly. *Good. 1ˢᵗ 3ʳᵈ & 2ⁿᵈ in the final.*

Aurora: ☺☺☺ *Way to go. Wish I was there.*

Nate: *You were. ;) In my heart.*

She sat in her chair smiling like an idiot. Yeah, she was in a slow fall for this man.

Nate: *I'll be leaving the track in a couple hours. Do you want to meet for supper?*

Aurora: *No. I'll make supper. Come hungry.*

Nate: *I'm salivating already.* ☺

Aurora: *Dinner will be ready at 5.*

Now, she had something to do, and she jumped at the chance to get it done. Tonight's dinner would be cheese and prosciutto stuffed chicken with steamed veggies and twice baked potato. She made a quick shopping list and raced to the grocery store. Fearing she wouldn't have time to make a dessert, she scoured the bakery section, settling on a couple slices of cheesecake. She returned minutes before the rain started and swallowed a Xanax.

"He's here," she said to no one as she raced to the buzzer.

A soft knock sounded moments later and she opened the door to see Nate standing there, holding an envelope and small package. He looked good, no scratch that, he looked fucking gorgeous. His mop of dark hair brushed off to the side, exposing his forehead more than normal. A clean-shaven face and his chocolate eyes sparkled. And he was in normal clothes– jeans and a Henley top.

She gestured him in and he set the items on the edge of the kitchen table, grabbing her and firmly planting a kiss on her lips. Breathless and wanton, she pressed back, parting her lips as she did. "Hi," she said when they separated.

He glanced around the apartment. "You cleaned." Candles cast a soft orange glow on the table, where matched dishes were set out for supper. "Wow. Very romantic." His eyes danced. "But first, these are for you." Two packages thrust into her hands. "The envelope is from Mom, the box is from me."

"To what do I owe this honour? It's not my birthday."

"Just open it, will you?"

"Okay." She set the small box down and tore open the heavy envelope, slowly removing a picture frame. Turning it over, she gasped. "Oh my god." It was a picture of her and Nate, sitting in the cage, her head resting on his shoulder, her hand over his heart. Her eyes were closed but a small smile edged her lips. Nate's head was leaning against hers, a look of satisfaction on his face as his finger stroked her cheek. They looked relaxed with each other, and over-the-moon happy. "Wow," she said unable to make a more coherent sentence. "How—when–"

"Obviously when you were at the track." He rolled his eyes mocking her. "Seriously though, there's always a professional photographer around, taking car shots mostly. Guess he thought we were happy."

"We were, I mean, we are." She couldn't remove her eyes from the picture, and it rendered her speechless. She touched the edges as if it were alive. "Thank you."

"Gosh, if I knew you'd like it that much, I should've had you open mine first."

She set the picture frame down and picked up the little box. Unwrapping it, she froze when she saw the velvet-covered box.

"Relax," he said, "it's not a ring." She released her breath as he lifted the lid, revealing a necklace charm. "It's the universal symbol for hope."

It was gorgeous. A silver pendant with three symbols as one– a cross, a heart and an anchor, hung on a black satin string.

"I saw it and it instantly made me think of you." His cheeks flooded with colour. "If you don't like it I can take it back."

"Over my dead body," she said, trembling as she removed it from its velvet confines. She draped it over her head, letting it settle near her heart. "It's perfect. Thanks."

"You really like it?"

"I do."

He smiled. "Good. Because I did this." He lifted his shirt, pulling it high over his sculpted chest. There above his heart was the same symbol. "Maybe I should've waited until after I gave you the present, but I couldn't help myself."

She reached out and gingerly touched the dark ink, running her finger over the fresh scar. "I don't know what to say."

"How about dinner's ready, because it smells delicious and you told me to come hungry."

They dined on her fancy meal, and Nate ate up and moaned with every morsel. His carnal groaning ignited the fires in her. Ones she desperately wanted, *and needed,* him to put out.

Speechless, she stared up at him as her breaths raced alongside her pulse. Her blood pumped fast and like a hungry monster her body fed off it. "Dessert now, or later."

He propped his chin on his hand. "Later, I'm stuffed." She watched his full lips as he spoke. "You are quite something."

"Quite something, eh? Those are words to warm the cockles of my heart."

"Ha-ha, you said cockles."

"What are you, five?"

His head tipped to the side as a smile tickled its way out. "Maybe."

"I can't date a five-year-old," she said as she nudged him.

His face turned to wanton desire, and he threaded his fingers through hers. "I can be twenty-two."

She pulled him to the centre of the living room and pressed play on the stereo. The room filled with soft, sultry music. "Dance with me?"

His calloused hand was softer than usual as he held hers as if it were a piece of delicate china, placing his other on her hip. Pulling her closer, he pressed up against her and she breathed in his warm, intoxicating spicy cologne. Her hand rested against the tattooed part of his chest, and she swore she felt the race of his beating heart.

Arms held the other tightly, dancing and swaying in time to the music. He bent down, lowering his full, soft lips to hers, kissing and tasting as his hands escaped hers and threaded through her long hair. She prodded him over towards the couch, pushing him playfully into the seat while she straddled him, and hiked up her skirt.

Tongues entwined, hearts raced, moans escaped. She leaned back and removed her shirt, allowing it to slip off her shoulders as her breasts, covered in bright tangerine silk revealed themselves. The necklace rested against her chest. She heard his low, throaty groan, and the bulge in his pants was hard to miss. Tenderly she picked up his hand, kissed each of his fingers and placed his hand over her heart. Another moan, and the bulge moved beneath as if it were a caged beast.

Not holding back, he kissed her, keeping her close as one hand slipped behind her back. His hand danced underneath the band of her bra as if trying to free it single-handedly. Aurora reached behind and unhooked it for him, his face lighting up with joy at seeing her naked breasts. She tossed the bra to the floor and resumed her kisses, grabbing and tugging his shirt up and over his head.

"Aurora, wait," he said breathless. His face so close she could lick it. "I need to tell you something." She leaned closer, kissing the fleshy lobes of his ears while trying to become a part of him.

"It's okay, I have condoms," she whispered as her eyes closed.

"It's not that." He moaned as she sucked on the lobe. "Aurora, my love...I'm a virgin."

She sat ramrod straight, her eyes flashed open. "What?"

"I know you heard me." His gaze cast down as if in shame.

"Okay," she whispered, lifting his chin and looking deep into his eyes. "That's a first for me. I've never been someone's first." She wiggled back a little, giving him some space, shocked to hear that. I mean, c'mon, he was a living god. "Do you want to stop? Because I'm okay if you do." Desperate, she hunted for any sign he was scared or confused.

"No, I just need you to know. Mom had Chris at fifteen, and I swore to myself that I'd never have a sexual relationship if I couldn't handle any possible accidents. Children are a huge commitment."

"I can assure you that accidents won't happen with me. I can't have children." His face saddened, but he never let go of her. "But I understand what you're saying." She kissed him softly. "And I thank you for–" What was the word she was searching for? Was it trust? No, because it was more than that. Was it devotion? Maybe. Her mind blanked out.

"Plus... I'm–" His hands wrapped tight around her waist. "Very nervous."

"Not here." She wrapped her hands into his, and pulled him to a stand. *His first time can't be on a couch where I've done others. Needs to be more personable. More romantic.* "To the bedroom."

Before she could make a step towards her room, a strong arm swept her off her feet, and carried her down the hall, placing her gently on the made-up bed. After unzipping his pants and stepping out of his clothes, he shyly climbed onto the bed, covering himself as he did.

You're too cute, Nate. She stood and slipped her skirt off, letting it puddle on the floor as the sunshine-yellow silk panties joined it heartbeats later. Parading around in the buff wearing her new necklace, she popped into the bathroom, and returned in a breath with a box of condoms she tossed onto the bedside table.

The bed bounced as she pulled back the blanket, resumed the straddle position and moved around, playing with her hair as she moved her hips against his. He curled around her, his warm breath on her collar bone, his tender hands on the small of her back.

In no time at all, Nate was groaning, hard, into her ear. He alternated kissing her lips and moving south to her breasts.

"Are you ready?" she asked as her hands ran over his sculpted chest, kissing the tender skin above his heart. "We can just do this, if you don't want more. There doesn't have to be penetration."

He pulled her tight. "I want you," he breathed hard. "To be in you."

She pushed him down so he lay prone on the bed. Her hand over his belly button as she stretched across him for the box and withdrew a foil pouch. It rolled amongst her fingers and she held it between her thumb and finger. "I'm disease free, as are you obviously." The packet flipped between her fingers again and a playful smile crossed her face. "I don't want your first experience to be dulled from the lack of sensation." She wiggled against him, her heart pounding loudly as it swelled with desire for the handsome man beneath her. "But if you wear it, *I* get to put it on."

"God woman, hurry up and make a decision before I explode right now." His head fell back, and he closed his eyes as moans of ecstasy escaped his lips.

Scooting back towards his knees, she tugged on his boxer shorts, releasing the bulge. *Impressive.* With the foil packet in her teeth, she ripped it open, and rolled it over top of him and down his length. Heavy with excitement, she asked, "Are you ready?"

"Never better," he gasped.

One breath at a time, she lowered herself over his tip, allowing him to fill her from the bottom up. His chest heaved as her fingertips walked up from his hips to his shoulders.

"Good lord, Aurora," he breathed, and another gasp slipped from his lips.

Her hips moved back and forth while her fingertips trailed the length of his muscular arms. Fingers entwined together, she placed his hands on her breasts while slowly wiggling her hips. He sat up, moving his hands to her hips, as his lips found hers. As his tongue pressed deep into her, she gyrated more, his hands pulling and pushing her hips, her hands sliding through his thick hair.

"Ooohhh." A low, throaty rumble.

Instead of hot core-bashing sex, she wanted their first time together to be romantic and sensual. Slowing her pace, her fingers danced over the sculpted muscles on his back. "Just roll with it," she whispered in his ear and proceeded to flick and suck on his lobe. Being with Nate, felt good. Natural. Perfect. Repositioning herself, she allowed him to glide back into her, slowly, gently, until they were one solid piece of flesh and soul.

He grunted "OH GOD" over and over as her hips mashed against his. Her fingers moved deep in his hair, her tongue danced around his piercing. Pushing herself close to his chest, their hearts raced together in perfect synchronization.

She knew the moment he released as his hands grabbed the fleshy part of her thighs before they went limp and he fell back against the bed.

"Oh my god," he whispered. "Thank you," he breathed when he opened his eyes. "That… was everything… I ever hoped… it would be." Unable to stop herself, she kissed him until she couldn't breathe, knowing this wonderful, loving man forever held her heart.

She removed the condom, tossing it onto the ripped foil package on the bedside table. Her head rested against his shoulder, and she placed her hand over the pulse of his heart, which raced along at top speed. "You're good?"

"Never better." He kissed her forehead. "I love you, Aurora, so much."

She closed her eyes and breathed in his sweaty, sexy scent. Nothing in the world could ever smell as wonderful to her as he did right now.

"So was that the best sex you've ever had?" He laughed as he spoke.

"No," she said as she turned into him, draping a leg over him. "We didn't have sex." She breathed hard. Her heart raced in time to her thoughts. "We made love."

He rolled her over, kissing her hard, and trailed his tongue stud over her breasts, down to her naval. He halted as his eyes took in her hips.

"Yes," Aurora said as she followed his gaze, feeling no shame. "Those are my accident scars."

"I knew there'd be a few, but there are so many." He ran his finger over one of many long scars dotting her pelvis like a connect-the-dots pattern.

"That long one," she said, touching his hand, "is my surgery scar where they cut me open to fix my shattered pelvis. The little ones surrounding it are from the external fixator I wore. This long scar," she rolled over to give him a better view, "is where my skin was torn apart on impact. The console snapped and lodged itself there." His face was attentive and full of sympathy. It broke her heart seeing Nate's pained expression as she explained all her scars. "There are more on my legs too." His eyes followed the curve of her hips, the length of her thigh.

"I didn't realise that you were as badly damaged– I mean hurt." Panic crossed his eyes.

"I know what you mean, and I don't take offense, honestly. I am damaged. I get that. It just means something different to me than the rest of the general population." She forced a smile.

"You're one of a kind."

"Thank God. Could you imagine two of me?" She laughed, easing away the start of tension.

He lowered his head, and kissed the scars above her knee, and every scar on the way up her leg, and across her hips. "I'm so sorry," he murmured over and over again. In her mind, it was the most romantic buildup to her oncoming orgasm. Each kiss tenderer than the previous, and yet each kiss filled with sorrow. However, each also overflowed with love and *that* made her heart swell.

He kissed her lips, and allowed his hand to wander south, brushing her heated skin. A finger slipped between her legs, and he released a groan that matched hers in bass, as he caressed and explored, taking his time with this uncharted territory.

Oh geez! The rise of an impending orgasm came fast and furious. *Slow down, let me enjoy–* Panting and gripping his shoulders, she looked at him. He gazed at her, a smile cracking his once serious face. *Oh, oh, oh.* A heartbeat or two later. "Nate–" she groaned, rasping and trying to catch her breath. Tears fought their way to the surface as her heart rate maintained top speed. "Oh, Nate," she sighed. A lump formed in her throat. "I love you." And she meant it. Every. Single. Word. She nuzzled her nose into the crook of his neck where her tears fell.

Breathless and silent, they held each other tight. The room lit up with a flash of light from the approaching storm, and she curled tighter into Nate before the thunder cracked.

An arm tightened around her waist, and a hand covered her visible ear. Pressed against his chest, the beating of his heart tried to drown out the roll of thunder.

Without a thought, her body trembled and shimmied closer.

"Operation Baby Steps," he said as he kissed her lips. "Replace the fear with something positive." His hand caressed her arm, following the length of it as they trailed their way down across her hips, and over her soft behind. In response, his ample package grew and pulsed beside her.

Her fingers ran through his hair and apprehensively she rolled back on top of him, a slight quiver in her legs as she moved. The storm rolled again, and she covered her chest, tipping her head down, her hair falling over her face.

A gentle touch, so perfect she wanted to ignore the fear pressing upon her. She squirmed against him and tried to replace the horrible thoughts flooding into her brain with his voice, his touch, his taste. But it wasn't working. The closer the storm, the higher her fear. A cold sweat blanketed her body, and nausea took up residence in her stomach. Nate's hands traced along her backbone, leaving a trail of heat in its wake.

A sob overtook her body, and she collapsed against his body. "I can't," she whispered, her voice breaking as she spoke.

Although she was beyond terrified, his arms were the perfect security blanket she craved and needed. Until the storm passed, neither said a word as she quietly cried into his shoulder. His warm hands held her tight and his kisses on her forehead tamed the wild beast of fear inside her.

❤ Chapter Thirty ❤

The next day Aurora awoke in Nate's arms, very much in love. With Derek, she thought she was in love, but it was never like this. Honest and free, tender and pure. Saying goodbye to him, so they could get ready for work was hard. It helped ease the discomfort knowing she'd see him in an hour.

Feeling courageous and to pass the time, she gave her father a call.

"Princess?" he asked when he answered.

She rolled her eyes, but resumed with why she was calling. "Daddy, I need something from you. I need a couple more of those pills." A long pause. "The Isas."

"So the only reason for you to call me is to ask for more pills? You were completely irresponsible with the last set I gave you."

"Fuck, Daddy." She stomped her foot on the living room floor. He wouldn't hear it, but it made her feel better. "We forgot, okay? And we made it home safely. Like made it into the apartment as it wore off."

"And you don't think I worried? I waited for you or Nate to call. We had a deal." His voice terse, but a hint of concern leaked through.

"Daddy, it was an oversight. I talked to you the next day."

"No, you hung up on me."

"Oh, for fuck's sake." She stomped her foot again and then kicked at a throw pillow which landed on the side table, nearly taking out her lamp. "I'm an adult, and you control me like a child."

"Because you act like a child."

She growled. "I need a couple more pills. Please. I want to go back to the track on Saturday and I need them to get there."

"He means that much to you?"

A long pause as she paced around the living room, glancing out the patio window. "Yeah. I'm in love with him." A smile bubbled up as she spoke.

"Well–"

"Please, Daddy."

He sighed long and paused longer. "I'll overnight a couple to you."

She punched the air. "Thank you."

"I expect more responsibility from you this time."

"I promise." She hung up, excited to tell Nate the good news but figured she should wait until the package arrived. No point getting excited if the pills never came.

Aurora checked her mailbox Tuesday, expecting the package to be there. Nothing. She checked again on Wednesday. Still nothing. She debated calling her daddy to ask where the hell the pills were. Thursday, she ran home to check on her lunch break, and cheered when she saw mail addressed from him. It was hard to contain her excitement and surprise, and she worked hard to make sure she finished her shift before Nate.

The pills were a part of a complete package, so she swallowed a Xanax as she grabbed her purse from her locker. Hoping he finished *only* a few minutes after her, she walked out to his car and dropped her belongings beside it. She inhaled deeply before she leaned against the side. Deep breath in, one, two, three, exhale. Repeat. With a quick thrust from her arms, she jumped up and sat on the hood. *Breathe.*

The bottom of her lip became raw from biting it, but she didn't waver from her spot. "Hey, good looking," she breathed out when Nate strode over with a smile as wide as the Grand Canyon, and his dimple just as deep.

"Look at you." He whistled and kept his gaze on her.

She slipped off the car, relief relaxing her shoulders. Her arms found their home around his neck as she reached up to kiss him. "I have something for you." She retrieved the envelope from her back pocket. Watching his face, she read the excitement as he tore it open and dumped a little bag containing two pills into his hand.

"Are these–" His eyes wide with joy. "Really?"

"Yep."

"You're talking again? What did you say to him?"

She shrugged. "Enough that he sent them." Nate stuffed the envelope into his pocket. "Don't lose those, otherwise I can't come down on Saturday."

The snug distance between them narrowed as he asked, "Would you come with me tomorrow night and spend the weekend?"

"Does everyone go out Friday night?"

"No, but Mom and Lucas will be there. Most of the other drivers come out on Saturday."

She rubbed her chin in mock thought. "Okay. I've never camped before."

"Never?" She shook her head. "It's not so bad." Strong arms wrapped around her. "I love you," he said, kissing her before she could speak.

"So, when do we leave tomorrow?"

"I'll pick you up around seven? I need to get everything loaded up with Lucas first." Excitement written all over his face. "I'm thrilled you're coming, and that you want to."

"I do. I really do." She placed her hand on his shoulder and grasped a wad of shirt in her other hand, tugging him in closer. Standing on her tippy-toes, she raised her lips to his, wanting to taste him. As she linked her hands behind his neck, his gently lifted her higher. Eyes closed, the sensations heightened and electrified her skin, making it tingle with carnal desire. It pooled in her panties and she couldn't wait to taste more of him.

Friday after work, she raced home and packed a weekend bag, throwing a sexy negligee and a few condoms on top. She didn't know if they'd have privacy or not, but she wanted to be prepared in case. Topping up her pill containers, she added them to her purse.

Fresh from a shower, she dropped her bag at the door and grabbed the box of homemade pastries she made the night before.

Nate knocked on her door, and being so excited she opened the door rather harshly. It banged into the door jamb, and marked up the wall. "Easy, tiger."

"Rawr," she said. "I missed you today."

"I'm here now," he said, enveloping her in a long hug. "Ready to go?"

"Yes and no. This part I'm not looking forward to." Eyes locked on his, she lifted her trembling hand to him as she opened it.

"I promise," he pulled the bag free from his pocket, "to keep you safe. To protect you and watch over you." Cupping her twitching hand, he poured one out.

Her breath caught in her throat as she listened to the sincerity in his voice. She swallowed her fear. "I believe you." With a quick movement, the pill slid down her throat. "Let's go."

Nate grabbed her bag. "This it?"

"And this," she said as she snapped up a Tupperware container of pastries. "I made snacks."

"You carry that, I've got this." Her lips quivered as he brushed them with his own. "I promise."

"Tick, tock." Her empty stomach growled. She hadn't eaten since lunch, hoping the Isa would take effect faster and last longer that way.

"Right." Locking up, they walked out the main entrance where Lucas stood beside a pickup truck with a trailer holding the white race car.

"Hey," she said to Nate's little brother, surprise in her voice.

"I hope you don't mind," Nate said, "Mom's already out at the track, and Lucas needed the ride."

She looked between the men. "I don't mind."

Nate set her overnight bag in the back seat of the extended cab. "Lucas will ride in the back, unless you think it would be better for you there?"

The idea bumped around inside her brain. Would the backseat be better? It would be easier for the men to chat while she drifted away. She looked between the front and back seat. "I'll take the back."

Lucas opened the passenger door and unlatched the back seat's mini door, so she could enter. Nate walked around and held her hand as she apprehensively placed a foot on the running board. Yanking it off as if she'd been shocked, she said, "Nope, not ready."

Nate stroked the top of her hand. "Keep trying, and I'll take good care of you."

"I know you will." Her foot touched the running board again. "Send Dad a text, will you?"

What the hell is that screeching? She stretched out her ears only to realise the awful noise was coming from her own lips. "What the fuck?" she said.

"Hang on, Aurora. Keep singing."

"I was singing?"

"I hope it was you or I just ran over a pack of wild cats."

She wanted to laugh, but she froze in place. Everything came into focus like a slap to the face. "Nate," she whimpered as the unmistakable view of trees and grasslands passed beyond the boundaries of his truck. "I'm scared." Her eyes slammed shut. "No, no, no."

"Hang on, we're nearly there."

"I can't do this, Nate." A violent shudder rocked her body, and she threw her head against the front seat.

"You *are* doing it. I promise."

She covered her ears as if that would help. "I can't stop them," she said as headlights blinded her view and a scream drowned out her thoughts. "They're here." Cold and wet, she choked on the metallic taste of her own blood, gagging as she did. It felt real and yet– it felt as though she were in a nightmare where a pinch would bring her out. "Stop! Stop!" Fighting against an unseen monster, she screamed and thrashed in her seat. Darkness descended up on her, dropping her into a pit of terror where the only way out was to let go.

It was warm–uncomfortably warm–when she blinked again. Squinting and focusing, she took in her surroundings. It must be inside the Johnson's trailer. A tiny space with a one-person kitchen across from a small table. Beneath her, a pull-out sofa. Her ears perked up as she heard two voices outside.

"I like her, I really do, but how can you put up with this every time?"

"We need to find a better drug. This one doesn't last long enough."

"Drugs aren't the answer and you know it." Someone coughed. "Last time she was here she fainted, and today she screamed herself into a blackout *while* you were driving. You're lucky Lucas was with you, otherwise– God only knows what could've happened if she'd been successful in opening the door."

She recoiled on the sofa. What the fuck had gone down? She'd tried to escape?

Nate's voice boomed. "It's PTSD, mom, and she's trying. I'm not giving up on her."

"That's not what I'm asking. I'm concerned for you, Nate, just as much as I am for her."

"She's come so far. If you only saw how bad it used to be."

"Nate, you can't fix her."

"I have faith that I can."

The door to the trailer opened and slammed shut, shaking her. "Nate." Her throat was raw as if she'd swallowed a cheese grater, but after hearing that, she understood why.

"Sorry, did I wake you?"

"No, I just woke up." Fighting to sit up, his warm hands settled on her.

He kissed her forehead and pulled out his phone. "I need to call your dad again so I don't get in shit."

Okay. She closed her heavy eyes again, listening to his voice as he spoke. "She's up... I'll know more in when I talk to her... Yeah, I'll keep you posted." He sounded despondent.

"Nate?" She shuffled over, giving him room to sit.

He exhaled loudly. "Just rest."

"Want to tell me what the hell happened?"

He shook his head and rubbed his face, looking years older than when they left her apartment. "I wish I knew. You came off the drug so fast, and early I might add." A finger stroked her cheek. "Then you started screaming." He curled into himself and stared at his hands. "The worst. I shouldn't even tell you."

She whispered, "Please. Tell me."

His shoulders rolled. "It's a good thing you chose the backseat. There's no door handle back there. You yelled stop over and over again, and threw yourself against the door. Then you screamed and passed out. We pulled over to check on you, and thankfully you still had a pulse and were breathing. Then I called Chris and talked."

Waves of shame covered her. "And Lucas? How's he?"

"He's shaken up, but he's okay."

Unable to be more shocked by her behaviour, she pulled back. "I'm sorry. I'm so sorry."

His eyes shut and his voice cracked as he said, "I don't know how– how to get you home. There's not enough time."

"How... early?"

"Fifteen minutes."

She recoiled in her spot. "Oh, Nate." How the hell was she going to get home if the Isa wasn't lasting long enough? "Maybe Daddy could overnight another?"

"If we want to stay until Tuesday. Maybe?"

She pushed herself into a sitting position and rubbed her face. Surely, an idea would come to her if she could only think. She refused to be stuck here. But worse, she hated to see the scared desperation on his face. And all because of her. "What time is it now?"

"Nine-thirty."

"Seriously?"

"I wish I was joking." She stroked his cheek to soothe him, but it comforted *her* more to touch his stubbled cheek. "But I know you had no control. You warned me, I didn't think–" He sighed. "I didn't think it'd be like that." His forehead touched her arm. "And your blackout? You didn't come out of it until now. I talked to your dad, and he said to wake you and shake you until you responded, and my sister said to give it time."

"Obviously you listened to your sister."

"Yeah, no offence to your dad, but she's a doctor."

Shrugging, she agreed thankful that she was. "Your mom hates me, doesn't she?"

"Not in the least, so please don't think that." He raised his head and looked at her.

Wishing she could erase his worry, she kissed him, but the kiss lacked intimacy. She shuddered.

After a few breaths he passed her his phone. "Call your dad."

"I'll text. It's easier to avoid him that way." She sat up and tucked her legs underneath her, throwing a heavy blanket off to the side. "Let's go out. I don't want to make things any more uncomfortable."

A quick glance to Nate revealed a man who looked spent and worn. His normal smile flipped into a frown, his forehead creased with tension. It didn't matter how much he loved her, because her problem seemed to threaten his, and her, happiness.

"I promise you they won't be." But he didn't look sure.

She took a deep breath and walked to the door, stepping outside ahead of Nate. Brenda and Lucas sat around a campfire where Lucas toasted marshmallows.

Brenda was the first to notice her when the door opened and advanced to greet her. "Hi. Welcome back to the track."

"Hey," she said as she was engulfed in a hug. "A million apologies for what happened on the way here," she said in a self-depreciating tone.

"We're glad you're okay."

"Yeah, I'm more embarrassed than anything. Guess I need to find a better pill to swallow." Nate stood a few feet behind her.

She patted Lucas on the shoulder. "I'm truly sorry you had to witness that."

With a shrug he pulled a chair out for her and passed her a roasting stick along with the bag. "You like marshmallows?"

Plopping into the chair, she didn't miss the silent exchange between Nate and Brenda as they took the other two seats. "Sure, who doesn't?" She stabbed a round white puff onto the end of her stick and held it over the fire, unable to take her eyes off them, trying hard to be discreet.

"So, Lucas," she said, filling a need to put something in the air aside from her own nervousness. "Are you looking forward to university? Nate tells me you're going into engineering."

"Figured I'd do okay in there."

"Okay?" Nate said as he chucked a marshmallow at his little brother. "You know more about cars and shit than anyone I know."

"So, you're going into mechanical engineering?"

"Yeah," Lucas said, a smile sneaking out onto his face. "Sort of up my alley." He looked at Nate. "Following his lead."

"I'm not in mechanical, Bro."

"Still, I'll get to hang out with you on campus."

"In your dreams," he said, but he was laughing, or at least trying to. "Like I'd let you hang out with me."

Their friendly banter relaxed her a bit. It reminded her of Carmen and how they used to be. She wondered if Nate and Lucas were best friends. She and Carmen were.

They made small talk for the next little bit, but the tension in the air hung like a dark cloud over Brenda and Nate, refusing to blow over. Brenda said little to Nate. Mind you, she didn't say much to her or Lucas either. Maybe she was one of those people more content to listen to the conversations than to actually be a part of them. Or perhaps she was one of those moms who never thought any girl her son brought home was good enough. And based on how things have started between them already, she banked on the latter. She wasn't good for Nate and it didn't matter how much she loved him.

After a few burnt marshmallows, Brenda said good night to everyone, reminding Lucas to lock up when he came in.

Aurora frowned, crinkling her eyebrows.

Nate leaned closer. "We can go to sleep whenever you'd like," he told her, keeping his voice low.

She yawned. "You wouldn't think I'd be tired after that nap earlier."

"I don't think anyone would call *that* a nap." Stuffing a chunk of white onto his stick, he held it over the fire. "We're sleeping in Bill's trailer. He's not coming until tomorrow."

Relieved to not be bunking with Brenda, a slight flush warmed her cheeks. "I thought we'd be–" She cocked her head to the trailer Brenda entered.

"Well, if you'd rather–" He pulled her chair close.

She shook her head and squeezed his hand as her chest tightened. Maybe they would be okay.

"And that's my cue to say good night." Lucas folded up his chair. "Need help with anything?"

"Nah, we're good," Nate said. "Sleep well, Dorkus." They high-fived each other in passing.

After staring at the fire, and yawning a few more times, Nate declared it was bedtime. He turned off the propane and tucked it beside the trailer. She folded up the chairs and blankets. They walked behind the trailer, stopping to grab their bags from his truck before moving two trailers away to Bill's.

He unlocked it and waved her in, using the flashlight on his phone to light the space. "There's no power to this trailer. No water either. You can clean up in our trailer in the morning."

"Bathroom?"

Nate walked her over to the pit's port-a-potty and when they finished, they sat huddled together on the edge of the wall.

"I'm really sorry for what happened."

He turned his body, draping a leg on either side of the wall, and cupped her face. "I don't want you to worry about it."

"But I can see it's upsetting you." She stroked his cheek as he closed his eyes.

"It is." His breathing was quick. "Because I failed." His head tipped down.

"How?"

"I promised to keep you safe and to protect you."

"You did. I'm still here, right?"

He nodded. "Yeah, but how do I get you home safely? How do I protect you from– You?"

A million dollar question if ever there was one. "I don't... I don't know." She leaned into him, relishing the warmth from his strong arms as they held her together. She had a feeling deep down she was going to self-destruct.

❤ Chapter Thirty-One ❤

The moment Aurora's eyes opened, she was searching for her purse. Thank god, it was within reach. Her body desperate as she dug, finding and popping a perc after a painful stretch screamed from her hip. It would only take a few minutes for relief. That fold-out table was no five-star hotel.

Alone in the trailer, Aurora dropped her jammies and dug out the fresh panties and bra from her bag. She'd just finished zipping her jeans when the trailer rocked and the door flung open. *Shit!* Instinctively, her arms covered her chest.

"Coffee's ready," Nate said, his voice flat.

She brushed the hair away from her eyes and looked up into his, hoping the strain from last night had disappeared. Although he seemed more relaxed, his eyes still held tension. "Hey, handsome."

He closed the distance between them in a heartbeat. "Mom's making breakfast right now, and the coffee's really good."

"Can I shower?"

He laughed his warm, endearing laugh that melted her heart. Maybe things *were* improving. "Not here. But I can wet you a washcloth for a sponge bath."

Little daggers flew in his direction. "No, thanks." Her arms fell to her side, and she batted her eyes. *Does he still want me?*

"As much as I like what you're wearing, you'll need to get dressed and I'll take you to the pit to clean up."

Well, there goes that. She pulled on a shirt, and a zip up jacket. "So what's the plan for today?"

"I need to tinker on the beast. When I drove her onto the track, I could feel her sticking."

The way he talked of his car as if it were a living, breathing entity amazed her. It didn't have the same effect on her. "What should I do then?"

"Make yourself comfortable? Maybe even learn about my car? It might make it less scary."

It didn't sound like a fun way to spend her time, but what else could she do. Essentially, she was trapped.

"Let's go eat before Mom sends out a search party." He loosely held her hand on the way over to the other trailer.

After eating and cleaning up, she and Nate wandered over to the pit, neither saying anything. The silence pained her, and made her heart ache. Worse was the distance between them. They walked hand in hand, but the intimacy lacked. Until she was back home safe and sound, the return trip hung between them. After tinkering on the beast, and getting in a few laps around the track, he seemed pleased with the fix and a small smile appeared briefly.

Desperate to talk to him, she begged Nate to join her for a walk. Somewhere private, away from his family and the pit. Sitting in the grandstand, her mind swirled. So many questions and zero answers. First at the top of the list, she needed to make sure they'd be okay. "Nate?" she asked, as his phone buzzed.

He held up a finger. "Hey… Great… I'm in the grandstand… Give me five." He turned to her. "Chris is here and I need to go talk to her."

"If this is about me, I should come."

He rose as he held her hand. "I want to see her alone."

"Seriously?" She sulked and sighed. "I hate everyone tip-toeing around me. Breakfast was uncomfortable at best, and now you're off to talk to Chris. About me. Yet it's my problem."

"We're trying to help you."

"So *include* me."

"I need to discuss–" His chin tucked into his chest. "How it's been affecting me."

"Nate," she said with panic in her voice, "talk to *me* about that. *I* want to know how this affects you, but you're shutting me out. Like Dad does. I'm not so delicate that I can't handle your emotions."

The chocolate brown eyes she loved to look at, closed to her pleading. "I won't be long." As he walked away, her hand fell onto her lap. Either he was excited to see his sister, or he was in a hurry to leave her, but no time was wasted putting more distance between them. He quickly disappeared from sight. Hurt and lonely, she texted Kaitlyn.

Aurora: *Something bad happened last night.*

Kaitlyn: *What?*

Aurora: *I came off the drug way too early and screamed myself into a blackout.*

Kaitlyn: *OMG. R U okay? Where R U?*

Aurora: *The track. I'm fine but I freaked the hell out of Nate. He's very distant.*

Kaitlyn: *Probably just worried sick.*

Aurora: *He is. About the ride home.*

Kaitlyn: *Oh. ☹ How will that work?*

Aurora: *Don't know. He went to talk to his shrink sister. Hopefully she'll have an idea.*

Kaitlyn: *Let me know if I can help.*

Aurora: *Thanks. <3 you.*

Kaitlyn: *U2.*

Pocketing her phone, she walked over to the pit alone. The pit hummed and roared as it came to life when the other drivers unloaded trailers, tires and toolboxes. She spotted a folded chair and parked herself by Nate's car.

It was lonely sitting there. No one looked familiar. At this point, she'd even settle on seeing Marissa Montgomery, at least she could get in a dig. But she didn't see her. After several minutes of wringing her hands and shifting uncomfortably in her seat, a meek smile crossed her face as Lucas approached.

"Where's Nate?"

"With your sister."

"Ah." He grabbed another chair. "You okay?"

She shrugged, but didn't make eye contact. "I'm worried about Nate."

"Well, he's really worried about *you*."

"The trip home—"

"He'll figure it out. If it's one thing Nate's great at, it's problem solving."

She hung her head and pulled on her sleeves until her hands disappeared inside. "I'm worried that my PTSD will drive us apart."

He tapped her foot with his own, and she looked at him. "It hasn't so far. If anything, I'd say it's brought you together."

"But—"

"You'll get through it. Intact."

"How can you be so sure?"

"Because Chris is here. She was at a convention, but ditched it when he begged her last night to come down and help." She blinked. "He loves you, and he desperately wants to help you. His faith in that is unshakeable."

It helped hearing that, and she melted into her chair. She hoped everything would work out with Chris' help. Shrinks can prescribe the best medicines.

"I know you're opposed to vehicles, but are you okay with tools?"

She crinkled her forehead. "Why?"

"Are you able to help me move the toolboxes and set up the area? Nate left it in a mess."

She laughed as she rose. "I think I can handle that."

After swearing the toolbox weighed more than she did, she rolled it into its spot. Thank god the blessed thing was on wheels. If it wasn't, her back would ache way more than the dull throb it had now. About to head to the trailer for relief, she spotted Nate marching across the track with a huge smile on his face.

He grabbed her, spun her around and kissed her hard on the lips. "We have a plan or two to get you home." True happiness replaced his tension-filled eyes.

"What? What's the plan?"

"It's so simple, I don't know why we never thought of it. Well, probably because it risky, but really, it's no different than those Isas you take. Which, by the way, Chris has never heard of." He raised an eyebrow.

"Really? Dad gets them from his doctor."

"Hmm, I doubt that–" His voice low. "Very much." Shaking his head, a wide and easy grin reappeared on his face. "Anyways, about the plan. We're going to give you sleeping pills. Knock you out the old-fashioned way."

She crossed her hands over her chest. "I thought you said your sister was new and would change things in the industry, and yet she's resorting to sleeping pills?" Part of her hoped she'd had something better than that.

"It sounds crazy, right? But it's just to get you home. The safest plan is to move you late tonight, then we won't need too much. You should be naturally tired."

"A we'll-move-the-body-after-midnight type of thing?" Unsure, she mulled the idea over in her head. She'd be dead weight, but should have no memory of the transport. Maybe it'd work, and at this point, she was willing to try anything. "Okay, let's do it."

♥ Chapter Thirty-Two ♥

Nate readied for his time trials. He tapped the toolbox where they'd locked up her purse. "Do you need anything?"

"I have them here." She patted her pocket. "I'll be fine. It's just you on the track for four laps. I was okay last time."

"Are you going to watch?"

She turned and saw the board behind her. "Nah. I can see your score from here."

He laughed. "My time, not my score."

So much to learn. She vowed to pick up a few books on Monday.

Preparations complete, she gave him a kiss before he slid into the car. "I'll be right back."

She stared at the board after he left. His car number flashed, and his car thundered onto the track. First lap– 15.9. Her eyes bugged out. She knew enough to know that wasn't very fast. Second lap– 16.3. What the hell was going on? Third lap– 16.2. Terrible. The car screamed as he pulled it back into the pit.

Angry, he exited the car rather harshly, dropping his helmet onto his seat. "Something's wrong," he said to Lucas. "Now, it's too tight."

"Rear springs or sway bar?"

"We'll check both." He rolled the toolbox closer to the car. "Let's hoist her up."

"Hey, Nate." A sultry voice from behind her caused her head to whip back. *Marissa Montgomery.* "What's up with fifteen?"

"Nothing," he said as he turned from her.

"Doesn't look like nothing." Her hand touched his shoulder. "You don't crawl all over her for nothing. Let me help."

Aurora stood there dumbfounded. Was Marissa trying to put the moves on her boyfriend right in front of her? *Bold little bitch.* A smile stretched across her face though as Nate pushed her hand away.

"Seriously. It's under control, Marissa."

Her face remained determined. "Well, if you need me or my knowledge, I'm over there."

A forced grin cut across his face. "I'm aware of where you are. I'll call if I need your help." Nate slammed the toolbox drawer shut as she strutted away.

Aurora stepped closer to him. "You're a lot nicer than I would've been."

"Yeah, well, I have to be." He fumed in Marissa's direction. "Her father supplies everyone with their tires at cost plus ten. I can't afford to pay full price."

"Well, she doesn't have to be so obvious about it." She searched for Marissa as she wanted to give her the finger, but in the end was glad she didn't. Nate didn't need to deal with her revenge, he was having enough problems as it was.

As Nate and Lucas tinkered with the beast, she tested out her power of invisibility, blending into the background. It was almost five o'clock when the heats were ready to start. How could she spend so much time doing nothing? The next time she comes, she'd have to bring a book. "Good luck," she told Nate as he washed his hands with an orange wipe.

"I wish I had time to test her out before the heat. I hope she handles better." The fire suit rolled over his tight body. "Are you going to watch me?"

"Oh I've been watching you all afternoon. Bending, squatting."

"I mean–"

She kissed him. The first chance she had in a while. "Of course, I'll watch."

"Need anything?"

Double-checking her pocket, she shook her head. "I'll try without. I've been good so far, right?" Hell, she hadn't even taken a perc since the morning.

"Yes, you have." He started walking away but stopped, turning to face her. "I'll be right back."

"I'll be here. Or up there." She pointed to the spotters' cage.

Standing on the raised platform, Lucas joined her as the stock cars readied. Due to Nate's despicable times, he was at the back of the pack, shaking and shimming the car. The flag dropped and Aurora gripped the railing, holding her breath as they started their ten lap heat.

"Something still ain't right," Lucas said beside her after the cars lapped twice. "He shouldn't be pulling so far to the outside on the turns like that."

"Does that mean he could... hit the wall?" Fear gripped her heart.

Lucas mulled it over. "Maybe, but not likely. Nate should be able to correct out of the turns before that point."

"You don't sound confident."

Lucas ignored her, focusing his attention on Nate's car.

"Oh, please, let him maintain control of it," she whispered.

Nate struggled to keep the pace, and by the seventh lap, he pitted the car.

"Oh dear," Lucas said and scaled the ladder.

Climbing down, she met Nate at his spot. And he looked pissed as he exited. "Okay, now it's way too loose. Stupid gremlins." Aurora didn't know what that meant, but it didn't take too long for the car to be jacked up again, and the hood lifted.

Brenda walked over, appraising the car. "What's going on?"

"Loose in the corners."

Nate, Lucas and Brenda disappeared into a discussion of possible solutions. Hands waved all over the place and she became lost in words like chassis, steering angles, and front and rear grips. She watched in amazement as Brenda pulled herself under the engine and called out for a variety of tools. Not knowing the difference between a socket wrench and pliers, she felt pretty useless. A couple other drivers also appeared after the heat to help out as well.

"It's so great how you all work together. Even the other drivers helped you," she told Nate as he wiped his hands clean after fixing what she hoped was the issue.

"Of course we help each other. We need someone to race against." He winked. "But the guys that helped out are more engine guys, so they understand a little more than I do."

"I can't believe your mom just slid under the car."

"She's been working on cars since she was a kid. Helped Granddad all the time."

She didn't care if he brushed it off, she still thought it was pretty fucking cool of Brenda.

Aurora chose sit out the next heat staying in the chair. The next heat wasn't any better, or so she heard. Although Nate finished the heat, in sixth, the car started making an awful grinding noise upon return to its spot. Back up on the jack, and everyone pitched in.

Feeling useless and with intermission upon them, Aurora headed over to the main concession and grabbed food for everyone. She pulled a few chairs together and placed warm food at each spot. Slowly Brenda, Lucas and Nate crawled out from inside or under the vehicle to nosh. Then she passed around the pastries she brought, revelling in the delicious sounds as they enjoyed her food.

"With any luck, the gremlins are out," Brenda told her as they gathered up the garbage. "But it's not like he can take it for a test drive or anything to verify."

"Guess I'll found out in the feature." He stood and stretched, revealing gorgeous taunt abs she desperately wanted *and needed* to touch. "Hey, Buddy," he said to Lucas, "time for you to get ready." Nate turned back to her, and held her arm rests as he lowered. "Come watch him race with me." His voice was deep.

She made eye contact with Brenda, who appeared disinterested. It was either hang out with her or watch Lucas race and neither sounded particularly fun. She liked Lucas, and the thought of him racing gave her goosebumps. Holding Nate's hand, she chose him.

There were two others in the cage when Nate and Aurora arrived. "I'll stand behind you," Nate said, as he secured them a corner.

"I'd like that," she smirked as his body pressed into her. His arms graced her sides as he held the railing. Trapped, but totally okay with it.

The cars filed out, with Lucas's #67 in the middle. She counted twelve cars. "There's so many tonight."

"Yeah, it's a great turnout."

The flag guy waved the green flag, and they sped off. Lucas did a great job of passing two cars in his first lap, and three more in the second.

"You're trembling," Nate whispered in her ear.

"Sorry."

He turned her around, and faced her. "You're pale too."

"I'm nervous."

A sexy little smile leaked its way onto his face. "You got a thing for my little brother?"

"Yeah," she said, "I don't want him to get hurt." Her back against the railing, she took a quick breath.

He kissed her forehead before he enveloped her in a tight embrace. "You're too sweet."

Content to be safe in his arms, she didn't move. Didn't even open her eyes. Nate watched, and she supported him in it because they were together. It was perfect. They both cheered when Lucas came in second.

"Now it's my turn." Nate rolled on his fire suit and zipped it up as he stood beside his car.

She looked at the beautiful white beast, with the orange and yellow stripes, and hoped that whatever gremlins were there, had now left. Still quivering, she patted her pocket, double-checking her meds were handy.

"It's okay, take one," Nate said.

Somehow, shaking as much as she was, she managed to get a pill under her tongue.

"I'll be right back."

"You promise?"

"Always."

She gave him a good luck kiss before he slipped into the seat. Harnessed in, Lucas passed him his helmet, then the steering wheel. When Nate waved that was her cue to let him get into the zone he needed.

Lucas walked with her over to the cage. "The first laps will tell us if we solved the problem or not."

Her hands shook against the cool metal bar and her heart pounded loudly in her chest. *Come on, Xanax, do your job. Work faster.*

"You okay?" Lucas asked.

"Just nerves." She swallowed hard and wiped her brow. She didn't want to be up here, and stole a quick glance to the pit's office. It wasn't far away. Checking her band, she still had instant access if she needed it.

"Do you want the headphones?"

She was about to say no until an asshole in a supped-up car drove into the pit. Before he shut it off, he gave it a good rev which nearly caused her to soil her pants. Unable to speak after that, she nodded. And then regretted it because she was alone again. Even the Xanax left her. Dejected, she leaned against the metal railing as the super stocks rolled out.

Nate drove his vehicle hard from side to side, probably testing it out or getting his wheels warm, she couldn't remember why. However, she could hear the scream from his engine as he revved it while in low gear.

Lucas reappeared with the headphones, and she looped them over the bar. For later. "Thanks."

The cars moved around the track, some racing ahead, others falling back.

"They're getting into order," Lucas said.

Nate unfortunately, was at the back. The starting order fixed, and the green flag dropped to the thunderous roar of the nine cars. Tonight's feature was thirty-five laps– long enough to give her heart a workout of cardio proportions, if the fucking Xanax didn't kick in quick.

"I think we fixed it," Lucas said after the first dozen corners. "He's managing the turns okay."

Nate had even managed to catch and pass a few of his opponents. She glanced at the board. He was in fifth and closing in rapidly on fourth place.

Her heart raced along, and her breathing quickened. Watching him take the corners two wide was nauseating.

"Do they have sun visors?" she asked. The sun, low in the sky, appeared to blind the drivers out of turn three and four. As she followed the cars around into turns one and two, she shielded her own eyes.

"No." His eyes stayed trained on the cars. "But they know the track well and their spotters radio them constantly as to the location of the other cars."

"Should he be slowing down that much?" Lucas shook his head. "What's going on?" Her voice pitched and her knuckles almost broke skin.

"I don't know," he said and leaned over the cage as if searching for someone.

Coming into corner three, Nate slowed considerably. The scream from his engine was easily heard from where she stood. The hairs stood up on the back of her neck. Exiting corner three, he gained some speed, but in doing so, started fishtailing as he entered corner four. His car spun out in the middle of the turn to face oncoming traffic and stopped. Dead.

Time ceased to exist and everything moved in slow-motion. Whipping her head, she checked the flags. The yellow had just waved. A caution to the other drivers. Her full attention back on Nate, she caught the glimmer of a red car–the leader, #33–as he left corner three still at full speed.

Aurora screamed at the top of her lungs. The caution flag was out. Either #33 didn't hear his spotter over the radio or didn't see the flag or the setting sun was the problem. Whatever his reason, he didn't slow down. He slammed head first into Nate's car at top speed.

The crunching sound of the cars silenced the grandstand and stopped her heart. Nate's car smashed into the outside wall, pieces of fibreglass flying everywhere. She couldn't blink. Smoke and steam escaped between the two crushed cars and fluids poured out onto the track, dark streaks like scratches against the pavement.

"NATE! NO!!" Aurora screamed and nearly launched herself off the cage.

Lucas grabbed her by the arms. "He'll be okay. Shit like this happens," Lucas said although his voice betrayed that sentiment.

"NO!! NO!!!" Aurora said over and over again, fighting against Lucas' hold. She couldn't breathe anymore. Her legs gave out and the metal bottom of the cage reached up to catch her.

A few people from the pits ran out to help, and the #33 driver pulled himself out of his car to the clapping of the audience.

Why isn't Nate getting out?

The safety truck sped over and parked above the wreckage, and a tow truck drove out of the pit. Her stomach soured and a bad feeling shuddered violently through her body.

"Oh my god, Nate," she whimpered as Lucas dropped beside her. She buried into him, curling herself into a tight ball. "It can't happen, not again," she said, tears trailing down her face. "I can't do this. I can't."

Lucas' hand ran down her back. He wasn't saying anything which made her panic more.

"No," she repeated over and over, covering her ears as if that would help. In her mind, the sounds of the crash replayed, the staccato of the popping fibreglass bumpers, the crunching of the car's metal cage banging into each other, the sound of her heart beat at once racing and then coming to a full stop in a millisecond. A feeling of doom washed over her and she couldn't hold back anymore. Turning her head, she threw up into the corner.

❤ Chapter Thirty-Three ❤

"He's getting out," Lucas said, and she whipped her tear-stained face around to see for herself.

Nate sat propped up on the window ledge for a breath before waving to the crowd. Slowly he turned his head in her direction and gave a thumbs up sign. Stepping out onto the track, he walked around the wreckage with a slight limp as he headed towards the pit.

"He's okay," Lucas said full of relief. And in that moment, she hated him for pretending everything was okay when he himself had worried.

As the tears rolled down her face like a flash flood, she saw he was right. Nate was walking away from the head-on collision–literally–with nothing more than a limp. No broken bones, no gashes, no serious injury.

She jumped off the cage and ran across the pit to meet him, bulldozing him over when she reached him.

"Hey," he said, unhooking his helmet from the device on his shoulders as he pulled it off. "Hey, I'm okay." He wiped away a trail of her tears with a swipe of his finger.

"I was... so scared..." she said breathlessly.

"I can see that."

Lucas appeared from behind and took the helmet from Nate. "Not a scratch on it."

"No. I saw Dean coming, and I threw my hands back."

"You saw him coming?" Her head felt woozy as her legs gave out. Thank god she was in his arms as he caught her on the way to meet the ground.

"Yeah. But the car wouldn't move. There was an issue with the–" He looked at her and back to Lucas who seemed eager for more details. "Talk to Mom. I was chatting with her on the radio."

"I figured. Oh, watch out for her, she's puked already," he said and walked away.

Still terrified at what she witnessed, she shook and struggled to breathe.

Nate turned to her. "I'm okay. Promise."

The tears had yet to stop flowing. Her heart beat wickedly fast, and her breathing put her in danger of hyperventilating. "I... I..."

He escorted her to a chair. "Breathe." His fingers searched her pockets, pulling out the pill box. "Which one?"

Her hands shook she couldn't pick up a pill, so he helped her. They sat in silence for a few minutes until her breathing was back under control.

"I was chatting with mom and Terry, my spotter. I was communicating with them."

"Yeah, well, no one was communicating with me." She wanted to be angry, but couldn't find the energy.

"But Lucas was with you."

"He wasn't overly confident himself."

"Yeah, he tends to feed off of other's emotions. Remind me to punch him later for that." Nate kissed her quivering hand. "But I swear I'm okay. The crash was obviously more terrifying for you to watch than it was for me to be in. We're protected and safe." He removed his fire suit and examined his knee. "Ah, that'll bruise," he said to himself as he gave his left knee a rub. "I banged it pretty hard, but other than that–" He extended his arms out and spun. "All good."

She slumped into the seat, and pulled her legs up. "I can't do it, Nate."

Throwing his suit over the toolbox, he raised an eyebrow. "Can't do what?"

"I can't watch this anymore." He pulled a chair as close to her as possible. "Last time I was here, you got clipped. This time you were in a head-on collision." Her breath caught as she saw the impact play again in her mind. She rested her cheek on her knees and stared hard at him, watching his expression. "I can't. I can't watch you and wonder if you're going to die when you're out here having fun." She air-quoted 'having fun' to get her point across. "It's dangerous."

"I can assure you *that*," he pointed to his incoming wrecked car, "is as bad as it gets. And look what happened. I. Walked. Away. Like I'm supposed to." She said nothing. "We have a saying around here when it comes to our cars. Money for safety first and foremost, then money to make it faster and stronger. Safety is not something taken lightly in these parts."

"But it's so dangerous."

"And that's part of the appeal." He rubbed her legs as if that would make it all better. But the truth was, she was beyond scared. What if he was seriously hurt? Or worse, what if she lost him? That thought alone scared the hell out of her.

The tow truck parked in front of his spot as Brenda and Lucas appeared. "Out with some gremlins, in with new ones and then Dean plows into you," Brenda said, laughing while surveying the damage. "But it could be worse."

Yeah, he could've died! She looked at Nate who continued to stare at her.

"I need to attend to this, sorry, he should lower it right on the trailer." A quick peck on the cheek before he ran over to the tow truck driver.

Nodding, she turned away, unable to look at the car hanging in the air. Lost in her own thoughts, she wondered if her momma and sister had been harnessed, would they have survived with nothing more than a bruised knee. The thought caused another stream of tears. She missed them so much.

A tissue appeared in front of her eyes. A gift from Brenda. "Hey, honey, how you doing?"

"Not well." Nothing in her body felt right. Her chest hurt, her stomach rolled and her brain resembled a war zone.

"Bringing back a few repressed memories?"

She sniffed and wiped her nose. "Something like that." Brenda spoke so calm and collected, it was hard to make eye contact. "You're right, though. This isn't fixing me. Seeing this–" She pointed towards the car she refused to look at, "makes it worse. Reminds me of *how* I lost. And I don't want that to happen again. Not to him."

Brenda sighed. "I know Chris has some wild ideas, and Nate's willing to play along, but you need to do what's best for you."

"So, you're saying I should stop coming?" Deep down shame and anger settled in for a comfy little nap. A part of her enjoyed seeing Nate so deliciously happy, but another part–a bigger part–was scared shitless every time he slipped behind the wheel. She'd never be as relaxed as Brenda was.

"That's not at all what I'm saying, but if this is too much for you, *right now,* then maybe?" She shrugged, but never took her eyes off her. "I know Nate adores you, but it's not good for him to worry about how you'll react to everything. That whole screaming fit yesterday nearly caused him to drive into oncoming traffic. THAT was more dangerous than anything he's done on the track. At least he's protected out there."

Her whispered voice said, "I make it hard for him." Not a question, but a statement. And not loud enough for anyone to hear.

"When he's out here, in order to do his best, he needs full concentration. If you're fainting, or freaking out over every little thing, it affects him and his ability to do well." Brenda's face was tight with concern for her child. "He has a lot riding on this. He may say it's all fun and games, but the money he wins if he places first overall, will pay for university."

Completely understanding, Aurora nodded again and turned further into her chair, pulling her legs as close to her chest as she could manage.

"That being said, Honey, I like you. And I think you're good for Nate. But you're just not ready for Nate's lifestyle, and that's where the problem lies." She looked away. "'Scuse me, I need to talk to her." Brenda stood and walked over to a lady carrying a clipboard.

Sniffing again, she stole a glance around the pit. Once again she was alone, and she wanted to go home. Right fucking now. But Nate was with his car, as was Lucas, most likely. She texted Kaitlyn.

Aurora: *Can you pick me up?*

Kaitlyn: *Aren't you out at the track?*

Aurora: *Yes. I'll give you gas money. I can't be here anymore.*

Kaitlyn: *Did you have a fight?*

Aurora: *It's complicated. Please. You know I wouldn't ask if it wasn't a big deal.*

Kaitlyn: *Drop me a pin, and I'll be there ASAP.*

Now she needed to think through the impossible ride home. Nate had the other Isa, but she knew where he put it. It was in the pocket of his jeans. However, getting to it was a problem. She only had an hour to retrieve it and meet Kaitlyn at the front gate. How was she going to get through the entire ride though? Kaitlyn drove under the speed limit, or at least that's what she claimed. Forty-five minutes wasn't enough time. Hell, based on the last experience, even thirty minutes wasn't enough. What if she mixed the Isa with a couple Xanax? Could that work? Or would a perc or two be better? Or what about the Flexeril? It was a muscle relaxant. Perhaps a combo of Flexeril and a Xanax before the Isa? She had no idea, but one of those combos had to work. *Fuck!*

Nate, Lucas and Brenda returned to his area and closed up the toolbox after she grabbed her purse. Once the track officials and safety crew declared the track free of debris and fluids, the final race of the night continued. She zoned out from time to time, and glazed over the people who came to talk to Nate, never missing the peculiar looks on the stranger's faces when they glanced her way. *I'm the girlfriend that can't handle his lifestyle. I'm the one who screamed. And yep, I'm the one that puked on the platform. This is my worst fucking nightmare come to life and you can all fuck off for thinking I'm weak. You don't know shit.*

Thirty minutes after calling Kaitlyn, the feature was nearly over, but she only knew because she looked up to the board. Twelve laps remained for the night. Fuck! She just wanted to sneak over to the trailer, get her overnight bag, and be gone already. Time was tight. She looked over at Nate, who had his phone pressed into his ear. He looked at her once, his face distressed.

The last race ended, and the trophy presentation lasted forever. She stayed curled up in her chair, keeping her back to Nate. Still crying, but for different reasons now.

Nate stood over her, his head looking anywhere but at her. "When everyone's gone, we'll talk okay? Chris is coming back with the sleeping pills and we'll get you home."

"And then you'll leave me, and I'll wake up alone?"

His eyes narrowed, and a frown formed. "No, not at all." But he didn't reach for her.

An ache spread across her chest. "I need to go to the bathroom and then I'll hang out in the office. I don't want to be here when the fans come and ask about–"

On her way to the shack, she popped a Xanax and a Flexeril.

As the last car pulled into the pit, she darted across the south end of the track, grabbing her bag and the last pill from Nate's jeans. Across the pit on the other side of the track, the gate guard lowered the stairs. In minutes, the fans would be able to enter the pit. That was her chance to escape, and she snuck around the far end of the pit to the stairs. A quick check towards the pit where the guests milled, asking for autographs and admiring the cars. She popped the Isa, stepped through the gate, and as she passed the grandstands Kaitlyn texted. *I'm here.*

Focusing hard, she looked for Kaitlyn's car, feeling light headed and off balance.

Kaitlyn high-beamed her, and she staggered over. Taking a deep breath, she opened the car door and stared. She wasn't ready yet, but felt she was close. *Something* was working. "Thanks for picking me up."

"What's going on?"

She leaned in and said quickly, "Ask me later. I took a Flexeril and a Xanax about twenty minutes ago, and an Isa two minutes ago. It's all on my phone should you need the info. Drive as fast as you can and get me home." She looked at her best friend. "I apologize now for anything that may happen on the ride."

Kaitlyn's eyes bugged out.

Typing rapidly while the tears streamed, she sent a text to Nate. *Sorry, I had to go. Kaitlyn picked me up. This isn't working. It's too hard.*

She knew he wouldn't get the text until later, he'd be too busy talking with his fans. Time to test out the combo, so she put one foot on the floorboard. Aside from some minor nervousness, it was bearable. "Time to go," she said, falling in and the fringes of darkness wrapped around her.

♥ Chapter Thirty-Four ♥

"Stop fucking calling her," Kaitlyn's voice yelled. Aurora heard her clear as day and Kaitlyn wasn't even in the room. "I don't know what happened, but she wanted to come home immediately... If she wants to explain it to you, she will." Kaitlyn sounded somewhere between severely pissed off and borderline sympathetic. "Since I had nothing to compare it to, I don't know... Not what I expected, that's for fucking sure... That's a bad idea, Nate. Really bad... Oh yeah, well I fucking dare you..." The apartment quieted.

"Kait?" she yelled.

A head popped into the bedroom. "Oh good, you're awake." She didn't look as angry as she sounded as she walked over and turned on a lamp. "Your boyfriend won't stop calling."

"Kind of figured that'd happen." The clock on her bedside table flash two. "It's two a.m., right?"

"Yeah," she said as she sat on the bed and smoothed out the bedspread. "Want to tell me what happened?"

"Want to tell me what the ride home was like?"

"No." Kaitlyn avoided eye contact. "Is that how you are each time?"

"You're not giving me any info, how the hell am I supposed to know what I did?"

Kaitlyn grimaced and rubbed her eyes. "It doesn't matter. You're home now, and everything's worn off, right?"

Running a mental checklist of symptoms over her body, she said, "My head aches a little, and my heart's beating faster than normal, but–" She shrugged. "Tell me, Kait, what happened?" She cringed remembering what Nate told her of the trip there.

"Your basic drug-induced psychosis. I've never heard such gibberish in all my life. It was like watching you have an out-of-body experience. Seriously, Aurora, whatever the hell combo you took, it fucked you up."

"I'm sorry."

"I debated driving you straight to the hospital. Had you started frothing at the mouth–" Kaitlyn fiddled with a loose thread on the bed. "Your boyfriend phoned twenty minutes after we left, and called every five minutes after that. I finally answered a few minutes ago because I'm exhausted and I want some fucking sleep." Aurora opened the blanket, allowing Kaitlyn to slide under. "I left your phone and your bazillion messages out on the kitchen table." Her eyes were closing as she said, "I'm glad you're okay. You worried me."

"I love you, Kaitlyn. Thanks for taking care of me." Thankful for her friendship, she waited until Kaitlyn filled the room with her gentle snores before slipping off the bed. In the living room, she huddled on the couch under a blanket, and flipped through the multiple messages. One after another, the messages were one of three; *WTH happened? Where are you? Call me please.*

She couldn't call him though, the thought of hearing his irresistible voice made her legs quiver, and she needed to resist him. His mom didn't think she was good enough for him, and she was right– one-hundred percent correct. PTSD and racing were not a match made in heaven. More like a recipe for disaster. She was crazy to have ever thought it would work. There were too many barriers between them.

Stretching out on the couch, she stared at one message in particular, and read it over and over until her eyes were as heavy as lead weights. A final ping before sleep washed over her.

Please, Aurora. I love you.

She texted her father later that morning, pretending they were leaving the track. In keeping up with the charade, fifty minutes later, she called him. "Hey, Daddy."

"Princess." He sounded sleepy, although he should've been expecting her call. "You're home, good."

"Safe and sound."

"How'd the weekend go?"

"Oh good, it was lots of fun." She rolled her eyes.

"No strange reaction to the pills?"

"No, I didn't seem to come out of the haze any earlier than before and Nate didn't say anything about this morning's trip." Which was true, but only because he wasn't around and there was no morning trip. Her eyes roved from the patio to Kaitlyn, who leaned against the wall, her arms crossed tightly over her body.

"It was so strange to hear that you had on Friday." She said nothing, meeting Kaitlyn's glare head on. "Anyways, I can tell it's still in your system as you're not paying attention."

"Sorry, Daddy."

"It's okay, Princess. I'll be down Tuesday and Wednesday for a few meetings, so I'll see you Tuesday night?"

"See you Tuesday." She hung up and said to Kaitlyn, "What?"

"You're a filthy liar."

"There were no lies." She nervously tightened her grip around the phone. "Just the absence of the complete story."

"You didn't tell him you left Nate at the track and that I drove you home, did you?"

She shook her head. "It's too complicated and would only lead to more questions I'd rather not answer right now."

Kaitlyn crossed the room in a hurry and she yanked her legs out of the way before Kaitlyn dropped on them. "Want to tell me what happened between you and Nate?"

"No."

"Why? Whatever it was, it was important enough for you to ask me to pick you up and ingest some sick combo of drugs to get you home."

A lump of self-pity lodged in her throat and she tugged her sleeves down. "I'm not good enough for him," she said, tears building and blurring her vision as her heart ached.

"He said that?" Kaitlyn sat up straight, her tone filled with anger.

"No, but his mom did."

"What a bitch."

"But she's right, Kait, because Nate's lifestyle is not conducive to mine. He LOVES the thrill of being behind the wheel, where it terrifies me to the core." She hung her head. "So Friday I came out of it early, right, and screamed myself into a blackout. Well, yesterday Nate was in a head-on crash– which I watched happen, by the way."

Kaitlyn's face moulded from anger to horror to sadness. "That had to have been hell."

"Yeah it was. He walked away from it, like I mean he really walked away from it, just a bruised knee. But still. It freaked me out. And his mom said that was a distraction to him. I was distracting Nate because now he spends his time thinking of me instead of preparing for his races."

"So what? You're his girlfriend. He can think about you if he wants."

"Yeah, maybe. But I'm not sure."

Kaitlyn turned to face her and pulled the blanket out of her hands. "Of what?"

"We're so different. How can I be a part of his life when it scares me so much?"

She huffed. "I wish I had answers for you."

"Seeing him in that crash… it was my nightmare– the live version."

"Oh my. I'm truly sorry."

"And he didn't get it. Said it was fine and the worst it would ever be. Yeah, he survived because of all the safety gear and shit. What if? What if Momma and Carmen had that type of protection, would they have lived?" Kaitlyn's eyes saddened, and she shrugged, but never answered. "I'll never know and the bastard who killed them gets to live his life."

"Well, not really. He's in jail."

"Yeah, but he's alive. He breathes. Eventually he'll get out and have a life, but not Momma or Carmen."

"He killed three people in that crash, I hardly think he'll ever be a free man."

"Well, we'll find out soon enough. His court date got changed. He goes Wednesday."

"I thought your dad didn't talk about it."

"He doesn't. Matthew texted me." She flipped to the message.

Thomas Anderson's court date was changed. He'll see a judge and get his just rewards. Wednesday morning @ 10:15 a.m. I'm flying up to give my Victim Impact Statement. Are you coming, or is a lawyer reading yours?

Kaitlyn leaned her head back. "Does your dad know?"

She shrugged. "Not to me. But he said he's here for meetings Tuesday and Wednesday. I'll bring it up."

"You'd better." Kaitlyn looked at her phone again. "What's a Victim Impact Statement?"

"Fuck if I know."

"Well, the scumbag thinks you have one." Opening Safari, Kaitlyn typed and scrolled, her eyes getting bigger the longer she read. "You need to talk to your dad. He's been keeping shit from you."

"What?"

"Look." She pointed to the article on the phone. "A Victim Impact Statement is a chance for you to voice what you lost in the accident and how it affected your life. It could make the difference on his sentencing."

"Why would he not tell me?" Aurora rubbed her face and pushed on her temples. "What am I going to do?"

Kaitlyn pulled her close, her hands running up and down her spine. "I really wish I had answers for you. But I'm drawing a blank."

Normally a back rub would soothe her, but today it rubbed her the wrong way. "Stop, please." She shook her head.

"Why don't you go take a shower, and I'll make you something to eat and get you a tea or something. My mom says that's supposed to help."

A long, hot shower and a warm cup of coffee did little to soothe her mind. However, the couple of Xanax did. At least it kept the swirling thoughts of Matthew, the impact statement, Brenda, and the mysterious Isas to a minimum. It did nothing though to quell her heartache over Nate, knowing it was in both of their best interests to let go. Then he wouldn't need to worry about her reactions and she'd never worry that he could die in front of her eyes.

Kaitlyn passed her the remote. "Movie?"

She nodded and flipped through the TV channels, stumbling across one of her favourite movies. Hopped up on pills that relaxed her emotional state, but needing to expel the hurt and sorrow she felt, she hoped watching it would bring on the ugly cry.

And it did. By the end of the movie, she wasn't crying over Hazel's loss, she was bawling over her own.

♥ Chapter Thirty-Five ♥

A loud bang on the door woke Aurora. "What the hell?" *Where's Kaitlyn?* She looked around the apartment and spotted the note on the table. *Needed to run home for a bit. Call me when you wake up.* Another bang came from the door, this one more insistent. The clock on her phone said it was a few minutes after noon.

"Aurora, please, open the door and talk to me."

How did he get in?

Nate's voiced thundered through the door. "I'm not leaving until you open the door. I have nowhere I need to be and can stay all day long if necessary."

Tenderly, she touched her eyes, wondering if they looked as bad as they felt. And they felt puffy and sore. Dragging herself over to the door, she pulled it open. "There, I opened it, now please leave." There was no fight left in her, the heartache destroyed everything.

"Please, Aurora. Talk to me." His face twisted as he spoke. "You're not answering your phone, you're not returning my texts–" His voice cracked.

"Please, go away." Her hand shook on the doorknob. "It's... It's... It's not going..."

"NO," he said, his voice just shy of shouting. "You owe me an explanation and I'm not leaving until I get one."

She owed him one, right? It was the least she could do. *Let's get this over with.* She opened it and stared. Nate stood there with a forlorn expression, looking wrecked as if he hadn't slept in days. "Then stay, whatever." Resigned, she walked back over to the couch, huddling under the blanket her momma made for her sixteenth birthday.

It took a minute, but finally Nate closed the door and walked over to her. "What the hell happened last night?" His voice changed from an upset curious tone to one laced with sympathy. "I get you were spooked by my accident, but it was more than that. You tell me you're going to the office, and then I go to find you and it was like you'd vanished. Poof." He snapped his fingers. "I get my phone to call you and there's a message telling me you're sorry. What the hell, Aurora?"

Wanting to speak, but unable to think of a proper answer, she remained silent.

Brow furrowed, eyes narrowed and his lips drawn tightly. However, he carried on, not giving her a chance to answer. "Then I call and call you, getting your voicemail. Finally, your friend answers but tells me nothing. How the hell did she get you home in time?"

She closed her eyes. It was hard to face him and see him hurting. "My friends Xanax and Flexeril. And the Isa."

He slumped into a nearby chair and ran his fingers through his hair. As he sat up, he said, "Well that explains why she sounded like the ride home was hell." A minute passed.

A pained voice she didn't recognise spoke, "It's over, Nate. It's best for everyone." A loud sigh escaped her lips.

He crawled on his knees and sat in front of her. "Is it really?" Something tugged around her neck and her eyes watched as his sparkled for the briefest of moments. "You're still wearing the necklace." He fingered the silver pendant. "Please, Aurora. Please tell me what happened."

Her heart pulsed beneath his fingers as he lay the pendant back on her skin. "The accident, Nate."

"But I'm fine."

"You don't get it, and that's okay."

"What don't I get? Please, tell me. I'm desperately trying to understand."

She sat up straighter, tugged down her sleeves and folded her hands in her lap. "I don't need the constant reminder of *how* my momma and sister died. I see it every damn day in here," she pointed to her head.

"Every fucking day I live with the nightmare of how they died." Her eyes rolled skyward.

Nate nodded, and reached for her arm. "That I get."

Why does his touch feel so good? She closed her eyes again and sighed as the images played over in her mind. "Seeing you in that crash, well, for a moment, I thought I'd lost you." Her eyes roved over his face. She gripped her chest tight, trying to hold herself together. The air was frozen in her lungs and she couldn't breathe. A tear fell. "I can't watch you die." Her voice resembled a whisper as her chin tucked into her chest.

"Aurora," he said softly, holding her hands against his chest. "I'm not going to die."

"Plus, I'm a huge distraction to you."

"I promise, you're not a distraction."

Her head tipped up with the tug of his finger, but she kept her eyes closed. "If I'm not there, you're able to concentrate on the race ahead instead of worrying about me and how I'll react to any little situation." A breath forced its way out.

"Sure, I'm going to worry, but only because I love you. I'd worry just the same if you weren't there. Maybe even more." He stroked her cheek, wiping away the stream of tears.

"How?" Her eyes opened, and she stared at him. His brow tight, and his expression grim. He looked so hot, which only made it harder to be strong. She knew this wasn't going to work. Why did he have to be so damn adorable?

"Well, I wouldn't be able to prove to you that I'm okay immediately after, right? When you're not there, I wonder what you're doing, if you'd be proud of me if I won. Trust me, when you're not there, my thoughts are still with you. But I've told you that." He placed her hand over his beating heart and pressed it against it. His heart raced. "You're always here."

"But your mom said—"

He pulled back. "What? Wait. What did mom say to you?"

Brenda's words played over and over in her head. "She was worried because of the trip there, and how hard I made it on you, and how that wasn't fair to you. And how right now isn't the best time for us to be together."

She saw the tongue stud as his mouth fell open. Any other day it'd turn her on, but her heart wasn't there today. "Wait? She what? Yes, the trip down was hell, and I won't downplay that. Your screaming was... umm... well, anyways, we handled it. You and I–" He pointed to her and back to him. "We made it through. Together." He huffed and shifted on his knees. "What the hell does she mean by it not being the best time for us to be together?" He ran his hands through his brown hair and judging by the force of it, removed a few strands too.

"She thinks it's too much all around, and I agree with her. You need to focus. This'll help pay for university."

His eyes enlarged and his tone changed to shock. "You agree with her?"

"Nate, your hobby doesn't mesh with my fear. They're polar opposites. I don't know how to make it work."

"Let's leave my mom out of this equation, since she doesn't belong in it the first place, what do you mean you don't know how to make this work? We *have* been making it work." The heat on her knee from his hand soothed her rattled soul. "Yes, there have been hiccups, some unexpected surprises along the way, but we've made it through. You're so much further ahead than where you were when we first met. You couldn't even touch a car. And now? You just spent a weekend at the track *surrounded* by cars." He stroked her hair as a proud grin tugged at the corners of his mouth. "I've given my heart to you. You can't walk away with it. Please tell me we're not over? Please tell me *this* we can make it through." His dark brown eyes held more than the fear in his voice, they held sorrow and forgiveness. "We'll find a way to make it work. I'll talk to my sister, and you should too." He cupped her chin as his own quivered. "Please don't give up on me."

Shaking as she rose, the tears fell hard and fast. "I'm sorry," she breathed, and wiped her eyes. "As long as you're racing, I can't be with you. And I don't want you giving up your love, so I need you to give up on me." One step in front of the other, she made it to the door and pulled it open. "I'm sorry."

A sniffle came from behind her, and the footsteps approached. She slammed her eyes shut as he whispered, "Aurora, *you* are my love."

She sighed. "I won't be anymore." Her voice softened. "I can't be." *He needs to leave me, needs to understand that I'm not the one for him. And only one thing would hit him where it hurts.* "I slept with someone else." His gasp was soul-crushing, and it stung to hear his pain. But it was what she wanted, right? To push him away, and give him another reason why they weren't meant to be together.

His breath caught, and a moment later his voice shook and cracked as he asked, "Who?"

With her heart beating in her throat, she couldn't breathe. Eyes firmly closed, she shook her head as the tears ran. "It doesn't matter."

"The hell it doesn't." A hurtful moan. "Who?"

He's not leaving. "Yours, Nate, he may have been in my body–"

Another painful gasp from him cut her off. "When?"

On the cusp of a full out sob, she whispered, "The weekend before your birthday." She wasn't proud of it, even though she'd thought of him. Still... she'd been with another guy. Sometimes there are moments in life you wish you could take back, and sleeping with Matthew ranked in the number two position.

Unsure why she needed to see the destruction, she turned to face him and instantly regretted it. His face was flushed, and his eyes were glassy. Those five words didn't waste time destroying him. Maybe now he'd leave, and she'd never have to worry about coming between him and his love of racing.

Her head fell, but her hand remained on the door knob. As he shuffled out, she heard his ragged breathing which further broke her heart. With a click of the lock, she sobbed as she slid to the floor.

♥ Chapter Thirty-Six ♥

Tuesday afternoon a key twisted in the apartment door. "Hello?" the voice called out, as bags dropped to the floor.

"Hey, Daddy," Aurora said with no emotion in her voice. She hadn't said much over the last forty-eight hours, hadn't eaten much and hadn't even touched the percs that called out to her. She told herself there was no pain to feel because she was dead inside. Barely breathing, she resumed staring at the blank screen.

Kaitlyn rose from beside her to greet Cole.

"Kaitlyn, how nice to see you," her father said but looked at Aurora. "What's a matter, Princess, not feeling well?"

"Something like that," Kaitlyn muttered.

He stepped around Kaitlyn and blocked the view of the silent TV. "What's wrong?"

As if he were a ghost, she looked right through him. "I don't want to talk about it."

Kaitlyn stepped closer. "She's having a rough time, Cole."

"Obviously." His eyes darted back and forth between her and Kaitlyn. "Why?"

Kaitlyn's whisper was loud enough to hear. "Just be there for her. Don't push her though." Kaitlyn walked back to her. "I'm heading out for a while to give you some time alone. Call me when you want me to come back." A soft kiss fell upon her cheek as she rubbed her arm.

He sat on the floor in front of the couch. "You look terrible." Delicately, he picked up her arm and felt her pulse. "Wow, your heart's racing and you've got goosebumps. Are you cold?"

"Freezing," she said, adjusting the blanket.

He sighed. "If you've got a tummy issue, I'm not good at dealing with that."

You're not good at dealing with anything, but that's neither here nor there, right now. Instead of speaking her mind, she said, "It's not a flu, Daddy."

"Okay," he said, relaxing his shoulders. "That's a relief. Your mother was always the one that helped with that. Always had a magical healing touch. You were never sick for long."

She didn't want to hear about her momma right now, especially when she wanted her by her side to hold her and help her and soothe her heartache. "Shut up please, Daddy."

"What?" He snapped his head to her. "The last few times here you beg me to talk about her, and now when I do you tell me to shut up?"

Her breath stumbled on its way out. "I need her, right now, Daddy. And you talking about her only adds to the hurt I'm feeling."

"Aw, shit, something happen between you and Nate?" A fresh wave of tears ran down over her nose, hitting the couch below. "Aw, Princess. I thought you were falling in love?" His voice softened.

She sniffed. "Nate was in–" The image of his car slamming into the wall projected to the front of her mind, causing her voice to shake. "A head-on collision."

Blanching, he swallowed. "Shit. Did he–"

"No, he didn't die. It was at the track." She pulled her legs up to her chest, her arms holding them in place. "But I can't do it, Daddy. I can't be with him anymore. His mom's right, it's too hard on us both when I'm there."

"Back the truck up. What does this have to do with his mom?"

She relayed the conversation to him, ending with, "She said I'm not ready for Nate's lifestyle and that's a problem."

"Yet, he still brought you home? Did you two not discuss this before you left? Or once you got home?"

Whoops. "Well, actually, Kait brought me home."

"How? How *exactly* did she bring you home?" With his eyes growing large, he looked poised to freak out.

As she rested her chin on her knees, she took a deep breath. "The Isa plus a Flexeril and a Xanax."

"Oh dear God." Cole paled further before her eyes.

She swallowed back the bitter taste building in her mouth. "Speaking of Isas, where do you get them? Chris, Nate's shrink sister, said she's never heard of them."

"I get them from my doctor." His eyes failed to meet hers.

"Dr. Who?"

"Does it matter? I get them for you when you need them." He stood and started walking away.

"Stop. Right. Now." Finding strength, she stood. "Tell me the truth."

He turned, anger rolling off him in waves. "Right. Like I owe you any form of the truth. Have you been entirely honest with me?" he yelled.

"No," she said, pained to have the truth thrown back at her.

"So stop prying into my life."

"Prying? I'm not prying, I'm asking a goddamn question." She stomped her foot. "I talked to Chris yesterday, and it came up in conversation. Again. She thinks they're actual Rohypnols, Daddy. A date-rape drug. You don't get *those* from a doctor." Her father glanced around, and didn't answer. "You've been giving me street drugs? How could you? I'm your daughter." Her hands flew wildly through the air, missing the nearby kitchen chair.

"They're safe in small quantities."

"What?" Her eyes bugged out. "Listen to you. You gave me– YOUR DAUGHTER–a street drug that has no regulations. What the hell?"

"Now you just stop!" He held up his hand. "I bought them from the best supplier, and kept them under lock and key. You didn't get them willy-nilly whenever you felt you needed it, they were dispensed under care." A frown crossed his stern face as he pointed a finger at her. "You're the one mixing drugs, not me. You're the reckless one here, so stop losing your shit on me, Princess. I gave you the Isas to help you." Fatherly concern replaced his anger as he lowered his head.

"Right. Like by helping me, you kept me from learning about Thomas Anderson's trial?"

His head snapped up. "How do you know about that?"

"Does it matter?" She threw his own words back at him. "Were you ever going to mention the Victim Impact Statement? Do we even have a lawyer?"

"Of course we do, and I've paid quite handsomely for him."

Defeated, she sat beside him. "Why didn't you tell me?" Her tone softened as her energy level depleted and the need to sit overwhelmed her.

"I didn't need you flying off the handle. You're a little uncontrollable when you lose it."

Seeing an image of Nate's face as he told her about her trying to open the truck door flashed. She shivered knowing he was right. "But that doesn't excuse you from telling me. If anything, I can tell them how my life has changed. The medications I'm on, the fears I have, what holds me back. I'm a victim in this. I was there." She crossed her arms over her chest, fearing her heart had more cracks in it than a sidewalk, and she feared all her heartache would eventually kill her.

"I know, Princess."

"Can I still write the statement? I assume you're going tomorrow."

"Yes, I am. And no you can't." He scratched his nose and shrugged. "Everything had to be given to the lawyer before his court date last week. Seriously, how did you hear about this?"

Matthew James, but I won't get into that with you. I'd rather never have to think of him again. She shook her head. "It doesn't matter anymore." Grabbing her laptop, she opened her word processor. "So, can I still write it? I swear it won't take me long."

A hand clasped her shoulder. "Aurora, it's over. Thomas Anderson will be going to jail for a long time. Your letter won't change that." After glancing at his watch, he said, "I have to go. I have a meeting in twenty minutes. I didn't think you'd be here when I dropped my stuff off." His eyes narrowed. "By the way, why aren't you at work?"

"Because Nate works there too, and right now, it hurts too much to see him. I feel sick to my stomach just thinking of that look on his face." A shiver ran through her.

He studied her to the point it made her uncomfortable. A weak mumble escaped his lips as he once again checked her pulse. One eye squinted as the other scanned the area. "When was the last time you took *any* drugs?" His lips moved, but no words escaped.

Any drugs? It was hard to remember. Surely she had something yesterday. Right? Fuck, why was it so hard to think? Did she have one yesterday? No, she didn't think so.

"When, Princess?"

"Shut up, Daddy. I'm thinking." Seriously, when was it? The anger started boiling in her again. *I had to have had one yesterday, right? Or was that Sunday?*

Her daddy sat across from her. "You're right when you said you don't have the flu. You have withdrawal." Eyes ringed in fear and concern bored straight into her heart.

Her eyebrow shot up. "There's no withdrawal, because I don't abuse drugs." Even though she said it, she didn't believe it. Not anymore. Saturday night's fiasco was the icing on the cake. Kaitlyn was terrified at what she took and refused to leave her alone. Nate had also worried. Her daddy paled when he heard. "No!" She hadn't taken anything over the last couple of days because she was dead inside over pushing Nate away. It wasn't withdrawal. It was heartache she was going through. She battered her fists on the table. "NO! I'm not going through withdrawal. My heart's fucking snapping in two." Storming down the hall, she slammed the door so hard the pictures on the wall fell. Another door slammed immediately after, and she presumed her daddy left.

❤ Chapter Thirty-Seven ❤

Picking up one of the fallen picture frames, she looked at her dresser where her friends sat waiting expectantly for her. They sat in their containers, staring out from behind the labels, eyeing her as she walked by, almost yelling 'pick me, pick me'. She could hear their whispers, hear them calling out to her, how taking one of them in her mouth would make her feel better, so much better. They would help her, and reassure her and make her feel good inside. She stared at the bottles and with a right arm that would please a pitcher, she launched them all into her dresser mirror, shattering it into a million pieces as she screamed at the top of her lungs.

Collapsing into bed, she begged for sleep to take her under, but it was only four o'clock, too early to turn in for the night and too late for a nap. Besides, she wasn't tired, she was angry. And she had no way to rid herself of her sudden energy. She stepped around the shards of glass and marched into the kitchen. She started baking—anything and everything—until the wee hours of the morning, and had exhausted her baking ingredients, filling her fridge and freezer full of homemade yum-yums. It was two a.m. when she climbed back into bed, and her father had yet to return.

In the morning, she heated a muffin, and her daddy stumbled out of the spare room, right into the heart of the disaster zone.

He rubbed his eyes as he surveyed the mess. "What the hell happened?"

"I baked."

"And you forgot to clean?"

She shrugged and tossed her muffin wrapper onto the table. "By time I was done, I wasn't interested in cleaning."

"You never are," he said as he reached through the stack of pans to grab a coffee cup.

She rolled her eyes. Biting into a muffin she'd made with pancake mix instead of flour, she was impressed at the taste. Better than she thought it would be. She took another bite. "What time did you roll in?"

"Four."

"What the hell were you doing out so late?"

"What are you, my mother?" he snapped.

Aurora glared and tore off a chunk of muffin. Obviously he was in a mood to fight and amazingly enough, she wasn't. She took a deep breath and said, "Oh, just so you know, I broke a mirror yesterday."

"And you didn't bother to clean it up?"

"No. But I have a reason for that, a theory if you will."

He raised an eyebrow as he grabbed a muffin and walked over to the table.

"I'm working on it. Trying to be all metaphoric about it and what it stands for and what it represents."

"And?"

"I'm still thinking on it."

He chomped on the muffin and as she looked at her father, his eyes were bloodshot and rimmed in red. "These are good."

"I know." A sip of warm coffee dripped down her throat. "You look like hell, Daddy."

"Thanks." Reaching for another muffin, he asked, "How are you feeling this morning?"

"Emotionally? Physically? And which version? Sugar coated or hit you between the eyes truth?"

"Too many options for first thing in the morning." He tapped his watch. "Why aren't you at work, yet?"

"I took today off. You know, to deal with things."

"What's to deal with? So you broke up, whatever. You got over Derek, and he was–" He stopped whatever words wanted to fall from his mouth. "You'll get over this."

Snap. Never mind, she *was* ready for a fight. Anger coursed through her hands and she gripped her mug until her knuckles turned white. "Like hell. Nate was the best thing that ever happened to me. It fucking hurts that we're not together. And it's all my fault. I pushed him away. I told him to go. It killed me inside to do it, but I had to. For him, I had to do it." She took a sip of coffee even though what she wanted to do was throw it at her father. "So get over it?" She stood, anger propelling her off her seat like a rocket. "Fuck you, Daddy. It'll never happen."

He rose in response. "Excuse me?"

"I'm so fucking tired of you telling me how *not* to deal with something. How to sweep it under the carpet like it never existed. I've tried that and it doesn't fucking work for me. I need to talk it through. I need to feel emotions. I need to hurt, and I need to cry. I *need* to fucking deal with things. You telling me that there's nothing to deal with negates my feelings and makes me feel unworthy. And I am worthy, Daddy."

"Of course you're worthy. No one's saying you're not." Sympathy rolled off him. His shoulders fell, and he looked exhausted.

"Then stop. Let me deal with it. My way. Just because it works for you, which I'm not entirely believing anymore, doesn't mean it works for me."

"Do you want to know how it works for me? I'll tell you." He fell into the chair, rubbing his face. "But I'd rather I didn't." A loud sigh. "Your mother had kicked me out. That weekend–that horrible weekend–I was already packing. Then it happened, and she was gone, your sister too. You were here, at the university hospital for weeks. What was I supposed to do? I couldn't stay here at the apartment, and yet, I couldn't sit at home and sulk. I had two funerals to plan. TWO. So I worked. Every. Fucking. Day. Because I had to. I had to carry on. Bills still had to get paid. So that's how *I* dealt with it."

"Geezus." Her tone softened. Shocked and more than a little curious to learn why her mother had kicked him out. Had he done something? Had she? What happened between them? "Did you ever deal with her death? Ever climb into bed at the end of the day and miss that warmth? Did you ever miss her voice, or the sweet way she'd make everything better with a hug?"

"It wasn't like that with us."

"It had to be at some point. You were married for twenty-four years."

His chest relaxed, and he propped himself up. "We'd stopped loving each other a long time ago. It was all too easy to do. I was away, you know three on, one off. And the one off was always filled with tension. She managed perfectly fine raising you girls while I was away, and my week home it was like I was a huge imposter, messing up routines and schedules. It got easier to stay away than to be yelled at for getting involved. But I'm an honourable, responsible man, so I started a small job on the sly, and made extra money. Lots of it. Enough to pay for you and your sister's education and the apartment here, without it affecting my income and the life you'd all grown accustomed to. Thanks to this side job, I could work smarter, not harder. The new job became my love."

She sat and stared at him, trying to process everything he said. "But you never dealt with it."

"I already had. Before she died."

"What about Carmen?"

"I didn't know her, we saw each other so briefly, especially after she moved here for school. I was more a stranger to her than a father. If someone asked me to name five things she loved spending her time on, I'd be guessing at four of them."

"Oh, Daddy."

"It's no different than you." He looked at her, and his face became tight. "We're family, so I drop in on you from time to time, and we speak often. But we don't know each other, do we?"

Her eyebrows formed a deep V, and she shook her head. There was the truth– they really *didn't* know each other. His life was his own, and as much as he helped her with her living expenses, he didn't get involved in her life, so she was on her own. They were each other's family, and yet they'd shut the other out.

She looked at her father, and a lightbulb flashed over her head. "The colour yellow, the smell of coconut, sex, this necklace and Nate."

"Huh?"

"These are five things I love. One you knew, and now you know the other four so you won't have to guess." A smile spread across her face.

He laughed. "Sex? Really?"

"I had to see if you were still listening." She moved closer to him. "There, now I'm not a stranger." Gripping his hand, she reflected how similar their hands looked. His was more masculine for sure, but the long shape was identical. "We have the same hands."

He held her hands up, looking at them. "Indeed."

She cocked her head. "So, now it's your turn. Five things you love."

He stretched back, and pulled his hand away. "Five? Okay. Fort Mac– I love it there, the smell of oil, a fine bottle of wine, warm socks and money."

"Guess I'll stop getting you a tie for Christmas," she laughed. "And get you warm socks instead."

"If my feet are dry and warm, then I'm a happy guy." Her daddy smiled and said, "So back to you. Nate's one of the things you love, eh?"

The colour rose in her cheeks. "Yeah. I really do. Even if we have such different lifestyles. But I fucked up, Daddy. Big time." There was no need to mention Matthew. It was best to keep that info on a need to know basis. If shame were a blanket, it would be made of lead, trapping her beneath it forever.

"So how do you fix that?"

"I'm thinking on it. Weird and wild ideas passed through this brain as I baked like a maniac last night."

He glanced to the kitchen. "Want to tell me about them while I help you clean?"

"You want to know?" Perplexed the direction the conversation had gone when it started out so poorly.

"Yes. You're my daughter–my family–and I should get to know all about you."

Feeling a lightness in her heart she hadn't felt in days, she walked into the kitchen, wondering where to start.

❤ Chapter Thirty-Eight ❤

I t had been hard returning to work a few days after decimating Nate's heart, knowing he was there and avoiding her. Not that she blamed him. And even though she shouldn't, she looked for him. Every. Damn. Day. Just a glimpse of his face. His perfect body. That sweet dimple in his cheek she could put her finger in. It would help the heartache, right?

There was nothing in her medicine cabinet to dull that hurt. If there was, it wouldn't be found within her apartment. After finally admitting she was in withdrawal, she begged her daddy to clean out all her pills. The first day knowing they were gone was okay, but the second day was harder. Her body ached, and she craved something. Anything. But her daddy had removed everything– there wasn't even cold meds around. Jerk. She never knew she could hate someone as much as she loved him.

Nightmares plagued her, filling her mind with horrid visions of Nate's devastated expression. The sorrow he wore as he stepped away from her, a mixture of deep pain and disgust. But he was free of her. Free of her reactions, free of her guilt. Free to find someone who'd be a part of his life, the way she never could. Someone else deserved him and it pained her that it would never be her.

She remembered a frightening dream. The pills had grown to ten feet tall, and hovered over her–

"Aurora?"

Shaking her head, the visions disappeared. "Huh?"

"Can I see you in my office, please?" Sara, usually the most chipper staff member, looked most displeased, and beckoned her.

Once behind the closed office door, she sat in the chair across from Sara.

"Aurora, I've been watching you over the past few days. You're not very happy."

Bing. Bing. Bing. And the award for most observant boss goes to...

"I've been hearing complaints from the other staff members."

Aurora glanced out the window. *Go ahead and fire me. Please. It would be the icing on the cake. I swear I won't take it personally.* "Yeah, so?" Her fingers twitched as she waited for the inevitable.

"What's up with you? I want to dismiss you, but I can't. Matthew James has threatened to pull his summer event if I do." Sara folded her hands in her lap, and stared hard at her. Under her breath, she whispered, "I really hate that man and the hold he puts over us."

Anger roared to life inside her. "Seriously, that man is out to ruin my life." *Why can't he just leave me alone?*

"Actually, it's because of him you still have a job."

"And if I quit?" *I don't want to be a part of his spectacle.*

"That never came up," Sara said, looking down.

Oh, really? Interesting.

"As much as I–" She stopped and glared. "Never mind."

Aurora turned and faced her boss. "Oh, just say it. It's not like anything you can tell me, I haven't told myself over the past nine days."

Sara opened her mouth, and snapped it shut. "You're difficult, aren't you?"

A shift in her seat. "Yes, I am. But you would be too if you were in my shoes." *Oh, what I wouldn't give for a Xanax right now. So sweet and intoxicating. I could just drift–*

"Aurora?"

Tired of being there, waiting to be fired, she figured she had nothing more to lose. "Listen, I show up, I do my job and I go home. I'm not here to make friends or to have a career in the library field. If you think I'm terrible at shelving books, then please, you have my blessing. Fire me. I'll talk it over with Matthew James personally so he doesn't leave you scrambling."

"I couldn't ask you to do that," Sara said, although the implication was ripe in her voice.

"Why not? It's not like I have anything to lose. My life is falling apart. I've pushed the love of my life away and I'm struggling with drug addiction. Stir-rug-a-ling!" Her fingers spread wide as she tightened and shook them. "My body feels like it's being eaten alive with pain."

Sara's eyes widened, and she leaned away from her. "I'm sorry, Aurora. I had no idea."

"Of course you didn't. You just thought I was being a bitch." A blank expression told her everything she needed to know. "So, are you firing me?" Sara hung her head. "Am I free to go?" Sara nodded, and she bolted from the room.

A few days later, she pushed around a cart full of novels. As she shelved a few books, a voice said, "Excuse me, where can I find a book on getting two people back together?"

She knew that voice, a familiar little brother. "Lucas, what are you doing here?" Her voice dropped to a whisper, but her face broke out in a smile. The first in a long, long time.

"Checking on you. Had to see if you're as miserable as him."

A pinch to the bridge of her nose. "Well, I'm fine." The heartache grew every time Nate texted. Nothing more than "Can we talk? Please?" but each time she ignored it. Even as much as she wanted to be back in his arms, she couldn't do it just yet. The whole he-could-still-die-in-front-of-her remained an issue she didn't know how to solve, or work through.

The visions of his pained face didn't disappear or reduce their occurrence. Her brain had replayed the crash over and over, taunting her. The fucking insomnia wasn't helping either, nor the constant sensation of doom that washed over her. Although, her daddy told her *that* was a minor withdrawal effect.

"If that's true, then great."

She looked at him, studied the way he was looking at her. There was mischievousness behind those eyes– she remembered how Nate's eyes sparkled exactly the same way. Geezus she missed him. Lowering her head, she grabbed another small stack of books and shoved them onto the shelf. "I'm not, but there's no future for us. We're too different." Curious, she sighed and asked, "How is he?"

"Miserable." He looked over her head towards the construction area. "And he'd kill me if he found out I was here." As he stood in front of her, he held her gaze.

"So what are you doing here then?"

"I wanted to tell you something." Stepping closer, he put his hands in his pockets. "Nate's decided to retire. At the end of the season."

Her eyes widened and her mouth hit the floor. "He can't. He loves racing."

"I know that. Hell, everybody knows that." He leaned back on the shelf, and suddenly her heart ached a whole lot more. Aside from the difference in hair colour and the fact that Lucas was a touch taller, they had identical mannerisms. He leaned exactly the same way Nate would. And she missed him even more.

"Why then?" She moved closer to take in his every word.

"Says his heart's not in it anymore."

Two male voices approached from behind, jolting her to spin around and see who it was. Disappointment filled her soul. Although it was a pair of construction workers, Nate was not one of them. She looked back over to Lucas, who had ducked behind the shelves.

The area clear, he said, "But, to be honest, I think—no, I know—he still loves you. Very much." He kicked at an invisible rock on the floor. "He doesn't want the racing to be an issue between the two of you."

It's not the only issue, but maybe he didn't share the other reason with you. Thanks for keeping that a secret, Nate. "But he can't retire. He loves it so much."

Lucas shrugged and a hint of a smile leaked out. "Guess you know where you stand in the scheme of things."

"I've been thinking about something and I wonder if you'd be willing to help me?" She leaned closer to him and whispered her idea in his ear.

He rocked back on his heels. "That's a mighty tall request."

"I know. Believe me, *I* know. But will you help me?"

Lucas gave her a hug—a long, tight hug—which she didn't want to break free from. It felt nice to be embraced. If given a choice, she'd prefer Nate, but at this moment, Lucas was a close second and she'd take every hug handed out. "Of course I will, just tell me how."

"Thank you." She pulled out her phone and gave it to him. "I'll text you the details."

He punched in his contact information. "I expect to hear them soon. I will need some time with this."

"Promise. You'll know before the day is through. I need to try something first."

Nodding, Lucas patted her shoulder, and peered between the shelves. Slinking along the row, his head popped out and darted around.

"What are you doing?" she whispered, holding back a giggle.

"Making sure the coast is clear."

To help him, she limped out to the aisle and checked the area. Having spent the last two weeks looking for him, searching for any little nook and cranny where he could hide had become second nature. "All clear."

"Sweet. Bye." He smiled as he patted her arm again, and dashed past the construction zone, his head moving left and right until he disappeared.

Putting her plan into motion was a monumental task. While the details filled every moment of her free time, it also gave her something to look forward to at the end of a Nate-less viewing day. The insomnia, for once, helped her as she now had extra hours to plan and execute. She affectionately dubbed it Operation Save Nate.

It was brilliant in concept, but dangerous in execution. There were many nights when she wondered if she'd mentally and physically survive it.

♥ Chapter Thirty-Nine ♥

"Dude, you need to stop this."

Nate straightened up and turned to face Jason. "Stop what?"

"Watching her." He thumbed toward the main part of the library. Towards Aurora.

"I'm not watching her."

"Dude, if you spent half as much time on this project, as you did spying on her, we'd be finished by now." Jason shook his head and muttered, "Come on," as he stepped away.

Nate turned back around and peered through the shelves. Maybe it was true he watched her too much. But he also texted her too much, telling her he wanted to talk and work things out. It had been a long month, and he was trying to forgive her. "Baby steps," he'd said unable to stop himself.

Upon hearing ramblings from the library staff that Aurora had turned into a major bitch and was close to being fired, didn't sound right and sit well with him. It was true she was snappy that was who she was. One just needed to get through the cracks to see how soft she was inside, but he doubted anyone tried. The library was too busy and hell bent on getting everything ready for the Matthew James event. God, he hated that man.

His heart broke as he followed her, hidden in the shadows. Day after day, she'd slam book after book onto the shelves. *Oh, Aurora.* He sympathized with her, it must be hard staying clean. But he only knew because he'd accidentally overheard a conversation Chris had where she'd mentioned a drug detox clinic at the hospital. He'd pieced together what was going on. But that was all he found out. Chris shut him out of any further conversations bearing her name.

But today she looked different. There was a hardness to her that hadn't been there before. He wanted to ask what caused the change, but stopped himself, choosing instead to follow her with his eyes. Geez, she was beautiful. And he missed her so much. Missed holding her, missed her witty banter and the way she smiled at him. He was so close to forgiving her. Just needed a little more time, even if his every waking thought was of her. Things will be different when he retires, and the racing won't be an issue between them. He could stop racing although he'd never actually leave the track. He'd need to help Lucas. But at least he wouldn't have her worry about any more crashes. She'd be devastated to learn he'd been in another, and just two weeks after finally getting the #15 back on the track.

"Nate," Jason yelled, "Come on."

Before he spun around, Aurora had turned in his direction and for a fraction of a second he thought she spotted him. But she couldn't have. He'd gotten too good at hiding from her.

Finishing up for the day, he was leaving the bathroom in the staff area, and stopped cold in his tracks when two voices spoke from the other side of the lockers. One he knew by heart.

"Matthew," she said, a tinge of surprise in her voice.

Matthew? As in the jerk, Matthew James? The one they're naming the new wing after?

"There you are, my lady. I figured I'd find you in here."

"Yeah, here I am." *Was she rolling her eyes?* At least her tone sounded like an eye roll. A locker door slammed, startling him, and he presumed she was grabbing her things.

"I wanted to tell you. My lady, the trial's over. It's done."

What trial? He stepped a little closer to the end of the lockers and turned his ear towards the conversation. He wanted to hear Aurora's reaction. There was only silence.

"You, we, can put it to rest now. Thomas Anderson will spend the rest of his life in prison. Three counts of vehicular manslaughter causing death."

Someone banged against the locker, and he assumed it was her. Was Matthew connected to her accident? And if he was, why didn't she tell him?

"That's," Aurora said, her voice cracking, "great news."

"Aw, don't cry. It's what we hoped for."

She's crying? His heart ached hearing those two words, and he inched closer. Quietly.

"No–" Her voice fell to a barely audible whisper. "I wish it'd never happened and they would all," she stumbled over the last words, "be here."

"I know." His voice soft in understanding. "Come here."

The urge to make himself known overwhelmed him as fury fuelled up inside. Was she snuggling into him? Chancing a look, he took a quick peek. In a microsecond, he saw everything and regretted it, wishing he could undo his movements.

Matthew wiped away her falling tears with his thumbs. Her beautiful face held up in Matthew's direction. Her eyes were closed, but that hadn't stopped the rivers of tears. She looked wrecked, but made no hesitation as Matthew leaned to kiss her.

A sound escaped him, and it was raw and full of emotion, and unlike anything he'd made in his life.

Her eyes flashed open as she turned to stare at him. Not wanting to look at her, he stormed away and banged against the lockers on his way out.

Sitting in his car, he smacked the steering wheel, his anger at what he witnessed growing. Just when he was getting ready to forgive her too. He'd understood and was coming to terms with her mistake. He'd remembered back to the weekend before his birthday, when she'd slammed the door in his face, and later explained she believed they had broken up. If that's what she thought, then in her mind she hadn't done anything wrong. And he understood her point of view on it, even if he didn't agree with it. But now?

Matthew James, the pretentious jerk, and the love of his life were together. By the way he'd touched her, they'd been together for a while at least. But when, and why? It's not as if Matthew lived here, that much he knew. If they were connected because of her accident, was that why she was always so hell bent on defending Matthew? Previous conversations rolled over and over in his mind.

Suddenly it dawned on him. *Oh my god. That's who she slept with. She'd slept with Matthew James.* Of all the men in all the world, why did it have to be with *him?*

Looking up from his dashboard, he saw her as she ran through the doors, eyes wide, searching for him.

He peeled out of the parking lot, spinning onto the nearby road, redlining the engine. Afraid of the damage he'd do, he pulled into a nearby parking lot. *All this time, it had been Matthew?* He slammed the car into park, narrowly missing the curb.

Matthew? Really? He shook as anger raced through him. Grabbing his phone, he flipped through his contact list. Sure, women weren't beating down his door, but one always was. His thumb hovered over the button. Maybe it was time to stop pushing *her* away and expand company relations.

He hit dial and before her sultry voice answered, he said, "Hi, Marissa."

❤ Chapter Forty ❤

"Stop pacing, you're making *me* nervous," Kaitlyn said as Aurora completed her millionth lap around the living room.

Aurora shook her hands, trying to disperse her energy. "What if it doesn't work?"

"Then it doesn't work."

Scowling, she stopped pacing for a moment. "Thanks."

"Well, it's the truth." Kaitlyn said as she rose and intercepted her on another pass. "Besides, it'll be fine. It has to be. You've worked too hard on this to fail."

Aurora rolled her eyes. "But so much can go wrong. You and I both know that."

"Yeah, but let's not dwell on that." Like a speck of dust, she fanned that incident away. "Focus on the end goal. Let that be what pushes you forward." Kaitlyn swept her hair off her trembling shoulders. "You look lovely, by the way."

Aurora had spent half the day deciding what to wear. After rummaging through her closet, she decided simple was best and selected a white v-neck t-shirt to go with her black capris. She wanted to blend in, not stand out. "Kait, I'm so nervous." She extended her hands which shook as if leaves on a windy day. "What if he still hates me?"

"He's never hated you."

She hung her head. *That's not how I remember it.*

"I'd tell you to stop worrying, but that's not what you want to hear." She gripped her shoulders. "Breathe. You can do this."

Pushing her hands away, she stepped to the side, and breathed as instructed. "I know. I know." She wiped her brow.

"What time did he say he was coming?"

"Around three?"

"He'll be here soon. Do you have everything?"

"It's on the table so I don't forget. Purse, jacket, poster." She rubbed her neck, the black satin of the necklace rolling against her palm. Her heart raced so fast she wondered if it were visible to Kaitlyn.

Her phone pinged an incoming message from her father.

Good luck, Princess.

She flashed it to Kaitlyn who smiled.

"I'm so glad you two are getting along."

"Me too. Who knew he'd be the one I needed most coming off the drugs." The phone dropped into the pocket of her capris, as she paced, shaking her hands with each loop.

"He told me once, it was probably harder for him to watch you detox, than it was for you to actually detox."

Halfway through another lap, she paused and said, "He did. When?"

"It doesn't matter." Kaitlyn smiled a shy little smile. "Anyways, you're clean now. A little rougher around the edges, but clean nonetheless."

Grabbing Kaitlyn's hand, she trembled. "Let's go downstairs. I think some fresh air will make me feel better." She opened the door and stepped into the hallway.

"You're the boss," Kaitlyn said, adding, "Forgetting anything?"

The poster. Her jacket. Her purse. "You're a lifesaver. What would I do without you?"

"Oh, I'm sure you'd be fine." Kaitlyn patted her on the arm as they stepped into the elevator.

Aurora took deep breaths all the way down and her heart skipped a beat when the doors opened and Lucas stood beyond them at the entrance. "He's here," she whispered.

"Go get 'em, Tiger," Kaitlyn said, pushing her towards the door.

Aurora managed one foot in front of the other, through the glass doors to where Lucas waited.

"You all set?" he asked, stepping closer to meet them.

She swallowed and lifted her things.

Kaitlyn walked up behind them, draping an arm on her shoulders. "She's a nervous wreck."

"Good," Lucas said, smiling, "it gives us something to focus on." He reached for her bag, coat and poster, which he placed in the trunk of his white sports car. Opening the passenger door, he motioned for her to get in.

"Good luck," Kaitlyn said, giving her a quick peck on the cheek. She whispered in her ear, "I want all the details later."

"Sure, you won't follow us?"

"As much as I'd love to see how this plays out, I can't. But call me later."

"Okay," she said, shaking so hard she could barely stand as she braced herself against the car door.

Kaitlyn blew a kiss and walked away.

Aurora looked from Lucas to the passenger seat and back to him. She swallowed again.

"Whenever you're ready. We have lots of time."

I can do this. I can do this. Huffing and puffing like a swimmer reading for a long dive, she breathed and fell in against the seat. Her legs trembled, and a fresh band of sweat formed in her armpits. *I am doing this. This is what I've been working on all this time. Focus. Think of Nate. And breathe.*

"All good?" Lucas asked as he propped himself against the car.

The door closing was the hardest part. At least with it open, there was still a chance to escape. *I can do this. Breathe. Focus. Remember why you're doing this.* When she gave him a nod, he closed it and rushed to his side. He slipped behind the wheel, waiting to start the car until she gave him the signal. A flat hand meeting her opposite palm was code for stop. A thumbs up was go.

Breathe. She gave him the thumbs up.

"Alrighty," he said, putting the car in gear. "First stop, Tim Hortons."

Building up to sit in a car and then drive around in one–without the need for drugs–was a tough pill to swallow. She wanted to do it so badly, but her first few times were exhausting, and terrifying experiences for both her and Lucas. However, the more she did it, and the harder she focused on Nate, the more tolerable it became. Thankfully, Lucas was a patient partner and willing to try as often as she was. Aurora knew he enjoyed being part of the plan.

The first part of the trip was doable. Unable to look out the window, she instead focused on a phrase Lucas printed and taped to the dash. It was a long passage on faith and hope, and she focused on every letter, every word and every breath she took in between. At the Tim Hortons they stopped and stretched.

"You did great."

"Thanks," she said, unsteady on her feet. Driving was such a different feeling than walking. And she much preferred walking.

She paced around the parking lot, shaking out her limbs and wiping the sweat off the back of her neck, her palms and the back of her knees. At this rate, she'd need a shower before she even arrived. She bought Lucas an Iced Capp, and they leaned against his car for a few minutes. Breathing hard, she shook out her hands. "I'm ready for more. Let's continue."

"Alrighty then," he said as he once again opened the door and patiently waited for her to make the first move. He never lost his smile. So much like Nate. God she missed him.

After patting his arm, she folded back into the seat, heart racing as she clicked herself in.

Lucas waited for the thumbs up. "Great. We'll stop in Leduc and watch the airplanes, okay?"

"That works." She looked at the clock on the dash. It was approaching 3:30–two hours until race time–and they still had at least one more stop and a good thirty minutes of drive time ahead of them.

They were approaching the turnoff into Leduc, and a memory of *that* night floated in when she chanced a glance at Lucas. *That night,* when the last time she saw her strong and beautiful momma, she was sitting motionless beside her. Her breathing increased, her heart raced and her palms became little sweat generators. Wiping them harshly on her pants, she started huffing.

"Aurora?"

The breaths grew shallower and shallower. "It's sneaking in. It's sneaking in." Her fists clenched as tight as her eyes.

"Okay," he said with a calmness in his voice. This had happened before. "I want you to think of Nate. Right now." His voice edged with firmness. "Tell me what you see."

Her nails dug into her palms. "I see Momma beside me." An inhale of air.

"Where's Nate?"

"He's not there." The memory changed shape. Instead of sitting beside her, a ghostlike version of her momma, stood alone in a long, wispy dress, stretching out her hand towards her. So beautiful and youthful. The air around her dark and swirly.

"Look harder, do you see him? Is he in the background somewhere?"

She searched and searched, looking beyond the spot where Momma stood. Faintly in the background, there was another shape. But it was far away from her. Too far to reach out and touch. "It's too dark."

"Keep looking. I'm sure he's there. Take a few more steps."

In her mind, she did just that. Left foot first. And the image became a little clearer. Her momma faded off to the side and when she reached to touch her, she'd disappeared. Facing towards the image, she slid her right foot forward. A smile broke out across her face. "I found him."

"What's he doing?"

"He's looking at me, but he's smiling and seems very happy." The Nate in her mind reached out his hands for her, pulled her close to whisper in her ear. His breath tickled her and made her giggle. But she wasn't going to share that with his eighteen-year-old brother. Acutely aware she was no longer moving, she popped open one eye when a blast of fresh air came from her right side.

"I figured you needed some air," he said.

"I thank you for that," she said, escaping the confines of the car and wasting no time stepping over to a picnic table. Leaning against the edge, she stretched out. "One more leg and we'll be there." A loud sigh blew from her lungs and her hands shook off their restless energy.

"And you're doing great."

"I was worried there for a bit."

"I gathered."

As he eclipsed the sun, she thought of Nate. Handsome and rugged. She missed him so much and reminded herself she was only twenty minutes away from seeing him.

Lucas interrupted her thoughts. "What was she like? Your mom, I mean."

"Beautiful, wonderful, smart. Kind-hearted, but firm. She'd be the first to scold us, and the first to tell us how proud she was." She stretched out her arms above her head. "What about you? What was your dad like?"

A gentle shrug. "I don't remember as much anymore. But I remember little things. The way he adored my mom and was always such a gentleman."

"A trait he passed on well to his boys."

Lucas blushed, and the colour flooded across his face and into his strawberry-blond hair. It was cute to watch. "Thanks. We try to keep him smiling… wherever he is." Lucas looked up.

Watching the cars zoom by, she asked, "Is this going to work out? Our big plan?"

He stepped closer to her. "It has to. You're meant to be together. He wasn't happy with her the way he was with you."

Marissa Montgomery. Nate's girlfriend for a few weeks.

"Maybe." She shrugged. "Part of me wishes I hadn't found out."

"Well, part of me wishes you hadn't asked why he'd suddenly stopped texting you, because then *I* wouldn't have found out either." Lucas smirked, a look of amusement on his face.

"Touché." While it pained her to see the same mischievous expression on Lucas' face that Nate sported, it was also comforting. She knew she'd chosen correctly when she picked him to help with her plan.

"You need a hug?" he asked but didn't wait for an answer as he wrapped his arms around her. "It's all good. You'll see." Lucas let go, grabbed his Iced Capp and offered her a sip.

She shook her head. "Remember last time?" During one of their training events, she had foolishly eaten before they attempted a ten-minute drive, and regretted it as soon as they stopped. She'd covered the parking lot in her partially digested supper. After that, every lesson was on an empty stomach. "Well, shall we go? My destiny awaits."

"Yeah, and he doesn't know you're coming. This'll be so awesome." Buckled in and ready to go, Lucas asked, "Are you sure you're ready? This is the longest leg."

"I think I can handle it. I've made it this far."

"Yes, you have," he said. Within minutes they were flying down the highway. "Music?"

She had clenched up tight again, as if in doing so, it would keep out the memories, flashbacks and trauma. Her legs pulled tight, her arms rigid, and her muscles stiff as a board. "Yeah, sure. Something to focus on." *Think of Nate. Handsome. Imagine his hand stroking your cheek.* Her breath moved from deep to shallow in a few heartbeats. Her eyes shut to the peripheral visions of movement flying by.

He fiddled and inserted a CD. When it kicked in, the most amazing symphony surrounded her and she listened to pick out the instruments. A violin, a clarinet, a harp in the distance. The most beautiful high-pitched voice she'd ever heard started singing in a foreign language.

She laughed slightly. "What is this?"

"Italian opera." He turned it up a notch. "I have no idea what she's singing about, but I can make up my own ideas based on the sound of her voice."

Listening harder, she allowed herself to be consumed in the music. Not knowing a word of Italian, she did as Lucas did, and tried to imagine what she was singing of. Most likely love– true and powerful. She pictured the singer standing on the edge of a stage, her hands once close now thrust towards the sky in declaration of her love. She was so engrossed into something so completely foreign, time slipped away and before she realised it, Lucas rubbed her hand.

"We're here."

"What? We're here?" Carefully she opened her eyes, checking out her surroundings. Dozens and dozens of cars occupied the many stalls. Lucas parked outside the main entrance where a few people mingled. "Oh my god, I did it. I really fucking did it." She unlatched herself and climbed out of the vehicle, racing over to him before he stepped out. "Thank you, Lucas." She jumped and gave him a big hug. The background roared to life with the sound of a racing car. Probably a late qualifier or something.

"My pleasure." He set her on the ground. "Thank you for listening to the opera with me. No one likes opera."

"Nate does." She remembered hearing it once in his car.

"'Cept him. Mom hates it."

"Really? I'm going to listen to it more, it was fascinating."

He beamed. "You go in through there." He pointed at the main gate. "Sit up near the announcer's booth and I'll come back after I go say hi to the family."

"You won't say anything, right?"

"Not a word, promise. They know I'm not racing tonight, obviously," he cracked a grin, "so it would be weird if I didn't at least drop in and say hi." She nodded, and he opened the trunk. "Your things."

With a last glance towards the car, she held her gear and approached to the main gate.

♥ Chapter Forty-One ♥

Like a girl on a first date, Aurora was nervous. Beyond nervous. She bought her ticket and ambled her way through the small gathered crowds. Searching for the announcer's box, she spotted it and made the slow climb up, her hip giving her a pinch of grief over it. *I can do without the drugs. They don't help me; they hurt me.* A motto she'd learnt over weeks of unrelenting therapy. If it wasn't a session for the PTSD, then it was one for the drug abuse. *The pain reminds me I'm still alive and I can survive.*

As she sat on the bleachers, she glanced into the pit below, her heart jumping in place when she spotted the white #15 sparkling in its spot. Today was the final race of the season, and it appeared every racer was in the pit. Similar to a live version of 'Where's Waldo?' she tried to locate Nate.

The September day was mild and perfect, so she enjoyed soaking up the autumn sun as a few cars made their qualifying laps. She wondered how Nate did, and where he'd be in the heats. She looked for Brenda and Chris, but they were invisible amongst the crowd. With divine intervention, the crowd parted like the Red Sea and she saw him. *Nate.* And he was talking to her– Marissa Montgomery. Her blood boiled instantly although she had no right to be upset. He'd run to Marissa after catching Matthew's lips on her. Too bad he missed the terrible right hook she threw at Matthew. If he saw it, perhaps he wouldn't have caved to the bitch.

But seeing them together in the pit fuelled her goal. Desperate to be a part of his life, to make things up to him, she practised and did car homework daily. Once she heard he wanted to retire, she tested her limits, pushing herself to the edge of her breaking point.

She knew Nate still loved her as he often told Lucas. The guys were close, so how Lucas managed to keep a straight face and not spill the beans about the plan was a mystery to her. She guessed this secret was worth keeping. And Lucas told her most challenges were worth overcoming.

She only needed to wait a touch longer to put the rest of the plan into motion. There was a time for everything. But seeing him with Marissa made her want to run to the pit and jump into his arms. Screw waiting for a big reveal. However, after watching Nate and Marissa talk for a few minutes more, she saw them drift apart.

As her heart smiled, two heads bobbed through the pit and sprinted onto the track. Lucas and a friend bounced over the wall. Spotting her, he nudged his friend and took the bleachers two at a time.

"Aurora, meet Ian, my decoy."

"Decoy?"

"They'd think it weird if I was going to sit up here by myself. So I brought a buddy."

She leaned over and shook his hand. "Pleased to meet you, Decoy Ian."

Ian, a tall lanky individual sporting a baseball cap that seemed to tame most of his wild hair, pumped her hand. "Pleased to meet you, I've heard all about you."

Shame caused her to cover her face and turn away. "I can only imagine."

Lucas smacked him. "Don't be a jerk."

Ian said, "Sorry. Didn't mean to upset you."

Lucas sat between her and Ian. He passed a water bottle her way. "Figured you'd be thirsty. You haven't had anything to drink since we left your place, and it's starting to warm up." He discussed how Nate did in qualifications, and which class of cars raced tonight and in what order. Nate's group would be the second to last race of the night.

She tucked herself in for a long night, however, Lucas and Ian proved to be good company. The men never excluded her from conversations and helped explain what she didn't understand, which was plenty even with the reading she found time for.

As Nate drove in his heats, she only focused on the board, counting down the remaining laps and order of the cars. Nate's number moved into fifth, disappeared for a few laps, only to reappear with three laps left. He finished in fourth for the first heat, and didn't make it into the top five for the second heat. She guessed Lucas was right when he said his heart wasn't in it anymore.

At intermission, the trio snuck over to the concession for supper.

Lucas stepped back. "I need to hop into the pit for a bit. You know, check in with Mom and Nate. But I'll be back before the finals start." He gave her shoulders a squeeze and to Ian he said, "Don't embarrass yourself."

Ian's ears glowed with that comment, but he nodded anyways.

After grabbing their food, they found shade under the awning, getting much needed relief from the heat and the sun. She dropped the tray with burgers and cold drinks onto the table furthest back and sat facing toward the track. A bite into her burger, she saw him standing in line. *Nate.*

"Quick, loan me your hat." She gestured to Ian.

He looked around, confusion written over his face, but passed her his cap anyways.

She pulled and twisted her hair, pulling the baseball cap overtop. "He's standing in line," she whispered, cocking her head in that direction.

Ian turned and looked. "Oh," he said, understanding. He gave his rowdy hair a tussle. "So it doesn't look like I gave you my cap." His hair flew in many directions as he gave it another shake.

"Thank you." She lowered her head and tried to be out of Nate's line of sight. His gaze darted all around, but thankfully never reached the back where she peered over Ian's shoulders. Would the sunglasses in the shade make her stand out? "Did Lucas fill you in?"

"Sort of. He said you're here to prove something to Nate, but Nate doesn't know you're here?"

She shrugged. "Yep." *That's basically it in a nutshell.* She stared at Nate as he moved through the busy line. Damn he looked good. The fire suit rolled down to his hips, the arms tied at his waist. His tank top hung on him as though he'd lost a little weight, his hair was longer, and he sported a sexy five o'clock shadow. Desperate to touch him, or at least call out his name but it wasn't time yet.

Ian interrupted her ogling. "Did you want to stay here and stare at him, or should we sneak out? I know another way out of this area." She looked at him. "It's not my first time at the track."

Right. Lucas had mentioned Ian raced here a few years back. Not wanting to leave, but not wanting to spoil the surprise, she nodded and pulled the ball cap low enough to touch her sunglasses. They grabbed their food, and Ian escorted her to the fence behind them, slipping through the gate he unlatched. Quietly, so as not to get caught, he re-latched it and they walked back to the main gate unnoticed. Flashing their wristbands, they walked back through the gate and up to their seats.

Once sitting, she texted Lucas. *Nate showed up. Moved back to our seats.*

Lucas responded: *That's why I can't find him.*

Aurora: *LOL. Hope he didn't see me.*

Lucas: *Hope not. But I wonder why he went up there for food.*

Aurora: *Better selection? LOL*

No further texts from Lucas and she saw him sprint across the track, meeting Nate at the gate where they exchanged words. Unable to read their lips, she couldn't figure out what they said. Suddenly they both glanced over in her general direction. *Not yet, not yet.* Hoping with Ian's hat pulled low and the sunglasses on he wouldn't recognise her, she watched him carefully. His head tipped sideways and studied her for a second before he shrugged and walked away. She didn't know who was more relieved, her or Lucas.

He dropped beside her a moment later. "Shit, that was close."

"You don't need to tell me." Aurora sighed as she breathed again. "Do you think he suspected anything?"

"Nah. He thinks you're Ian's girlfriend." Lucas smirked.

Her eyes grew bigger. "What? Why would he think that?"

"Because I told him that."

She playfully smacked him across his arms and took off Ian's hat, letting her hair fall back over her shoulders. "Thanks for the hat," she said, passing it to him.

"Anything for my girrrrlll-friennnnddd," he sung out and laughed. "So do I get to hold your hand?"

"Not a chance." She stared back into the pit. There was Marissa again, and it looked as though she had her hand on his arm. "You never mentioned they were back together?"

Lucas piped up. "Don't worry, they're not. She wants to get back together, but he told her no. Persistent little thing. Reminds me of someone I know." He rubbed his chin in mock amusement.

"Oh, shut up," she said, smiling.

By the time the moon rose, Nate's class of cars were reading. A whole new wave of nervousness descended upon her as the cars shimmied and shook on the track, warming their tires and getting into their placements. Nate was seventh of ten. She twisted in her seat and picked at her nails while reminding herself to breathe.

"You're doing great." Lucas wrapped an arm over her shoulders. "You've managed fantastically so far. You should be proud of yourself." He gave her a comforting squeeze. "Don't watch if you don't want to."

"I think it's important that I do." She stared at his car. Thirty laps and she'd be executing the final step in her plan, and with a little faith, it would all work out.

The cars zoomed around the track after the green flag dropped. A few laps in, and Nate advanced from seventh to fourth. Marissa maintained the lead, with the #33 and #7 ahead of Nate's #15. Ten laps completed, and the order had changed slightly as Nate overtook the #7. Halfway done and the top three were Marissa, #33, and Nate, and they fought to hold the top three.

"I thought you said Nate's heart wasn't in it?" She nudged Lucas, a nervous smile edging the corners of her lips.

"Maybe he changed his mind for his final race. You know, go out a winner and all?"

Focused on the board, she sighed as there were only seven laps remaining. Marissa slowed enough out of turn three that #33 passed her. On the straightaway, the distance between first and third was microseconds. Marissa came within inches of #33, and Nate was right on her tail. The battle for first began. Nate took to the outside wall on turns one and two, as Marissa clipped #33, causing him to spin out and take Marissa with him.

Aurora gasped, fearing for Nate, but caught her breath as he sailed around them both as the new leader. However, the caution flag dropped, and the race slowed to a crawl.

Lucas pushed closer to her and held her hand. "It's all good. Remember, we watched all those videos?"

"Ah huh," she said, unable to move her eyes off Nate's car.

Those videos, or as Lucas called them "The Phobia Desensitizers" were not the best way to spend a Monday night. However, after the seven-hundredth crash, she finally understood that most truly did walk away un-injured. Only four NASCAR drivers had died in the past ten years, none of them at this track.

The drivers lined back up– Nate in first, #33 in second and Marissa in last place, as she was the instigator. The flag dropped green and the final seven laps were gripping nail-biters, as Nate held on to the lead, but just.

Aurora couldn't take her eyes off Marissa, who passed car after car attempting to catch up to the leaders. She showed off her aggressiveness, weaving in and around the others. With two laps left, she'd caught up to fourth place. Nate still held first, with #33 a close second.

The white flag flew–the final lap–and Aurora sat on the edge of her seat. Nate still had first and just had to hang on for four more turns. Three turns. Two turns. Final turn. She screamed with untold joy as he crossed the line, the checkered flag his. Taking a victory lap around, he parked his car in the number one spot as Aurora raced down the stairs, poster in hand. She'd been hoping for a podium: first, second or third. Nate getting first meant she had a couple more minutes to sweat it out.

The announcer went to the track, as he always did, to interview the drivers. He started with third–Marissa–and asked her thoughts on the race. She blabbed for a few minutes while Aurora moved along the fence and stood in front of Nate's car. Nothing but the chain-link fence and eight feet of air separating them. God he looked good, sweaty and smiling, even though the smile didn't touch his eyes.

The announcer talked to the second place driver, but Aurora only had eyes for Nate who sat on the edge of his window, his helmet on the roof. He wasn't looking into the crowds, but rather down the line towards Marissa. His hand raised with his thumb rubbing against his fingers. Had they placed a bet?

As the announcer walked over to him, he hopped out of his car and she pressed the poster against the chain-link fence. Her face smiled with nervous tension above it.

The announcer asked, "So how was the race for you?"

Nate held the mic. "It was good. I was a little nervous that Marissa was going to take me out at one point." He laughed as he pointed towards her, giving her a friendly wave. "But it's all good. It's the spirit of the game, right?" Continuing on, he thanked his competitors for making the sport fun, and his sponsors for making it possible.

The announced handed him the first place trophy.

Aurora took a deep breath. As Nate held it, his mouth froze in a firm smile. Was he feeling overwhelmed? She knew what was coming. God, he really did love racing. It must be killing him to think he just raced his final race and was now preparing to announce his retirement. Because of her. The trophy held his focus while he remained at a loss for words. Very un-Nate like.

"Thank you," he finally spoke. "I have an announcement to make, and tonight's win makes it even harder."

She saw the tension in him, his shoulders high and tight. "Look in my direction," she willed him. "Please."

"Tonight's race is my–" As he glanced around the stands, his eyes stopped on her. Curiously he stepped forward. He saw the poster as she hoped. Looking at it, his eyes roved upwards. "What the hell?" he said, unaware he still held the mic, and it was still broadcasting. The air was electric. "Aurora?" Her name boomed through the grandstand, silencing the crowd as he walked towards the outside wall and fence. "Seriously?" His voice held shock, but his face held something else. Joy? Curiosity?

She felt a hand on her shoulder, and Lucas' voice in her ear. "Go to him."

As she turned, the crowd beside her stepped back when they noticed who Nate was looking at. Lucas pushed her towards the now open gate where the guard stood smiling.

Nate met her at the wall. "You're here. You're really here." She nodded and stepped over to the edge of the wall. "How?"

"Lots and lots of practising."

His face lit up like a thousand-watt bulb. Noticing the mic in his hand, he passed it to the announcer a couple feet behind him and returned his focus to her. "But–"

"I did it for you and me." Footsteps approached from behind her, and she looked to see Lucas. "He helped me. We wanted it to be a surprise."

Nate looked from her up to his little brother and back to her again. "I... I'm totally surprised."

"Please don't retire. I know how much this sport means to you." She looked beyond him to see Brenda rushing onto the track, Chris and Max a few short steps behind. "You said you'd never give up on me, so here I am today." She pulled the necklace out from under her shirt. "Love, hope and faith, right?"

She squatted, ready to hop onto the track. Instead Nate lifted her onto the asphalt. Her voice echoed throughout the track as the announcer hadn't stepped away yet. "You had faith in me that I'd overcome my fear, and I'm working on it because I'm standing here before you. Drug free, I may add."

No flood lights needed as he could've lit up the entire track with the smile on his face.

"The racing is part of who you are. I was a fool to say your hobby and my fear don't belong together because it's *what* brought us together. You told me you loved me, and with all my heart I am so in love with you, and I have faith that we can be together again. Can you ever forgive–"

His lips pressed into hers.

The crowd roared around them.

As they broke apart, the announcer declared, "Our first place winner, Nate Johnson, is going home with more than just a trophy tonight." He clapped with the crowd and leaned closer to the couple. "Congrats."

For a moment, it was only her and Nate, but as the crowd clapped and cheered, she remembered they weren't alone. Many members of the pit stood along the inside wall, and fans lined the fence. The grandstand was on their feet. She hated being the centre of attention.

"I need to get off the track so the super-trucks can race," he said, giving her another kiss. "Go to my spot?"

She nodded. "I promise." With Lucas beside her, she joined Brenda, Chris and Max and they walked together into the pit.

"I owe you a huge apology, Aurora," Brenda said. "You've come a long ways since Nate's accident. I'm taking back what I said. You are good for Nate and I'm so glad everything worked out the way you hoped." Motherly arms wrapped around her, which she melted into.

"Well, I suppose I have you to thank for all of this. Because if you hadn't confirmed out loud what I was already thinking, I wouldn't have had the drive to do what I needed to do." She looked at Brenda. "You have amazing children. Lucas and Chris have been so helpful over the past couple of months, especially Lucas. You've done a great job raising your children, and I love them to pieces." It felt fucking awesome to be a part of a family.

Lucas jumped into the conversation. "You should've seen the look on his face, Mom. I wish I had video'd it. He was so surprised."

"Well, I think you've kept him from retiring," Brenda said.

She linked arms with Brenda. "I hope so."

They stopped at Nate's spot, watching as he drove in. He launched himself out from his car and raced over to where she stood, lifting and spinning her in his arms.

"I can't believe you're really here," he said, holding her tight. "It feels like a dream."

She pinched him.

"Ow, what was that for?"

"See, it's not a dream." She smiled as she basked in delirious joy of being back in his arms where she felt safe and happy.

After a moment, he pushed her out of his arms, leaving his hands on her shoulders. "Wait a minute, aren't you with Matthew?"

She laughed, harder than she meant to but it was so funny to see the twisted, confused look on Nate's face. "No fucking way!"

"But, that day I saw you two, and he kissed you."

"Yeah, he kissed *me*. I was not kissing him back. In fact, if you'd hung around longer, you could've watched me punch him. Or try to. I wasn't very successful." She stared into his eyes. "I chased after you to tell you that, but you sped away." Hanging her head, she whispered, "As much as Matthew may have wanted it, there was never anything between us. Just that one night. One stupid night I'll regret for the rest of my life."

"But why him? That's the part I never understood."

She swallowed. "His wife, Rebecca, was the passenger in the other car in my accident. She died that night, alongside my mom and sister."

"Oh wow." He wrapped his arms back around her. "Well, that conversation now makes a little more sense."

She breathed him in, each breath healing her broken heart. "It was never him. Always you."

He kissed her again and lifted her. "I still can't believe you're here. And everyone knew?"

Right, she forgot the others were standing there still. Oh well, she'd confessed her sins so many times over, there was nothing left to hide. "Only Lucas and Chris, and your mom to a small degree." Her feet touched the pavement again. "Once I heard you planned on retiring, I pushed myself harder, knowing it was important to be out here before you said anything."

"How'd you know?" When she didn't speak, he turned to face Lucas, who stood there smiling. "Never mind. I'll deal with you later."

"Don't." She playfully punched him. "You owe him. He spent all his free time with me, going through everything over and over again. Sometimes Chris would be there too. Your family's pretty fucking awesome." Pride filled her heart and soul. They had taken a damaged bird and helped bring her back to life.

A look of concern filled his face. "How'd they do it?"

She explained although Lucas filled in the details of the first few trips. "Simple rides home from the library to start with. Two-minute drives that seriously felt like *hours*." Talk about testing an eighteen-year-old's perseverance to distraction. They discussed the many smaller trips around, some trips taken four or five times a day. Lucas had practically lived at her place over the summer.

"Well, I started sessions with a new therapist, one of Chris's colleagues," Aurora said. "She encouraged me to pour out every single fear I have, or had, about being in a vehicle, and to write them down in point form." She shook, remembering the long list. "When I finished, I'd listed over fifty separate fears. So she put together game plans and agendas to help each fear become less. Well, more accepted than feared. Then Chris would show up once a week and offer suggestions, overseeing a few rides." She looked around for her, and in spotting her, waved her over. "I took every bit of her advice to heart."

Chris smiled. "She really did. We role played and practised. Sometimes into the wee hours of the morning. Whatever it took. She never gave up."

Lucas added, "It was incredible watching her transform. To see her push herself over and over until something as simple as buckling herself into the car could be done without panic."

Aurora watched the sadness crawl across Nate's face when Lucas spoke.

"I wish I was there to watch, or help," Nate said.

She grabbed his hand and gave it a gentle squeeze. "You were. You were here," she pointed to her head, "and here." She pointed to her heart. "You may be the driving force behind the need to get this done, but don't get all smug thinking I *only* did this to keep you from retiring."

He raised an eyebrow, and she melted on the spot. Oh how she'd missed that.

"I didn't do it just for you, I did it for me. I love you so much and each day without you was worse than the day before. I needed to do this, to make it manageable, so I can hopefully be a part of your life." A deep sigh. "I'm not cured, not by a long shot, but it's doable now. I can't promise any cross-country trips, but I can get safely around town."

"Can you drive again?"

Laughter rang out behind her. "Baby steps, man." Lucas clapped Nate on the shoulder. "I'm leaving that for you," he said, winking at Nate. "Besides, there's still the return trip home."

"I'm so amazed," Nate said, shaking his head. "Like, you have no idea how amazed. Seeing you there, I was shocked. At first I wondered how many drugs you took, and then I wondered who drove you here." He looked at Lucas and pointed a finger at him. "You're a sneaky bugger. All this time I thought you were hanging out with a girlfriend."

"I was," he said. "Aurora's my friend, and she's a girl." He stuck his tongue out at his big brother and laughed as he walked away.

"So, my brother, eh?" His voice a joking, happy sound.

Aurora smiled, but cast her gaze down. "Yeah, he's become a great friend. It was comforting having that time with him. I'll cherish it. But he's not the one I want to be with."

A smug look crossed his face. "Oh yeah, who do you want to be with?"

She stood on her tippy-toes and kissed him. "Who do you think?"

"Ian, maybe?" His eyes never left hers.

A playful nudge. "No thanks. I want to be with you."

"Duly noted." He kissed her and swung her around. "And how is everything, you know, with the detox?"

Her eyes widened in shock. "You knew about that?" She glanced around to see who would've mentioned anything.

"I overheard a conversation between you and Chris. And... I watched you like a hawk at work. You know, I heard they were going to fire you at one point."

Arrogance filled her face. "I quit at one point."

"What?"

"You didn't know?" He shook his head. "That day you saw Matthew and me together? After I chased you, I went back into the library and quit."

"Ah, I see. Thought maybe they moved you to evenings as I didn't see you anymore. Then we moved job sites a couple weeks later, so–" His hand waved through the air. "But back to my question, Miss Avoidance. How are things with the detox?"

"Okay." Stretching her neck, she turned her head and sighed before answering. "Had a few relapses and setbacks, and some *really* bad days, but I'm getting there. I've been clean for twenty-two days now. The anxiety's more manageable and I'm finding other ways to deal with the chronic pain."

"Really? How so?"

"I hate physical therapy, but it works. And because it's so fucking brutal, I'm allowed one Advil after a session but I have to take it there." Her last session was the first one where she'd actually refused the pain killer as it was tolerable, something she'd been rather pleased about. "And as far as Xanax goes, I'm allowed two pills out at a time. Chris has taught me other forms of distraction, which we used today in fact. However, now I have guilt when I take one because it feels so good."

"Say what?"

"It's like chocolate. You know, you want a piece so bad, and then when you have it, you feel guilty because you know what it's doing to your body?" Nate squinted at her as he shook his head. "Must be a girl thing. Anyways, I'm working on it and trying my best. Day to day." A loud sigh blew from her chest. It felt good being able to catch Nate up on everything. "Between your sister, the new therapist, the physical therapist and Lucas, I'd say we crammed over a year's worth of therapy sessions into a few short weeks."

He shifted on his feet. "Love, hope and faith, right?"

"I hope you'll never give up on me."

He beamed. "I'll just continue to have hope and faith for our future."

"God, I love you, Nate Johnson."

"I love you more, Aurora MacIntyre."

"I love you most."

"Duly noted."

What's Next?

keep reading for an excerpt of

THAT SUMMER

by H.M. Shander

❤ Chapter One ❤

"Again."

"No!"

"Yes. Dammit, we're going to try this again." She smacked her hand against the roof of the car for effect.

"Aurora..." Lucas said as he walked around and stood in front of her. "It's finished for tonight." Gentle, soothing hands gripped her shoulders as his reddish-blond head tilted down, his hair teasing the edges of his dark eyebrows. "And that's okay. We can try again tomorrow."

The parking lot was half-full of tenant vehicles, but the spots around Lucas' car were empty. It was the perfect location to play 'touch-the-car', and endeavor to sit in it. Tonight, she had tried. Multiple times. And failed miserably. The first shot at it, she could sit and touch the seatbelt, but with each successive endeavor, she worsened. Her last attempt to sit in the car, she launched back out as soon as her butt hit the seat. It didn't matter how many times she tried, staying any longer than a few seconds caused instant panic. At least she'd stopped puking. PTSD was a complete bitch.

Her gaze cast toward the other vehicles around them. Anywhere but him. Shame and hatred blanketed her—shame that she couldn't physically handle anymore, and hatred because of what she was trying to overcome. Normal people didn't need to fight post-traumatic stress disorder. Normal people didn't worry about their next car ride leading them straight to death. There was more hate than shame lately, which in itself was a good thing. It gave her something to fight against.

"Again, please Lucas." Her voice almost a whine. "Just one more time."

The tall man stood strong before her, his stance unchanging. "As much as I'd like to see you conquer this tonight, it's not gonna happen. You've pushed yourself all day. You're on the edge of falling apart." He flicked his hair away from his grey-blue eyes as they settled over her.

"But I can do it. I just need another…"

I can do this. I know I can. I just need another shot.

He shifted and closed the gap between them. "Your body and your mind need a break, okay?" When she didn't respond, he squeezed again. "Okay? Look at me." His hands smoothed out the wrinkles of her sleeves.

His soothing touch grounded her. When she flew off the handle, swore like a sailor, and lost all control, his gentle stroke from her shoulders to her fingertips brought her back to her senses. She couldn't explain the way it instantly calmed her racing heart, steadied her breathing, and focused her. Only that it worked. Every. Damn. Time.

She was so lonely and her body craved human contact. Since she'd quit her drug addiction cold turkey, all chemical relaxers were completely out of the question. Touch had become her drug of choice. She was allowed two Xanax weekly, and she saved them for those times where she was so overwhelmed she couldn't think straight. This wasn't one of them. She needed his comfort more.

She and Lucas had been working on Operation Save Nate for the past few weeks. Every day two steps forward, one and a half steps back. It was maddening. She was never going to conquer her fears in time.

Lucas tipped up her chin and said, "Take a deep breath."

Cool night air rushed into her lungs.

"Hold it for one… two… three… exhale." Long fingers tapped out the count on her shoulder, ending with a tender squeeze.

His gaze held hers as she released the air. "Thank you," she said.

"You're welcome."

Her shoulders sagged as she leaned against the car defeated. "Now what?"

"Tonight, we pack it in." The passenger door latched. "Tomorrow's a new day."

Her voice dropped. "Yeah."

He draped an arm across her shoulders. She leaned into him as they headed into the apartment building. Punching the correct floor, the elevator doors rolled shut in front of them.

"And what, may I ask, is on the docket for you tomorrow?"

Aurora faced him. "Work and back-to-back therapy appointments. Physio at three, shrink at four."

"With Chris?"

Chris Johnson was Lucas' older sister; a highly skilled psychologist working on her master's degree, and Aurora's mental health specialist. Or was.

"No, Chris thinks it's best to sever my dependency on her. Claims it's a conflict of interest or something because you're helping me win back Nate, so she keeps referring me out to other shrinks in her office." A small, awkward laugh escaped her lips. "But I haven't found anyone there yet that I'm comfortable with. We're running out of staff. I think there's one or two left, if the one tomorrow isn't right."

"You'll find someone."

"And if I don't?"

"There are others. Chris will find you someone awesome. She wants to help you just as much as I do."

And as much as Nate did. A long, low exhale. With it came another squeeze on her arm.

He pulled her closer. "I know that sigh."

"I know you do." She turned her body toward him. "Can I ask?"

"You can, but you know I won't tell you anything."

"But…"

"He's my brother."

The elevator dinged announcing her floor, and he held the door as she stepped through into the darkened corridor. The dingy carpet softened their footsteps as they walked the length of the hall.

"I just figured, being my best friend and all, that you'd–"

"I'm your best friend?" A playful smile erupted on his face, lighting him up.

She pushed him further down the hall. "Shut up. You know that."

He gave a low, throaty chuckle. "Yes, I do and I promise I won't tell Kaitlyn." Even in the lull of the dim light, his grey-blues sparkled.

Kaitlyn. Her cheerleader, former roommate and female bestie who was expected back from a month-long Russian holiday in the next forty-eight hours. A smile instinctively tickled the corners of her mouth as she yearned to catch up with her and show her how hard she'd worked to overcome her car phobia. She'd be a great trial. If Kaitlyn was impressed, Nate was sure to have his socks blown off.

Her heart ached. For Nate. God, how she wanted Nate to be the one standing in the hall with her now. Wanted his chocolate-coloured eyes on her, his lop-sided, one-dimpled smile lighting the area. Wanted to run her fingers through his ridiculously soft brown hair, but she'd screwed up. Not only had she screwed up, she'd also told him about it. Maybe at the time she thought she was doing him a favor or maybe she was sabotaging herself. Either way, he'd walked out, and her heart had shattered to pieces at the same time. But she knew, via Lucas, that Nate still loved her. In fact, he loved her so much despite her major screw up, he was preparing for his final race. He planned on retiring from his first love in nine weeks so the racing and car issues she had wouldn't be a problem between them. She didn't like that—not at all—and a plan to foil his career ending move was born.

Nine weeks. Sixty-three days to stop his retirement. The only way she figured she could succeed would be to show up at the track. It would prove she could handle his lifestyle, even if her PTSD from her automobile accident fought against that. In order to do that, she needed to get over her fear of touching cars, of sitting in them, of being strapped to them while they transported her around. It was the last one holding her back the most, but at the same time, she knew she was close to having a breakthrough on. Oh so close.

Dear Reader,

I hope you enjoyed *Duly Noted!* I have to tell you, I really loved Aurora and Nate. Many readers have wrote to me and asked "What's next for them? And what about Lucas?" Well, stay tuned because things haven't quieted down for the MacIntyres nor the Johnsons. ☺ My personal favourite question is the one asking "What was on the poster?" Hmm....only I know the answer to that, but I'm curious—What do *you* think is on it?

When I wrote *Run Away Charlotte* and *Ask Me Again*, I received many emails from fans who had fallen in love with Charlotte and Andrew. Some had very strong opinions on the characters, and many others wanted to know more about them. As an author, it makes my day when someone shares their thoughts, and gives me feedback. It's because of this early feedback on *Duly Noted* that another story has come alive. So share with me what you liked, what you loved, or even what you hated. I'd love to hear from you. Contact me via email at hmshander@gmail.com or via my website www.hmshander.com.

Finally, I need to ask you a favour. If you are so inclined, I'd love a review or a rating of *Duly Noted!* Loved it or hated it, I will enjoy your feedback. You'll even get a *bonus* chapter emailed to you for doing so when you send me the link to your rating/review.

As I'm sure you can tell from my books, reviews are tough to come by. As a reader, you have the power to make or break a book. If you have the time, please visit my author page on Goodreads. You can also leave your rating/review wherever you purchased *Duly Noted!*

Thank you so much for spending your valuable time with me.

Yours,
H.M. Shander

300

Acknowledgements

☺ Wow! You made it this far and are still reading. Thanks. ☺

I'd like to thank my family and friends for your unwavering support. You've helped me achieve a dream. I'm in total shock that I've written (and published) three full-length novels. Even more shocking, is how you all want to read and devour them. From the bottom of my heart, THANK YOU.

To my hubs — Still a half-million books shy of being a millionaire, but hopefully one day I'll be your sugar momma and we'll have it made. ☺ But you know what, we already do, so thanks, babe. Thank you for allowing me to do what I love, and supporting me in the process. Thanks for reading, even though this is not your genre, and you takes you months to get through it, I appreciate your thoughts. Love ya.

To my boys Bear and Buddy — what would I do without you? You two make me laugh, and cry, and proud to be your mom. It warms my heart to know you're proud of me and when you go out for an evening with Dad, you tell me to write some more. I love that you want to explore your creative side and write, and I love reading your adventures with Bob, and bombs and all things boy. Be true to yourselves. And what was the saying about Batman? LOL.

To my BFF — Thank you for your support, for filling a void in my life, and for the gift of your friendship — I will treasure it forever. Thanks for your constant desire for "another chapter", for wanting more Aurora & Nate, for drooling over him, for forgiving her and for your thoughts on where they go next.

To my CP extraordinaire — Where would my story be without you? Your questions, comments and expressions were perfect. I knew when the email arrived with the heading "Don't hate me" that I had some work ahead. But you made it better, and stronger, and I'm *forever* grateful. Our partnership has evolved, and I'm blessed to know and work with you. Now hurry up and get your story out there. People need to read it!

To my beta readers — thank you for your edits, your comments, and all your help. It means a lot to me to know you're in my corner, rooting for the right people.

To my editor, and my creative designer — Thanks for the last minute changes I worried about. It turned out beautifully, just as we envisioned.

About the Author

- Knows four languages— English, French, Sarcasm and ASL. Speaks two of them exceptionally well. Any guesses which two?

- Lives in Edmonton, AB. A big city with a small-town feel. As much as she'd love the beach under a blanket of stars, this is her home.

- Is a coffee addict, and when she gave it up for Lent, totally felt Aurora's dependency and struggle through withdrawal. Sunday morning coffees were a Godsend.

- Terrified of scary clowns, although she once wanted to be a "Happy Clown" as she enjoys making people smile.

- Is a self-proclaimed nerd (and friends/family will back this up), reveling in all things science, however likes to be creative when there's time. Right brain, left brain? Both. ☺

- Has worked many jobs, her favourite being a birth doula and librarian, in addition to being an author and writing romances. Because, let's be honest, who doesn't love falling in love?

- Five things she loves, in no particular order; The Colour Blue, The Smell of Coconut & Shea Butter, Star Wars, The Ocean, and Chocolate

- Follow her on Facebook, Twitter and Goodreads. She also has a blog (hmshander.blogspot.ca) she writes on from time to time.

Thanks for reading—all the way to the end.
See you in the next book.

Made in the USA
Lexington, KY
14 May 2018